THE PENGUIN CLASSICS

FOUNDER EDITOR (1944–64): E. V. RIEU

GUSTAVE FLAUBERT, a doctor's son, was born in Rouen in 1821, and sent at eighteen to study law in Paris. While still a schoolboy, however, he professed himself 'disgusted with life', in romantic scorn of bourgeois society, and he showed no distress when a mysterious nervous disease broke off his professional studies. Flaubert retired to Croisset, near Rouen, on a private income, and devoted himself to his writing.

In his early works, particularly *The Temptation of St Anthony* (begun in 1848), Flaubert tended to give free rein to his flamboyant imagination, but on the advice of his friends he later disciplined his romantic exuberance in an attempt to achieve total objectivity and a harmonious prose style. This ambition cost him enormous toil and brought him little success in his lifetime. After the publication of *Madame Bovary* in the *Revue de Paris* (1856–7) he was tried for offending public morals; *Salammbô* (1862) was criticized for the meticulous historical detail surrounding the exotic story; *Sentimental Education* (1869) was misunderstood by the critics; and the political play *The Candidate* (1874) was a disastrous failure. Only *Three Tales* (1877) was an unqualified success with public and critics alike, but it appeared when Flaubert's spirits, health and finances were at their lowest ebb.

After his death in 1880 Flaubert's fame and reputation grew steadily, strengthened by the publication of his unfinished comic masterpiece, *Bouvard and Pécuchet* (1881) and his remarkable *Correspondence*.

ROBERT BALDICK, Fellow of Pembroke College, Oxford, and of the Royal Society of Literature, and joint editor of Penguin Classics, translated the works of a wide range of French authors, from Chateaubriand, Flaubert, Huysmans and Verne to Montherlant, Sartre, Salacrou and Simenon. He also wrote a history of duelling, a study of the 1880 Siege of Paris, and biographies of Huysmans, the Goncourts, Frédérick Lemaître and Murger. He was married to the American writer and translator, Jacqueline Baldick. Robert Baldick died in 1972.

GUSTAVE FLAUBERT

SENTIMENTAL EDUCATION

*

Translated with an introduction by

ROBERT BALDICK

PENGUIN BOOKS

Penguin Books Ltd, Harmondsworth, Middlesex, England
Penguin Books, 625 Madison Avenue, New York, New York 10022, U.S.A.
Penguin Books Australia Ltd, Ringwood, Victoria, Australia
Penguin Books Canada Ltd, 2801 John Street, Markham, Ontario, Canada L3R 1B4
Penguin Books (N.Z.) Ltd, 182–190 Wairau Road, Auckland 10, New Zealand

—

This translation first published 1964
Reprinted 1969, 1970, 1972, 1974, 1975, 1976, 1978, 1979, 1980, 1981, 1982

—

—

Set, printed and bound in Great Britain by
Cox & Wyman Ltd, Reading
Set in Monotype Fournier

Contents

Introduction

Sentimental Education, undoubtedly the most influential French novel of the nineteenth century, and to many minds the greatest, was completed on Sunday, 16 May 1869, after nearly five years of unremitting labour. During that period Flaubert often admitted feeling exhausted by the intellectual effort involved, worried by the problems his huge enterprise presented, and uncertain of the aesthetic merits of the novel he had planned. But not for a single moment did he deviate from the concept of the work which he had stated in October 1864 in a letter to Mademoiselle Leroyer de Chantepie: 'For the past month I have been hard at work on a novel of modern life set in Paris. I want to write the moral history, or rather the sentimental history, of the men of my generation.'

This ambition to paint the moral portrait of a whole generation was new to Flaubert. On the other hand, the basic, personal theme of a young man's romantic passion for an older woman was not. Already, in three early works, *Memoirs of a Madman* (1837), *November* (1842), and a first version of *Sentimental Education* (1845) – works full of a youthful, Byronic lyricism which the mature novelist abandoned – Flaubert had treated in different forms the decisive encounter of his life. At Trouville in 1836, at the age of fourteen, Flaubert had met Élisa Schlésinger, the dark, beautiful, twenty-six-year-old wife of a well-known music-publisher, Maurice Schlésinger, and had promptly fallen in love with her. During the next few years his love would appear to have cooled, only to rekindle in the eighteen-forties when he came to Paris to study law and became a friend of the Schlésingers. Ruined by a series of disastrous speculations similar to those of Arnoux in *Sentimental Education*, Schlésinger eventually left for Germany with his wife and children and settled at Baden. Flaubert kept in touch with 'Madame Maurice', who in 1862 was committed to an asylum near Mannheim for seventeen months. In the years that followed, the years when Flaubert was writing *Sentimental Education*, the two may have met on several occasions, and there seems little doubt that the scene of Frédéric's reunion with the white-haired Madame Arnoux in the penultimate chapter of the novel had its counterpart in real life. In the eighteen seventies Madame Schlésinger was once again committed to an asylum, this time at Illenau, where she died insane, eight years after Flaubert's own death, in 1888. We shall probably never know whether Flaubert's love for her was ever consummated. For some time at least, and possibly until the very end of their relationship, Madame Schlésinger, like Madame Arnoux, apparently opposed a mysterious, unshakable reserve to her admirer's pleas; for, unknown to him, she lived and suffered under the burden of a monstrous secret. Born Élisa Foucault, in 1829 she had married a certain Lieutenant Émile-Jacques Judée, who in order to escape prosecution for embezzlement had one day sold his wife to Maurice Schlésinger in return for the money he needed to avoid arrest; Schlésinger had been unable to marry her until Judée died, and the child Flaubert had seen in Élisa's arms at Trouville had been illegitimate. Most Flaubert critics, knowing the secret which was kept from the novelist, and assuming that the account of Frédéric's relationship with Madame Arnoux corresponds to reality, maintain that Madame Schlésinger was deterred by mingled feelings of fear and gratitude towards Schlésinger from yielding to Flaubert's advances; but a recent discovery suggests that she may have become his mistress after all. In one of Flaubert's notebooks in which he first sketched out the plot of *Sentimental Education*, referring to Madame Schlésinger–Arnoux as Madame Moreau, the name he would eventually give his hero, Flaubert wrote: 'She loves him when he no longer loves her. It is at that moment that he possesses her – or she offers herself ... It would be better not to have Madame Moreau making love, but remaining physically chaste and eating her heart out with love ...'

Just as Madame Arnoux is a portrait of Madame Schlésinger, so Frédéric is basically a self-portrait of the author. Flaubert had conceived the same romantic love as Frédéric, had led the same sort of life in Paris, had dreamt the same extravagant dreams and suffered the same eventual disillusionment. But there is a vital difference between the hero of *Sentimental Education* and his creator. Frédéric is a weak, timid creature, suffering from an incurable debility of will – on the first printed copy of the book the novelist altered the subtitle: *Histoire d'un jeune homme* to the patronizing diminutive: *Histoire d'un jeune hommet* – whereas Flaubert had a virile strength of purpose derived from his literary vocation and the discipline of his craft. That is not to say, however, that Frédéric is a worthless nonentity: he is not, any more than Madame Bovary is the contemptible trollop Henry James held her to be. True, Frédéric is the undoubted ancestor of all the 'unheroic heroes' and 'anti-heroes' of the twentieth century, while Emma is the forerunner of all the middle-class heroines of modern literature. But just as Emma acquires a certain tragic nobility from the sensibility which raises her above the level of an Homais, so Frédéric is not sufficiently mediocre or mean-minded to admire or approve the greedy, stupid, vulgar people of all classes with whom he comes in contact. Both characters lack the means or the will-power to succeed in life, but success in Flaubert's eyes – witness Homais and Martinon – is not a sign of merit.

The other characters in *Sentimental Education* are just as firmly rooted in reality as Madame Arnoux and Frédéric; and Maxime du Camp could write in his memoirs: 'There is not a single one of the actors whom I cannot name; I have known them and rubbed shoulders with them all.' Du Camp himself, indeed, served as the model for the envious, ambitious Deslauriers, who also owes something – his more attractive qualities – to Flaubert's other close friend, Louis Bouilhet. It was du Camp too who furnished Flaubert with the details of his successful seduction in 1851 of Valentine Delessert, the Madame Dambreuse of *Sentimental Education*, and the sometime mistress of Mérimée, Rémusat, and Victor Cousin. The other leading feminine character in the novel, Rosanette Bron, alias the Marshal, was chiefly inspired by the famous Aglaé Sabatier, alias the President, who was courted with more or less success by Gautier, Baudelaire, and Flaubert himself, and whom Clésinger immortalized in the most erotic piece of sculpture of the nineteenth century, his 'Woman stung by a snake'; but the story of the Marshal's sexual initiation is that of Suzanne Lagier, Flaubert's favourite among the courtesans of the Second Empire. Names have likewise been put to all the subsidiary characters in the novel: thus Martinon has been linked with Mérimée, Sénécal to Lucien de la Hodde, Hussonnet with the boulevardier journalist Gustave Claudin, Pellerin with the cartoonist photographer Nadar, Monsieur Dambreuse with the financier Pouyer-Quertier, and Louise Roque with Flaubert's childhood friend Henriette Collier. As for Jacques Arnoux, at once the mean, scheming business-man and the generous, reckless dreamer, he is by all accounts a faithful likeness of Maurice Schlésinger, whom Flaubert, despite his love for Schlésinger's wife, has painted with affectionate, almost admiring sympathy.

While there is inevitably some discrepancy, however slight, between the characters in *Sentimental Education* and their prototypes, Flaubert allowed himself no such licence in the matter of background details and historical facts. His notebooks and his correspondence bear witness to the immense efforts he made in the interests of authenticity – visiting Sèvres and Creil to document himself for the passages on Arnoux's factory; reading medical treatises and attending an operation at the Sainte-Eugénie Hospital in order to describe the illness and death of Frédéric's child; touring the Forest of Fontainebleau, notebook in hand, in preparation of his hero's excursions with the Marshal; asking Jules Duplan for details of the sort of working-class house in Lyons in which he intended to situate Rosanette's childhood; questioning Ernest Feydeau about the kind of speculation in which an ignorant young man could have lost a small fortune on the Stock Exchange in 1847; or consulting undertakers and exploring Père-Lachaise in order to plan Monsieur Dambreuse's funeral down to the smallest detail. As might be expected, the 1848 Revolution gave him more trouble than any other background event in the novel. 'I am slaving away at the Revolution of '48,' he told Bouilhet in 1867. 'Do you know how many books I have read and annotated in the last six weeks? Twenty-seven, old fellow, and in spite of that I have managed to write ten pages.' Here again he did not rely simply on his own recollections or documentary evidence, but consulted his friends about such various matters as the position of the guard-posts in Paris, the meetings of the political clubs, and the nature of the fighting in both February and June. The result is a vivid reconstruction of incomparable value, which no historian or student of the period can afford to neglect.

Flaubert was well aware of the danger involved in setting the personal adventures of an ordinary individual – especially one as unheroic as Frédéric Moreau – against a historical background as tumultuous as that of Paris in 1848. 'I am afraid,' he told Jules Duplan, 'that my background will eat up my foreground: that is the trouble with the historical novel. Historical figures are more interesting than fictional characters, above all when the latter have moderate passions: the reader finds Frédéric less interesting than Lamartine.' Flaubert's solution to this problem was to make the most decisive or absorbing events in his hero's love-life coincide with the most dramatic events in his country's history, so that Frédéric either fails to realize what is happening or arrives only in the aftermath of revolution, insurrection, or *coup d'état*. Thus the February Revolution breaks out just when Frédéric is obsessed with his abortive rendezvous with Madame Arnoux; the June insurrection takes place while he is enjoying a belated honeymoon with Rosanette in the Forest of Fontainebleau; and he returns from his fruitless visit to Nogent after Louis-Napoleon has brought off his *coup d'état*, and when only a few isolated demonstrators such as Dussardier remain to be cut down by the police.

The same skill is evident in Flaubert's handling of the problem of time, the most vexatious of all the problems which plague the author of a novel whose action is spread over a number of years. Anybody reading *Sentimental Education* for the first time is apt to regard it as a continuous narrative stretching from December 1840 to December 1851, with an epilogue of two chapters set in 1867–8; and this impression is confirmed by dozens of historical references which – with the exception of the Pritchard Affair and the first use of the title *The Human Comedy* – are all placed in their correct sequence and hence lull the reader into a sense of security. But in fact the narrative is far from being continuous; quite apart from the famous passage beginning 'He travelled,' which leapfrogs the sixteen years between 1851 and 1867, there are three places in the novel where Flaubert surreptitiously moves the clock on. The first instance is at the end of Part One, when a whole year, from September 1843 to September 1844, is casually dropped; then, at the beginning of Part Two, the year 1846 mysteriously disappears, and Frédéric, returning to Paris in December 1845, throws a housewarming party in January 1847; and finally, in the third chapter of Part Three, the reader is taken swiftly and imperceptibly from August 1848 to May 1850, within the space of a few pages. In this last instance Flaubert's sleight-of-hand is so brilliant that it deceived the author himself; as mathematically-minded critics have pointed out, Rosanette announces her pregnancy in January 1849 and gives birth to the child in February 1851, twenty-five months later. But this mistake is no more apparent to the ordinary reader than the earlier tricks with time; Flaubert is so careful to avoid precise dates and so skilful at muddling the cards that only an eagle-eyed reader armed with an index of names and a calendar of historical events is likely to catch him out.

The composition of *Sentimental Education* is indeed of such a high order that it seems non-existent. Thus when the novel was published in 1869, critics such as Edmond Scherer dismissed it as 'a collection of photographs', failing to appreciate either the skilful manipulation of time, or the subtle balance between bourgeois and revolutionaries, or the recurring pattern of Frédéric's adventures in politics, finance, and love. The younger generation of Naturalist writers, on the other hand, considered *Sentimental Education* the greatest novel in French literature – Huysmans called it their Bible, while Henry Céard and others performed the fantastic feat of committing the entire work to memory – but in their uncritical admiration for the book they too failed to realize the art which had gone to the making of it, and some of them produced long, uneventful novels consisting of disconnected tableaux in the naïve hope that the result would be comparable to Flaubert's masterpiece.

It was not the form of *Sentimental Education*, however, which provoked the severest criticism in 1869, but the ending of the novel. A howl of fury went up from the critics at what they considered a statement of gratuitous immorality, for they one and all understood Flaubert to be saying through Frédéric that the happiest moment in a man's life is his first visit to a brothel. Even present-day critics, though not so easily shocked, tend to make the same assumption, and shake their heads sadly at what they regard as a crude, provocative attempt to *épater le bourgeois*. But there is surely another explanation of that final comment, more in keeping with the seriousness of the novel as a whole. It is that Frédéric, like other disillusioned figures in Flaubert's novels – whether Emma Bovary who 'discovered in adultery all the platitudes of marriage', or Salammbô who, touching the sacred veil of Tânit, 'remained melancholy in the fulfilment of her dream' – comes to realize that the happiest moment in his life was when he stood on the threshold of adult life, as on the threshold of the Nogent brothel, with all his hopes and illusions intact, and dazzled by the glorious possibilities which, like the young women in their white dressing-gowns, appeared to be his for the taking. On that particular summer evening he had run away and kept his illusions; but a day would come when he would go into the brothel, just as a day would come when he would try to fulfil his dreams of love and fortune – and then the long, heartbreaking process of disillusionment which is the story of *Sentimental Education* would begin.

It was this overall theme of disillusionment rather than a supposedly shocking ending which was responsible for the novel's failure when it first appeared; and Flaubert knew it. In his memoirs

Henry Céard recounts how, one evening in Flaubert's Paris flat in the Rue Murillo, he told the veteran novelist of the admiration he felt for *Sentimental Education*. Obviously moved by this unexpected tribute, Flaubert drew himself up to his full height and answered in a gruff voice: 'So you like it, do you? All the same, the book is doomed to failure, because it doesn't do this.' He put his long, powerful hands together in the shape of a pyramid. 'The public,' he explained, 'wants works which exalt its illusions, whereas *Sentimental Education* . . .' And here he turned his big hands upside down and opened them as if to let his dreams fall into a bottomless pit . . .

The public still wants works which encourage and exalt its illusions, and consequently many readers are still bound to find *Sentimental Education* distasteful and even abhorrent. Politicians of every party loathe the book, since it shows up the politics of Right and Left, of the twentieth century as much as of the nineteenth, with impartial ferocity and disgust; young people shy away from it, because it exposes the hollowness and fragility of their ideals; while women regard it with suspicion and dislike, on account of its insidious devaluation of the power of love. Yet for all the hopes it kills and the illusions it destroys, Flaubert's novel is not a barren, dispiriting work. 'I know nothing more noble,' he once wrote, 'than the contemplation of the world'; and any reader who is capable, as he was, of accepting both pleasant and unpleasant experiences as an inevitable part of life, and deriving an ironic pleasure from acquiescence in the human condition, will find *Sentimental Education* a work of profound, mature, satisfying beauty.

R. B.

PART ONE

I

On the 15th of September 1840, at six o'clock in the morning, the *Ville-de-Montereau* was lying alongside the Quai Saint-Bernard, ready to sail, with clouds of smoke pouring from its funnel.

People came hurrying up, out of breath; barrels, ropes and baskets of washing lay about in everybody's way; the sailors ignored all inquiries; people bumped into one another; the pile of baggage between the two paddle-wheels grew higher and higher; and the din merged into the hissing of the steam, which, escaping through some iron plates, wrapped the whole scene in a whitish mist, while the bell in the bows went on clanging incessantly.

At last the boat moved off; and the two banks, lined with warehouses, yards, and factories, slipped past like two wide ribbons being unwound.

A long-haired man of eighteen, holding a sketchbook under his arm, stood motionless beside the tiller. He gazed through the mist at spires and buildings whose names he did not know, and took a last look at the Île Saint-Louis, the Cité, and Notre-Dame; and soon, as Paris was lost to view, he heaved a deep sigh.

Monsieur Frédéric Moreau, who had just matriculated, was returning to Nogent-sur-Seine, where he would have to hang about for two months before going to read for the Bar. His mother had sent him to Le Havre, giving him just enough money for the journey, to see an uncle who she hoped would leave his fortune to her son; he had returned to Paris only the previous day, and he was making up for the impossibility of staying in the capital by taking the longest route home.

The noise began to die down. The passengers had all taken their places, and some of them stood round the engine, warming themselves, while the funnel spat out its plume of black smoke with a slow, regular breath. Tiny drops of moisture trickled over the brasses, the deck shook with a gentle vibration, and the two paddle-wheels, turning swiftly, beat the water.

The river was lined with sand-banks. The boat kept coming across timber rafts which rocked in its wash, or a man sitting fishing in a dinghy. Then the drifting mists melted away, the sun came out, and the hill which followed the course of the Seine on the right gradually grew lower, giving place to another hill, nearer the water, on the opposite bank.

On the crest of this second hill there were trees in between low-built houses with Italianate roofs. These houses had sloping gardens separated by new walls, iron gates, lawns, greenhouses, and vases of geraniums placed at regular intervals along terraces with balustrades to lean on. At the sight of these peaceful, pretty dwellings, several passengers felt a longing to possess one and spend the rest of their days there, with a good billiard table, a launch, a wife, or some other object of desire. The novel pleasure of a trip on the river banished any feeling of shyness and reserve. The practical jokers started getting up to their tricks. A good many began singing. Spirits rose. Glasses were brought out and filled.

Frédéric thought about his room at home, about the plot of a play, about subjects for pictures, about future loves. He considered that the happiness which his nobility of soul deserved was slow in coming. He recited melancholy poems to himself; striding along the deck, he went forward as far as the bell, and there, in a group of passengers and sailors, he noticed a gentleman flirting with a peasant-girl, and toying with the gold cross which she wore on her breast. He was a big fellow of about forty, with crinkly hair. His sturdy figure filled out a black velvet tail-coat, a couple of emeralds glittered in his cambric shirt, and his wide white trousers fell over a pair of strange red boots of Russian leather, which were decorated with a pattern in blue.

Frédéric's presence did not embarrass him. He turned towards him several times, giving him conspiratorial winks; then he offered cigars to all the men around him. But he probably found the company boring, for he moved away. Frédéric followed him.

To begin with, the conversation touched on the different kinds of tobacco, and then turned quite naturally to women. The gentleman in the red boots gave the young man advice, expounded theories, told anecdotes, and quoted himself as an example, reeling all this off in a fatherly tone of voice, with an ingenuous wickedness which was quite amusing.

He was a Republican; he had travelled; he knew the secrets of the theatres, restaurants, and newspapers; and he was acquainted with all the celebrities of the stage, whom he referred to familiarly by their

Christian names. Before long Frédéric had confided his plans to him; he took a favourable view of them.

Suddenly he broke off to examine the funnel, and then rapidly muttered a lengthy sum to himself, in order to discover 'the force of each piston stroke, at so many a minute'. Having found the answer, he expatiated on the beauties of the landscape. He said how happy he was to have escaped from business.

Frédéric felt a certain respect for him, and on a sudden impulse asked his name. The stranger replied all in one breath:

'Jacques Arnoux, proprietor of *L'Art Industriel*, Boulevard Montmartre.'

A servant with gold braid on his cap came up to him and said: 'Would Monsieur please go below? Mademoiselle is crying.'

He disappeared.

L'Art Industriel was a hybrid establishment, comprising both an art magazine and a picture shop. Frédéric had seen the title several times in the window of his local bookshop, printed on huge prospectuses which bore the name of Jacques Arnoux in a prominent position.

The sun blazed down, glittering on the iron bands round the masts, the plating of the bulwarks, and the surface of the river; and the prow of the boat sliced the water into two furrows which spread out as far as the meadow banks. At every bend of the river the same curtain of pale poplars came into view. The countryside was deserted. Some little white clouds hung motionless in the sky, and a vague sense of boredom seemed to make the boat move more slowly and the passengers look even more insignificant than before.

These, apart from a few well-to-do people in the first class, were workmen and shopkeepers with their wives and children. As it was the custom in those days to put on one's oldest clothes for travelling, nearly all of them were wearing old skull-caps or faded hats, threadbare black jackets worn thin by desk-work, or frock-coats with buttons which had burst their covers from too much service in the shop. Here and there a coffee-stained calico shirt showed under a knitted waistcoat, gilt tie-pins pierced tattered cravats, and trouser-straps were fastened to list slippers. Two or three louts, carrying bamboo canes with leather thongs, glanced shiftily from side to side, while the family men opened their eyes wide as they asked questions. Some stood about, chatting, or squatted on their luggage; others slept in corners; several had something to eat. The deck was littered with nutshells, cigar stubs, pear skins, and the remains of sausage-meat which had been brought along wrapped in paper. Three cabinet-makers in overalls stood in front of the bar; a harpist dressed in rags was resting with his elbow on his instrument; now and then one could hear the sound of the coal in the furnace, a burst of voices, or a roar of laughter. On the bridge the captain kept striding from one paddle-wheel to the other, without ever stopping. To get back to his seat, Frédéric pushed open the gate leading to the first-class section of the boat, disturbing a couple of sportsmen with their dogs.

It was like a vision:

She was sitting in the middle of the bench, all alone; or at least he could not see anybody else in the dazzling light which her eyes cast upon him. Just as he passed her, she raised her head; he bowed automatically; and stopping a little way off, on the same side of the boat, he looked at her.

She was wearing a broad-brimmed straw hat, with pink ribbons which fluttered behind her in the wind. Her black hair, parted in the middle, hung in two long tresses which brushed the ends of her thick eyebrows and seemed to caress the oval of her face. Her dress of pale spotted muslin billowed out in countless folds. She was busy with a piece of embroidery; and her straight nose, her chin, her whole figure was silhouetted clearly against the background of the blue sky.

As she stayed in the same position, he took a few turns to right and left, in order to conceal the purpose of his movements; then he stationed himself close to her sunshade, which was leaning against the bench, and pretended to be watching a launch on the river.

He had never seen anything to compare with her splendid dark skin, her ravishing figure, or her delicate, translucent fingers. He looked at her workbasket with eyes full of wonder, as if it were something out of the ordinary. What was her name, her home, her life, her past? He longed to know the furniture in her room, all the dresses she had ever worn, the people she mixed with; and even the desire for physical possession gave way to a profounder yearning, a poignant curiosity which knew no bounds.

A negress with a silk scarf round her hair appeared, holding a little girl by the hand. The child, who had tears in her eyes, had just woken up. The lady took her on her knee.

'Mademoiselle was a naughty girl, for all that she was nearly seven; her mother wouldn't love her any more; people forgave her pranks too easily.'

Frédéric was overjoyed to hear all this, as if he had made a discovery or an acquisition.

He supposed her to be of Andalusian origin, a creole perhaps. Possibly she had brought the negress back from the West Indies with her.

There was a long stole with purple stripes hanging over the brass rail behind her. How many times, out at sea, on damp evenings, she must have wrapped it round her body, covered her feet with it, or slept in it! Now the fringe was pulling it down, and it was on the point of falling into the water when Frédéric leapt forward and caught it. She said:

'Thank you, Monsieur.'

Their eyes met.

'Are you ready, my dear?' Arnoux called out, appearing in the hood of the companion-way.

Mademoiselle Marthe ran up to him, threw her arms round his neck, and pulled his moustache. The sound of a harp came through the air, and the child asked to see the band; soon the player was brought into the first-class section by the negress. Arnoux recognized him as a former artist's model, and greeted him familiarly, to the surprise of the onlookers. Finally the harpist flung his long hair back over his shoulders, stretched out his arms, and began to play.

It was an eastern romance, all about daggers, flowers, and stars, which the man in rags sang in a biting voice. The throbbing of the engine provided the melody with an uneven accompaniment; he plucked harder, the strings vibrated, and it seemed as if their metallic sounds were sobbing out the sad story of a proud, unhappy love. On both sides of the river woods leaned down to the edge of the water; a cool breeze blew up; Madame Arnoux gazed vaguely into the distance. When the music stopped she fluttered her eyelids several times, as if she were emerging from a dream.

The harpist came up to them humbly. While Arnoux was looking for some change, Frédéric stretched out his closed hand towards the man's cap and, opening it discreetly, dropped in a gold louis. It was not vanity that led him to make this charitable offering in front of her, but a feeling of generosity in which he included her, an almost religious impulse of the heart.

Leading the way, Arnoux cordially invited him to come below.

Frédéric declared that he had just had luncheon, although in fact he was starving and had not a centime left in his purse.

Then he reflected that he had as much right as anybody else to sit in the saloon.

Some worthy citizens were eating at the round tables, with a waiter serving them. Monsieur and Madame Arnoux were at the far end, on the right; he picked up a newspaper from the long, plush-covered bench, and sat down.

At Montereau they were to take the Châlons coach. Their trip to Switzerland was going to last a month. Madame Arnoux accused her husband of spoiling his child. He whispered something in her ear – presumably a compliment, for she smiled. Then he got up to draw the curtain of the window behind her neck.

The low white ceiling gave off a harsh light. Frédéric, sitting opposite Madame Arnoux, could make out the shadow of her eyelashes. She dipped her lips in her glass and broke a crust of bread between her fingers; her lapis lazuli locket, fastened to her wrist by a thin gold chain, tinkled against her plate every now and then. Yet the other people in the saloon did not seem to notice her.

From time to time, through the portholes, they could see a small boat coming alongside the steamer to take passengers on or off. The people at the tables kept leaning out of the openings and naming the villages on the river banks.

Arnoux complained about the cooking; he made a tremendous fuss about the bill and had it reduced. Then he took the young man forward for a toddy. But Frédéric soon came back under the awning, where Madame Arnoux had resumed her seat. She was reading a thin volume with grey covers. The corners of her mouth moved every now and then, and a gleam of pleasure lit up her face. He felt jealous of the man whose writings she seemed to find so fascinating. The longer he gazed at her, the more conscious he became of abysses opening up between the two of them. He reflected that he would have to part from her soon, part from her irrevocably, without having drawn a single word from her, without leaving her a single memory of himself!

A plain stretched away to the right; on the left a meadow sloped gently up to a hill, on which vineyards and walnut-trees could be distinguished, with a mill in the midst of the greenery. Further up, paths zigzagged across the white rock which seemed to touch the sky. What bliss it would be to climb up there beside her with his arm round her waist, listening to her voice and basking in the radiance of her eyes, while her dress swept the yellow leaves along the ground! The boat could stop, and they had only to disembark; it was all so simple, yet budging the sun would have been an easier proposition.

A little further on, a mansion came into sight, with a pointed roof and square turrets. There was a flower-bed in front of the house, and avenues stretched away like dark tunnels under the tall lime-trees. He imagined her strolling past the hedgerows. Just then a young lady and a young man appeared on the steps, between the orange-trees in their tubs. Then the whole scene vanished.

The little girl was playing near him. Frédéric tried to kiss her. She hid behind her nursemaid, and her mother scolded her for not being nice to the gentleman who had rescued her stole. Was this an indirect overture?

'Is she going to speak to me at last?' he wondered.

Time was running out. How could he get an invitation to Arnoux's house? He could not think of any better way than to point out the autumn tints of the landscape, adding:

'Soon it will be winter, the season of balls and dinner-parties.'

But Arnoux was worrying about his luggage. The Surville shore came into view; the two bridges drew nearer; they passed a ropery, then a row of low-built houses; in front there were cauldrons of pitch and chips of wood; and boys were running about on the sand and turning cartwheels. Frédéric recognized a man in a sleeved waistcoat, and called out to him:

'Hurry up!'

They had arrived. He eventually found Arnoux in the crowd of passengers, and as they shook hands the other said:

'I hope we shall meet again, my dear sir.'

Once he was on the quay, Frédéric turned round. She was standing by the tiller. He threw her a look into which he tried to put his whole heart and soul; but she remained motionless, as if he had done nothing at all. Then, taking no notice of his servant's greeting, he said:

'Why didn't you bring the carriage here?'

The poor fellow apologized.

'What a fool! Give me some money.'

And he went off to have a meal at an inn.

A quarter of an hour later he was tempted to go into the coach-yard, as if by chance. Perhaps he might see her again.

'What's the use?' he said to himself.

And the phaeton carried him away. The two horses did not both belong to his mother. She had borrowed the one belonging to Monsieur Chambrion, the tax-collector, to harness beside her own. Isidore had set off the day before, resting at Bray until the evening and spending the night at Montereau, so that the animals were fresh and trotted along at a brisk pace.

Fields of stubble stretched away as far as the eye could see. Trees lined the road on both sides; there were heaps of stones one after another; little by little he recalled Villeneuve-Saint-Georges, Ablon, Châtillon, Corbeil and the other villages, and the whole of his journey on the boat came back to his mind, so clearly that he could now remember fresh details, more intimate particulars: her foot, in a brown silk boot, peeping out under the lowest flounce of her dress, the drill awning forming a wide canopy over her head, and the little red tassels on the fringe trembling perpetually in the breeze.

She looked like the women in romantic novels. He would not have wanted to add anything to her appearance, or to take anything away. His world had suddenly grown bigger. She was the point of light on which all things converged; and lulled by the movement of the carriage, his eyelids half closed, his gaze directed at the clouds, he gave himself up to an infinite, dreamy joy.

At Bray he did not wait until the horses had been given their oats, but went ahead down the road, by himself. Arnoux had called her Marie. He shouted 'Marie!' as loud as he could. His voice faded into the air.

A broad, deep-red band of colour lit up the western sky. Huge corn-ricks, standing in the midst of the stubble, cast gigantic shadows. A dog started barking on a distant farm. He shivered, seized with a nameless anxiety.

When Isidore caught up with him, he climbed up on to the box and took the reins. His moment of weakness had passed. He was firmly determined to get into the Arnoux home somehow or other, and to become a friend of the family. It was sure to be an interesting household. Besides, he liked Arnoux; and then, who knew? At this point a flush rose to his cheeks and his temples started throbbing; he cracked his whip, shook the reins, and drove the horses at such a pace that the old coachman kept saying:

'Easy, now! Easy! You'll spoil their wind.'

Little by little Frédéric calmed down, and he gave his attention to what his servant was saying.

Monsieur's arrival was impatiently awaited. Mademoiselle Louise had cried to be allowed to go in the carriage to meet him.

'Who's Mademoiselle Louise?'

'You know, Monsieur Roque's little girl.'

'Oh, I'd forgotten,' Frédéric replied casually.

By now the horses were tired out. They were both limping, and the Saint-Laurent clock was striking nine when he drew up in the Place d'Armes, outside his mother's house. This house, which was large and spacious, with a garden leading into open country, enhanced Madame Moreau's position as the most highly esteemed person in the neighbourhood.

She came of an old and noble family, now extinct. Her parents had married her to a man of plebeian origin, who had died of a sword wound while she was pregnant, leaving her an encumbered fortune. She received visitors three times a week, and every now and then gave a splendid dinner-party. But the number of candles was calculated in advance, and she waited impatiently for her farm rents to come in. Her financial difficulties, which she concealed like a vice, gave her a certain gravity. Yet in the practice of virtue she showed neither prudery nor harshness. Her smallest gifts took on the appearance of great benefactions. People consulted her about the choice of servants, the education of young girls and the art of jammaking, and the bishop stopped at her house on his episcopal tours.

Madame Moreau harboured lofty ambitions for her son. She disliked hearing criticism of the Government, out of a sort of anticipatory prudence. Frédéric would need patronage to begin with; then, thanks to his own ability, he would become a counsellor of state, an ambassador, a minister. His successes at Sens College justified her confidence in him; he had carried off the first prize.

When he went into the drawing-room, the whole company rose noisily to their feet; they kissed him, and arranged the easy chairs and upright chairs in a wide semicircle round the fireplace. Monsieur Gamblin promptly asked him his opinion of Madame Lafarge.[1] This case, which was the great subject of conversation at the time, inevitably provoked a violent argument. Madame Moreau put a stop to the discussion, much to the annoyance of Monsieur Gamblin, who considered it useful for the young man in his capacity as a future lawyer, and he left the room in a huff.

This sort of thing was only to be expected from a friend of old Roque's. Talking of old Roque, they mentioned Monsieur Dambreuse, who had just acquired the estate of La Fortelle. But in the meantime the tax-collector had taken Frédéric aside, to ask what he thought of Monsieur Guizot's latest book. Everybody wanted to know about his financial affairs; and Madame Benoît went about it skilfully by asking after his uncle. How was this worthy relative? Frédéric never gave them any news of him. Hadn't he a distant cousin in America?

The cook announced that Monsieur's soup was served. The company tactfully withdrew. Then, as soon as they were alone in the room, his mother asked him in a low voice:

'Well?'

The old man had received him cordially, but without revealing his intentions. Madame Moreau gave a sigh.

'Where is she now?' he thought to himself.

The stage-coach was rolling along; and inside, doubtless wrapped in her stole, she was asleep, with her lovely head resting against the cloth lining the carriage.

They were just going to their rooms when a waiter from the Cygne de la Croix brought in a note:

'What is it?'

'Deslauriers wants to see me,' he said.

'Oh, your friend!' said Madame Moreau with a sneering laugh. 'He picks his time well, I must say.'

Frédéric hesitated. But friendship won the day. He picked up his hat.

'Don't stay out too late, anyway,' said his mother.

II

CHARLES DESLAURIERS' father, a former infantry officer who had resigned his commission in 1818, had returned to Nogent to marry, and with his bride's dowry he had purchased a post as bailiff which was barely sufficient to keep him alive. Embittered by long-standing grievances, tormented by his old wounds, and constantly harking back to the days of the Emperor, he vented his choking rages on his family. Few children were thrashed more frequently than his son, but the beatings failed to break the lad's spirit. When his mother tried to intervene, she was given the same rough treatment. Finally the captain put the boy in his office, and all day long he kept him bent over his desk, copying legal documents, an occupation which made his right shoulder perceptibly more muscular than his left.

In 1833, at the request of the president of the court, the captain sold his post. His wife died of a cancer. He went to live at Dijon, and after that set up as a 'dealer in men' at Troyes, providing substitutes for military service. Obtaining a small scholarship for Charles, he sent him to Sens College, where Frédéric recognized him as a native of Nogent. But he was twelve years old and Charles fifteen; besides they were separated by countless differences of character and breeding.

In his chest of drawers Frédéric kept all sorts of provisions, and various objects of luxury such as a toilet-case. He liked sleeping late in the morning, watching swallows, and reading plays; he missed the comforts of his home and found school life rough.

It seemed good to the bailiff's son. He worked so hard that at the end of his second year he moved up into the fourth form. However, either because of his poverty, or on account of his hot temper, a veiled hostility surrounded him. But one day a servant called him 'a paupers' child' in the middle-school yard; he flew at the man's throat, and would have killed him but for the intervention of three of the masters. Carried away by admiration, Frédéric clasped him in his arms. From that day on, their friendship was complete. The affection of a senior doubtless flattered the younger boy's vanity, while the other gratefully accepted the devotion offered to him.

His father left Chárles at school during the holidays. A translation of Plato which he opened by chance aroused his enthusiasm. He conceived a passionate interest in metaphysics and made rapid progress in the subject, for he approached it with youthful energy and the pride of an intelligence tasting freedom for the first time. He read Jouffroy, Cousin, Laromiguière, Malebranche, the Scottish philosophers – everything the library had to offer. He even stole the key, to obtain the books he wanted.

Frédéric's distractions were of a less serious character. He did a drawing of Christ's family-tree, which was carved on a door-post in the Rue des Trois-Rois, and another of the cathedral porch.

After reading some medieval plays, he embarked on a series of books of memoirs: Froissart, Commines, Pierre de l'Estoile, Brantôme.

The pictures which these books conjured up in his mind haunted him so persistently that he felt an urge to copy them. He nursed an ambition to become the Walter Scott of France. Deslauriers pondered over a vast philosophical system which would have the most far-reaching applications.

They talked about these things during break, in the yard, opposite the motto painted underneath the clock; they whispered about them in chapel, under the very nose of Saint-Louis; they dreamt of them in the dormitory, which looked on to a cemetery. When the form was taken for a walk, they took their places behind the others and talked incessantly.

They talked about what they would do later on, when they had left school. To begin with, they would go on a long voyage with the money Frédéric could deduct from his fortune when he came of age. Then they would come back to Paris and work together, never leaving each other; and as a relaxation from their labours, they would have love affairs with princesses in satin boudoirs, or wild orgies with famous courtesans. But doubts followed on their transports of hope. After fits of wordy gaiety they would relapse into profound silences.

On summer evenings, after walking for miles along the stony paths beside the vineyards, or on the highroad in the open country, with the fields of corn waving in the sunshine and the scent of angelica filling the air, a feeling of suffocation came over them and they lay down on their backs, dazed and elated. The others, in shirtsleeves, played prisoners' base or flew kites. The usher called them. On the way back they went past gardens traversed by little streams and along the boulevards shaded by the ancient walls; the empty streets echoed with the sound of their footsteps; the gate opened, and they climbed the stairs again, feeling as sad as if they had been indulging in wild debauchery.

The headmaster maintained that they over-excited each other. Yet if Frédéric worked hard in the upper forms, it was in response to his friend's exhortations; and in the holidays of 1837 he brought him home to his mother.

Madame Moreau disliked the young man. He ate enormously, refused to go to church on Sunday, and aired republican views; worse still, she formed the opinion that he had taken her son to places of ill repute. A close watch was kept on their relationship. This only strengthened the affection between them; and there was a painful scene the following year, when Deslauriers left the school to go to study law in Paris.

Frédéric expected to join him there soon. They had not seen each other for two years, and once their embraces were over, they went on to the bridge in order to be able to talk more freely.

The captain, who now ran a billiard saloon at Villenauxe, had flown into a rage when his son had asked him for an account of his trusteeship of his mother's fortune. He had even stopped his allowance on the spot. Since Deslauriers wanted to try later on for a chair at the Law School and he had no money, he had taken a post as chief clerk to a solicitor at Troyes. By dint of careful economy, he hoped to save four thousand francs, so that even if he never obtained any of his mother's money, he would still have enough to enable him to work on his own for three years, while he was waiting for a post. The consequence was that they would have to give up their old idea of living together in the capital, at least for the time being.

Frédéric hung his head. The first of his dreams had come to nothing.

'Cheer up,' said the captain's son. 'Life is long, and we are young. I'll join you one day. Don't think about it any more.'

He shook him by the hands, and, in order to turn his thoughts in another direction, asked him about his journey.

Frédéric had nothing much to tell. But at the memory of Madame Arnoux his sorrow vanished. He did not mention her, restrained by a sense of delicacy. Instead he talked at some length about Arnoux, recounting his conversation, his manners, and his connexions; and Deslauriers urged him to cultivate this acquaintance.

Frédéric had not done any writing recently; his literary opinions had changed; he now prized passion above all else; Werther, René, Franck, Lara, Lélia, and other less distinguished characters roused him to almost equal enthusiasm.[2] Sometimes it seemed to him that only music was capable of expressing his inner anguish, and then he dreamt of symphonies; or else the surface of things attracted him, and he longed to paint. Yet he had written some poetry; Deslauriers expressed his admiration for one poem, but did not ask for more.

Deslauriers himself had abandoned metaphysics; political economy and the French Revolution now occupied his attention. He was now a tall, thin fellow of twenty-two, with a wide mouth and a look of determination. This evening he was wearing a shabby lasting overcoat, and his shoes were white with dust, for he had walked all the way from Villenauxe, especially to see Frédéric.

Isidore came up to them. Madame begged Monsieur to come in, and sent him his cloak in case he felt cold.

'Do stay!' said Deslauriers.

And they went on strolling from one end to the other of the two bridges which rest on the narrow island formed by the canal and the river.

When they were walking in the direction of Nogent, they had in front of them a group of slightly lopsided houses; on the right the church could be seen behind the wooden water-mills with their sluice-gates closed; and on the left, all along the bank, there were hedges of shrubs marking the boundaries of gardens which were only just visible. Looking towards Paris, on the other hand, they could see the highroad stretching away downhill in a straight line, and there were meadows which disappeared in the distance, among the evening mists. The night was silent and lit by a whitish light. The smell of damp leaves drifted up to them; and a hundred paces further on, the water of the weir murmured with the soft, heavy sound that waves make in the darkness.

Deslauriers stopped and said:

'They make me laugh, all these good folk sleeping peacefully in their beds. Just you wait; there's a new revolution brewing! People are sick and tired of constitutions and charters, lies and evasions. Oh, if I had a newspaper or platform, I'd shake them up, I can tell you that! But you can't do anything without money. What a curse it is to be born the son of a publican and have to waste your youth trying to earn a living!'

He bowed his head, and bit his lips, shivering in his thin clothes.

Frédéric threw half his cloak over his shoulders. The two of them wrapped themselves in it and walked along underneath it, side by side, holding each other round the waist.

'How do you expect me to live there without you?' said Frédéric, whose sadness had been reawakened by his friend's bitterness. 'If I had a woman to love me, I might have achieved something. What are you laughing for? Love is the food and air of genius. It's powerful emotions that produce great works of art. As for looking for the woman of my dreams, I've no intention of doing that. Besides, even if I find her, she'll only reject me. I belong to the race of the disinherited, and I shall die without ever knowing whether the treasure within me is diamond or paste!'

Somebody's shadow fell across the paving-stones, and at the same time they heard these words:

'Your servant, gentlemen.'

The speaker was a little man in a voluminous brown frock-coat, with a pointed nose poking out under the peak of his cap.

'Monsieur Roque?' said Frédéric.

'The same,' the voice replied.

Monsieur Roque explained his presence by saying that he had just been inspecting the man-traps in his garden, down by the water.

'So you're back in our parts?' he went on. 'Excellent! I heard about it from my little girl. Keeping well, I hope? You're not leaving us again, are you?'

And off he went, doubtless put out by Frédéric's cool reception. The truth of the matter was that Madame Moreau was not on calling terms with old Roque. He lived in illicit union with his house-keeper and was held in very low esteem, for all that he was the electoral registrar and Monsieur Dambreuse's steward.

'The banker who lives in the Rue d'Anjou?' Deslauriers asked. 'You know what you ought to do, old fellow?'

Isidore interrupted them again. This time he had orders to bring Frédéric back with him. Madame was growing anxious about his absence.

'All right, all right! He's on his way,' said Deslauriers. 'He'll sleep at home tonight.'

And when the servant had gone:

'You ought to ask that old boy to introduce you to the Dam-breuses; there's nothing like mixing with the rich. Seeing that you own a tail-coat and a pair of white gloves, why not make the most of them? You really must get into that circle. You can introduce me later on. A millionaire – just think of it. Make sure you can get into his good books – and his wife's too! Become her lover!'

Frédéric protested.

'But all I'm saying to you is in the best tradition. Remember Rastignac in *The Human Comedy*. You'll succeed, I'm sure of that!'

Frédéric had so much confidence in Deslauriers that he felt shaken. Forgetting Madame Arnoux, or else including her in Deslauriers' prediction about the other woman, he could not help smiling.

The clerk added:

'One last word of advice: pass your examinations. A label is always safe: drop your satanico-Catholic poets: their philosophy is about as up-to-date as the twelfth century. Your despair is absurd. Plenty of great men have had harder beginnings than you – Mirabeau for one. Besides, we shan't be apart for long. I'll make my old swindler of a father cough up. But I must be getting back now. Goodbye. Have you got a hundred sous for my dinner?'

Frédéric gave him ten francs, all that was left of the money he had taken from Isidore that morning.

A few yards from the bridges, on the left bank, a light was burning in the attic window of a low-built house.

Deslauriers noticed it, and sweeping his hat off, he pompously declaimed:

'Venus, queen of the skies, your servant! But Poverty is the mother of Continence, and heaven knows we've been slandered enough about that!'

This reference to an adventure they had shared amused them. They roared with laughter as they walked along the street.

Then, having paid his bill at the inn, Deslauriers accompanied Frédéric as far as the Hôtel-Dieu crossroads; and after a long embrace, the two friends parted.

III

Two months later, alighting from the coach one morning in the Rue Coq-Héron in Paris, Frédéric decided to pay his momentous call.

Luck had been with him. Old Roque had brought round a bundle of papers which he had asked Frédéric to deliver personally to Monsieur Dambreuse; and he had attached an unsealed note introducing his fellow townsman.

Madame Moreau had appeared surprised at this request. Frédéric had concealed the pleasure it afforded him.

Monsieur Dambreuse was really the Comte d'Ambreuse; but after 1825 he had gradually abandoned both his title and his party, and had turned his attention towards commerce. Always on the look-out for a bargain, with an ear in every office and a finger in every pie, as wily as a Greek and as hard-working as an Auvergnat, he had amassed what was said to be a considerable fortune. What is more, he was an officer of the Legion of Honour, a member of the General Council of the Aube, and a deputy with a good chance of becoming a peer of France sooner or later. Being of an obliging nature, he pestered the Government with continual requests for subsidies, decorations, and licences to run tobacconists' shops; and in his tiffs with officialdom, he inclined towards the Left Centre. His wife, the lovely Madame Dambreuse, who was always being quoted in the fashion papers, presided at meetings of charitable organizations. By flattering the duchesses, she soothed the rancour of the noble faubourg and created the impression that Monsieur Dambreuse might yet repent and render useful service.

The young man felt nervous on his way to their house.

'I ought to have put on my tail-coat. They will probably invite me to their ball next week. What are they going to say to me?'

His self-confidence was restored by the thought that Monsieur Dambreuse was just a member of the middle class like himself, and he leapt gaily out of his cab on to the pavement of the Rue d'Anjou.

After pushing open one of the two main gates, he crossed the courtyard, climbed the steps, and entered a hall paved with coloured marble.

A double staircase, fitted with a red carpet and brass stair-rods, was built against the high walls of shining stucco. At the bottom of the stairs there was a banana-tree, whose broad leaves hung over the velvet-covered banister-rail. Two bronze candelabra supported porcelain globes hung in little chains; hot air came from the gaping vents of the radiators, and nothing could be heard but the ticking of a grandfather clock which stood at the other end of the hall, under a wall-trophy.

A bell rang; a footman appeared, and showed Frédéric into a small room where there were two strong-boxes containing pigeon-holes filled with files. Monsieur Dambreuse was in the middle of the room, writing at a roll-top desk.

He glanced through old Roque's letter, cut open the cloth wrapper containing the papers, and examined them carefully.

From a distance, on account of his slender build, he could still pass for a young man. But his thinning white hair, his emaciated limbs, and above all the extraordinary pallor of his face, all revealed a decrepit constitution. A pitiless energy lay in his grey-green eyes, which were colder than eyes of glass. He had prominent cheekbones, and the joints of his hands were knotted.

Standing up at last, he asked the young man a few questions about common acquaintances, about Nogent, and about his studies; then he dismissed him with a bow. Frédéric went out by another corridor, and found himself in the lower part of the courtyard, next to the coachhouse.

A blue brougham, with a black horse in the shafts, was standing at the foot of the steps. The carriage door opened, a lady climbed in, and with a dull rumbling noise the brougham moved off across the sandy ground.

Frédéric reached the main gate from the other side of the yard at the same moment as the brougham. As there was no room for him to pass, he was obliged to wait. The young woman, leaning out of the window, was talking to the concierge in a low voice. All he could see of her was her back, covered with a purple cloak. In the meantime he peered into the inside of the carriage, which was upholstered in blue rep, with silk fringes and trimmings. The lady's clothes seemed to fill the whole carriage, and out of this little padded box there drifted a perfume of orris, an indefinable scent of feminine elegance. The coachman loosened the reins, the horse turned sharply round the corner-stone, and the carriage disappeared.

Frédéric walked home along the boulevards. He was sorry that he had not been able to get a closer look at Madame Dambreuse.

A little way past the Rue Montmartre, a traffic block made him turn his head; and, on the other side of the street, he read on a marble tablet:

JACQUES ARNOUX

Why had he not thought of her earlier? It was Deslauriers' fault. He went over to the shop, but did not go in; he waited for her to appear.

The high plate-glass windows revealed an ingeniously arranged display of statuettes, drawings, engravings, catalogues, and numbers of *L'Art Industriel*; and the subscription prices were given again on the door, the middle of which was adorned with the publisher's initials. On the walls could be seen some large pictures gleaming with varnish; at the back there stood two cabinets loaded with pieces of china, bronzes, and other attractive curios, and between them there was a little staircase, closed at the top by a velvet curtain. A chandelier of old Dresden china, a green carpet, and an inlaid table made this interior look more like a drawing-room than a shop.

Frédéric pretended to be examining the drawings. After countless hesitations he went in.

An assistant lifted the curtain and in answer to his inquiry said that Monsieur would not be 'at the shop' before five o'clock. But if he could take a message . . .

'No . . . I'll come back,' Frédéric replied softly.

The following days were spent in looking for lodgings; and he decided on a second-floor room in a private hotel in the Rue Saint-Hyacinthe.

Carrying a brand new blotter under his arm, he went to the opening lecture at the Law School. Three hundred bare-headed youths sat in an amphitheatre listening to an old man in a red gown whose voice droned on to the accompaniment of the scratching of pens on paper. This lecture-hall reminded Frédéric of the classrooms at school, with the same dusty smell, the same sort of chair, the same boredom. He attended the lectures regularly for a fortnight. But he dropped the Civil Code before they got to Article 3, and he abandoned the Institutes of Justinian at the *Summa divisio personarum*.

The joys he had looked forward to failed to materialize; and after exhausting the resources of a lending-library, inspecting the collections at the Louvre, and going to the theatre several nights in succession, he lapsed into a state of utter lethargy.

Countless novel experiences added to his melancholy. He had to check his laundry himself, and put up with the concierge, a boorish fellow with the build of a male nurse, who came in every morning to make his bed, smelling of drink and muttering under his breath. He disliked his room, which was adorned with an alabaster clock. The partitions were thin, and he could hear the students in the adjoining rooms making punch, laughing, and singing.

Tiring of this lonely life, he sought out one of his former schoolmates, called Baptiste Martinon. He found him in a boarding-house in the Rue Saint-Jacques, grinding away at his rules of procedure, in front of a coal fire.

Opposite him, a woman in a printed calico dress was darning socks.

Martinon was what people call a good-looking fellow: tall and plump, with regular features and prominent bluish eyes. His father, a prosperous farmer, intended him to become a magistrate; and in his eagerness to look serious even at this early age, he wore his beard trimmed in a fringe.

Since Frédéric's distress had no rational cause, and since he could not ascribe it to any actual misfortune, Martinon utterly failed to understand his lamentations about life. He for his part went to the Law School every morning, took a walk in the Luxembourg Gardens afterwards, drank his cup of coffee in some café in the evening, and, with fifteen hundred francs a year and the love of this working woman, was perfectly happy.

'What an idea of happiness!' Frédéric exclaimed inwardly.

He had made another acquaintance at the Law School. This was Monsieur de Cisy, the scion of a noble family, who was like a girl, his manners were so gentle.

Monsieur de Cisy drew as a pastime, and was fond of the Gothic style. They went together several times to admire the Sainte-Chapelle and Notre-Dame. But the young nobleman's distinguished manner concealed an extremely mediocre mind. Everything astonished him; he laughed uproariously at the smallest joke, and showed such complete innocence that Frédéric began by taking him for a humorist and ended up by regarding him as a fool.

Thus there was nobody in whom he could confide, and he was still waiting for an invitation from the Dambreuses.

On New Year's Day he sent them visiting cards, but received none from them.

He had gone once again to *L'Art Industriel*.

He paid a third visit to the shop and at last managed to see Arnoux, who was arguing in a group of five or six people and barely replied to his greeting. Frédéric was offended, but did not give up looking for means of getting in touch with *her*.

The first idea he had was to call frequently at the shop to haggle over the price of some of the pictures. Then he thought of slipping some 'powerful' articles through the magazine's letter-box, in the hope that this would bring about closer relations. But perhaps it would be better to go straight to the point and declare his love? He composed a twelve-page letter full of lyrical outbursts and appeals; but he tore it up, and did nothing, attempted nothing, paralysed by the fear of failure.

Over Arnoux's shop, on the first floor, there were three windows which were lit up every evening. Shadows moved about behind them, and one in particular – hers. He used to come a long way in order to look at those windows and gaze at that shadow.

A negress whom he passed one day in the Tuileries Gardens, holding a little girl by the hand, reminded him of Madame Arnoux's negress. She was sure to come here like other women; and every time he crossed the Tuileries Gardens the hope of meeting her made his heart beat faster. On sunny days he continued his walk as far as the end of the Champs-Élysées.

Women lolling in barouches, their veils fluttering in the breeze, passed close to him, moving at the same steady pace as their horses, with a scarcely perceptible swaying which made the polished leather creak. More and more carriages appeared, slowing down beyond the Rond-Point so that they filled the entire roadway. Mane brushed against mane, lamp against lamp; steel stirrups, silver curb-chains, and brass buckles threw out points of light here and there among the knee breeches, the white gloves, and the furs hanging over the crests on the carriage doors. He felt as if he were lost in a remote world. His eyes wandered over the women's faces; and vague resemblances reminded him of Madame Arnoux. He imagined her in their midst, in one of those little broughams, like Madame Dambreuse's brougham. But now the sun was setting, and the cold wind stirred up swirling clouds of dust. The coachmen tucked their chins into their neckcloths, the wheels started turning faster, the macadam grated; and all the carriages swept down the long avenue at a brisk trot, touching occasionally, overtaking, swerving away from each other, and finally scattering in the Place de la Concorde. Behind the Tuileries, the sky took on the same colour as the slates. The trees in the gardens formed two huge masses, tinged with purple at the top. The gas-lamps were lit; and the Seine, a greenish colour as far as the eye could see, was torn into strips of silvery silk by the piles of the bridges.

He went and dined for forty-three sous in a restaurant in the Rue de La Harpe.

He looked distastefully at the old mahogany counter, the stained napkins, the greasy cutlery, and the hats hanging on the wall. Those around him were students like himself. They were talking about their professors and their mistresses. What did he care about professors? And since when had he had a mistress? To avoid their display of happiness he arrived as late as possible. The tables were all covered with scraps of food. The two waiters, tired-out, were asleep in corners, and a smell of cooking, lamp-oil, and tobacco filled the empty room.

After dinner he went slowly home through the streets. The lamps swung to and fro, casting long patches of flickering yellowish light on to the mud. Shadows with umbrellas stole along the kerb. The pavement was slimy, a mist was falling, and he felt as if the moist darkness enveloping him was sinking endlessly into his heart.

Remorse overtook him, and he went back to the Law School lectures. But as he knew nothing about the matters being elucidated, the simplest things puzzled him.

He started writing a novel entitled *Sylvio, the Fisherman's Son*. The setting was Venice. The hero was himself, the heroine Madame Arnoux. She was called Antonia; and in order to possess her he murdered several gentlemen, burnt down part of the town, and sang under her balcony, where the red damask curtains of the Boulevard Montmartre quivered in the breeze. The echoes from other writers which he noticed in his novel discouraged him; he dropped it, and his feeling of aimlessness grew worse.

Then he begged Deslauriers to come and share his room. They would manage somehow or other on his allowance of two thousand francs; anything was better than this intolerable life. But Deslauriers could not leave Troyes yet. He urged Frédéric to enjoy himself, and to cultivate the acquaintance of Sénécal.

Sénécal was a teacher of mathematics, a strong-minded fellow with Republican convictions, a future Saint-Just according to the clerk. Frédéric climbed his five flights of stairs three times without receiving a single call in return. He did not go back.

He decided to enjoy himself and went to the balls at the Opéra. These wild entertainments chilled his blood as soon as he set foot in the place. Besides, he was inhibited by the fear of a financial humiliation, imagining that supper with a domino was a formidable undertaking involving considerable expense.

Yet it seemed to him that he deserved to be loved. Sometimes he awoke with his heart full of hope, dressed carefully as if he were going to a rendezvous, and wandered endlessly around Paris. Every woman walking in front of him or coming towards him made him say to himself: 'This is she!' But every time he suffered a fresh disappointment. The thought of Madame Arnoux intensified these longings of his. Perhaps he would find her in his path; and, in order to accost her, he imagined odd coincidences, and extraordinary dangers from which he would rescue her.

So the days went by, in the repetition of the same boring activities and the same habits. He glanced through leaflets in the Odéon arcade, read the *Revue des Deux Mondes* in some café or other, and dropped into the Collège de France to spend an hour listening to a lecture on Chinese or on political economy. Every week he wrote a long letter to Deslauriers, dined now and then with Martinon, and occasionally saw Monsieur de Cisy.

He hired a piano and composed some German waltzes.

One evening, at the Théâtre du Palais-Royal, he saw Arnoux in a stage box sitting beside a woman. Was it *she?* The green taffeta screen drawn across the edge of the box concealed her face. At last the curtain rose and the screen was lowered. The woman was a tall, faded creature of about thirty, with thick lips which revealed splendid teeth when she laughed. She was talking familiarly to Arnoux and tapping him on the fingers with her fan. Then a fair-haired girl, whose eyes were a little red as if she had just been crying, sat down between them. From then on Arnoux talked to her, half leaning over her shoulder, while she listened without answering. Frédéric racked his brains trying to guess the social rank of these women, who were modestly dressed in dark dresses with flat, turned-down collars.

At the end of the performance he hurried out into the corridors, which were crowded with people. In front of him, Arnoux was going down the staircase, step by step, with the two women, one on each arm.

All of a sudden, the light of a gas-jet fell on him. He had a black mourning-band round his hat. Perhaps she was dead? This idea tormented Frédéric so violently that the next day he hurried round to *L'Art Industriel*, and, quickly paying for one of the prints displayed in the window, asked the shop-assistant how Monsieur Arnoux was keeping.

The man replied:

'Why, very well.'

Turning pale, Frédéric added:

'And Madame?'

'Madame is well too.'

Frédéric went off without his print.

The winter came to an end. He felt less melancholy in the spring, started working for his examination, passed it without distinction, and then left for Nogent.

He did not go to Troyes to see his friend, so as to avoid his mother's comments. Then, at the beginning of the next term, he left his lodgings and took a couple of rooms on the Quai Napoléon, which he furnished. He had given up hope of receiving an invitation to the Dambreuses'; and his grand passion for Madame Arnoux was beginning to fade away.

IV

ONE morning in December, on his way to attend a lecture on procedure, he thought he noticed more animation than usual in the Rue Saint-Jacques. Students were rushing out of the cafés or calling to each other from house to house through the open windows; the shopkeepers were standing in the middle of the pavement, watching uneasily; shutters were being closed; and when he reached the Rue Soufflot he saw a large crowd assembled round the Panthéon.

Youths in groups of anything from five to twelve were strolling around arm in arm, occasionally going up to larger groups which were standing here and there; at the far end of the square, against the iron railings, men in smocks were holding forth, while policemen were walking up and down beside the walls, their three-cornered hats cocked to one side and their hands behind their backs, making the pavement ring with the sound of their heavy boots. Everybody wore a mysterious, anxious expression; clearly something was in the air; and on each person's lips there was an unspoken question.

Frédéric found himself standing next to a fair-haired young man with a pleasant face, who sported a moustache and a little beard like a dandy of the age of Louis XIII. He asked him what all the excitement was about.

'I've no idea,' the other replied; 'and neither have they. It's a habit of theirs nowadays. It's a good joke, isn't it!'

And he burst out laughing.

The petitions for reform which had been circulated among the National Guard, together with the Humann census and other events,[3] had led during the past six months to inexplicable demonstrations. Indeed, these now took place so often that the newspapers no longer mentioned them.

'All this lacks form and colour,' Frédéric's neighbour continued. 'I do trow, honoured sir, that we have degenerated. In the good old days of Loys the Eleventh, nay even of Benjamin Constant, there was more of a rebellious spirit among the scholars of the town. I deem them as meek as sheep, as stupid as gherkins, and by my troth, well fitted to be grocers. And this is what folks call the Youth of the Schools.'

He spread his arms out wide, like the actor Frédérick Lemaître in *Robert Macaire*.

'Youth of the Schools, I give you my blessing!'

Then, speaking to a rag-picker, who was poking around among some oyster shells outside a wine-merchant's shop:

'You, my good man – are you a member of the Youth of the Schools?'

The old man turned a hideous face towards him, in which, in the midst of a grey beard, a red nose, and two stupid, bleary eyes could be distinguished.

'No! You look to me rather like "one of those men of criminal appearance who can be seen, in various groups of people, scattering money in handfuls". Oh, scatter away, venerable greybeard! Corrupt me with the treasures of Albion! *Are you English?* I do not reject the gifts of Artaxerxes! Let us talk a little about the Customs Union.'[4]

Frédéric felt somebody touch him on the shoulder, and turned round. It was Martinon, looking astonishingly pale.

'Well,' he said with a deep sigh, 'another riot!'

He was afraid of getting involved, and was very sorry for himself. Men in smocks he found particularly worrying, because they were sure to belong to secret societies.

'What secret societies?' said the young man with the moustache. 'That's just an old dodge of the Government's, to scare the middle classes.'

Martinon begged him to lower his voice, for fear of the police.

'You mean to say you still believe in the police? Come to that, Monsieur, how do you know that I'm not a police spy myself?'

And he looked at him in such a way that Martinon, thoroughly upset, failed to see the joke at first. The crowd was pushing them back, and all three of them had been forced to climb up on to the little staircase which led, by way of a corridor, into the new amphitheatre.

Soon the throng split up of its own accord; several people bared their heads; they were greeting the famous professor, Samuel Rondelot, who, wrapped in his thick frock-coat, raising his silver-rimmed spectacles in one hand, and wheezing asthmatically, was ambling along on his way to give his lecture. This man was one of the great jurists of the nineteenth century, rivalling even Zachariae and Ruhdorff. Although he had recently been raised to the peerage, this had not altered his behaviour in the slightest. He was known to be poor, and was greatly respected.

Meanwhile, on the far side of the square, some people started shouting:

'Down with Guizot!'

'Down with Pritchard!'[5]

'Down with the traitors!'

'Down with Louis-Philippe!'

The crowd surged forward, and, pressing against the closed door of the courtyard, prevented the professor from going any farther. He stopped at the foot of the staircase. Soon he could be seen on the lowest of the three steps. He spoke; a loud murmur drowned his voice. A popular figure a moment before, he was hated now, for he represented authority. Every time he tried to make himself heard the shouting began again. With a sweeping gesture he urged the students to follow him. He was answered by a general uproar. He shrugged his shoulders contemptuously and disappeared into the corridor. Martinon had taken advantage of his position to vanish at the same time.

'What a coward!' said Frédéric.

'He's a sensible fellow,' the other replied.

The crowd broke into applause. They regarded the professor's retreat as a victory for themselves. People were looking out of every window. Some started singing the *Marseillaise*; others suggested marching to Béranger's house.

'To Laffitte's!'

'To Chateaubriand's!'[6]

'To Voltaire's!' yelled the young man with the fair moustache.

The policemen tried to push their way through the crowd, saying as gently as they could:

'Move along, gentlemen, move along now.'

Somebody shouted:

'Down with the butchers!'

This insult had become customary since the troubles in September.[7] Everybody took it up. They hissed and jeered at the guardians of the law, who began to turn pale. One of them could not stand it any longer, and seeing a boy who had come too close to him and was laughing in his face, he gave him such a violent shove that he fell on his back five yards away, in front of the wine-merchant's shop. Everybody drew away, but almost immediately the policeman himself was on the ground, felled by a sort of Hercules whose hair protruded like a bundle of tow from under an oil-cloth cap.

After standing for the past few minutes on the corner of the Rue Saint-Jacques, he had suddenly dropped a large cardboard box he was carrying, in order to throw himself at the policeman; and now, holding him prostrate beneath him, he was punching him in the face with all his might. The other policemen came running up. The big fellow was so strong that it took at least four of them to overpower him. Two shook him by the collar, two others pulled him by the arms, and a fifth pounded him in the small of his back with one knee, and all of them called him a brigand, a murderer, and a rabble-rouser. With his chest bare and his clothes in tatters, he protested his innocence; he had been unable to stand by and see a child struck down.

'My name is Dussardier! I work for Messieurs Valincart Frères, laces and fancy goods, Rue de Cléry. Where's my cardboard box? I want my box!'

He kept on repeating:

'Dussardier! . . . Rue de Cléry. My box!'

However he calmed down and, with a stoical air, allowed himself to be marched off in the direction of the guard-house in the Rue Descartes. A stream of people followed him. Frédéric and the young man with the moustache walked immediately behind him, full of admiration for the shop-assistant and indignant at the brutality of authority.

The further they went, the thinner the crowd became.

Every now and then the policemen looked round and glared ferociously; and as the rowdy characters could find nothing more to do, and the inquisitive nothing more to see, they gradually drifted away. Passers-by whom they met looked Dussardier up and down and indulged in loud and insulting comments. One old woman, standing on her doorstep, even shouted that he had stolen a loaf; this injustice added to the exasperation of the two friends. At last they arrived at the guard-house. There were only about twenty people left. The sight of the soldiers was enough to disperse them.

Frédéric and his companion boldly asked to see the man who had just been taken to the cells. The sentry threatened to put them inside themselves if they persisted. They demanded to see the superintendent in their capacity as law-students, refused to give their names, declaring that the prisoner was a fellow pupil of theirs.

They were shown into a bare room in which there were four benches placed against walls of smoke-blackened plaster. A hatchway opened at the far end, and Dussardier's robust face appeared. With his dishevelled hair, his little honest eyes, and his square-tipped nose, he looked vaguely like a good-natured dog.

'Don't you recognize us?' said Hussonnet.

This was the name of the young man with the moustache.

'But . . .' stammered Dussardier.

'Oh, stop playing the fool,' the other went on. 'Everybody knows that you're a law-student like ourselves.'

In spite of the winks they gave him, Dussardier failed to grasp their meaning. He seemed to reflect for a moment, and then suddenly asked:

'Have they found my box?'

Frédéric, discouraged, raised his eyes to the ceiling. Hussonnet replied:

'Ah, you mean the box you put your lecture notes in! Yes, yes! Don't you worry about it!'

They started their dumbshow again. Dussardier finally realized that they had come to help him; and he kept quiet, not wanting to compromise them. Besides, he felt a sort of shame at seeing himself raised to the social rank of a student, on a par with these young men who had such white hands.

'Do you want to send a message to anybody?' asked Frédéric.

'No, thank you, nobody.'

'But what about your family?'

He hung his head without answering; the poor fellow was a bastard. The two friends were astonished by his silence.

'Have you got anything to smoke?' Frédéric went on.

Dussardier felt his clothes, then took out of the depths of his pocket the debris of a pipe, a splendid meerschaum pipe, with an ebony stem, a silver lid, and an amber mouthpiece.

For three years he had been working on this pipe to make it a masterpiece. He had taken care to keep the bowl constantly encased in a chamois leather sheath, to smoke the pipe as slowly as possible, never putting it down on a marble surface, and to hang it up every night beside his bed. Now he shook the broken pieces in his hand, the nails of which were bleeding; and, with his chin sunk on his chest and his eyes staring, he gazed at these ruins of his happiness with a look of ineffable melancholy.

'What if we gave him some cigars?' whispered Hussonnet, reaching towards his pocket.

Frédéric had already put a full cigar-case on the edge of the hatch.

'Take these. Good-bye, and keep your chin up!'

Dussardier threw himself on their two outstretched hands. He clasped them in a sort of frenzy, his voice broken with sobs.

'What? ... For me? ... For me? ...'

Evading his expressions of gratitude, the two friends left the guard-house, and went to lunch together at the Café Tabourey, in front of the Luxembourg.

While he was cutting his steak, Hussonnet informed his companion that he worked for several fashion magazines and designed advertisements for *L'Art Industriel*.

'Jacques Arnoux's business,' said Frédéric.

'You know him, do you?'

'Yes. No ... I mean, I've seen him, I've met him.'

He asked Hussonnet casually if he ever saw his wife.

'Now and then,' the Bohemian replied.

Frédéric did not dare to go on asking questions; this man had just assumed a position of immense importance in his life; he paid the bill for their lunch without the other raising the slightest objection.

Their liking was mutual; they exchanged addresses, and Hussonnet cordially invited him to accompany him as far as the Rue de Fleurus.

They were in the middle of the garden when Arnoux's employee, holding his breath, twisted his face into a horrible grimace and started crowing like a cock, whereupon all the cocks in the neighbourhood replied with prolonged cock-a-doodle-doos.

'It's a signal,' said Hussonnet.

They stopped near the Théâtre Bobino, in front of a house which was approached by way of a passage. In an attic window, between pots of nasturtiums and sweet-peas, a young woman appeared, bare-headed, in her stays, leaning on the roof-gutter.

'Good-day, my angel, good-day, my duck,' said Hussonnet, blowing kisses to her.

He kicked open the gate and disappeared.

Frédéric waited the rest of the week for him. He did not dare to go to Hussonnet's lodgings, for fear of appearing impatient to have his hospitality repaid; but he searched for him all over the Latin Quarter. One evening he met him, and took him to his room on the Quai Napoléon.

They talked for hours, opening their hearts to one another. Hussonnet hankered after the fame and profits of the theatre. He collaborated on musical comedies which were never produced, had ideas galore, and wrote the words for songs: he sang one or two for Frédéric's benefit. Then, catching sight of a volume of Hugo and another of Lamartine in the bookcase, he launched out on to a sarcastic attack on the Romantic school. Those poets lacked both common-sense and grammar, and above all they were not French! He prided himself on knowing his language and criticized the finest phrases with that cantankerous severity, that pedantic taste which characterizes frivolous-minded people when they come face to face with serious art.

Frédéric was offended in his preferences, and felt like breaking off relations. Why should he not risk, here and now, the question on which his happiness depended? He asked the young writer if he could take him to Arnoux's house.

Nothing could be simpler, and they agreed to meet next day.

Hussonnet missed this appointment; he missed three others. One Saturday about four o'clock, he suddenly turned up. But taking advantage of Frédéric's carriage, he stopped first of all at the Théâtre-Français to buy a ticket for a box; he had himself set down at a tailor's and a dressmaker's; he wrote notes in concierges' lodges. At last they reached the Boulevard Montmartre. Frédéric crossed the shop and climbed the stairs. Arnoux recognized him in the mirror in front of his desk; and, without stopping writing, held out one hand to him over his shoulder.

Five or six people filled the narrow room, which was lit by a single window looking out on the courtyard. A settle upholstered in brown wool occupied a recess at the far end, between two curtains of the same material. On the mantelpiece, which was littered with papers, there was a bronze Venus, flanked by a pair of candelabra fitted with pink candles. On the right, beside a filing-cabinet, a man was sitting in an armchair, reading a newspaper with his hat on; the walls were covered with prints and pictures, rare engravings, or sketches by contemporary masters, all adorned with dedications indicating the sincerest affection for Jacques Arnoux.

'How are things with you?' he asked, turning to Frédéric.

And without waiting for his reply, he whispered to Hussonnet: 'What's your friend called?'

Then aloud:

'Have a cigar. They're in the box on the filing-cabinet.'

L'Art Industriel, situated in the very heart of Paris, was a convenient meeting-place, a neutral territory where rival factions could rub shoulders. Among those present that particular day were Anténor Braive, the painter of kings; Jules Burrieu, whose drawings were beginning to popularize the Algerian wars; the caricaturist Sombaz; the sculptor Vourdat; and others, none of whom was as Frédéric had imagined him. Their manners were simple, their conversation free. The mystic Lovarias told a smutty story; and the famous Dittmer, the inventor of the Oriental landscape, wore a woollen spencer under his waistcoat and went off to catch an omnibus.

They talked at first about a certain Apollonie, a former model, whom Burrieu claimed to have seen riding along the boulevard in a carriage with four horses and two postilions. Hussonnet attributed this metamorphosis to her succession of protectors.

'That young fellow knows the girls of Paris, and no mistake,' said Arnoux.

'After you, sire, if there's anything left,' the Bohemian replied with a military salute, parodying the grenadier who offered his water-bottle to Napoleon.

Then they discussed some paintings in which Apollonie's head had been depicted. Absent colleagues were criticized. Surprise was expressed at the prices fetched by their works; and everybody was complaining of not earning enough when there entered a man of medium height, with bright eyes and a rather wild expression, wearing a coat which was fastened by a single button.

'What a bunch of shopkeepers you are!' he said. 'Good God, what difference does it make? The old boys who turned out master-pieces never bothered about the money. Correggio, Murillo. . .'

'Not to mention Pellerin,' said Sombaz.

But without answering this witticism, he went on speaking with such vehemence that Arnoux was obliged to say to him twice:

'My wife wants you to come along on Thursday. Don't forget.'

These words brought Frédéric's thoughts back to Madame Arnoux. No doubt the little dressing-room next to the divan led to her bedroom. Arnoux had just opened the dressing-room door to fetch a handkerchief, and Frédéric had caught sight of a washstand at the far end. But suddenly a sort of grumbling mutter came from the chimney corner; it was the man reading his paper in the arm-chair. He was five foot nine inches tall, with eyelids which drooped slightly, grey hair, and a majestic bearing; and his name was Regimbart.

'What is it, Citizen?' asked Arnoux.

'Another scurvy trick of the Government's!'

He was referring to the dismissal of a schoolmaster. Pellerin returned to his comparison of Michelangelo and Shakespeare. Dittmer was just going when Arnoux stopped him and put a couple of bank-notes in his hand. Then Hussonnet, thinking that this was an auspicious moment, said:

'Governor, I suppose you couldn't advance me . . .'

But Arnoux had sat down again and was chiding a shabby-looking old man with blue spectacles.

'Ah, you're a fine one, I must say, Papa Isaac! That's three pictures shown up and finished. Everybody's laughing at me. They know the damn things now. What do you expect me to do with them? I'll have to send them to California . . . or to the devil! No, shut up!'

The old fellow's speciality consisted of putting the signatures of old masters at the bottom of his own pictures. Arnoux refused to pay him, and told him harshly to get out. Then, changing his manner, he greeted a haughty-looking gentleman with side-whiskers and a white cravat, who wore a decoration in his buttonhole.

With his elbow on the window-hasp, Arnoux talked to him for a long time in a honeyed voice. Finally he burst out:

'You know, Monsieur Le Comte, it's an easy matter for me to find jobbers!'

The nobleman having submitted, Arnoux paid him twenty-five louis, and, as soon as he was outside, exclaimed:

'What a bore those high-and-mighty nobles are!'

'All rascals!' murmured Regimbart.

As the afternoon wore on, Arnoux grew busier and busier; he sorted out articles, opened letters, balanced accounts; at the sound of hammering in the shop, he went out to supervise the packing, then resumed his work; and all the time, while his pen was speeding over the paper, he kept up his repartee. He was due to dine with his lawyer that evening, and the next day he was leaving for Belgium.

The others chatted about the topics of the day: Cherubini's portrait, the hemicycle at the Beaux-Arts, the forthcoming exhibition.[8] Pellerin railed against the Institut. Gossip and argument intermingled. The low-ceilinged room was so crowded that nobody could move; and the light from the pink candles pierced the cigar-smoke like rays of sunshine in a mist.

The door near the divan opened, and a tall, slim woman came in, her brusque movements making all her watch-charms tinkle together on her black taffeta dress.

It was the woman he had glimpsed at the Palais-Royal the previous summer. Some of those present, greeting her by name, shook hands with her. Hussonnet had finally succeeded in obtaining fifty francs. The clock struck seven; everybody left.

Arnoux told Pellerin to stay behind; and led Mademoiselle Vatnaz into the dressing-room.

Frédéric could not hear what they were saying; they were talking in a whisper. But once the woman raised her voice:

'It was all settled six months ago, and I'm still waiting!'

There was a long silence. Mademoiselle Vatnaz reappeared. Arnoux had once again promised her something.

'Oh, later on, we'll see!'

'Farewell, happy man!' she said as she left.

Arnoux strode back into the dressing-room, put some pomade on his moustache, hitched up his braces to tighten his trouser-straps, and, while he was washing his hands, called out:

'I want two panels to go above the door. Boucher style. Two hundred and fifty francs each. All right?'

'All right,' said the artist, blushing.

'Good. And don't forget my wife!'

Frédéric accompanied Pellerin as far as the top of the Faubourg Poissonnière, and asked if he might come to see him occasionally, a favour which was graciously granted.

Pellerin used to read every book on aesthetics he could lay his hands on, in the hope of discovering the true theory of Beauty, for he was convinced that once he had found it he would be able to paint masterpieces. He surrounded himself with every conceivable accessory – drawings, plaster casts, models, engravings – and hunted around fretfully, blaming the weather, his nerves or his studio, going out into the street to seek inspiration, thrilling with joy when he had found it, but then abandoning the work he had begun, to dream of another which would be even finer. Tortured by a longing for fame, wasting his days in argument, believing in countless ridiculous ideas, in systems, in criticisms, in the importance of the codification or reform of art, he had reached the age of fifty without producing anything but sketches. His robust pride prevented him from feeling any discouragement, but he was always irritable, and in that state of excitement, at once natural and artificial, which is characteristic of actors.

Going into his studio, one's eye was caught by two large pictures, in which the first tints, scattered here and there, formed patches of brown, red, and blue on the white canvas. Over them there stretched a tracery of chalk lines, like the meshes of a net which had been mended time and again; indeed it was absolutely impossible to make anything of it. Pellerin explained the subject of these two compositions by indicating the missing parts with his thumb. One was intended to represent 'The Madness of Nebuchadnezzar', the other 'The Burning of Rome by Nero.' Frédéric admired them.

He admired some studies of nudes with dishevelled hair, some landscapes abounding in storm-twisted tree-trunks, and above all some pen-and-ink sketches, inspired by Callot, Rembrandt, or Goya, the originals of which were unknown to him. Pellerin thought very little of these early works of his; now he was for the grand manner; he pontificated eloquently on Phidias and Winckelmann. The objects around him gave added force to his argument; there was a skull on a prayer-stool, some scimitars, and a monk's frock, which Frédéric put on.

When Frédéric arrived early, he used to find the other in his wretched truckle-bed, screened by a ragged piece of tapestry; for Pellerin was an assiduous theatre-goer and went to bed late. An old woman in rags looked after him, he dined in cheap eating-houses, and he had no mistress. His learning, which he had picked up all over the place, lent spice to his paradoxes. His hatred of the vulgar and the mediocre found expression in sarcastic outbursts of superb lyricism, and he held the old masters in such veneration that it almost raised him to their level.

But why did he never mention Madame Arnoux? As for her husband, sometimes he called him a good fellow, sometimes a charlatan. Frédéric waited for him to take him into his confidence.

One day, looking through one of Pellerin's sketchbooks, he came across a portrait of a gipsy who bore a certain resemblance to Mademoiselle Vatnaz, and, as that lady interested him, he asked what her circumstances were.

She had started as a schoolteacher in the provinces, Pellerin thought; now she gave lessons and tried to write for the cheap magazines.

The way she behaved with Arnoux, in Frédéric's opinion, suggested that she was his mistress.

'Oh, I don't know. He's got others.'

Then the young man, turning his face away, for he was blushing with shame at the vileness of the thought which had entered his head, remarked in a breezy manner:

'I suppose his wife pays him back in kind?'

'Not a bit of it! She's a virtuous woman.'

Frédéric was stricken with remorse, and took to visiting the shop more frequently.

The big letters spelling out the name of Arnoux on the marble slab above the shop seemed to him to be unique of their kind and charged with meaning, like a sacred script. The wide, sloping pavement appeared to speed him along, the door opened almost by itself, and the handle, which was smooth to the touch, seemed as gentle and sensitive as a hand in his own. Imperceptibly he became as punctual as Regimbart.

Every day, Regimbart would sit down in his armchair by the fire, get hold of the *National*[9] and hang on to it, expressing his opinion by exclamations or simply by shrugging his shoulders. Now and then he would wipe his forehead with his rolled-up handkerchief, which he usually wore on his chest, tucked in between two buttons of his green frock-coat. He wore trousers with a crease in them, half-boots, a long cravat, and a hat with a turned-up brim which made it possible to pick him out in a crowd a long way off.

At eight o'clock in the morning he would come down from the heights of Montmartre to drink his white wine in the Rue Notre-Dame-des-Victoires. His lunch, which was followed by several games of billiards, took him until three o'clock. He then made for the Passage des Panoramas to drink his absinthe. After his visit to Arnoux, he went into the Estaminet Bordelais for his vermouth; then, instead of going home to his wife, he often chose to dine alone, in a little café on the Place Gaillon, where he insisted on 'home cooking, good wholesome food'. Finally he moved on to another billiard-saloon, and he stayed there until midnight, until one in the morning, until the moment when, with the gas turned out and the shutters closed, the exhausted proprietor begged him to go away.

It was not love of the bottle which drew Citizen Regimbart to these haunts, but the ingrained habit of talking politics; with age his verve had diminished, and he had become silent and morose. From his serious expression anybody would have thought that his mind was full of the most profound ideas. But he expressed none of them; and nobody, even among his friends, had ever seen him working, although he gave out that he had a business agency.

Arnoux seemed to have a boundless admiration for him. One day he said to Frédéric:

'He's a deep 'un, that fellow! He's got a good head on his shoulders!'

On another occasion, Regimbart spread out on his desk some papers concerning china-clay mines in Brittany; Arnoux set great store by his experience.

Frédéric showed added politeness to Regimbart, even offering him a glass of absinthe now and then; and although he considered him stupid, he often spent a full hour in his company, simply because he was Jacques Arnoux's friend.

Having helped certain contemporary masters at the outset of their careers, the picture-dealer, as a man who believed in progress, had tried to increase his profits, while at the same time maintaining his artistic pretensions. His aim was the emancipation of the arts, the sublime at a popular price. All the Paris luxury trades came under his influence, which was good in small matters, but baneful when larger issues were involved. With his passion for pandering to the public, he led able artists astray, corrupted the strong, exhausted the weak, and bestowed fame on the second-rate, controlling their destinies by means of his connexions and his magazine. Young painters longed to see their works in his window and upholsterers came to him for their patterns. Frédéric regarded him as an amalgam of a millionaire, a dilettante, and a man of action. But a good many things about

Arnoux surprised him, for the latter was a cunning business-man.

A picture which he had bought in Paris for fifteen hundred francs would be sent to him from some distant part of Germany or Italy, and, displaying an invoice pricing it at four thousand, he would resell it, for a favour, at three thousand five hundred. A common trick of his with painters was to demand, as an extra commission, a small-scale copy of their picture, under the pretext that he was going to publish a print of it; he always sold the copy, and the print never appeared. To those who complained of being exploited, he replied with a playful dig in the ribs. An excellent fellow in other respects, he lavished cigars on all and sundry, spoke familiarly to strangers, and was often moved to sudden enthusiasm for a picture or a man, sticking to his opinion when this happened, sparing no expense, and throwing himself into a frantic round of visits, letters, and advertisements. He considered himself to be the soul of honesty, and, under the impulse of his expansive nature, he would naïvely recount his unscrupulous tricks.

Once, in order to annoy a colleague who was giving a big banquet to launch a rival art magazine, he asked Frédéric, just before the dinner was due to be held, to write out in front of him some notes putting off the guests.

'There's nothing dishonourable about that, you understand.'

And the young man did not dare to refuse him this service.

The next day, going into his office with Hussonnet, Frédéric saw the hem of a dress disappearing through the door which opened on to the staircase.

'I'm terribly sorry,' said Hussonnet. 'If I'd thought there were ladies . . .'

'Oh, that was only my wife,' said Arnoux. 'She just came up to see me as she was passing.'

'What!' said Frédéric.

'Why, yes. She's going home now.'

The things around him suddenly lost their charm. The vague atmosphere of which he had been conscious here had just vanished, or rather had never existed. He felt an immense surprise, and something akin to the anguish of a betrayal.

Arnoux, rummaging in his drawer, was smiling. Was he laughing at him? The shop-assistant placed a bundle of damp papers on the table.

'Ah, the posters!' the dealer exclaimed. 'It'll be ages before I can have dinner tonight!'

Regimbart picked up his hat.

'What, are you going?'

'It's seven o'clock!' said Regimbart.

Frédéric followed him.

On the corner of the Rue Montmartre he turned round; he looked at the first-floor windows; and he laughed inwardly, pitying himself, as he remembered how lovingly he had often gazed at them. Where did she live then? How could he meet her now? Solitude opened up once more about his desire, which was vaster than ever.

'Are you coming along to have one?' asked Regimbart.

'To meet whom?' said Frédéric, who had misheard.

'To have an absinthe!'

And yielding to Regimbart's addiction, Frédéric allowed himself to be taken along to the Estaminet Bordelais. While his companion, leaning on his elbow, was gazing at the decanter, he glanced from side to side. Catching sight of Pellerin's profile among the people on the pavement, he tapped sharply on the window-pane; and the painter had scarcely sat down before Regimbart asked him why he was no longer to be seen at *L'Art Industriel*.

'I'll be damned if I ever go back there. The man's a bore, a philistine, a scoundrel, a ruffian!'

These insults gratified Frédéric's anger. However, they wounded him too, for it seemed to him that they reflected to some extent on Madame Arnoux.

'Why, what's he done to you?' asked Regimbart.

Pellerin stamped on the floor and breathed hard instead of replying.

He secretly turned out portraits in charcoal and chalk, and pastiches of old masters for ignorant art-collectors; and as he was ashamed of these pieces of work, he generally preferred to say nothing about them. But 'that swine Arnoux' infuriated him too much, and he gave vent to his feelings.

Commissioned to paint a couple of pictures, as Frédéric could testify, he had delivered them to Arnoux – and the dealer had dared to criticize them! He had found fault with the composition, the colour, and the drawing, particularly the drawing; and, to cut a long story short, he had refused to take them at any price. Pellerin, finding himself in difficulties over a bill which had fallen due, had let the

Jew Isaac have them; and a fortnight later, Arnoux himself sold them to a Spaniard for two thousand francs.

'Yes, two thousand francs! What a filthy trick! And he's pulled off plenty more like that too. One of these days we'll see him in the dock.'

'You're exaggerating,' said Frédéric in a timid voice.

'Oh, so I'm exaggerating, am I?' shouted the artist, crashing his fist down on the table.

This violent gesture restored all the young man's self-assurance. No doubt Arnoux could have behaved better; but if he really thought those two paintings were . . .

'Bad, eh? Go on, say it! Have you seen them? Is it your profession? Because you'd better get this into your head, my boy: I don't brook criticism from amateurs.'

'Oh, it's none of my business,' said Frédéric.

'Then what are you defending him for?' Pellerin asked coldly.

The young man stammered:

'But because he's a friend of mine.'

'Give him a kiss from me! Good night!'

And the painter stormed out, without saying anything, of course, about the drink he had just had.

Frédéric had convinced himself, in defending Arnoux. In the warmth of his own eloquence, he felt a sudden affection for that kindly, intelligent man who was slandered by his friends and who now, deserted by them all, was working on his own. He gave in to a strange longing to see him again, straight away. Ten minutes later he pushed open the door of the shop.

Arnoux was working with his assistant on some enormous posters for an exhibition of pictures.

'Well, now! What brings you back?'

This simple question embarrassed Frédéric; and, not knowing what to reply, he asked if anybody had happened to find his notebook, a little notebook in blue leather.

'The one you keep your love letters in?' said Arnoux.

Frédéric, blushing like a virgin, repudiated this supposition.

'Your poems, then?' said the dealer.

He picked up one proof after another, discussing their shape, their colour, their margins; and Frédéric found himself becoming increasingly irritated by his thoughtful expression, and above all by his hands as he fingered the posters: big, rather flabby hands, with flat nails. At last Arnoux stood up, and, saying: 'That's that!' chucked him familiarly under the chin. This liberty annoyed Frédéric; he stepped back, and then walked out of the office, so he thought, for the last time in his life. Madame Arnoux herself was somehow lowered in his eyes by her husband's vulgarity.

In the course of the same week he received a letter from Deslauriers saying that he would be arriving in Paris on the following Thursday. In a violent reaction he fell back on this stronger and loftier band of affection. A man like Deslauriers was worth all the women in the world. From now on he would have no further need of Regimbart, Pellerin, Hussonnet, or anybody else. In order to make his friend comfortable, he bought an iron bedstead and a second armchair, and divided his bedding into two; and on the Thursday morning he was getting dressed to go to meet Deslauriers when the doorbell rang. Arnoux came in.

'Just a word! Yesterday I was sent a fine trout from Geneva. We're counting on you to come along this evening, at seven o'clock sharp . . . It's 24 *bis*, Rue de Choiseul. Don't forget!'

Frédéric was obliged to sit down. His knees were shaking. He kept saying to himself: 'At last! At last!' Then he wrote to his tailor, his hatter, and his bootmaker, sending the three notes off by three different messengers. The key turned in the lock, and the concierge appeared, with a trunk on his shoulder.

Seeing Deslauriers, Frédéric began to tremble like a guilty wife under her husband's gaze.

'What's the matter with you?' said Deslauriers. 'Surely you got my letter?'

Frédéric had not the courage to lie.

He opened his arms and threw himself on his friend's breast.

Then the clerk told his story. His father had refused to give an account of his trusteeship, imagining that the legal period for such accounts was ten years. But Deslauriers, being well up in procedure, had finally managed to extort the whole of his mother's legacy – seven thousand francs clear – which he had there on him, in an old pocket-book.

'It's a reserve fund in case of accidents. Tomorrow morning I must find a way of investing it, not to mention lodgings for myself. Today I'm on holiday and entirely at your disposal, old fellow.'

'Oh, don't put yourself out!' said Frédéric. 'If you've something important to do tonight . . .'

'Oh, come now! I'd be a selfish wretch . . .'

This epithet, flung out at random, cut Frédéric to the quick, like an insulting allusion.

On the table by the fire the concierge had set out some chops, galantine, a lobster, some dessert, and a couple of bottles of claret. Deslauriers was touched by this hospitable reception.

'Upon my word, you're treating me like a king!'

They talked about their past and about the future, and every now and then they clasped each other's hands across the table, exchanging a brief, affectionate glance.

A messenger arrived with a new hat. Deslauriers remarked on the shiny lining.

Then the tailor himself came in, to deliver Frédéric's coat, which he had pressed for him.

'Anybody would think you were getting married,' said Deslauriers.

An hour later, a third person appeared on the scene and drew a pair of shining patent-leather boots from a big black bag. While Frédéric was trying them on, the bootmaker looked superciliously at the country visitor's footwear.

'Does Monsieur require anything?'

'No, thanks,' replied the clerk, tucking his old laced shoes under his chair.

This humiliation annoyed Frédéric. He kept putting off his confession. Finally, as if an idea had suddenly struck him, he exclaimed:

'Good Lord! I was forgetting!'

'What?'

'I'm dining out tonight.'

'At the Dambreuses'? Why don't you ever mention them in your letters?'

It was not at the Dambreuses' he was dining, but at the Arnoux's.

'You should have let me know,' said Deslauriers. 'I'd have come a day later.'

'Impossible!' Frédéric retorted abruptly. 'I only got the invitation this morning, a little while ago.'

And in order to redeem himself, and to take his friend's mind off the matter, he untied the tangled cords round his trunk, arranged all his things in the chest of drawers, and offered him his own bed, saying that he would sleep in the boxroom. Then, at four o'clock, he started washing and changing.

'You've plenty of time,' said the other.

At last he got dressed and went off.

'That's the rich for you,' thought Deslauriers.

And he went to dine in the Rue Saint-Jacques, at a little restaurant kept by a man he knew.

Frédéric's heart was beating so hard that he stopped several times on the stairs. One of his gloves was too tight and burst; and while he was tucking the torn part under his shirt-cuff, Arnoux, who was coming up the stairs behind him, took him by the arm and led him in.

The hall, decorated in the Chinese style, had a painted lantern hanging from the ceiling, and bamboos in the corner. Crossing the drawing-room, Frédéric tripped over a tiger skin. The candelabra had not been lit, but a couple of lamps were burning in the boudoir beyond.

Mademoiselle Marthe came in to say that her mamma was dressing. Arnoux lifted her up to kiss her; then, as he wanted to go to the cellar himself to select certain bottles of wine, he left Frédéric with the little girl.

She had grown a lot since the journey to Montereau. Her dark hair hung down in long ringlets over her bare arms. Her dress, which was puffed out like a ballet-dancer's skirt, showed her pink calves, and the pretty child smelt as fresh as a bunch of flowers. She received the visitor's compliments with a coquettish air, fixed her dark eyes on him, and then, slipping in between the furniture, vanished like a cat.

He no longer felt ill at ease. The globes of the lamps, covered with shades of lacelike paper, gave off a milky light, softening the colour of the walls, which were hung with mauve satin. Through the bars of the fireguard, which looked like a big fan, the coal could be seen in the fireplace; and a little box with silver clasps stood next to the clock. Here and there, homely objects were lying about: a doll in the middle of the sofa, a fichu against the back of a chair, and on the worktable some knitting from which two ivory needles were hanging with their points downwards. It was altogether a peaceful room, with an intimate yet innocent atmosphere.

Arnoux returned, and, through the other doorway, Madame Arnoux appeared. She was in the shadows, and at first he could only make out her head. She wore a black velvet dress, and, in her hair, a long Algerian headdress of red silk net which was caught in her comb and hung over her left shoulder.

Arnoux introduced Frédéric.

'Oh, I remember Monsieur perfectly,' she replied.

Then the other guests arrived, almost at the same time: Dittmer, Lovarias, Burrieu, the composer Rosenwald, the poet Théophile Lorris, two art-critics, colleagues of Hussonnet's, a paper-manufacturer, and finally the illustrious Pierre-Paul Meinsius, the last representative of the grand school of painting, who carried his fame, his eighty years, and his great paunch with sprightly good humour.

When they moved into the dining-room, Madame Arnoux took his arm. A chair had been left empty for Pellerin. Arnoux, though he exploited him, was fond of him. Besides, he was afraid of his terrible tongue; so much so that, in order to appease him, he had published his portrait in *L'Art Industriel*, accompanied by a fulsome eulogy; and Pellerin, more sensitive to fame than to money, appeared about eight o'clock, quite out of breath. Frédéric assumed that they had been reconciled for a long time.

The company, the food, everything delighted him. The dining-room was hung with embossed leather, like a medieval parlour; a Dutch whatnot stood opposite a rack of chibuqs; and, round the table, the Bohemian glasses, variously coloured, gleamed among the flowers and fruit like illuminations in a garden.

He had ten sorts of mustard to choose from. He ate daspachio, curry, ginger, Corsican blackbirds, Roman lasagna; he drank extraordinary wines, lip-fraoli, and tokay. Arnoux indeed prided himself on his hospitality. With a view to keeping his larder well stocked, he cultivated the acquaintance of all the mail-coach drivers; and he was on friendly terms with the cooks at several great houses, who gave him the secrets of their sauces.

But it was the conversation that Frédéric found most entertaining. His taste for travel was indulged by Dittmer, who talked about the East; he gratified his curiosity about the theatre by listening to Rosenwald's gossip about the Opéra; and even the horrors of Bohemian life struck him as amusing when seen through the gaiety of Hussonnet, who gave a picturesque account of how he had spent an entire winter with nothing to eat but some Dutch cheese. Then an argument between Lovarias and Burrieu about the Florentine school revealed masterpieces and opened new horizons to him, and he could scarcely contain his enthusiasm when Pellerin exclaimed:

'I don't want any of your hideous reality! What do you mean by reality, anyway? Some see black, some see blue, and the mob see wrong. There's nothing less natural than Michelangelo, and nothing more powerful. The cult of external truth reveals the vulgarity of our times; and if things go on this way, art is going to become a sort of bad joke inferior to religion in poetry and inferior to politics in interest. You'll never attain the purpose of art – yes, its purpose! – which is to give us an impersonal sense of exaltation, with petty works, however carefully they're produced. Look at Bassolier's pictures, for instance: they're pretty, charming, neat, and not at all heavy. You can put them in your pocket, or take them with you on your travels. Solicitors pay twenty thousand francs for them, and there isn't tuppence-worth of ideas in them; but without ideas, there is no grandeur, and without grandeur there is no beauty! Olympus is a mountain. The proudest of all monuments will always be the Pyramids. Exuberance is better than taste, the desert is better than a pavement, and a savage is better than a barber!'

Frédéric watched Madame Arnoux as he listened to these words. They sank into his mind like metals into a furnace, adding to his passion and filling him with love.

He was sitting three places below her on the same side of the table. Now and then she bent forward slightly, turning her head to say a few words to her little daughter; and as she smiled when she did this, a dimple puckered her cheek, giving her face a look of rarer kindness.

When the liqueurs were served she disappeared. The conversation became very free; Monsieur Arnoux shone in it; and Frédéric was astonished at the obscenity of these men. However, their preoccupation with the subject of women established a sort of equality between him and them which raised him in his own estimation.

They returned to the drawing-room, and to keep himself in countenance, he picked up one of the albums lying about on the table. The great artists of the day had illustrated it with drawings; some had written pieces of prose or verse, or simply their signatures. Among the famous names there were a great many nonentities, and the original thoughts were lost in a mass of platitudes. All these entries contained a more or less direct expression of homage to Madame Arnoux. Frédéric would have been afraid to write a single line beside them.

She went into her boudoir to fetch the little box with the silver clasps which he had noticed on the mantelpiece. It was a present from her husband, a piece of work of the Renaissance. Arnoux's friends complimented him, and his wife thanked him; he was touched, and suddenly kissed her in front of all the guests.

After that they all chatted in scattered groups. The worthy Meinsius was with Madame Arnoux, sitting in an easy chair by the fire. She was leaning forward to say something into his ear, their heads were touching, and Frédéric would gladly have been deaf, infirm, and ugly to have a famous name and white hair – in other words, to have something which would establish him in an intimacy such as this. He ate his heart out, furious at being so young.

But then she came into the corner of the room where he was standing, and asked him whether he knew any of the guests, whether he was fond of painting, how long he had been studying in Paris. Every word that fell from her lips seemed to Frédéric something new, something exclusively hers. He gazed attentively at the fringes of her hair, the ends of which were caressing her bare shoulder; he could not tear his eyes away, and plunged his soul into the whiteness of this female flesh; yet he did not dare to raise his eyes and look straight at her, face to face.

Rosenwald interrupted them by asking Madame Arnoux to sing something. She waited while he played some introductory chords; then her lips parted, and a pure, long-drawn, silvery sound rose into the air.

Frédéric did not understand a single one of the Italian words.

The song began with a solemn measure, like plainchant; next, growing faster and livelier, it broke into repeated bursts of sound; then it suddenly subsided, and the melody returned tenderly, with a lazy, sweeping lilt.

She stood next to the piano, with her arms by her sides and a far-away look in her eyes. Occasionally she bent her head forward to read the music, blinking her eyes for a moment. In the low notes her contralto voice took on a mournful intonation which had a chilling effect on the listener, and then she leant her lovely head with its great eyebrows towards her shoulder; suddenly she raised it again, with flames in her eyes; her bosom swelled, her arms stretched out, her neck bent slightly as she warbled, as if under ethereal kisses; she sang three piercing notes, came down the scale again, threw out one higher still, and after a moment's silence, finished with a sustained cadence.

Rosenwald did not leave the piano, but went on playing for his own amusement. Every now and then one of the guests disappeared. At eleven o'clock, as the last of them were leaving, Arnoux went out with Pellerin, under the pretext of seeing him home. He was one of those people who say they are ill if they fail to 'take a turn' after dinner.

Madame Arnoux had come out into the hall; Dittmer and Hussonnet were saying good-bye to her, and she held out her hand to them; she held it out to Frédéric too, and he felt as if it were something permeating every particle of his skin.

He left his friends; he wanted to be alone. His heart was overflowing. Why had she offered him her hand? Was it a casual gesture, or an encouragement?

'Come now, I'm mad!'

Besides, what did it matter when he could now call on her when he pleased, and live in the same atmosphere she breathed?

The streets were deserted. Now and then a heavy cart rolled by, shaking the roadway. He passed rows of houses with grey fronts and closed shutters; and he thought disdainfully of all the human beings lying asleep behind those walls, who lived without seeing her, and not one of whom even knew that she existed. He was no longer aware of his surroundings, of space, of anything; and, striding out, tapping the shutters of the shops with his stick, he went on walking along at random, carried away by his emotions. Some damp air enveloped him, and he realized that he was on the quays.

The street-lamps shone in two straight lines, stretching away into the distance, and long red flames flickered in the depths of the water. The river was the colour of slate, while the sky, which was brighter, seemed to be supported by the huge masses of shadow that rose on each side of the river. Buildings which the eye could not distinguish intensified the darkness. Further away, a luminous haze floated over the roof-tops; all the noises of the night melted into a single murmur; a light breeze was blowing.

He had stopped in the middle of the Pont-Neuf, and, bareheaded, with his coat open, he breathed in the air. At the same time he felt something inexhaustible welling up from the depths of his being, a surge of tenderness which made him giddy, like the motion of the waves under his eyes. A church clock struck one, slowly, like a voice calling out to him.

Then he was seized by one of those tremors of the soul in which one seems to be transported into a higher world. He had been endowed with an extraordinary talent, the object of which he did not know. He asked himself in all seriousness whether he was to be a great painter or a great poet; and he decided in favour of painting, for the demands of this profession would bring him closer to Madame Arnoux. So he had found his vocation! The object of his existence was now clear, and there could be no doubt about the future.

When he had shut his door, he heard somebody snoring in the dark closet next to his bedroom. It was his friend. He had forgotten all about him.

His own face presented itself to him in the mirror. He liked the look of it, and remained there for a minute gazing at himself.

V

BY noon the next day he had bought himself a box of paints, some brushes, and an easel. Pellerin agreed to give him lessons, and Frédéric brought him along to his rooms to see if there was anything he needed to complete his painting equipment.

Deslauriers had come back, and there was a young man sitting in the second armchair. The clerk pointed at him and said:

'Here he is! Sénécal!'

Frédéric did not like the fellow. His hair was cut short like a brush, giving added height to his forehead. There was a cold, hard look in his eyes; and his long black frock-coat, his whole costume, smacked of the pedagogue and the priest.

First of all they talked about the topics of the hour, including Rossini's *Stabat*; Sénécal, in answer to a question, declared that he never went to the theatre. Pellerin opened the box of paints.

'Is all that for you?' asked the clerk.

'Yes, of course.'

'Well, I never!'

And he leant over the table, where the mathematics tutor was looking through a volume of Louis Blanc which he had brought with him. He read passages from it in a low voice, while Pellerin and Frédéric inspected the palette, the knife, and the bladders. Then the talk came round to the dinner at Arnoux's.

'The picture-dealer?' asked Sénécal. 'He's a fine fellow if you like.'

'What do you mean?' said Pellerin.

Sénécal replied:

'He's a man who makes money by political skulduggery.'

And he went on to talk about a well-known lithograph which showed the entire royal family engaged in edifying occupations: Louis-Philippe had a copy of the Code in his hand, the Queen a prayer-book; the Princesses were doing embroidery; the Duc de Nemour was buckling on a sword; Monsieur de Joinville was showing his young brothers a map; and in the background could be seen a bed with two compartments. This picture, which was entitled 'A Good Family', had been a source of delight to the middle classes, but the despair of the patriots. Pellerin, speaking in an offended tone as if he had drawn the picture himself, remarked that everybody was entitled to his own opinion. Sénécal objected to this. Art should aim exclusively at raising the moral standards of the masses. The only subjects that should be reproduced were those which incited people to virtuous actions; all the rest were harmful:

'But that depends on the execution!' cried Pellerin. 'I might produce masterpieces!'

'So much the worse for you, then. You haven't any right . . .'

'What's that?'

'No, Monsieur, you haven't any right to interest me in matters of which I disapprove. What need have we of elaborate trifles from which it is impossible to derive any benefit – those Venuses, for instance, in all your landscapes? I can see no instruction for the common people there. Show us the hardship of the masses instead. Rouse our enthusiasm for their sacrifices. Good God, there's no lack of subjects: the farm, the workshop . . .'

Pellerin, stammering with indignation and thinking that he had found an argument, said:

'What about Molière? Do you accept him?'

'Certainly!' said Sénécal. 'I admire him as a precursor of the French Revolution!'

'Oh, the Revolution! What art! There's never been a more pitiful period!'

'There's never been a greater, Monsieur!'

Pellerin folded his arms, and, looking him straight in the face, said:

'You talk just like a member of the National Guard.' [10]

His opponent, who was used to arguing, retorted:

'I'm not one of *them*, and I hate them as much as you do. But principles like that corrupt the masses. Besides, that sort of thing is just what the Government wants. It wouldn't be so powerful if it hadn't the support of a lot of rogues like Arnoux.'

The painter took up the picture-dealer's defence, for Sénécal's opinions exasperated him. He even went so far as to maintain that Jacques Arnoux was a man with a heart of gold, devoted to his friends and deeply attached to his wife.

'Ho! If you offered him enough, he wouldn't refuse to let her pose as a model!'

Frédéric turned pale.

'He must have done you some great injury, Monsieur?'

'Me? No! I've only seen him once, at a café with a friend. That's all.'

Sénécal was telling the truth. But he was irritated every day by the advertisements for *L'Art Industriel*. In his eyes, Arnoux was the representative of a world which he considered fatal to democracy. An austere Republican, he scented corruption in every form of elegance, since he wanted nothing himself and was inflexible in his integrity.

They found some difficulty in resuming the conversation. The painter soon remembered an appointment, the tutor his pupils; and, when they had gone, after a long silence, Deslauriers asked a number of questions about Arnoux.

'You will take me along to his place one day, won't you, old fellow?'

'Of course,' said Frédéric.

Then they set about planning their life together. Deslauriers had obtained without much trouble a post as junior clerk to a barrister, enrolled at the Law School, and bought the necessary books. The life which they had so often dreamt about began.

It was delightful, thanks to the beauty of their youth. As Deslauriers had not mentioned any financial arrangement, Frédéric did not refer to the subject. He paid all their expenses, kept the larder well-stocked, and looked after the housekeeping; but if the concierge had to be given a dressing-down, the clerk undertook the task, still playing the part he had assumed at college of elder and protector.

Separated all day long, they met again in the evening. Each took his place by the fire and set to work. But it was interrupted before very long. There would be endless confidences, unaccountable bursts of merriment, and occasional arguments about a smoking lamp or a mislaid book, brief quarrels which were quenched by laughter.

They left the door of the boxroom open, and chatted from a distance, in bed.

In the morning they strolled up and down their balcony in their shirtsleeves. The sun rose, light mists floated over the river, they could hear shrill voices in the near-by flower-market; the smoke from their pipes coiled up into the clear air, which freshened their sleepy eyes; and, as they breathed it in, they had a sense of boundless expectation.

On Sunday, when it was fine, they would go out for a walk, strolling through the streets arm-in-arm. The same thought nearly always occurred to them at the same time, or else they talked without noticing anything around them. Deslauriers longed for wealth, as a means of gaining power over men. He wanted to become a famous figure, to create a great stir, to have three secretaries at his beck and call, and to give a big political dinner once a week. Frédéric furnished a Moorish palace for himself, and spent his life reclining on cashmere divans, beside a murmuring fountain, attended by negro pages; and the things in these daydreams became so real that in the end they made him feel as miserable as if he had lost them.

'What's the use of talking about all this,' he used to say, 'seeing that we'll never have it?'

'Who knows?' replied Deslauriers.

In spite of his democratic views he urged Frédéric to get a footing in the Dambreuse circle. The other pointed to the failure of his previous attempts.

'Bah! Try again. They'll invite you one day.'

About the middle of March, among other fairly heavy bills, they received that of the caterer who supplied them with dinner. Frédéric, not having the entire amount, borrowed three hundred francs from Deslauriers; a fortnight later he repeated the request, and the clerk gave him a lecture on his extravagant purchases at Arnoux's shop.

The fact was that he had abandoned all restraint in this respect.

Views of Venice, Naples, and Constantinople occupying the centre of three walls, equestrian studies by Alfred de Dreux here and there, a group by Pradier on the mantelpiece, odd numbers of *L'Art Industriel* on the piano, and works in boards lying on the floor in the corners, filled the flat to such an extent that there was scarcely any book-room or elbow-room. Frédéric maintained that all this was necessary for his painting.

He worked at Pellerin's place. But Pellerin was often out, for it was his custom to attend all the funerals and other events which were likely to be reported in the papers, so that Frédéric spent hours at a time alone in the studio. The quiet of this spacious room – where there was nothing to be heard but the scampering of the mice – the light falling from the ceiling, and even the rumbling of the stove, filled him at first with a sense of intellectual comfort. But then his eyes, leaving his work, would roam over the scalloped mouldings of the wall, among the ornaments on the whatnot, and along the torsos on which the layers of dust looked like scraps of velvet; and like a traveller lost in the middle of a forest, whom every path brings back to the same spot, he invariably found, behind every thought, the memory of Madame Arnoux.

He chose days for calling on her; when he reached the second floor, he stood outside her door, hesitating as to whether to ring the bell or not. Steps approached; the door opened, and at the words: 'Madame is out,' he would feel a sense of deliverance, as if a weight had been lifted from his heart.

Yet there were occasions when he met her. The first time she was with three ladies; another afternoon, Mademoiselle Marthe's writing-master appeared on the scene. What is more, the men whom Madame Arnoux received never called on her. Out of discretion, he decided not to go again.

But to make sure that he was invited to the Thursday dinners, he took care to appear regularly, every Wednesday, at *L'Art Industriel*; and he stayed there after all the others, even longer than Regimbart, until the very last minute, pretending to be looking at a print or glancing through a newspaper. At last Arnoux would say to him: 'Are you free tomorrow evening?' and he would accept before the sentence was finished. Arnoux appeared to have taken a liking to him. He taught him how to become a good judge of wines, how to brew punch, and how to make a woodcock ragoût; Frédéric meekly followed his advice, for he was in love with everything connected with Madame Arnoux – her furniture, her servants, her house, her street.

He scarcely uttered a word during these dinners; he gazed at her. On her right temple she had a little beauty-spot; her bandeaux were darker than the rest of her hair, and always seemed a little moist at the edges; she stroked them occasionally, with two fingers only. He knew the shape of each of her nails; he delighted in listening to the rustle of her silk dress when she passed a door; he furtively sniffed at the scent on her handkerchief; her comb, her gloves, her rings were things of special significance to him, as important as works of art, almost endowed with life like human beings; they all took possession of his heart and strengthened his passion.

He had not had it in him to conceal it from Deslauriers. When he came home from Madame Arnoux's he would wake him up, as if by accident, so that he could talk about her.

Deslauriers, who slept in the little boxroom, next to the cistern, would give a great yawn. Frédéric sat down at the foot of his bed. At first he spoke about the dinner; then he described a host of insignificant details, in which he saw marks of contempt or of affection. On one occasion, for instance, she had refused his arm, in order to take Dittmer's, and Frédéric was utterly miserable.

'What nonsense!' said Deslauriers.

Or else she had called him her friend.

'Then get on with it!'

'But I daren't,' said Frédéric.

'In that case, forget about it! Good night!'

Deslauriers turned towards the wall and went to sleep. He could not understand this passion, which struck him as a final aberration of adolescence; and since his company was apparently no longer enough to content Frédéric, he had the idea of bringing together their common friends once a week.

They used to come on Saturday about nine o'clock. The three Algerine curtains were carefully drawn; four candles were burning as well as the lamp; the tobacco-jar, full of pipes, stood in the middle of the table, surrounded by bottles of beer, the tea-pot, a flagon of rum, and some fancy biscuits. They argued about the immortality of the soul, and drew comparisons between their professors.

One evening Hussonnet brought along a tall young man dressed in a frock-coat which was too short in the sleeves, and who looked very embarrassed. It was the young fellow they had tried to release from the guard-house the year before.

As he had been unable to recover the box of lace which he had lost in the scuffle, his employer had accused him of stealing it and threatened to prosecute him; he was now working for a firm of carriers. Hussonnet had come across him that morning on a street-corner; and he had brought him with him because Dussardier, out of gratitude, wanted to see 'the other one'.

He held out the cigar-case to Frédéric; it was still full, for he had taken scrupulous care of it, in the hope of being able to give it back. The young men invited him to come again. He took them at their word.

They all sympathized. At first their hatred of the Government had all the loftiness of an indisputable dogma. Martinon alone tried to defend Louis-Philippe. The others overwhelmed him with the commonplaces to be found in every newspaper – the fortification of Paris, the September Laws, Pritchard, 'Lord' Guizot[11] – so that Martinon held his tongue, for fear of giving offence. During his seven years at college he had not incurred a single imposition, and at the Law School he knew how to make himself agreeable to the professors. He usually wore a large putty-coloured frock-coat and rubber galoshes; but one evening he appeared dressed like a bride-groom, with a velvet shawl waistcoat, a white tie, and a gold chain.

The general astonishment was increased when the others learned that he had just come from Monsieur Dambreuse's. The fact was that the banker had just bought a stretch of woodland from Mar-tinon's father. The latter had introduced his son to him, and Dam-breuse had invited them both to dinner.

'Were there lots of truffles?' asked Deslauriers. 'And did you put your arm round his wife's waist in a dark corner, *sicut decet?*'

Here the conversation turned to women. Pellerin refused to admit that there were any beautiful women (he preferred tigers); besides, the human female was an inferior creature in the aesthetic hierarchy.

'What you find attractive about her is precisely what degrades her as an idea; I mean her breasts, her hair . . .'

'All the same,' said Frédéric, 'long black hair and big dark eyes . . .'

'Oh, that's old stuff!' cried Hussonnet. 'We've had enough of Andalusian women. As for the women of antiquity, no thank you! Because when all's said and done, a tart is a lot more fun than the Venus of Milo. Let's be Frenchmen, for God's sake, and regency rakes if we can! You know – "Flow, good wines, and women, deign to smile!" We must go from brunettes to blondes. Don't you agree with me, Dussardier?'

Dussardier did not answer. They all urged him to tell them what he preferred.

'Well,' he said, blushing, 'I'd like to love the same woman all the time!'

He said this in such a way that there was a moment's silence; some of them were taken aback by this innocent declaration, while others perhaps recognized in it the unspoken desire of their own hearts.

Sénécal put his mug of beer on the mantelpiece and asserted dogmatically that since prostitution was heartless and marriage was immoral it was better to abstain. Deslauriers regarded women as a distraction and nothing more. Monsieur de Cisy was frankly scared of them.

Brought up under the eye of a pious grandmother, he found the company of these young men as exciting as a place of ill repute and as instructive as a university. They were generous with their tuition, and he proved a willing pupil, even trying to smoke, in spite of the fit of nausea which affected him at every attempt. Frédéric lavished attentions on him. He admired the colour of his cravats, the fur on his overcoat, and above all his boots, which were as thin as gloves and seemed positively insolent in their immaculate elegance; his carriage used to wait for him down in the street.

One evening when he had just left, and it was snowing outside, Sénécal remarked that he was sorry for his coachman. Then he started inveighing against the dandies of the Jockey Club. A workman was better than all those fine gentlemen.

'At least I work for my living! I'm poor!'

'That's obvious,' said Frédéric at last, losing patience.

The tutor never forgave him for this remark.

However, since Regimbart had once said that he knew Sénécal slightly, Frédéric, wanting to be polite to Arnoux's friend, invited him to the Saturday parties. The two patriots enjoyed meeting each other.

They were different for all that.

Sénécal – who had a pointed skull – valued systems to the exclusion of all else. Regimbart, on the other hand, saw nothing in facts but facts. What worried him most of all was the Rhine frontier.[12]

He claimed to be an authority on gunnery, and had his clothes made by the tailor of the Polytechnic.

The first day, when he was offered some cakes, he shrugged his shoulders contemptuously, saying that such things were meant for women; and he was scarcely more gracious on subsequent occasions. As soon as the conversation reached a certain level he would murmur: 'Oh, no dreams and utopias, please!' On artistic matters – in spite of the fact that he was a frequent visitor to the studios of Paris, where he sometimes condescended to give a fencing lesson – his views were anything but transcendent. He compared Monsieur Marrast's[13] style to Voltaire's, and Mademoiselle Vatnaz to Madame de Staël, on account of an ode on Poland which 'had some feeling in it'. Altogether Regimbart annoyed everybody, and particularly Deslauriers, because the Citizen was on friendly terms with Arnoux. It was the clerk's ambition to be invited to Arnoux's house, where he hoped to make some useful acquaintances. 'When are you going to take me there?' he used to ask Frédéric. In reply he was told that Arnoux was up to his eyes in work, or that he was going on a business trip, or finally that it was not worth the trouble since the dinners were coming to an end.

If he had been called upon to risk his life for his friend, Frédéric would have done so gladly. But as he was bent on showing himself to the best advantage, and was extremely careful about his language, his manners, and his clothes, even to the extent of wearing immaculate gloves every time he visited the office of *L'Art Industriel*, he was afraid that Deslauriers, with his old black coat, his attorney-like behaviour, and his extravagant remarks, might make a poor impression on Madame Arnoux, and thus compromise him and lower him in her estimation. He did not mind the others, but somehow Deslauriers would have caused him much more embarrassment than anybody else. The clerk saw that he did not want to keep his promise, and Frédéric's silence struck him as adding insult to injury.

He would have liked to exercise absolute control over him, to see him develop in accordance with their youthful ideal; and his idleness aroused his indignation as a form of disobedience and treason. Moreover, Frédéric, obsessed with Madame Arnoux, often talked about her husband; and Deslauriers began an infuriating game, which consisted in repeating the man's name a hundred times a day, at the end of every sentence, like an idiot's nervous tic. Whenever there was a knock at the door, he would call out: 'Come in,

Arnoux!' At the restaurant he would ask for some Brie cheese 'of the Arnoux type'; and at night, pretending to be having a nightmare, he would awaken his friend by screaming: 'Arnoux! Arnoux!' Finally Frédéric could not stand it any longer, and said to him one day in a piteous voice:

'For God's sake stop going on about Arnoux!'

'Never!' replied the clerk. 'He's here, he's there, he's everywhere. In fire and ice, Arnoux's device . . .'

'Shut up, will you!' exclaimed Frédéric, raising his fist.

He went on less angrily:

'You know it's a painful subject with me.'

'Oh, I beg your pardon, old fellow,' retorted Deslauriers, bowing very low. 'In future we'll do our best to spare Mademoiselle's nerves. Once again, I beg your pardon. A thousand apologies!'

And that was the end of the joke.

But three weeks later, Deslauriers said to him one evening:

'Well, I've just seen Madame Arnoux.'

'Where?'

'At the Palais de Justice, with a barrister called Balandard. A dark woman, isn't she, of medium height?'

Frédéric nodded. He waited for Deslauriers to speak. At the least expression of admiration he would have opened his heart; he was ready to adore his friend. But the other remained silent. At last, unable to bear it any longer, Frédéric asked him with assumed indifference what he thought of her.

Deslauriers considered her 'not bad, but with nothing extraordinary about her'.

'Oh, really?' said Frédéric.

August came along, and the time for his second examination. The general opinion was that a fortnight was enough to prepare for it. Frédéric, confident of his ability, swallowed one after another the first four books of the Code of Procedure, the first three of the Penal Code, several chunks of criminal law, and part of the Civil Code, with Monsieur Poncelet's notes. The night before, Deslauriers revised the whole course with him, a process which lasted until the morning; and, in order to take advantage of the last quarter of an hour, he went on asking Frédéric questions while they were walking along the pavement.

As several examinations were being held at the same time, the courtyard was full of people, including Hussonnet and Cisy: it was the custom to attend these ordeals when one's friends were concerned. Frédéric put on the traditional black gown; then, followed by the crowd, he went with three other students into a big room lit by uncurtained windows and furnished with benches along the walls. In the centre some leather-covered chairs were placed round a table with a green cloth. This table separated the candidates from the examiners, who were all wearing red gowns with ermine shoulder-knots and gold-braided hats.

Frédéric was the last but one in the group – a bad position. In answer to the first question, on the difference between a covenant and a contract, he defined the one for the other; and the professor, who was a kindly man, said to him:

'Don't be nervous, Monsieur. Compose yourself.'

Then, after putting two easy questions which obtained obscure replies, he finally passed on to the fourth candidate. This poor beginning demoralized Frédéric. Deslauriers, sitting opposite him in the audience, signalled to him that all was not yet lost; and at the second round of questions, on criminal law, he did reasonably well. But after the third round, concerning the sealed will, during which the examiner remained completely impassive, his spirits sank; for Hussonnet brought his hands together as if to applaud, while Deslauriers shrugged his shoulders repeatedly. At last the time came for the examination on procedure. The questions were about third-party opposition. The professor, who had been shocked at hearing theories contrary to his own, asked Frédéric in a brusque voice:

'And what about you, Monsieur? Is that your opinion? How do you reconcile the principle of Article 1351 of the Civil Code with that extraordinary line of attack?'

Frédéric's head was aching after his sleepless night. A ray of sunlight, passing through one of the slits in a Venetian blind, shone into his face. Standing behind the chair, he wriggled about and tugged at his moustache.

'I am still awaiting your answer,' observed the man in the gold hat.

And, presumably annoyed by Frédéric's fidgeting, he added:

'You won't find it in your moustache!'

This sarcastic remark raised a laugh in the audience; flattered, the professor relented. He asked two more questions about the writ of summons and summary proceedings, then nodded his head in approval. The examination was over. Frédéric returned to the entrance-hall.

While the usher was taking off his gown, to put it straight on to another candidate, his friends gathered round him, putting the last touch to his bewilderment with their conflicting views as to the result of the examination. This was soon announced in a loud voice at the door of the hall: 'The third candidate was ... referred back!'

'Ploughed!' said Hussonnet. 'Let's be on our way!'

Outside the porter's lodge they met Martinon, flushed and excited, with a smile in his eyes and the halo of victory round his head. He had just passed his final examination without any trouble. All that remained was the thesis. Within a fortnight he would be a Bachelor of Law.

His family knew a minister: 'a fine career' lay before him.

'Say what you like, he's got the better of you,' said Deslauriers.

There is nothing more humiliating than seeing fools succeed where one has failed oneself. Thoroughly piqued, Frédéric replied that he didn't care. He had loftier ambitions; and, as Hussonnet looked like going off, he took him aside and said to him:

'Not a word about this to them, mind!'

The secret would be easy to keep, since Arnoux was leaving the next day for Germany.

When he came home that evening, the clerk found his friend singularly changed: he was whistling and dancing about; and when Deslauriers expressed surprise at his high spirits, Frédéric declared that he was not going home to his mother's but intended to spend his holidays working.

The news of Arnoux's departure had filled him with joy. He could go to the house when he liked, without fear of being interrupted during a call. The certainty of absolute security would give him courage. Above all, he would not be far away and parted from her. Something stronger than an iron chain bound him to Paris: an inner voice cried out to him to stay.

There were certain obstacles in his way. He overcame them by writing to his mother. First of all he admitted his failure, which was due to changes in the curriculum, bad luck, and injustice; besides, all the great lawyers (he gave their names) had failed in their examinations. But he intended to try again in November. So, seeing that he had no time to lose, he did not propose to come home that year; and, in addition to his quarterly allowance, he asked for two hundred and fifty francs for some private tuition in law which would be of great assistance to him. The whole letter was embellished with expressions of regret, condolences, terms of endearment, and protestations of filial love.

Madame Moreau, who was expecting him the following day, was doubly grieved. She concealed her son's misfortune and wrote to him 'to come all the same'. Frédéric held his ground. A quarrel ensued. Nevertheless, at the end of the week he received his quarterly allowance, together with the money for his private tuition – which helped to pay for a pair of pearl-grey trousers, a white felt hat, and a gold-headed stick.

When he had acquired all these things, he thought:

'Perhaps it's just a vulgar idea I've had.'

And he was assailed by serious doubts.

In order to decide whether he should go to see Madame Arnoux, he tossed a coin into the air three times. Each time the omens were favourable. Fate must have ordained it! He took a cab to the Rue de Choiseul.

He went nimbly up the stairs and pulled the bell-rope. It did not ring. He felt as if he were going to faint.

Then he tugged furiously at the heavy red silk tassel. A tremendous peal rang out, and gradually died away; nothing more was heard. Frédéric began to feel frightened.

He glued his ear to the door: not a sound. He put his eye to the keyhole; but he could see nothing in the hall except the tips of two reeds on the wallpaper, in the midst of the floral design. He was just about to go when he changed his mind. This time he gave a short, gentle pull. The door opened; and on the threshold, with tousled hair, a crimson face, and a bad-tempered expression, Arnoux himself appeared.

'Well, well! What the devil brings you here? Come in.'

He led him, not into the boudoir or into his own room, but into the dining-room, where there was a bottle of champagne and a couple of glasses on the table, and said in an abrupt tone of voice:

'You've got something you want to ask me, my dear fellow?'

'No, nothing, nothing at all!' stammered the young man, trying to think of some excuse for his call.

At last he said that he had come to ask if there was any news of him, because he understood from Hussonnet that he was in Germany.

'Nonsense!' said Arnoux. 'It's just like that feather-brained idiot to get everything wrong.'

To conceal his agitation, Frédéric walked up and down the room. Stumbling against a chair, he knocked down a parasol which was lying across it; the ivory handle broke.

'Oh, dear!' he exclaimed. 'I'm terribly sorry, I've broken Madame Arnoux's parasol.'

At this remark the dealer looked up and gave a peculiar smile. Frédéric, seizing the opportunity that was offered to talk about her, added shyly:

'Could I possibly see her?'

She had gone home to see her mother, who was ill.

He did not dare to inquire how long she would be away. He merely asked where her home was.

'Chartres. Does that surprise you?'

'Me? No! Why? Not in the slightest.'

After that they could find absolutely nothing to talk about. Arnoux, who had rolled himself a cigarette, walked round the table, puffing away. Frédéric, standing by the stove, gazed at the walls, the whatnot, the floor; and delightful visions flitted through his memory, or rather before his eyes. Finally he took his leave.

A piece of newspaper, rolled into a ball, was lying on the floor in the hall; Arnoux picked it up and, standing on tiptoe, pushed it into the bell, so that he could continue, he said, his interrupted siesta. Then, shaking Frédéric by the hand, he said:

'Please tell the concierge that I'm not at home.'

And he slammed the door shut behind him.

Frédéric went downstairs one step at a time. The failure of this first attempt discouraged him as to the possible success of any that might follow. Then began three months of boredom. As he had nothing to do, his idleness intensified his melancholy.

He spent hours on his balcony looking down at the river flowing between the grey quays, which were blackened here and there with smudges from drains; or at a pontoon for washerwomen moored to the bank, where children sometimes amused themselves by giving a poodle a mud-bath. His eyes, leaving the stone Pont de Notre-Dame and the three suspension bridges, invariably strayed in the direction of the Quai aux Ormes, towards a clump of old trees which looked like the lime-trees in the port of Montereau. Facing him, the Tour Saint-Jacques, the Hôtel de Ville, Saint-Gervais,

Saint-Louis, and Saint-Paul rose among a maze of roofs, and the genie on the July Column shone in the east like a great golden star, while in the other direction the dome of the Tuileries stood out against the sky in a solid blue mass. It was over that way, behind the dome, that Madame Arnoux's house presumably lay.

He would go back into his room, and, lying on his divan, give himself up to a vague reverie which combined working projects, plans of action, and dreams of the future. Finally, to escape from himself, he went out.

He sauntered idly up the Latin Quarter, usually bustling with life but now deserted, for the students had all gone home. The great walls of the colleges looked grimmer than ever, as if the silence had made them longer; all sorts of peaceful sounds could be heard, the fluttering of wings in bird-cages, the whirring of a lathe, a cobbler's hammer; and the old-clothes men, in the middle of the street, looked hopefully but in vain at every window. At the back of deserted cafés, women behind the bars yawned between their untouched bottles; the newspapers lay unopened on the reading-room tables; in the laundresses' workshops the washing quivered in the warm draughts. Every now and then he stopped at a bookseller's stall; an omnibus, coming down the street and grazing the pavement, made him turn round; and when he reached the Luxembourg he retraced his steps.

Sometimes, in search of amusement, he was drawn towards the boulevards. From the cool, damp air of dark alleys he emerged on to huge empty squares, full of dazzling light, where statues cast jagged black shadows on to the edge of the pavement. But soon he came upon more handcarts and shops; and the crowds made him dizzy, especially on Sundays, when, from the Bastille to the Madeleine, there was a vast torrent of humanity surging over the asphalt, in the midst of clouds of dust and a continuous din. He felt utterly nauseated by the vulgarity of their faces, the stupidity of their talk, and the imbecile satisfaction glistening on their sweating brows. However, the knowledge that he was worth more than these men lessened the fatigue of looking at them.

He went every day to *L'Art Industriel*; and in order to find out when Madame Arnoux was coming back, he made lengthy inquiries about her mother. Arnoux's reply was always the same: 'the improvement was continuing' and his wife, with the little girl, would be back the following week. The longer her return was delayed, the more anxiety Frédéric showed; so that Arnoux, touched by such persistent affection, took him out five or six times to dinner at a restaurant.

In the long conversations which they had together on these occasions, Frédéric came to realize that the picture-dealer was not a particularly witty talker. Arnoux might notice that his admiration was cooling; and besides, it was time that he did something to repay his hospitality.

Wanting to do things in style, Frédéric sold all his new clothes to a second-hand dealer for the sum of eighty francs; and adding to this a hundred francs which he had left, he called at Arnoux's to take him out to dinner. Regimbart was there. They went to the Trois-Frères-Provençaux.

The Citizen began by taking off his frock-coat, and, confident that the others would approve his choice, wrote out the menu. But it was in vain that he made his way to the kitchen to speak in person to the chef, that he went down to the cellar, where he knew every nook and cranny, or that he sent for the manager of the establishment, to whom he gave a 'dressing-down' – he found neither the food, the wine, nor the service to his satisfaction. At every new dish, at every fresh bottle, at the first mouthful, the first sip, he threw down his fork or pushed away his glass; then, leaning his elbows on the table and stretching out his arms, he would loudly lament that a man could no longer dine in Paris. Finally, not knowing what to eat, he ordered some kidney-beans in oil, 'and nothing else', which, although only a partial success, mollified him slightly. Then he had a conversation with the waiter about former waiters at the Provençaux. What had become of Antoine? And a fellow called Eugène? And little Théodore, who always served downstairs? In those days the food used to be really distinguished, and they had some Burgundies the like of which they would never see again.

After that there was some talk about the value of building-sites in the suburbs, an investment which Arnoux considered absolutely safe. In the meantime, however, he was losing on the interest, because he did not want to sell out at any price. Regimbart promised to find him somebody; and the two worthies did pencilled calculations until the end of the dessert.

They went out to have coffee at a tavern in the Passage du Saumon, upstairs. Frédéric remained on his feet, watching interminable games of billiards washed down with countless glasses of beer; and he stayed there until midnight without knowing why, out of cowardice or stupidity, in the vague hope that something might happen which would favour his love.

When could he see her again? Frédéric was in despair. But one evening towards the end of November, Arnoux said to him:

'My wife came home yesterday, you know.'

The next day, at five o'clock, he called to see her.

He began by congratulating her on the recovery of her mother, who had been so ill.

'Why, no! Who told you that?'

'Arnoux.'

She gave vent to a gentle 'Ah!' and then added that to begin with she had had serious apprehensions, which had now been dispelled.

She was sitting by the fire, in the upholstered armchair. He was on the sofa, with his hat between his knees; and the conversation went badly, as she kept letting it drop; he could find no opening for a mention of his feelings. But when he started complaining of having to study legal quibbles, she replied: 'Yes . . . I can imagine . . . business . . .' and lowered her eyes, suddenly absorbed in her own reflections.

He longed to know what they were, and indeed could think of nothing else. The dusk gathered shadows around them.

She stood up, having to go out on some errand, then reappeared wearing a velvet hood and a black cloak edged with squirrel fur. He plucked up his courage and offered to accompany her.

Outside they could scarcely see anything; it was cold, and a heavy, foul-smelling fog partially blotted out the fronts of the houses. Frédéric breathed it in with delight, for through the thickness of his coat he could feel the shape of her arm; and her hand, in a chamois-leather glove with two buttons – that little hand of hers which he would have liked to cover with kisses – was resting on his sleeve. The slippery pavement made them sway about slightly; it seemed to him as if they were being cradled by the wind, in the midst of a cloud.

The blaze of the lamps on the boulevard brought him back to earth. The opportunity was a good one; there was no time to lose. He gave himself as far as the Rue de Richelieu to declare his love. But almost at once she stopped short in front of a china-shop and said to him:

'Here we are. Thank you. We may expect you on Thursday, I hope, as usual?'

The dinners began again; and the more he saw Madame Arnoux, the more love-sick he became.

Looking at this woman had an enervating effect on him, like a scent that is too strong. The sensation penetrated to the very depths of his being, and became almost a habitual condition, a new mode of existence.

The prostitutes whom he came across in the gaslight, the singers warbling their ballads, the horsewomen galloping past, the house-wives on foot, the working-girls at their windows – each and every woman reminded him of her, through some resemblance or some violent contrast. As he walked past the shops, he looked at the cash-meres, the laces, and the jewelled ear-drops, imagining them draped about her waist, sewn on her corsage, or gleaming in her black hair. In the flowergirls' baskets, the blossoms opened for her to choose them as she passed; in the shoemakers' window, the little satin slippers edged with swansdown seemed to be waiting for her feet; every street led towards her house; and the cabs waited in the squares only to take him there more quickly. Paris depended on her person, and the great city, with all its voices, thundered like an immense orchestra about her.

When he went to the Jardin des Plantes, the sight of a palm-tree carried him off to distant lands. They travelled together on the backs of dromedaries, under the awnings of elephants, in the calm of a yacht among blue archipelagoes, or side by side on a couple of mules with bells on their harness, which stumbled over broken pillars in the grass. Sometimes he stopped in front of old pictures in the Louvre; and, his love embracing her even in vanished ages, he sub-stituted her for the figures in the paintings. Wearing a wimple, she prayed on her knees behind a leaded casement. A lady of Castille or Flanders, she sat dressed in a starched ruff and a boned bodice with puffed sleeves. Or she came down some great porphyry stair-case, under a canopy of ostrich feathers, surrounded by senators and wearing a gown of brocade. At other times he dreamt of her in yellow silk trousers on the cushions of a harem; and anything beautiful – the glitter of the stars, certain melodies, the turn of a phrase, or a sil-houette – brought her abruptly and unconsciously into his mind.

As for trying to make her his mistress, he was sure that any such attempt would be futile.

One evening Dittmer, on his arrival, kissed her on the forehead; Lovarias did the same, saying:

'You don't mind, do you? It's a friend's privilege.'

Frédéric stammered:

'We are all friends, aren't we?'

'Not all old friends!' she retorted.

This was rebuffing him in advance in an indirect manner.

Besides, how was he to set about it? Tell her that he loved her? She would probably repulse him, or else indignantly turn him out of her house. He preferred any sort of suffering to the awful possibility of never seeing her again.

He envied pianists their talent and soldiers their scars. He longed for a dangerous illness, hoping that he might arouse her interest in this way.

One thing astonished him, and that was that he did not feel jealous of Arnoux. Again, he could not imagine her otherwise than clothed, her modesty seemed so natural, hiding her sex in a mysterious darkness.

All the same he dreamt of the happiness of living with her, of talking familiarly with her, of passing his hand slowly over her hair, or of kneeling before her with both arms round her waist, gazing into her eyes and drinking in her soul. To bring this about he would have to conquer Fate; and so, incapable of action, cursing God, and accusing himself of cowardice, he turned restlessly about in his desire, like a prisoner in his dungeon. A perpetual anguish stifled him. He would remain motionless for hours at a time, or else he would burst into tears; and one day when he had found it impossible to contain himself, Deslauriers said to him:

'Heavens above! What's the matter with you?'

Frédéric's nerves were giving him trouble. Deslauriers did not believe a word of it. In the face of such keen suffering, he had felt his old affection reawakening, and he tried to cheer Frédéric up. What folly for a man like him to let himself feel depressed! When a fellow was in his youth it was all very well, but later on it was a waste of time.

'You're spoiling the Frédéric I used to know. I want the old one back. Waiter, the same again! I liked him. Come on, smoke a pipe, you old rascal! Pull yourself together – you're making me miserable!'

'You're right,' said Frédéric. 'I'm a fool.'

The clerk went on:

'Ah, old troubadour, I know what's the matter with you. Heart trouble, eh? I thought so! Bah, there are plenty of fish in the sea. A fellow consoles himself for the virtuous women with the other kind. Do you want me to introduce you to some women? You've only to come to the Alhambra.'

This was a dance-hall which had opened recently at the top of the Champs-Élysées, and which went bankrupt in its second season, on account of a luxury that was premature in this type of establishment.

'It's good fun, from what they tell me. Let's go! You can bring your friends if you like; I'll even allow you Regimbart!'

Frédéric did not invite the Citizen. Deslauriers dispensed with Sénécal. They took only Hussonnet, Cisy, and Dussardier; and a single cab dropped all five of them at the door of the Alhambra.

Two parallel arcades in the Moorish style extended right and left. The wall of a house took up the whole of the far end, opposite, and the fourth side, where the restaurant lay, was designed to look like a Gothic cloister with stained-glass windows.

A sort of Chinese roof sheltered the platform on which the musicians played; the ground all round it was covered with asphalt; and there were some Venetian lanterns hung on poles which, seen from a distance, formed a crown of multicoloured lights above the dancers. Every few yards there stood a pedestal supporting a stone basin from which a slender jet of water rose into the air. In the shrubberies plaster statues could be seen, Hebes and Cupids, all sticky with oil paint, and the countless paths, spread with bright yellow sand, carefully raked, made the garden look much bigger than it was.

Students were strolling up and down with their mistresses; shop-assistants strutted about with walking-sticks between their fingers; schoolboys puffed at cheroots; old bachelors stroked their dyed beards with combs; there were Englishmen, Russians, South Americans, and three Orientals in tarbooshes. Courtesans, working-girls, and prostitutes had come along in the hope of finding a protector, a lover, a piece of gold, or simply for the pleasure of the dance; and their tunic dresses in sea-green blue, cherry-red, and mauve, went swirling past among the laburnums and the lilacs. Nearly all the men had check suits; some were wearing white trousers, in spite of the coolness of the evening. The gas-lamps were lit.

Hussonnet, through his connexions with the fashion magazines and the little theatres, knew a great many women; he blew them kisses, and now and then, leaving his friends, went to chat with them.

This behaviour aroused Deslauriers' jealousy. He brazenly accosted a tall blonde, dressed in nankeen. After glancing at him irritably, she said: 'No. Don't like the look of you!' and turned on her heel.

He tried again with a big brunette, who must have been mad, for at his first word she jumped up and threatened to call the police if he went on. Deslauriers gave a forced laugh; then, finding a young woman sitting under a lamp apart from the rest, he invited her to dance.

The orchestra, perched like monkeys on the platform, scraped and blew with a will, while the conductor, standing in front of them, beat time mechanically. The dancers were crowded together and in high spirits; hat ribbons, coming undone, brushed against cravats; boots disappeared under skirts; and all this jumped up and down in time with the music. Deslauriers pressed the young woman against him, and, carried away by the intoxication of the can-can, flung himself about among the dancers like a great marionette. Cisy and Dussardier continued their walk; the young aristocrat eyed the girls, but, in spite of the clerk's encouragement, did not dare to speak to them, for he imagined that in the rooms of that sort of woman there was always 'a man hiding in the wardrobe with a pistol, who comes out and forces you to make out a bill of exchange in his favour'.

They rejoined Frédéric. Deslauriers had stopped dancing, and they were all wondering how to end the evening when Hussonnet exclaimed:

'Why, there's the Marquise d'Amaëgui!'

She was a pale snub-nosed woman with elbow-length mittens and big black curls which hung down over her cheeks like a dog's ears. Hussonnet said to her:

'Let's arrange a little party at your place – an Oriental orgy! Try and dig up some of your friends for these knights of France. Well, what's worrying you? Are you waiting for your hidalgo?'

The Spanish girl bowed her head; knowing her friend's simple tastes, she was afraid that she might have to pay for the refreshments. When she finally mentioned the word money, Cisy offered five twenty-franc pieces, the entire contents of his purse, and the matter was decided. But Frédéric had vanished.

Thinking he recognized Arnoux's voice, and catching sight of a woman's hat, he had promptly plunged into the next arbour.

Mademoiselle Vatnaz was alone with Arnoux.

'I beg your pardon. Am I intruding?'

'Not in the least,' replied the dealer.

From the last words of their conversation, Frédéric gathered that he had come hot-foot to the Alhambra to talk to Mademoiselle Vatnaz on an urgent matter; and it seemed that Arnoux was not completely reassured, for he asked her anxiously:

'Are you absolutely sure?'

'Absolutely! You are loved! Ah, what a man!'

And she pulled a face at him, pouting with her thick lips, which were so red they almost looked as if they were bleeding. But she had magnificent wild eyes, with specks of gold in the pupils, full of wit, love, and sensuality. They lit up the yellowish complexion of her thin face like lamps. Arnoux seemed to enjoy her teasing. He leant over to her and said:

'You're sweet. Kiss me.'

She took him by the ears and kissed him on the forehead.

At that moment the dancing stopped; and the conductor's place was taken by a handsome young man who was rather corpulent and as pale as wax. He had long black hair arranged in the style adopted by Christ, and a blue velvet waistcoat embroidered with big golden palms; he looked as proud as a peacock and as stupid as a turkey. After bowing to the audience, he launched out into a song. A villager was describing his trip to the capital; the singer imitated the dialect of Lower Normandy and played the drunkard. The refrain:

> I laughed and laughed, I'm telling thee.
> Ah, Paris is a place to see!

set the audience stamping their feet with enthusiasm. Delmas, who was billed as a 'soulful singer', was too artful to let them cool down. A guitar was hurriedly handed to him, and he wailed a ballad entitled 'The Albanian Girl's Brother'.

The words reminded Frédéric of those which the man in rags had sung on the boat, between the paddle-wheels. His eyes settled unconsciously on the hem of the dress spread out in front of him. After each verse there was a long pause, and the breath of the wind in the trees was like the sound of waves.

Mademoiselle Vatnaz, pushing aside with one hand the branches of a privet which was obstructing her view of the platform, gazed fixedly at the singer, her nostrils dilated, her eyes half-closed, as if absorbed in a solemn joy.

'Ah!' said Arnoux. 'Now I understand why you're at the Alhambra tonight. Delmas appeals to you, my dear!'

She would admit nothing.

'Oh, what modesty!'

And pointing to Frédéric, he said:

'Are you worrying about him? You needn't, you know. He's the soul of discretion.'

The others, looking for their friend, came into the arbour. Hussonnet introduced them. Arnoux distributed cigars and bought water-ices all round.

Mademoiselle Vatnaz had blushed at the sight of Dussardier. Soon she stood up and, holding out her hand to him, said:

'Don't you remember me, Monsieur Auguste?'

'How do you come to know her?' asked Frédéric.

'We used to live in the same house,' he answered.

Cisy tugged at his sleeve, and they went off. He was scarcely out of sight when Mademoiselle Vatnaz began a eulogy of his character. She even added that he had 'a genius for affection'.

Then the conversation turned to Delmas, who could have considerable success in the theatre as a mime; and an argument followed which touched on Shakespeare, the censorship, style, the lower classes, the takings at the Porte-Saint-Martin, Alexandre Dumas, Victor Hugo, and Dumersan. Arnoux had known several famous actresses; the young men leaned forward to listen to him. But his words were drowned by the din of the music; and as soon as a quadrille or a polka was over, everybody rushed for a table, called the waiter, and laughed; bottles of beer and sparkling lemonade exploded among the shrubberies; women cackled like hens; a couple of gentlemen started a fight; a thief was arrested.

When the galop was played, the dancers invaded the paths. Panting, smiling, and red-faced, they went by with dresses and coat-tails whirling; the trombones roared louder than ever; the rhythm grew faster; bangs could be heard behind the medieval cloister, as squibs went off; Catherine wheels started spinning; the emerald-green glow of Bengal lights illuminated the whole garden for a moment; and, at the final rocket, the crowd heaved a great sigh.

They moved away slowly. A cloud of gunpowder hung in the air. Frédéric and Deslauriers were edging their way along in the midst of the crowd when they saw something which brought them to a halt. Martinon was getting change from the cloakroom, and with him was a woman of about fifty, ugly, superbly dressed, and of doubtful social status.

'That fellow,' said Dussardier, 'is not as simple as people think. But where has Cisy got to?'

Dussardier pointed to the bar, where they saw the noble scion with a bowl of punch in front of him and a pink hat by his side.

Hussonnet, who had been away for five minutes, reappeared at the same moment.

A girl was hanging on his arm and calling him 'ducky'.

'No, no!' he said to her. 'Not in public! Call me Vicomte instead. That has something of Louis the Thirteenth, gay cavaliers, and soft boots about it that appeals to me. Yes, you fellows, this is an old flame. Isn't she sweet?'

He took her by the chin.

'Curtsy to these gentlemen. They're all sons of peers of France. I keep in with them so that they'll make me an ambassador.'

'You're absolutely mad!' sighed Mademoiselle Vatnaz.

She asked Dussardier to take her home.

Arnoux watched them move away, and then, turning to Frédéric, said:

'Would La Vatnaz appeal to you, I wonder? Now I come to think about it, you're not very open about these things. You keep your love affairs pretty quiet, don't you?'

Frédéric, turning pale, swore that he had no secrets.

'But nobody knows who your mistress is,' Arnoux went on.

Frédéric felt tempted to quote a name at random. But the story might be repeated to *her*. He replied that in point of fact, he had no mistress.

The dealer considered this deplorable.

'Tonight you had a splendid opportunity. Why didn't you do as the others, who've all gone off with a woman apiece?'

'Well, what about you?' said Frédéric, losing patience at this persistence.

'Oh, it's different for me, my boy! I'm going home to my own!'

He called a cab and vanished.

The two friends went off on foot. An east wind was blowing. Neither spoke. Deslauriers cursed himself for not 'shining' in front of a magazine proprietor, and Frédéric wrapped himself in his melancholy. Finally he said that he had found the dance-hall boring.

'Whose fault is that? You shouldn't have left us for your friend Arnoux!'

'Bah! Whatever I did would have been utterly futile.'

But the clerk had a theory. To get a thing, all you had to do was to want it badly enough.

'All the same, you yourself, just now . . .'

'I wasn't interested,' said Deslauriers, cutting the allusion short. 'If you think I'm going to get mixed up with women . . .'

And he inveighed against their affectation, their stupidity; in short, they did not appeal to him.

'Oh, don't put it on!' said Frédéric.

Deslauriers fell silent. Then suddenly he said:

'Will you bet me a hundred francs that I don't "make out" with the first woman we meet?'

'Yes! Done!'

The first they met was a hideous beggar-woman, and they were despairing of their luck when, in the middle of the Rue de Rivoli, they spotted a tall girl carrying a small cardboard box in her hand.

Deslauriers accosted her in the arcade. She turned off abruptly in the direction of the Tuileries, and soon afterwards started crossing the Place du Carrousel, darting glances right and left. She ran after a cab; Deslauriers caught up with her. He walked beside her, talking to her with expressive gestures. Finally she accepted his arm, and they proceeded along the quays. Then, opposite the Châtelet, they walked up and down the pavement for twenty minutes at least, like a couple of sailors on watch. Then, all of a sudden, they crossed the Pont au Change, the Flower Market, the Quai Napoléon. Frédéric went into the house behind them. Deslauriers gave him to understand that he would be in their way, and that he had only to follow his example.

'How much have you got left?'

'Two ten-franc pieces.'

'That's enough. Good night.'

Frédéric felt the sort of surprise one experiences when one sees a practical joke brought off successfully. 'He's just having me on,' he thought. 'Shall I go up?' But if he did, Deslauriers might think he envied him his catch. 'As if I hadn't a love of my own, a hundred times purer, nobler, and stronger!' A sort of fury drove him on. He arrived outside Madame Arnoux's door.

None of the outer windows belonged to her flat. All the same, he stood with his eyes glued to the front of the house, as if he thought that by staring hard he might penetrate the walls. Now she was probably resting, as peaceful as a sleeping flower, with her lovely black hair spread over the lace of her pillow, her lips parted, her head on one arm.

Arnoux's face appeared to him. He hurried away, to escape from this vision.

He remembered Deslauriers' advice; it horrified him. Then he wandered through the streets.

Whenever somebody came towards him, he tried to make out his face. Now and then a ray of light passed between his legs, describing a wide arc on the pavement; and a man emerged from the shadows, carrying a basket and a lantern. The wind, here and there, shook an iron chimney-flue; distant sounds arose, mingling with the buzzing in his head; and he seemed to hear the music of the quadrille echoing vaguely through the air. The motion of walking sustained this feeling of intoxication; he suddenly found himself on the Pont de la Concorde.

Then he remembered that evening the previous winter when, leaving her house the first time, he had been obliged to stand still, his heart had been beating so fast under the pressure of his hopes. Those hopes were all dead now.

Dark clouds scudded across the face of the moon. He gazed at it, thinking of the grandeur of space, the misery of life, the futility of everything. Dawn broke; his teeth were chattering; and, half asleep, soaked by the fog, and choked with tears, he asked himself why he should not put an end to it all. He had only to make a single movement. The weight of his head pulled him forward, and he imagined his corpse floating on the water. Frédéric leant over. The parapet was rather wide, and it was weariness that prevented him from clambering over it.

Panic seized him. He returned to the boulevards and slumped on a bench. Some policemen woke him up, thinking that he had 'been on the spree'.

He started walking again. But as he felt famished, and all the restaurants were closed, he went and had something to eat in a tavern in Les Halles. After that, imagining that it was still too early to go home, he wandered about in the vicinity of the Hôtel de Ville until a quarter past eight.

Deslauriers had long since dismissed his hussy, and he was writing at the table in the middle of the room. About four o'clock, Monsieur de Cisy came in.

Thanks to Dussardier, he had made the acquaintance of a lady the previous evening; and he had even taken her home in a carriage, together with her husband, as far as her front door. There she had given him an assignation, from which he had just come. And she did not have a reputation for that sort of thing.

'What does that matter to me?' asked Frédéric.

Then the nobleman began to digress; he spoke of Mademoiselle Vatnaz, the Spanish girl, and all the others. Finally, with a great many circumlocutions, he explained the purpose of his visit: counting on his friend's discretion, he had come to ask him for his help in an enterprise which, if successful, would establish him once for all in his own eyes as a man; and Frédéric did not refuse. He told the story to Deslauriers, but without explaining his part in it.

The clerk considered that 'he was doing very nicely now'. Frédéric's deference to his advice increased his good humour.

It was by virtue of this good humour that he had seduced, the first day they met, Mademoiselle Clémence Daviou, an embroideress who earned her living stitching gold braid on military uniforms. She was the sweetest person imaginable, and as slim as a reed, with big blue eyes which were always wide-open in astonishment. The clerk took advantage of her simplicity, even persuading her that he had the Legion of Honour; he decorated his frock-coat with a red ribbon when they were alone, but removed it in public, explaining that this was to avoid humiliating his employer. As a general rule, he kept her at a distance, allowed her to worship him like a pasha, and called her 'daughter of the people' by way of a joke. Every time she came to see him, she brought him a little bunch of violets. Frédéric had no desire for this sort of love.

All the same, when they went out arm-in-arm to dine in a private room at Pinson's or Barillot's, he felt a strange sadness. Frédéric did not know how much he had made Deslauriers suffer, every Thursday during the past year, when he scrubbed his nails before going to dine in the Rue de Choiseul.

One evening, after he had watched them go off from his balcony, he saw Hussonnet in the distance on the Pont d'Arcole. The Bohemian beckoned to him, and, when Frédéric had come down his five flights of stairs, he explained:

'The thing is this: next Saturday, the 24th, is Madame Arnoux's name-day.'

'How can it be? Her name is Marie.'

'Angèle too, but never mind. There's going to be a party at their country-house at Saint-Cloud; I've been asked to let you know. You'll find a carriage at the shop at three o'clock. That's settled, then. Sorry to have bothered you. But I've so much to see to!'

Frédéric had scarcely turned round when his concierge handed him a letter:

Monsieur and Madame Dambreuse request the pleasure of Monsieur F. Moreau's company at dinner on Saturday the 24th of this month. —R.S.V.P.

'Too late,' he thought.

All the same, he showed the letter to Deslauriers, who exclaimed:

'Ah! At last. But you don't look pleased. Why is that?'

After some hesitation, Frédéric said that he had received another invitation for the same day.

'Do me the pleasure of sending the Rue de Choiseul packing. No nonsense, now! I'll answer for you, if it embarrasses you.'

And the clerk wrote an acceptance in the third person.

Never having seen society except through the fever of his ambition, Deslauriers pictured it as an artificial creation, functioning in accordance with mathematical laws. A dinner in town, a meeting with an important official, the smile of a pretty woman, could, through a series of actions following logically upon one another, produce amazing results. Certain Paris drawing-rooms were like those machines which take in material in its raw state and give it out with its value increased a hundredfold. He believed in courtesans advising diplomats, in rich marriages obtained by intrigue, in the genius of criminals, in the submissiveness of fortune to a strong will. In short, he considered acquaintance with the Dambreuses so useful, and he argued so eloquently, that Frédéric did not know what to decide.

In any case, he would have to give Madame Arnoux a present on her name-day: and he naturally thought of a parasol to make up for his clumsiness. He happened to find a marquise sunshade in dove-coloured shot silk, with a little handle of carved ivory, which had just come from China. But it cost a hundred and seventy-five francs, and he had not a penny to his name; indeed, he was living on credit on his next quarter's allowance. Nevertheless, he wanted it, he had to have it, and swallowing his repugnance, he had recourse to Deslauriers.

Deslauriers replied that he had no money.

'I need it,' said Frédéric. 'I need it badly.'

And when the other repeated the same excuse, he lost his temper.

'I think you might, sometimes . . .'

'Might what?'

'Nothing.'

The clerk had understood. He withdrew the sum in question from his reserve, and, after paying it out coin by coin, he said:

'I shan't ask you for a receipt, seeing that I'm living on you.'

Frédéric threw his arms round his neck, with fulsome protestations of affection. Deslauriers remained cold. Then, the next day, seeing the parasol on the piano, he said:

'Oh, so it was for that!'

'I may send it,' said Frédéric weakly.

Luck was with him, for that evening he received a note on black-edged paper, in which Madame Dambreuse announced the death of an uncle of hers and expressed her regret at having to postpone the pleasure of making his acquaintance.

He was at the magazine office by two o'clock. Instead of waiting to take him in his carriage, Arnoux had gone off the day before, giving in to his longing for fresh air.

Every year, as soon as the first leaves appeared on the trees, he would set off every morning, for several days in succession, walk for miles across the fields, drink milk at farmhouses, joke with the village girls, inquire about the crops, and bring back a head of lettuce in his handkerchief. Finally, fulfilling an old dream, he had bought himself a country house.

While Frédéric was talking to the assistant, Mademoiselle Vatnaz came in, and was disappointed at not finding Arnoux. She was told that he might be away for another two days. The assistant advised her 'to go down there'; she could not go down there; to write a letter; she was afraid the letter might be mislaid. Frédéric offered to take it himself. She dashed off a note, and begged him to deliver it in private.

Forty minutes later he arrived at Saint-Cloud.

The house stood half-way up the hill, a hundred yards beyond the bridge. The garden walls were hidden by two rows of limes, and a wide lawn sloped down to the river bank. The gate in the railings was open. Frédéric went in.

Arnoux was lying on the grass, playing with a litter of kittens. He seemed to find this pastime utterly absorbing. The letter from Mademoiselle Vatnaz roused him from his lethargy.

'Damn it! What a nuisance! She's right. I must go back.'

Then, after thrusting the letter into his pocket, he showed Frédéric round his estate with obvious pleasure. He showed him everything: the stable, the barn, the kitchen. The drawing-room was on the right, and, on the Paris side, looked out on a trellis-work pergola covered with clematis. Suddenly a vocal flourish rang out above their heads; Madame Arnoux, thinking she was alone, was amusing herself by singing. She sang scales, trills, arpeggios. There were long notes which seemed to hang in the air; others fell swiftly, like the spray of a waterfall; and her voice, passing through the Venetian blind, cleft the profound silence and rose towards the blue sky.

Suddenly she stopped short, for Monsieur and Madame Oudry, a couple of neighbours, had arrived.

Then she herself appeared at the top of the steps; and as she walked down, he caught sight of her foot. She was wearing little open-work shoes of bronzed leather, with three cross-straps which formed a golden lattice-work against her stockings.

The guests arrived. Apart from Maître Lefaucheur, a lawyer, they consisted of the company which met round the table on Thursday evenings. Each had brought some gift: Dittmer a Syrian scarf, Rosenwald an album of ballads, Burrieu a water-colour, Sombaz a caricature of himself, and Pellerin a charcoal sketch depicting a sort of Dance of Death, a hideous fantasy of mediocre execution. Hussonnet had dispensed himself from bringing a present.

Frédéric waited until after the others before offering his.

She thanked him warmly for it. Then he said:

'But . . . it's almost a debt! I was so upset.'

'What about?' she asked. 'I don't understand.'

'Dinner's ready!' said Arnoux, seizing Frédéric by the arm.

Then, in his ear:

'You're not very bright, are you?'

Nothing could have been more delightful than the dining-room, with its sea-green walls. At one end, a stone nymph was dipping her toe into a basin shaped like a shell. Through the open windows, the whole garden could be seen, with the long lawn flanked by an old Scottish pine, three-quarters bare. The expanse of grass was broken by uneven clumps of flowers; and beyond the river, in a wide semi-circle, there stretched the Bois de Boulogne, Neuilly, Sèvres, and Meudon. In front of the railings, a sailing dinghy was beating up to windward.

First they talked about this view, then about landscapes in general; and an argument was starting when Arnoux gave instructions to his servant to get the phaeton ready for about half past nine. His cashier had sent him a letter calling him back to Paris.

'Do you want me to come back with you?' asked Madame Arnoux.

'Of course!'

And with a deep bow he added:

'You know very well, Madame, that it is impossible to live without you.'

They all congratulated her on having such an admirable husband.

'Oh, it's because I am not alone,' she replied gently, pointing to her little daughter.

Then the conversation returned to painting, and they talked about a Ruysdael which Arnoux hoped to sell for a considerable sum. Pellerin asked him if it was true that the famous Saul Mathias of London had come over the previous month and offered him twenty-three thousand francs for it.

'Absolutely true.'

And, turning to Frédéric, he went on:

'In fact that was the gentleman I was entertaining the other day at the Alhambra – very much against my will, I can assure you, because those Englishmen are poor company.'

Frédéric, suspecting that some feminine intrigue lay behind Mademoiselle Vatnaz's letter, had admired the ease with which Arnoux had found a plausible excuse for making off; but this new and utterly futile lie made him open his eyes wide.

The dealer added innocently:

'By the way, what's the name of that friend of yours, the tall young man?'

'Deslauriers,' said Frédéric quickly.

And, to make up for the wrong he felt he had done him, he praised him as a man of considerable intelligence.

'Oh, really? But he didn't look such a straightforward young fellow as the other, the one who works for the carriers.'

Frédéric cursed Dussardier. She would think that he mixed with the common people.

After that the conversation turned to the improvements in the capital, and the new districts; and the worthy Oudry happened to mention Monsieur Dambreuse as one of the leading speculators.

Frédéric, seizing the opportunity to make an impression, said that he knew him. But Pellerin launched into a diatribe against tradesmen; he saw no difference between them, whether they sold candles or money. Then Rosenwald and Burrieu started discussing porcelain; Arnoux talked gardening with Madame Oudry; Sambaz, a wit of the old school, amused himself by teasing her husband: he called him Odry, like the actor,[14] and declared that he must be descended from Oudry, the painter of dogs, for the bump of zoology was clearly visible on his forehead. He even tried to feel his skull; the other objected on account of his wig; and dessert ended in roars of laughter.

After they had had coffee and smoked under the limes, and strolled about the garden, they went for a walk along the river-bank.

The party stopped beside a fisherman, who was cleaning some eels in a tank for live fish. Mademoiselle Marthe wanted to see them. He emptied his box on to the grass; and the little girl went down on her knees to catch them, laughing with pleasure and screaming with fright. They were all lost. Arnoux paid for them.

After that he hit on the idea of going for a row.

One side of the horizon was beginning to grow pale, while on the other side a broad orange band stretched across the sky, deepening into purple above the tops of the hills, which were now quite black. Madame Arnoux was sitting on a big stone, with this fiery glow behind her. The others strolled about; Hussonnet, at the foot of the bank, played ducks and drakes.

Arnoux returned with an old long-boat, into which, despite the protests of the more prudent among them, he piled his guests. It started settling down in the water, and they had to get out.

By this time candles were already burning in the drawing-room, which was hung with chintz, with crystal candelabra on the walls. Old Madame Oudry dozed off in an armchair, while the others listened to Monsieur Lefaucheur holding forth on the glories of the Bar. Madame Arnoux was alone by the window. Frédéric went over to her.

They chatted about the subject under discussion. She admired orators; he preferred a writer's fame. But surely, she argued, one must derive a deeper pleasure from moving people directly, in person; from seeing the emotions of one's own soul entering into theirs. That sort of triumph did not greatly tempt Frédéric, who had no ambition at all.

'Ah, why?' she said. 'A man must have a little!'

They were standing close together in the window-recess. In front of them the night stretched out like a huge dark veil, studded with silver. It was the first time they had not talked about trivial matters. He even discovered her likes and dislikes: certain scents made her feel ill, history books interested her, and she believed in dreams.

He broached the subject of amorous adventures. She pitied the ravages of passion, but was revolted by hypocritical deceptions; and this rectitude of mind harmonized so well with the regular beauty of her face that the one seemed to be the natural outcome of the other.

Now and then she smiled, and her eyes rested on him for a moment. Then he felt her gaze penetrating his soul, like those great rays of sunlight which go down to the depths of the water. He loved her without any reservation, without any hope of return, unconditionally; and in those mute transports, which were like bursts of gratitude, he would have liked to cover her forehead with a rain of kisses. In the meantime an inner breath seemed to carry him beyond himself; it was a longing for self-sacrifice, a yearning for self-dedication, which was all the stronger because he could not gratify it.

He did not leave with the rest; nor did Hussonnet. They were to return in the carriage; and the phaeton was waiting at the foot of the steps when Arnoux went down the garden to pick some roses. Then, as he had tied the bouquet with a piece of thread, and as the stems were sticking out unevenly, he felt in his pocket, which was full of papers, pulled one out at random, wrapped the flowers in it, fastened his handiwork together with a large pin, and offered it to his wife, not without a certain emotion.

'Here you are, darling. Forgive me for having forgotten you.'

She gave a little cry; the pin, clumsily inserted, had pricked her, and she went back to her room. They waited nearly a quarter of an hour for her. At last she reappeared, picked up Marthe, and threw herself into the carriage.

'What about your bouquet?' asked Arnoux.

'No, no! It isn't worth the trouble.'

Frédéric ran to get it; she called out to him:

'I don't want it!'

He soon came back with it though, saying that he had wrapped it in the paper again, for he had found the flowers on the floor. She thrust them into the leather apron next to the seat, and they set off.

Frédéric, sitting beside her, noticed that she was trembling violently. Then, when Arnoux turned to the left after crossing the bridge, she cried:

'No! You're going the wrong way! It's over there, to the right.'

She seemed irritable; everything annoyed her. At last, when Marthe had closed her eyes, she extracted the bouquet and threw it out of the door; then she grasped Frédéric by the arm, motioning to him with her other hand never to mention what she had done.

After that she pressed her handkerchief to her lips and sat quite motionless.

The other two, on the box, talked about printing and subscribers. Arnoux, who was driving carelessly, lost his way in the middle of the Bois de Boulogne. They plunged down narrow paths. The horse went forward at walking-pace; the branches of the trees scraped the hood. Frédéric could see nothing of Madame Arnoux but her two eyes in the darkness; Marthe was lying across her lap, and he supported the child's head.

'She is tiring you,' said her mother.

He answered.

'No! Oh, no!'

Clouds of dust rose slowly into the air; they were passing through Auteuil; all the houses had their shutters closed; here and there a street-lamp lit up the corner of a wall, and then they were plunged back into darkness; once he noticed that she was crying.

Was it out of remorse? Or desire? Or what? This sorrow, whose cause was unknown to him, interested him as if it were a personal matter; now there was a new bond between them, a sort of complicity; and he said to her, in his gentlest voice:

'Are you unwell?'

'Yes, a little,' she replied.

The carriage rolled along, and the honeysuckles and syringas trailing over the garden fences sent whiffs of languorous perfume into the night. The ample folds of her dress covered her feet. It seemed to him that he was in communication with her whole being through the child's body which lay between them. He bent over the little girl, and, parting her pretty brown hair, kissed her gently on the forehead.

'You are a kind person!' said Madame Arnoux.

'Why?'

'Because you are fond of children!'

'Not all children!'

He said no more, but placed his left hand beside her and left it open, thinking that she might do likewise, and his hand would meet hers. Then he felt ashamed, and withdrew it.

Soon they reached the paved roads. The carriage went faster, the gas-lamps grew more numerous. They were in Paris. At the Garde-Meuble[15] Hussonnet jumped down from the box. Frédéric waited until they reached the courtyard before alighting; then he lay in wait at the corner of the Rue de Choiseul, and saw Arnoux slowly making his way back towards the boulevards.

The very next day he started working as hard as he could.

He pictured himself in an assize court, on a winter's evening, making the closing speech for the defence; the jury was pale, the breathless audience was almost bursting the partitions of the courtroom; he had been speaking for four hours now, and was recapitulating his arguments, finding new ones, and feeling that every phrase, every word, every gesture was lifting the blade of the guillotine suspended behind him. Then he was at the tribune in the Chamber, an orator carrying the safety of an entire people on his lips, overwhelming his opponents with his eloquence or crushing them with his repartee, speaking with thunder and music in his voice, ironic, pathetic, passionate, sublime. She was there somewhere in the crowd, hiding her tears of enthusiasm under her veil; they came together afterwards, and discouragement, slander, and abuse were powerless to touch him if she said: 'Ah, that was beautiful!' and passed her hands lightly over his forehead.

These pictures blazed like beacon-lights on the horizon of his life. Stimulated by them, his mind became quicker and more vigorous. He shut himself up until August, and passed his final examination.

Deslauriers, who had had tremendous trouble in pushing him through his second examination in December and his third in February, was astonished at his ardour. The old hopes were reawakened.

In ten years, Frédéric had to be a deputy; in fifteen a minister; why not? With his father's money, which would come to him soon, he could begin by starting a newspaper; that would be the first step; after that they would see. Deslauriers's own ambition was a chair at the Law School; and he sustained his doctorate thesis with such remarkable skill that he earned the compliments of the professors.

Frédéric sustained his own thesis three days later. Before leaving for his holidays, he hit on the idea of a picnic, to bring to a close the Saturday gatherings.

He was in high spirits on the day. Madame Arnoux was away at Chartres with her mother. But they would come together again soon, and he would end up by becoming her lover.

Deslauriers had been elected that very day to the Orsay debating society, and had made a speech which had won enthusiastic applause. Although he was an abstemious man, he got drunk and said to Dussardier at dessert:

'You're an honest fellow! When I'm rich, I'll make you my agent.'

Everybody was in a good mood. Cisy was not going to finish his law course; Martinon intended to continue his probationary period somewhere in the provinces, where he would be appointed deputy public prosecutor; Pellerin was embarking on a large picture representing 'The Genius of the Revolution'; while Hussonnet, the following week, was due to read the synopsis of a play to the manager of the Délassements, and was confident of success.

'Because everybody agrees that I'm good at constructing a play. I've knocked about long enough to know all about the passions. And as for witticisms, they're right up my street!'

He took a flying leap, landed on his hands, and walked for some time round the table with his legs in the air.

These antics failed to make Sénécal smile. He had just been turned out of his boarding-house for giving a thrashing to an aristocrat's son. As his poverty increased, he laid the blame on the social system, cursing the rich; and he opened his heart to Regimbart, who was becoming more and more disillusioned, melancholy, and disgusted. The Citizen was now giving his attention to the fiscal situation, and he accused the Camarilla of squandering millions in Algeria.

As he found it impossible to sleep without having paid a visit to the Alexandre tavern, he disappeared at eleven o'clock. The others left later; and Frédéric, as he said good-bye to Hussonnet, learnt that Madame Arnoux had been due back the previous day.

He accordingly went to the Messageries to change his seat on the coach for the next day, and about six o'clock he called to see her. The concierge told him that her return had been postponed for a week. Frédéric dined alone, then went for a stroll along the boulevards.

Pink clouds were floating like scarves above the rooftops; the awnings of the shops were being rolled up; water-carts were pouring a fine rain on the dust; and an unusual freshness was mingling with the smells from the cafés, where, through the open doors, between the silver and gilt decorations, bouquets of flowers could be seen reflected in the tall mirrors. The crowd moved along slowly. There were groups of men chatting in the middle of the pavement; and women went by with dreamy eyes and that camellia complexion which the fatigue of hot weather gives the female skin. An atmosphere of vast possibilities enveloped the houses. Never before had Paris seemed so beautiful to him. He could see nothing in the future before him but an endless succession of years filled with love.

He stopped to look at the poster outside the Porte-Saint-Martin; and, for want of anything better to do, he bought a ticket.

They were playing an old pantomime. There were few people in the audience; the windows in the gallery let in the daylight in small blue squares, while the oil-lamps of the footlights formed a single line of glowing yellow. The scene was a slave-market in Peking; there were bells, drums, sultans' wives, pointed hats, and bad puns. When the curtain fell, he wandered around the foyer by himself, and admired a big green landau, with two white horses and a coachman in knee-breeches, which was standing on the boulevard at the foot of the steps.

He was going back to his seat when a lady and gentleman came into the first stage-box, in the circle. The husband had a pale face with a thin grey fringe of beard; he was wearing the rosette of an Officer of the Legion of Honour, and that icy look which is supposed to be typical of diplomats.

His wife, who was at least twenty years younger than he, was neither tall nor short, ugly nor pretty; she wore her fair hair in long corkscrew tresses, had a dress with a flat bodice, and was carrying a large fan of black lace. The presence of people of that class at a theatre in that season of the year could only be explained by an accident, or by the tedium of spending an evening alone together. The lady chewed the edge of her fan, and the gentleman kept yawning. Frédéric could not remember where he had seen that face before.

During the next interval, he met the two of them as he was walking along a corridor. He made a vague gesture of greeting, whereupon Monsieur Dambreuse recognized him, went up to him, and promptly apologized for his unpardonable negligence. He was referring to the countless visiting cards which Frédéric, on Deslaurier's advice, had left at his house. However he got his dates mixed up, thinking that Frédéric was in his second year as a law student. Then he said that he envied his leaving for the country. He could do with a rest himself, but business kept him in Paris.

Madame Dambreuse, leaning on his arm, nodded her head gently; and the charm and intelligence of her face made a striking contrast with her bored expression a little earlier.

'But there are some wonderful amusements here!' she said, at her husband's last remark. 'This is such a stupid piece, don't you agree, Monsieur?'

And the three of them stood there talking about theatres and new plays.

Frédéric, accustomed to the affected grimaces of provincial housewives, had never seen such ease of manner in any woman, nor that studied simplicity which the ingenuous regard as a sign of immediate sympathy.

They counted on seeing him as soon as he got back; Monsieur Dambreuse asked to be remembered to old Roque.

On his return, Frédéric did not neglect to tell Deslauriers how he had been greeted.

'Splendid!' said the clerk. 'And now don't let your mamma talk you round. Come back straight away!'

The day following his arrival, after lunch, Madame Moreau took her son out into the garden.

She said she was happy to know that he had a profession, for they were not as rich as people thought; the land brought in very little; the farmers were slow in paying; she had even been obliged to sell her carriage. Finally she explained their financial situation.

During the first difficult period of her widowhood, an astute individual, Monsieur Roque, had lent her some money, renewing and prolonging these loans against her wishes. Then he had suddenly demanded repayment, and she had accepted his terms, letting him have the farm at Presles at a ridiculous price. Ten years later, her capital had disappeared in the collapse of a banking-house at Melun. Out of a horror of mortgages, and in order to keep up appearances for the sake of her son's future, she had once again listened to old Roque when he had reappeared. But now she was free. In short, they had about ten thousand francs a year left, of which two thousand three hundred were his – his entire inheritance.

'It can't be true!' exclaimed Frédéric.

With a nod of her head she indicated that it was perfectly true.

But surely his uncle would leave him something?

That was far from certain.

And they took a turn round the garden, without speaking. Finally she clasped him to her breast and, in a voice choked with tears, said:

'Oh, my dear boy! I have had to give up so many dreams!'

He sat down on the bench, in the shade of the tall acacia.

What she advised him to do was to become clerk to Monsieur Prouharam, a solicitor who would pass his practice on to him; if he made a success of it, he could sell it later, and then make a good marriage.

Frédéric was no longer listening. He was gazing unthinkingly over the hedge, into the garden opposite.

A little red-haired girl of about twelve was there all alone. She had made herself a pair of ear-rings with sorb-apples; her grey linen bodice revealed her bare shoulders, which were slightly bronzed by the sun; her white skirt was spotted with jam-stains; and her whole person had something of the grace of a wild animal, at once tense and slight. The presence of a stranger must have astonished her, for she had halted abruptly, with her watering-can in her hand, and was flashing her clear blue-green eyes at him.

'That is Monsieur Roque's daughter,' said Madame Moreau. 'He has just married his housekeeper and made his child legitimate.'

VI

RUINED, robbed, done for!

He had remained on the bench, as if dazed by a shock. He cursed fate, he wanted to fight somebody; and to increase his despair, he felt a sort of disgrace or dishonour weighing him down; for Frédéric had always imagined that his patrimony would one day amount to fifteen thousand francs a year, and he had hinted as much to the

Arnoux's. Now they would regard him as a boastful rogue, a worthless scoundrel who had wormed his way into their house in the hope of swindling them. And how was he going to see Madame Arnoux again, now?

That was out of the question, in any case, with only three thousand francs a year! He could not always live on the fourth floor, have the concierge as his servant, and pay calls wearing shabby black gloves going blue at the fingertips, a greasy hat, or the same frock-coat for a year on end. No, no! Never! Yet life was unbearable without her. Many people managed quite well without much money – Deslauriers for one – and he reproached himself with cowardice for attaching such importance to trivialities. Perhaps poverty would increase his talents a hundredfold. He grew excited at the thought of all the great men who had worked in garrets. A soul such as Madame Arnoux's would surely be stirred by a sight of that sort, and her emotions would be aroused. So this disaster was really a stroke of luck after all; like those earthquakes which uncover hidden treasure, it had revealed to him the secret riches of his nature. But there was only one place in the whole world where he could turn them to account: Paris! For, in his opinion, art, learning, and love – those three faces of God, as Pellerin would have said – were linked exclusively with the capital.

He told his mother, that evening, that he was going back there. Madame Moreau was surprised and indignant. It was preposterous, ridiculous. He would do better to follow her advice and remain near her in an office. Frédéric shrugged his shoulders: 'Oh, come now!' he said, considering the idea an insult.

The good lady thereupon tried another method. In a gentle voice, broken by sobs, she started talking to him of her loneliness, of her old age, of the sacrifices she had made. Now that she was unhappier than ever, he was deserting her. Then, referring to her approaching death:

'Good heavens, show a little patience! You will soon be free!'

These laments were repeated twenty times a day for three months; and at the same time the comfort of his home corrupted him; he enjoyed having a softer bed, and napkins which were not torn; so that in the end, exhausted, worn out, defeated by the terrible force of gentle persuasion, Frédéric allowed himself to be taken to Maître Prouharam's office.

There he showed neither knowledge nor skill. Until then he had been regarded as a young man of great ability, who would be the pride of the department. Everybody was disappointed.

To begin with he had thought to himself: 'I must let Madame Arnoux know.' And for a week he had planned in his mind dithyrambic letters, and brief notes in a sublime, lapidary style. He was held back by his reluctance to tell the truth about his past. Then he thought that it would be better to write to the husband. Arnoux knew life, and would understand.

Finally, after a fortnight's hesitation, he said to himself:

'Dammit, I shan't be seeing them again; let them forget me. At least I shan't have fallen low in her memory. She will think I am dead, and will miss me ... perhaps.'

As it cost him very little to make extravagant resolutions, he had sworn never to return to Paris, and even not to inquire after Madame Arnoux.

All the same, he missed the life of the capital, even down to the smell of the gas and the din of the omnibuses. He dreamt of all the words she had said to him, of the sound of her voice, of the light in her eyes; and, regarding himself as a dead man, he did absolutely nothing at all any more.

He used to get up very late and look out of the window at the waggoners' carts going past. The first six months were particularly horrible.

On certain days, however, he was seized with a fit of indignation against himself. Then he would go out and wander through the meadows, which in the winter were half-flooded by the Seine. They were separated by lines of poplars. Here and there rose a little bridge. He roamed about until the evening, kicking up the yellow leaves, breathing in the mist, jumping ditches; as his pulse beat faster, he was overcome by a longing for violent action; he dreamt of becoming a trapper in America, of entering the service of a pasha in the East, of signing on as a sailor; and he poured out his melancholy in long letters to Deslauriers.

The latter was struggling to make his way. His friend's cowardly behaviour and his eternal jeremiads struck him as absurd. Soon their correspondence dwindled to practically nothing. Frédéric had given all his furniture to Deslauriers, who had kept on his lodgings. His mother mentioned this furniture to him from time to time; one day he finally admitted that he had made a present of it, and she was scolding him when a letter arrived.

'What's the matter?' she said. 'You're trembling.'

'I'm all right,' replied Frédéric.

Deslauriers had written to let him know that he had taken Sénécal in, and that they had been living together for a fortnight. So now Sénécal was taking his ease among the things from Arnoux's shop! He might sell them, criticize them, make jokes about them. Frédéric felt deeply wounded. He went up to his room. He wanted to die.

His mother called him. She wanted to consult him about planting some flowers in the garden.

This garden, which was laid out like an English park, was divided down the middle by a wooden fence; and one half belonged to old Roque, who also had a kitchen-garden on the river-bank. Because of their quarrel, the two neighbours took care not to go into the garden at the same time. But since Frédéric's return, Roque appeared there more often, and he was lavish in his civilities towards Madame Moreau's son. He sympathized with him for living in a small town. One day he told him that Monsieur Dambreuse had asked after him. Another time he dilated on the custom in Champagne by which noble status was inherited through the mother.

'In those days you would have been a noble lord, because your mother was a De Fouvens. And you can say what you like, there's something in having a particule. After all,' he added, giving Frédéric a sly look, 'it depends on the Keeper of the Seals.'

These aristocratic aspirations were singularly out of keeping with his appearance. As he was short, his large brown frock-coat exaggerated the length of his torso. When he took off his cap, he revealed an almost feminine face with a sharply pointed nose; his yellow hair looked like a wig; and he greeted people with a very low bow, keeping close to the wall.

Until the age of fifty he had made do with the services of Catherine, a woman from Lorraine of the same age as himself whose face was pitted with smallpox. But about 1834 he brought back from Paris a pretty blonde with a face like a sheep and a majestic bearing. She was soon to be seen proudly flaunting a pair of huge ear-rings; and everything was explained by the birth of a daughter, who was registered under the names of Élisabeth-Olympe-Louise Roque.

Catherine, in her jealousy, expected that she would hate this child. In fact, however, she adored it. She lavished care, attention, and kisses on it, in order to take the mother's place and make the child hate her – an easy undertaking, for Madame Éléonore completely neglected the little girl, preferring to gossip with the shopkeepers. The very day after her marriage, she paid a visit to the sub-prefect, stopped talking familiarly to the servants, and decided that good form required her to be strict with the child. She sat in on her lessons; the tutor, an elderly clerk from the town hall, did know how to behave. His pupil rebelled, was slapped, and went to cry in the arms of Catherine, who invariably took her side. Then the two women would quarrel, and Monsieur Roque would tell them to hold their tongues. He had married out of affection for his daughter, and he wanted her to be left in peace.

Often she wore a tattered white dress with lace-edged drawers; and on great feast-days she went out dressed like a princess, in order to annoy the townspeople, who would not let their children play with her, on account of her illegitimate birth.

She lived by herself in her garden, swung on the swing, ran after butterflies, and suddenly stopped to look at the beetles settling on the rose-bushes. It was probably these games which lent her face an expression at once bold and dreamy. She also happened to be the same height as Marthe, so that Frédéric said to her, the second time they met:

'Will you allow me to kiss you, Mademoiselle?'

The little thing looked up and replied:

'I don't mind if you do!'

But they were separated by the fence.

'I'll have to climb over,' said Frédéric.

'No, lift me up!'

He leant over the fence, grasped her under her armpits, and kissed her on both cheeks; then he put her back by the same method, which was repeated on subsequent occasions.

As soon as she heard her friend coming, she ran to meet him, with no more shyness than a child of four: or else, hiding behind a tree, she barked at him like a dog, to frighten him.

One day when Madame Moreau was out, he took her up to his room. She opened all the bottles of scent and pomaded her hair liberally; then, without the slightest embarrassment, she stretched herself out at full length on the bed, and lay there with her eyes open.

'I'm pretending I'm your wife,' she said.

The next day he saw her in tears. She confessed that she was 'crying for her sins', and when he asked what they were, she lowered her eyes and answered:

'Don't ask me any more!'

Her first communion was drawing near, and that morning she had been taken to confession.

The sacrament did little to improve her character. She sometimes flew into a towering rage, and Frédéric had to be sent for to calm her. Often he took her with him on his walks. While he daydreamed as he strolled along, she picked poppies at the edge of the cornfields; and when she saw that he was more than usually depressed, she tried to comfort him with cheerful remarks. His heart, starved of love, fell back on the friendship of this child; he drew pictures for her, told her stories, and started reading to her. He began with *Les Annales romantiques*, a miscellany of prose and verse which was popular at the time. Then, so delighted by her intelligence that he forgot her age, he read one after the other *Atala, Cinq-Mars,* and *Les Feuilles d'automne.* But one night – she had listened that evening to *Macbeth,* in Letourneur's straightforward translation – she woke up screaming: 'The spot! The spot!' Her teeth were chattering, she was trembling, and, fixing her terrified eyes on her right hand, she kept rubbing it and saying: 'Still a spot!' Finally the doctor arrived and recommended avoiding any sort of excitement.

The townspeople saw nothing in all this but an unfavourable augury for her morals. It was said that 'young Moreau' was planning to make an actress of her later on.

Soon all the talk was about another event: the arrival of Uncle Barthélemy. Madame Moreau gave him her bedroom and pushed hospitality to the point of serving meat on days of abstinence.

The old man was far from affable. He made continual comparisons between Le Havre and Nogent, where he found the air heavy, the bread bad, the streets ill paved, the food poor, and the inhabitants lazy.

'Business is in a poor state here,' he said.

He criticized the extravagances of his late brother; he, on the other hand, had provided himself with an income of twenty-seven thousand francs a year. Finally he left at the end of the week, and, standing on the footboard of the carriage, he let fall these far from reassuring words:

'I'm glad to know that you are still comfortably off.'

'You'll get nothing!' said Madame Moreau, coming back into the parlour.

He had come only in response to a pressing invitation on her part; and for a whole week she had tried, too obviously perhaps, to extract a statement of his intentions. She regretted what she had done, and sat motionless in her armchair, her head bowed, her lips pursed. Frédéric, sitting opposite her, watched her; and both of them were silent, as they had been five years before, on his return from Montereau. This coincidence, striking him unexpectedly, reminded him of Madame Arnoux.

At that moment the crack of a whip sounded under the window, and a voice called him.

It was old Roque, alone in his waggonette. He was going to spend the day at La Fortelle, at Monsieur Dambreuse's, and cordially invited Frédéric to come with him.

'You don't need an invitation with me; don't worry on that account!'

Frédéric was tempted to accept. But how was he to explain his permanent residence at Nogent? He had no decent summer clothes; and then what would his mother say? He refused.

After that their neighbour was less friendly. Louise was growing up; Madame Éléonore fell dangerously ill; and the connexion was brought to an end, much to the relief of Madame Moreau, who was afraid that friendship with people of that sort might have an adverse affect on her son's career.

She dreamt of buying him the post of clerk of the court; Frédéric put up little opposition to this idea. He now accompanied his mother to Mass and played cards with her in the evening; he was growing accustomed to provincial life, sinking into it; and even his love had taken on a sort of funereal sweetness, a sleepy charm. By dint of pouring his sorrow out in his letters, mingling it with his reading, taking it on his walks in the country, and spreading it everywhere, he had practically exhausted it. Madame Arnoux was almost a dead woman for him, and he was surprised not to know where her grave was, his affection for her had become so calm and resigned.

One day, 12 December 1845, about nine o'clock in the morning, the cook brought a letter up to his bedroom. The address, in big letters, was in an unfamiliar hand; and Frédéric, who was half-asleep, did not hurry to break the seal. Finally he read:

Court of Conciliation of Le Havre. Third Arrondissement. – Monsieur: Your uncle, Monsieur Moreau, having died intestate . . .

He was the heir!

As if a fire had broken out on the other side of the wall, he jumped out of bed, in his nightshirt and bare feet; he passed his hand over his face, not believing his eyes and thinking that he was still dreaming; and, to make sure that he was really awake, he opened the window wide.

Snow had fallen; the roofs were white; and he even recognized a washtub in the yard which he had tripped over the evening before.

He read the letter again three times in succession: it was absolutely true! The whole of his uncle's fortune! Twenty-seven thousand francs a year! A frenzy of joy overwhelmed him at the thought of seeing Madame Arnoux again. With the clarity of a hallucination, he saw himself in her house, at her side, bringing her some present wrapped in tissue paper, while outside there stood his tilbury – no, a brougham rather – a black brougham, with a servant in brown livery; he could hear his horse snorting and the sound of the curb-chain mingled with the murmur of their kisses. This would happen day after day, indefinitely. He would entertain them in his own home; the dining-room would be hung with red leather; the boudoir in yellow silk; there would be divans everywhere! And what cabinets! What Chinese vases! What carpets! These pictures flooded in on him in such a torrent that he felt his head reeling. Then he remembered his mother; and he went downstairs, still holding the letter in his hand.

Madame Moreau tried to contain her emotion and fainted. Frédéric took her in his arms and kissed her on her forehead.

'Dear mother, you can buy back your carriage now. So smile now, don't cry, be happy!'

Ten minutes later the news had reached the outskirts of the town. Maître Benoist, Monsieur Gamblin, Monsieur Chambrion, all their friends came hurrying round. Frédéric slipped away for a moment to write to Deslauriers. Other people arrived. The afternoon was spent in receiving congratulations. Everybody forgot about Roque's wife, for all that she was 'very low'.

In the evening, when they were alone together, Madame Moreau advised her son to set up as a barrister at Troyes. Being better known in his own part of the country than any other, he would be more likely to make a good match there.

'Oh, that's a bit steep!' exclaimed Frédéric.

His happiness was scarcely in his hands before people were trying to take it from him. He stated his firm intention of living in Paris.

'What are you going to do there?'

'Nothing!'

Madame Moreau, surprised at his manner, asked him what he wanted to be.

'A minister!' replied Frédéric.

And he assured her that he was not joking; he intended to embark on a diplomatic career, for it was towards this career that his studies and his instincts impelled him. First of all he would become an official of the Council of State, under the patronage of Monsieur Dambreuse.

'You know him, then?'

'Why, yes! Through Monsieur Roque.'

'That's strange,' said Madame Moreau.

He had reawakened in her heart her old ambitious dreams. She inwardly yielded to them, and did not mention the others again.

If Frédéric had obeyed his impatience, he would have set off that very moment. But all the seats in the next day's coaches were taken; he fretted and fumed until seven o'clock in the evening of the day after.

They were sitting down to dinner when the church bell tolled three times, slowly; and the maidservant, coming in, announced that Madame Éléonore had just died.

All things considered, this death was not a calamity for anybody, not even for the child. The girl would only be the better for it later on.

As the two houses adjoined, they could hear a lot of coming and going, and the sound of voices; and the idea of the corpse next door cast a certain gloom over their parting. Madame Moreau wiped her eyes two or three times. Frédéric's heart was heavy.

When the meal was over, Catherine stopped him in the passage. Mademoiselle insisted on seeing him. She was waiting for him in the garden. He went out, stepped over the hedge, and, bumping slightly into the trees, made his way towards Monsieur Roque's house. Lights were burning at a window on the second floor; then a figure appeared in the darkness, and a voice whispered:

'It's me.'

She seemed taller than usual, probably because of her black dress. Not knowing what to say to her, he simply took her hands and sighed:

'Oh, my poor Louise!'

She did not answer. She gazed at him intently for a long time. Frédéric was afraid that he was going to miss the coach; he thought he could hear a rumbling in the distance, and to bring their encounter to an end he said:

'Catherine told me you had something . . .'

'Yes, that's true. I intended to inform you . . .'

Her formal phraseology surprised him, and, as she fell silent once more, he asked:

'Well, what?'

'I don't know. I've forgotten. Is it true that you are going away?'

'Yes, in a few minutes.'

She repeated:

'In a few minutes? . . . And for good? . . . Shall we never see you again?'

Sobs choked her.

'Good-bye! Good-bye! Kiss me, please.'

And she clasped him fiercely in her arms.

PART TWO

I

When he had taken his place in the back of the coupé, and the coach suddenly moved off as the five horses plunged forward together, he felt a wave of joy sweep over him. Like an architect designing a palace, he planned the life he was going to lead. He filled it with luxuries and splendours, so that it rose into the sky; countless things appeared in it, and this daydream of his was so all-absorbing that the outside world vanished.

At the foot of the hill at Sourdun, he noticed where they were. They had covered only three miles at the most! He was indignant. He lowered the window to look at the road, and asked the guard several times how long it would be before they arrived. However, he eventually calmed down, and sat in his corner, with his eyes open.

The lantern, hanging from the postilion's seat, lit up the wheelers' cruppers. He could see nothing beyond but the manes of the other horses, swaying up and down like white waves; their breath formed a mist on both sides of the shafts; the iron chains rattled, the windows trembled in their frames, and the heavy coach rolled along the paved road at a steady pace. Here and there they could make out the wall of a barn, or a solitary inn. Sometimes, as they passed through a village, a baker's oven would be throwing out a fiery glow and the monstrous shadows of the horses would race across the house opposite. At the posting-house, when the horses had been unharnessed, there was complete silence for a moment. Somebody started stamping on the roof of the coach, under the tilt, while a woman standing in a doorway sheltered her candle with one hand. Then the guard jumped on to the footboard and the coach set off again.

At Mormans they heard a clock strike a quarter past one.

'So I shall see her today,' he thought, 'this very day, quite soon now!'

But gradually his hopes and memories, Nogent, the Rue de Choiseul, Madame Arnoux, his mother, all merged together in his mind.

A dull rattle of planks woke him up. They were crossing the Pont de Charenton; it was Paris. His two companions promptly took off their headgear, a cap and a kerchief respectively, put on their hats, and started talking. The first, a fat, red-faced man in a velvet frock-coat, was a merchant; the other was coming to Paris to see a doctor; and Frédéric, fearing that he might have disturbed him during the night, offered him a spontaneous apology, his heart was so warm with happiness.

The Quai de la Gare was presumably flooded, for they went straight on, and the country began again. In the distance, tall factory chimneys were smoking. Then they turned into Ivry. They went up a street, and all of a sudden he caught sight of the dome of the Panthéon.

The plain had changed beyond recognition and looked like a town in ruins. The fortifications crossed it in a horizontal ridge, and on the unpaved paths edging the road stood small branchless trees protected by battens bristling with nails. Chemical factories alternated with timber-merchants' yards. Tall gateways, like those of farms, revealed between their half-open doors sordid yards full of refuse, with pools of dirty water in the middle. Long-fronted, dull-red taverns displayed a pair of crossed billiard cues in a wreath of painted flowers between their first-floor windows; here and there a little stucco shanty had been left half-finished. Then the double line of houses became continuous; at long intervals a huge tin cigar, indicating a tobacconist's shop, stood out against the bare façades. There were some midwives' signs showing a bonneted matron dandling a baby in a lace-trimmed quilt. Posters covered the corners of the walls, and, more than half torn off, they fluttered in the wind, like rags. Workmen in smocks went by, and also brewers' drays, laundry vans, and butchers' carts; a fine drizzle was falling, it was cold, and the sky was pale, but two eyes which meant more to him than the sun were shining behind the mist.

They stopped at the city gate for a long time, for it was blocked by poultry-farmers, carriers, and a flock of sheep. The sentry, his hood thrown back, walked up and down in front of his box in order to keep warm. The toll-clerk clambered on to the top of the coach, and a fanfare on a cornet rang out. They went down the boulevard at a brisk trot with swingle-bars rattling and traces flying. The thong of the long whip crackled in the damp air. The guard gave his ringing shout: 'Look sharp there! Hullo!' and crossing-sweepers stood aside, passers-by jumped out of the way, and mud splashed against the windows. They passed waggons, carriages, and omnibuses, and finally reached the iron gate of the Jardin des Plantes.

The Seine, which was a yellowish colour, had risen almost to the level of the bridges. It was giving off a chilly breath. Frédéric filled his lungs with it, savouring that wonderful Paris air which seems to contain exhalations of both love and intelligence. At the sight of the first cab he nearly cried. He felt that he loved even the straw-covered doorsteps of the wine-shops, the shoe-blacks with their boxes, the grocers' boys shaking their coffee-roasters. Women were tripping along under umbrellas, and he leant out to examine their faces: some chance might have brought Madame Arnoux out.

The shops sped by, the crowd increased, the noise grew louder. After going along the Quai Saint-Bernard, the Quai de la Tourelle, and the Quai Montebello, they took the Quai Napoléon; he tried to catch a glimpse of his own windows, but they were a long way off. Crossing the Seine again by the Pont-Neuf, they went as far as the Louvre; then, taking the Rue Saint-Honoré, the Rue Croix-des-Petits-Champs, and the Rue du Bouloi, they finally reached the Rue Coq-Héron, and entered the hotel yard.

To prolong his pleasure, Frédéric dressed as slowly as he could, and even made his way to the Boulevard Montmartre on foot, smiling at the thought that it would not be long before he saw the beloved name once more on the marble tablet. He raised his eyes. No shop-window, no pictures, nothing!

He ran to the Rue Choiseul. Monsieur and Madame Arnoux no longer lived there, and a neighbour was looking after the lodge for the concierge. Frédéric waited for him; at last he appeared. It was a different man, and he did not know their address.

Frédéric went into a café and consulted the commercial directory over lunch. There were three hundred Arnoux in it, but not a single Jacques Arnoux. Where the devil did they live? Pellerin would know.

He went to his studio, right at the top of the Faubourg Poissonnière. As there was neither a bell nor a knocker, he hammered on the door with his fist, called out, shouted. There was no answer.

Then he thought of Hussonnet. But where was he to find a man like that? Once he had accompanied him to his mistress's house in the Rue de Fleurus. Having arrived at the Rue de Fleurus, Frédéric realized that he did not know the lady's name.

He tried Police Headquarters, where he wandered from staircase to staircase, from office to office. The information office was just closing. He was told to come back the next day.

Then he went into all the art-shops he could find, to ask if they knew Arnoux. Monsieur Arnoux was no longer in business.

Finally, ill, disheartened, and depressed, he returned to his hotel and went to bed. Just as he was stretching out between the sheets, an idea occurred to him which made him sit up in delight:

'Regimbart! What a fool I was not to think of him before!'

The next morning at seven he was in the Rue Notre-Dame-des-Victoires, outside a dram-shop where Regimbart was in the habit of drinking a glass of white wine. It was not open yet; he went for a stroll in the neighbourhood, and came back to the shop half an hour later. Regimbart had just left. Frédéric rushed out into the street. He thought that he could recognize his hat in the distance; a hearse and some mourners' carriages intervened. When they had passed, the hat was no longer to be seen.

Luckily he remembered that the Citizen lunched every day on the stroke of eleven in a little restaurant in the Place Gaillon. He would have to be patient; and after an interminable stroll from the Bourse to the Madeleine and from the Madeleine to the Gymnase, Frédéric, on the stroke of eleven, went into the restaurant in the Place Gaillon, confident that he would find Regimbart there.

'Don't know him!' the owner said in a surly tone.

Frédéric insisted.

'I still don't know him, Monsieur!' the man repeated, raising his eyebrows superciliously and shaking his head in a way which suggested some mystery.

The last time they had met, the Citizen had mentioned the Alexandre tavern. Frédéric swallowed a brioche, and, jumping into a gig, asked the coachman if he knew of a certain Café Alexandre, somewhere on the Montagne Sainte-Geneviève. The cabby took him to an establishment of that name in the Rue des Francs-Bourgeois-Saint-Michel, and to his question: 'Monsieur Regimbart, please?' the proprietor replied with an ingratiating smile:

'He hasn't been in yet, Monsieur,' darting a meaning glance at his wife, who was sitting behind the counter.

And looking at the clock, he promptly added:

'But we expect to see him here within ten minutes, or a quarter of an hour at the most. Célestin, bring the papers! What does Monsieur want to drink?'

Although he did not feel like drinking anything, Frédéric downed a glass of rum, then a glass of kirsch, then a glass of curaçao, than a succession of toddies, both hot and cold. He read the whole of that day's *Siècle*, and then read it all over again, he examined the cartoon in the *Charivari*; down to the texture of the paper; he ended up by knowing the advertisements by heart. Now and then there was a sound of boots on the pavement: it was he! Somebody's profile was silhouetted against the window; but whoever it was always passed on.

To relieve his boredom, Frédéric kept changing his position; he went and sat at the back of the room, then on the right, then on the left; and finally he settled down in the middle of the bench, with his arms outstretched. A cat, stepping delicately along the back of the plush-covered seat, gave him a fright by suddenly jumping down to lick the drops of syrup on the tray; while the child of the house, an unspeakable brat of four, played with a rattle on the steps of the counter. His mother, a pale little woman with bad teeth, smiled stupidly. What could Regimbart be doing? Frédéric waited for him, sunk in a state of infinite depression.

The rain was rattling like hail on the hood of the gig. Through the gap between the muslin curtains he could see the poor horse standing in the street, as motionless as a vaulting-horse. The swollen gutter was flowing between the spokes of the wheels, and the coachman was dozing on his seat, sheltering under the apron. Every now and then, fearing that his gentleman might slip away, he opened the door of the café, dripping with rain. If one could wear things out by looking at them, Frédéric would have dissolved the clock with his fixed stare. Yet the hands went on moving. Alexandre walked up and down repeating: 'He'll come all right, he'll come,' and, to entertain Frédéric, chatted with him and talked politics. He even pushed his hospitality so far as to propose a game of dominoes.

At last, at half-past four, Frédéric, who had been there since midday, jumped to his feet and declared that he was not going to wait any longer.

'I can't understand it, Monsieur,' said the proprietor innocently. 'It's the first time Monsieur Ledoux hasn't turned up.'

'Monsieur Ledoux?'

'Why, yes, Monsieur!'

'But I said Regimbart!' cried an infuriated Frédéric.

'I beg your pardon, but that isn't true. Madame Alexandre, didn't Monsieur say Monsieur Ledoux?'

And appealing to the waiter, he said:

'You heard him, didn't you, the same as I did?'

But the waiter, presumably to score off his master, just smiled.

Frédéric had himself driven back to the boulevards, indignant about the time he had wasted, furious at the Citizen, imploring his presence like that of a god, and firmly resolved to extract him from the depths of the remotest of wine-cellars. His cab irritated him, and he dismissed it; his ideas became confused; then the names of all the cafés which he had heard that idiot mention flashed into his memory, all together, like a thousand fireworks – Café Gascard, Café Grimbert, Café Halbout, Estaminet Bordelais, Estaminet Havrais, Bœuf-à-la-Mode, Brasserie Allemande, Mère-Morel – and he went to all of them in succession. But at one, Regimbart had just left; at another, he might be coming; at the third, he had not been seen for six months; while at a fourth, he had ordered a leg of mutton the day before for Saturday. Finally, at Vautier's tavern, Frédéric, opening the door, bumped into the waiter.

'Do you know Monsieur Regimbart?'

'Do I know him, Monsieur? Why, I'm the one who has the honour of serving him. He's upstairs, just finishing his dinner.'

And the proprietor of the establishment himself came up to him, a napkin under his arm, and said:

'Are you looking for Monsieur Regimbart, Monsieur? He was here a moment ago.'

Frédéric uttered an oath, but the proprietor declared that he would find Regimbart at Bouttevilain's without fail.

'I give you my word of honour! He left a little earlier than usual, because he has a business appointment with some gentleman. But, as I've just said, you'll find him at Bouttevilain's, 92, Rue Saint-Martin, second staircase on the left, back of the courtyard, first floor, right-hand door!'

At last, through a cloud of tobacco-smoke, he caught sight of him, sitting by himself at the far end of the back room behind the billiard-saloon, a tankard in front of him and his chin sunk on his chest, in an attitude of contemplation.

'You know, I've been looking for you for ages!'

Without showing any emotion, Regimbart offered him just two

fingers, and, as if he had seen him only the day before, made a few insignificant remarks about the opening of Parliament.

Frédéric interrupted him by asking, as naturally as he could:

'How's Arnoux?'

The answer was a long time coming: Regimbart was gargling with his drink.

'All right.'

'Where does he live now?'

'Why . . . in the Rue Paradis-Poissonnière,' replied the Citizen in surprise.

'What number?'

'Thirty-seven, of course. You're a queer fellow, I must say!'

Frédéric got up.

'What, are you going?'

'Yes, yes, I've an appointment, something I'd forgotten! Good-bye!'

Frédéric went straight from the tavern to Arnoux's house, as if borne along by a warm wind, and with that extraordinary ease which is characteristic of dreams.

He soon found himself on a second-floor landing, in front of a door whose bell was ringing; a maid appeared; a second door opened; Madame Arnoux was sitting by the fire. Arnoux leapt to his feet and embraced him. She had a little boy of about three on her lap; her daughter, who was now as tall as herself, was standing on the other side of the fireplace.

'Allow me to introduce this gentleman to you,' said Arnoux, picking his son up by the armpits.

And for a few minutes he amused himself by throwing him high into the air and catching him with his outstretched arms.

'You're going to kill him! For heaven's sake, stop!' cried Madame Arnoux.

But Arnoux went on, swearing that there was no danger, and even lisping endearments in the Marseilles dialect, his native tongue.

'There, my poppet! There, my chickadee!'

Then he asked Frédéric why he had been so long without writing to them, how he had spent his time in the provinces, and what brought him back.

'As for me, my dear fellow, I'm in the pottery trade now. But let's talk about you!'

Frédéric blamed his silence on a long-drawn lawsuit and his

mother's health; he dwelt at length on the latter subject to make himself appear interesting. In short, he was settling in Paris, this time for good; and he said nothing of his legacy, for fear of showing up his past.

The curtains, like the chair covers, were in brown damask wool; two pillows lay side by side against the bolster; a kettle was warming among the coals; and the shaded lamp standing on the edge of the chest of drawers cast a dim light over the apartment. Madame Arnoux was wearing a dark blue merino dressing-gown. Gazing into the fire, she had one hand on the little boy's shoulder, and with the other she was undoing the laces of his vest; the child, in his shirt, was crying and scratching his head, like Monsieur Alexandre *fils*.

Frédéric had expected to feel paroxysms of joy; but passions wilt when they are transplanted, and, finding Madame Arnoux in a setting which was unfamiliar to him, he had the impression that she had somehow lost something, that she had suffered a vague degradation, in short that she had changed. The calm of his heart astounded him. He asked after his old friends, including Pellerin.

'I don't see much of him,' said Arnoux.

She added:

'We don't entertain as we used to.'

Was this a warning that he would not receive any invitations? But Arnoux, continuing his civilities, reproached him for not having dropped in to take pot-luck with them; and he explained why he had changed his occupation.

'What can a fellow do in an age of decadence like ours? Great painting has gone out of fashion. Besides, you can introduce art into every sphere of life. You know how devoted I am to the cause of beauty! I must take you to see my factory one of these days.'

And he insisted on showing Frédéric, there and then, some of his products in the shop on the storey below.

The floor was littered with dishes, soup-tureens, plates, and basins. Against the wall there stood some large tiles for bathrooms and lavatories, with mythological designs in the Renaissance style, while in the middle a double set of shelves which went right up to the ceiling bore ice-buckets, flower-pots, candelabra, small flower-stands, and large coloured statuettes representing Negroes or Pompadour shepherdesses. Arnoux's exhibition bored Frédéric, who was cold and hungry.

He hurried to the Café Anglais, where he had a splendid supper, and while he was eating he said to himself:

'What a fool I was, back home, with my lovesick sorrow. Why, she scarcely recognized me! What an ordinary creature she is!'

And in a sudden burst of animal health, he resolved to lead a selfish life. He felt as if his heart was as hard as the table on which his elbows were resting. Now he could throw himself into society life without fear. He thought of the Dambreuses; he would make use of them; then he remembered Deslauriers. 'Oh, so much the worse for him!' All the same, he sent him a note by a messenger, asking him to meet him the next day at the Palais-Royal, so that they could lunch together.

Fortune had not been so kind to Deslauriers.

He had entered for the State examination for teaching posts with a thesis on the right of making a will, in which he maintained that this right should be restricted as far as possible; his opponent had incited him to make some stupid remarks, and he had made a great many, but the examiners had not turned a hair. Then, as luck would have it, he had drawn by lot, as the subject for his lecture, the Statute of Limitations. Deslauriers had propounded the most unfortunate theories, arguing that old claims should be treated like new, and asking why an owner should be deprived of his property because he had no legal right to it until thirty-one years had elapsed. This was giving an honest man's security to the successful robber's heir. Every sort of injustice was consecrated by an extension of this right, which was nothing less than tyranny and the abuse of power. He had even exclaimed:

'Let us abolish it, and the Franks will cease to oppress the Gauls,[16] the English the Irish, the Yankees the Red Indians, the Turks the Arabs, the white men the Negroes, Poland . . .'

The chairman of the examiners had interrupted him:

'That's enough, Monsieur. We are not interested in your political opinions. You can present yourself again at a later date.'

Deslauriers had chosen not to present himself again. But that wretched Article 20 of the Third Book of the Civil Code had become a regular obsession with him. He was planning to write a vast work on *Limitations, viewed as the basis of civil law and of the natural rights of nations*; and he had plunged deep into Dunod, Rogerius, Balbus, Merlin, Vazeille, Savigny, Troplong, and other weighty authorities. So as to be able to give more time to his research, he had resigned his post as chief clerk. He lived by giving private lessons and writing theses; and, at the meetings of the legal debating society, the virulence of his arguments terrified the conservative members, all the young doctrinaires of Guizot's school, so that in certain quarters he enjoyed a sort of celebrity, mingled with suspicion.

He arrived at their rendezvous wearing a bulky overcoat lined with red flannel, like the one Sénécal used to have.

Out of deference to the passers-by, they refrained from a prolonged embrace, but they walked arm-in-arm to Véfour's, chuckling with delight, and with tears trembling in their eyes. Then, as soon as they were alone, Deslauriers exclaimed:

'By heavens, we're going to have an easy time of it now!'

Frédéric did not much care for the way in which Deslauriers promptly associated himself with his fortune. His friend displayed too much pleasure for the two of them, and not enough for him alone.

Then Deslauriers recounted his failure, and gradually told the story of his studies and the life he was leading, speaking of himself with stoic resignation and of other people with bitter rancour. Everything irritated him. There was not a man of position who was not either a fool or a rogue. He flew into a rage with the waiter because of a dirty glass, and to Frédéric's mild protest he replied:

'Why should I mince my words with fellows like that? They earn anything between six and eight thousand francs a year, they've got a vote, and they could probably even stand for election![17] Oh, no!'

Then he added gaily:

'But I was forgetting that I'm talking to a capitalist, to a Croesus, because you are a Croesus now!'

And coming back to the legacy, he expressed the following opinion: that collateral inheritance – something intrinsically unjust, although he was delighted about this particular instance – would shortly be abolished, in the coming revolution.

'You think so?' said Frédéric.

'I'm sure of it,' Deslauriers replied. 'Things can't go on like this. There's too much suffering. When I see people like Sénécal living in poverty . . .'

'Sénécal again!' thought Frédéric.

'But what's the rest of your news? Are you still in love with Madame Arnoux? It's all over, eh?'

Frédéric, not knowing what to say in reply, closed his eyes and bowed his head.

Talking of Arnoux, Deslauriers informed him that his magazine now belonged to Hussonnet, who had completely transformed it. It was called *L'Art*, 'a literary institution, consisting of a company with shares at a hundred francs each and registered capital of forty thousand francs'. Every shareholder was entitled to supply copy to the magazine for 'the object of the company is to publish the work of unknown writers and thus to spare authors of talent, perhaps of genius, those hardships which overwhelm, and so on . . . You know the line!' There was, however, something to be done, and that was to raise the tone of the magazine, then all of a sudden, keeping the same contributors and promising to continue the serial story, to provide the subscribers with a political journal; the sum required was not exorbitant.

'What do you think of the idea? Do you want to help?'

Frédéric did not reject the proposal. But he had to wait until his affairs were in order.

'Then, if there's anything you need . . .'

'No, thank you,' said Deslauriers.

After that they smoked cheroots, leaning their elbows on the plush-covered window-sill. The sun shone, the air was soft, flocks of birds fluttered down into the garden, the bronze and marble statues glistened after the rain, maids in aprons sat gossiping on chairs, and children's laughter could be heard together with the continuous murmur of the fountain.

Frédéric had felt disturbed by Deslaurier's bitterness; but under the influence of the wine flowing through his veins, half-asleep and slightly dazed, with the sun full in his face, he no longer felt anything but an immense, pleasantly stupid well-being, like a plant saturated with heat and moisture. Deslauriers, his eyes half-closed, was gazing vaguely into the distance. His chest swelled, and he said:

'Ah, those were the days, when Camille Desmoulins, standing on a table over there, urged the people on to the Bastille! That was a time when people really lived, when a man could assert himself, prove his strength! Mere lawyers gave orders to generals, and ragamuffins defeated kings, whereas nowadays . . .'

He fell silent, then suddenly added:

'Never mind. The future is full of promise.'

And drumming his fingers on the window-panes, he recited these lines by Barthélemy:

> The dreaded Assembly will appear once more,
> Just as inspiring as forty years before,
> A fearless colossus treading with mighty steps . . .

'I've forgotten the rest. But it's getting late. Shall we go?'

And he went on expounding his theories in the street.

Frédéric was not listening to him, but glancing in the shop-windows at materials and furniture which would be suitable for his new home; and it may have been the thought of Madame Arnoux which made him stop outside a second-hand dealer's shop, at the sight of three china plates. They were decorated with yellow arabesques, with a metallic sheen, and they cost three hundred francs apiece. He had them put on one side.

'If I were you,' said Deslauriers, 'I'd prefer to buy myself some silver plate,' revealing, by this taste for sumptuous display, the man of humble origin.

As soon as he was alone, Frédéric called on the famous Pomadère, from whom he ordered three pairs of trousers, two dress coats, a fur coat, and five waistcoats; then he went to a bootmaker's, a shirt-maker's, and a hatter's, giving instructions at each shop to make all possible speed.

Three days later, in the evening, on his return from Le Havre, he found his wardrobe complete. Impatient to make use of it, he decided to pay a call, there and then, on the Dambreuses. But it was too early, barely eight o'clock.

'What if I went to see the others?' he said to himself.

Arnoux was alone, shaving in front of his mirror. He offered to take Frédéric somewhere where he would have a good time, and at the mention of Monsieur Dambreuse he exclaimed:

'But that's splendid! You'll meet some friends of his there. Do come! It's going to be great fun.'

Frédéric was excusing himself when Madame Arnoux recognized his voice and greeted him through the partition, for her daughter was ill and she herself indisposed. The tinkle of a spoon against a glass could be heard, and that gentle rustling of things being carefully moved about which is inseparable from a sickroom. Then Arnoux disappeared to say good-bye to his wife. He multiplied his reasons for leaving her:

'You know how important it is. I simply must go; it's vital for me; they're expecting me.'

'Go, go, my dear. Enjoy yourself!'

Arnoux hailed a cab.

'Palais-Royal. No. 7 Galerie Montpensier.' And, sinking back on the cushions, he said, 'I'm so tired, my dear fellow! It'll be the end of me. I can tell *you* about it, anyway.'

He leant over and whispered mysteriously in his ear:

'I'm trying to find the copper-red of the Chinese potters.'

And he explained what a glaze was, and a slow fire.

When they arrived at Chevet's, he was handed a large basket, which he had taken out to the cab. Then he selected some grapes, pineapples, and other delicacies 'for his poor wife', and ordered them to be delivered early the next morning.

Next they went to a costumier's, for it was a fancy-dress ball which was being held that evening. Arnoux chose a pair of blue velvet breeches, a waistcoat to match, and a red wig; Frédéric a domino; and they drove off to the Rue de Laval, where they alighted outside a house lit up with coloured lanterns on the second floor.

At the foot of the stairs they could already hear the sound of violins.

'Where the devil are you taking me?' asked Frédéric.

'To see a sweet girl. Don't be frightened.'

A footman opened the door, and they went into the entrance-hall, where coats, cloaks, and shawls were piled on chairs. A young woman, dressed as a Louis Quinze dragoon, was just passing through. It was Mademoiselle Rose-Annette Bron, the mistress of the house.

'Well,' said Arnoux.

'It's all arranged,' she replied.

'Oh, thank you, my darling!'

And he tried to kiss her.

'Be careful, you idiot! You'll spoil my make-up!'

Arnoux introduced Frédéric.

'Go ahead, Monsieur. You're very welcome.'

She drew aside a curtain behind her and shouted with a flourish:

'Messire Arnoux, a scullery boy, with one of his noble friends!'

At first Frédéric was dazzled by the lights; he could see nothing but silk, velvet, bare shoulders, a mass of colours swaying to the strains of an orchestra hidden by some foliage, between walls hung with yellow silk, and adorned here and there with pastel portraits and crystal sconces in the Louis Seize style. Tall lamps, whose frosted globes looked like snowballs, rose above baskets of flowers which stood on little tables in the corners; and opposite, beyond a second, smaller room, a third could be seen, containing a bed with twisted posts and a Venetian mirror behind it.

The dancing stopped, and a burst of delighted applause greeted the spectacle of Arnoux advancing with his basket heaped with eatables on his head.

'Mind the chandelier!'

Frédéric raised his eyes; it was the old Dresden china chandelier which used to hang in the shop of *L'Art Industriel*. Memories of the old days came back to him; but just then an infantryman of the line in undress uniform, with that stupid expression which is traditionally attributed to conscripts, planted himself in front of him, stretching out his arms to show his astonishment; despite the disfigurement of a frightening black moustache with waxed points, he recognized his old friend Hussonnet. In a nonsensical mixture of Alsatian and pidgin French, the Bohemian overwhelmed him with congratulations, addressing him as 'colonel'. Frédéric, put out by the presence of all these people, did not know what to reply. A bow was tapped on a music-stand, and the dancers took up their positions again.

There were about sixty of them, most of the women dressed as peasant-girls or countesses, and the men, who were nearly all middle-aged, as carriers, stevedores, or sailors.

Frédéric, standing against the wall, watched the quadrille in front of him.

An old buck, dressed as a Doge of Venice in a long cassock of purple silk, was dancing with Madame Rosanette, who was wearing a green jacket, knitted breeches, and soft boots with gold spurs. The couple opposite consisted of an Albanian loaded with scimitars and a blue-eyed Swiss girl, as white as milk and as plump as a quail, in shirt-sleeves and a red bodice. In order to show off her hair, which came down to her knees, a tall blonde from the Opéra ballet had come as a savage; she had nothing on top of her brown tights but a leather loin-cloth, some glass bracelets, and a tinsel tiara adorned with a huge spray of peacock's feathers. In front of her a Pritchard in a ridiculously large black coat was beating time on his snuff-box with his elbow. A little Watteau shepherd, all blue and silver like a ray of moonlight, was striking his crook against the thyrsus of a

Bacchante, who was wearing a crown of grapes, a leopard skin on her left side, and buskins trimmed with golden ribbons. On the other side, a Polish girl in a spencer of orange velvet was swirling her gauze skirt over pearl-grey silk stockings encased in pink boots edged with white fur. She was smiling at a paunchy man of about forty, disguised as a choir-boy, who was leaping high in the air, lifting his surplice with one hand and holding on to his red skull-cap with the other. But the queen, the belle of the ball, was Mademoiselle Loulou, a star of the dance-halls. As she was temporarily well-off, she was wearing a broad lace collar over her plain black velvet jacket, and her wide trousers of flaming red silk, which clung to her buttocks and were fastened at her waist by a cashmere sash, were decorated all the way down the seams with little fresh white gard-enias. Her pale, somewhat puffy face, with its turned-up nose, seemed even more impudent than her tousled wig, to which a man's grey felt hat was clinging, knocked in and cocked over her right ear. When she jumped into the air, the diamond buckles of her shoes nearly touched the nose of her neighbour, a tall medieval baron imprisoned in a suit of armour. There was also an angel, with a golden sword in her hand and a pair of swan's wings on her back, who kept losing her escort, and, coming and going without under-standing the figures of the dance, threw the quadrille into confusion.

Frédéric, looking at these people, felt lost and ill-at-ease. He thought of Madame Arnoux again, and it seemed to him as if he were taking part in some kind of conspiracy against her.

When the quadrille was over, Madame Rosanette came up to him. She was panting slightly, and her gorget, which was as bright as a mirror, rose and fell gently under her chin.

'And you, Monsieur, aren't you dancing?'

Frédéric excused himself; he did not know how to dance.

'Really? Not even with me? You're quite sure?'

And standing with her weight on one leg, with the other slightly behind, she stroked the mother-of-pearl hilt of her sword with her left hand, and gazed at him for a moment, with an expression which was half-suppliant, half-ironic. Finally she said 'Well, that's that,' did a pirouette, and disappeared.

Frédéric, dissatisfied with himself, and not knowing what to do, started roaming about the house.

He went into the boudoir, which was lined with pale blue silk, embroidered with bunches of wild flowers, while on the ceiling, in a gilded wooden frame, cupids frolicked on pillowy clouds in an azure sky. These refinements, which would seem paltry to Rosanette's present-day counterparts, dazzled him; and he admired everything: the artificial convolvulus round the edge of the mirror, the curtains over the fireplace, the Turkish divan, and, in an alcove, a sort of tent lined with pink silk and covered with white muslin. The bedroom contained black furniture inlaid with brass, and, on a dais covered with swan's-skin, the great canopied bed decorated with ostrich feathers. Jewelled pins stuck in pincushions, rings lying about on trays, lockets in gold frames, and silver caskets could be made out in the dim light coming from a Bohemian bowl suspended by three chains. Through a little half-open door a conservatory could be seen which occupied the whole breadth of a terrace and was bounded at the far end by an aviary.

This was indeed a setting calculated to delight him. In a sudden explosion of youthful feeling, he swore to himself that he was going to enjoy it, and took courage. Returning to the door of the drawing-room, where there were more people now and everything seemed to be moving in a sort of luminous haze, he stood there watching the dancing, half shutting his eyes in order to see better, and breathing in the languorous scent of the women, which filled the room like a vast, ubiquitous kiss.

Near him, on the other side of the door, he suddenly noticed Pellerin – Pellerin in full evening dress, with his left arm tucked in his coat, and holding his hat and a torn white glove in his right hand.

'Well, we haven't seen you for a long time! Where the devil have you been? Travelling in Italy? Rather a bore, Italy, eh? Not the revelation they say it is? Never mind, bring along your sketches to show me one of these days.'

And without waiting for an answer, the artist started talking about himself.

He had made considerable progress, for he had realized once for all the stupidity of Line. One should not look for Beauty and Unity in a work of art so much as character and variety.

'Because everything exists in nature, and so everything is a legitimate subject for painting. It's just a matter of striking the right note – and I've discovered the secret.'

And giving him a nudge with his elbow, he repeated several times:

'I've discovered the secret, you see. For instance, look at that little woman with the sphinx headdress dancing with a Russian postilion: that's clear, crisp, and definite, all planes and crude colours. Indigo under the eyes, a dash of scarlet on the cheeks, a spot of sepia on the temples ... biff ... baff ...'

And he dabbed imaginary brush-strokes in the air with his thumb.

'Whereas that fat one over there,' he went on, pointing to a fishwife in a cherry-red dress with a gold cross on a chain round her neck and a knotted lawn kerchief hanging down her back, 'she's nothing but a collection of curves. Her nostrils are flared like the wings of her cap, her mouth turns up at the corners, and her chin is sagging; it's all lush, harmonious, rich, calm, and sunny – a real Rubens! Yet they're both perfect of their kind! So where's the ideal?'

He warmed to his subject.

'How would you define a beautiful woman? How would you define Beauty? Oh, Beauty, you'll say ...'

Frédéric interrupted him to ask about a pierrot with a profile like a goat who was blessing all the dancers in the middle of a quadrille.

'He's a nobody. A widower with three sons. He lets them run about in rags, while he spends his life at the club and sleeps with the housekeeper.'

'And that man dressed as a judge, who's talking to a Pompadour marquise over there in the window-recess?'

'The marquise is Madame Vandael, who used to act at the Gymnase; she's the mistress of the Doge, the Comte de Palazot. They've been together for twenty years; nobody knows why. Oh, what wonderful eyes that woman had once! The fellow talking to her is known as Captain d'Herbigny. He's one of the old guard, with nothing to his name but his Croix d'honneur and his pension. He acts as uncle to girls on the make on solemn occasions, arranges duels, and dines out at other people's expense.'

'A scoundrel?' said Frédéric.

'No, a decent fellow.'

'Oh!'

The artist pointed out other people to him, and then caught sight of a gentleman dressed, like Molière's doctors, in a long black serge gown which he wore open all the way down to show off the trinkets on his watch-chain.

'That character is Doctor Desrogis. He's livid at not being famous, has written a book of medical pornography, licks every-body's boots in high society, and is terribly discreet; the ladies love him. He and his wife – that scraggy lady-of-the-manor in the grey dress – trail around together in all the public places, and private palaces too. They're rather hard up, but they have an "at home" day for all that – artistic teas where people recite poetry. Look out!'

For the doctor was coming over to them; and soon the three of them were chatting in a group at the entrance to the drawing-room. Hussonnet joined them, followed by the Savage Woman's lover, a young poet whose short cloak, in the style of François I, revealed a puny anatomy underneath, and lastly a young wit dressed as a Turkish pedlar. His gold-braided jacket had travelled the road on the backs of so many itinerant dentists; his wide pleated trousers were such a faded red; his turban, rolled up like a fried eel, looked so shabby; in short, his whole costume gave such a successful impression of poverty, that the women did not conceal their disgust. The doctor comforted him by singing the praises of his mistress, who had come as a stevedore. This Turk was a banker's son.

In between two quadrilles Rosanette went over to the fireplace, where a fat little old man in a brown coat with gold buttons was sitting in an armchair. In spite of his withered cheeks, which drooped over his high white neckcloth, his hair was still fair and curled naturally like a poodle's coat, and this gave him a rather sprightly look.

She listened to what he was saying, bending down towards him. Then she brought him a glass of syrup; and nothing could have looked daintier than her hands under the lace cuffs which showed beyond the sleeves of her green tunic. When he had finished drinking, the old man kissed them.

'Why, that's Monsieur Oudry, Arnoux's neighbour!'

'Former neighbour,' said Pellerin with a laugh.

'What do you mean?'

A waltz began, and a postilion from Longjumeau[18] seized her by the waist. Then all the women, who were sitting on the wall-sofas round the room, sprang to their feet in a line, and their skirts, stoles, and headdresses started spinning around.

They came so close to him that Frédéric could see the beads of sweat on their foreheads; and this dizzy, whirling movement, growing ever faster and more regular, produced a sort of intoxication in his mind, filling it with other pictures, while the women passed him in a single dazzling vision, each with her distinctive beauty exciting a different emotion. The Polish girl, surrendering languidly to the music, made him long to hold her to his heart while the two of them travelled in a sleigh across a snow-covered plain. The Swiss girl, waltzing with her body erect and her eyelids lowered, opened up vistas of tranquil pleasure in a lake-side chalet. Then, all of a sudden, the Bacchante, leaning her dark head backwards, made him dream of greedy kisses in oleander groves, in stormy weather, to the dull beat of tabors. The Fishwife, out of breath from dancing so fast, was shrieking with laughter; and he felt he would have liked to go drinking with her at Les Porcherons and to crumple her neckerchief with both hands, as in the good old days. On the other hand, the Stevedore, whose light toes barely touched the floor, seemed to suggest, in the suppleness of her limbs and the gravity of her face, all the refinements of modern love, which combines the precision of a science with the mobility of a bird. Rosanette was whirling about with her hand on her hip; her knot-shaped wig, bobbing up and down on her collar, scattered orris-powder all around her; and, at every spin, she nearly caught Frédéric with the tip of her golden spurs.

At the final chord of the waltz Mademoiselle Vatnaz came in. She had an Algerian kerchief on her head, a number of piastres on her forehead, and mascara under her eyes; she was dressed in a sort of black cashmere coat falling over a light-coloured skirt spangled with silver; and she was carrying a tambourine in her hand.

Behind her walked a tall young fellow in the classical costume of Dante. He was – she no longer tried to conceal it now – the former singer at the Alhambra, who, his name being Auguste Delamare, had originally called himself Anténor Dellamare, then Delmas, then Belmar, and finally Delmar, altering and improving his name in this way to match his growing fame; for he had left the music-hall for the theatre, and had indeed just made a resounding début at the Ambigu, in *Gaspardo le Pêcheur*.

Hussonnet scowled at the sight of him. Since the rejection of his play, he loathed actors. People had no idea of the vanity of those fellows – and this chap was worse than the rest.

'Just look at him putting it on!'

After bowing slightly to Rosanette, Delmar had stationed himself with his back to the fireplace; and he stood there motionless, with one hand on his heart, his left foot forward, his eyes directed upwards, and his wreath of gilded laurels on top of his hood, trying to infuse poetry into his gaze in order to fascinate the ladies. People came up from all over the room to form a wide circle round him.

But Mademoiselle Vatnaz, after giving Rosanette a long kiss, went over to Hussonnet and begged him to revise the style of an educational book which she wanted to publish, a literary and moral anthology entitled *The Young Person's Garland*. The writer promised his help. Then she asked him if he could possibly puff her friend a little in one of the papers he wrote for, and even offer him a part in a play later on. Hussonnet was so taken aback by this that he forgot to take a glass of punch.

This punch had been brewed by Arnoux; and, followed by the count's footman carrying an empty tray, he handed it round with a self-satisfied air.

When he came to Monsieur Oudry, Rosanette stopped him.

'Well, what about that business matter?'

He flushed slightly: then, turning to the old man, he said:

'Our friend here tells me that you might be so kind ...'

'Why, neighbour, of course! I'm entirely at your service.'

And the name of Monsieur Dambreuse was mentioned. As they talked in low voices, Frédéric could not catch what they said. He went over to the other side of the fireplace, where Rosanette was chatting with Delmar.

The actor had a vulgar face, intended, like a stage-set, to be viewed from a distance, thick hands, big feet, and a heavy jaw. He was running down the most famous actors, speaking of 'my vocal organ, my physique, my resources', and embellishing his conversation with words which he liked but did not really understand, such as 'morbidezza', 'analogous', and 'homogeneity'.

Rosanette was listening to him with little approving nods of the head. Admiration could be seen blossoming under the rouge on her cheeks, and something moist passed like a veil over her pale eyes, which were of an indefinable colour. How could a man like that appeal to her? Frédéric inwardly incited himself to despise him more than ever, possibly in order to banish a kind of envy which he felt for him.

Mademoiselle Vatnaz was now with Arnoux; she was laughing loudly, but every now and then she darted a glance at Rosanette, whom Monsieur Oudry was watching intently.

Then Arnoux and Mademoiselle Vatnaz disappeared; the old man came and whispered to Rosanette.

'All right, then, it's settled. Leave me alone.'

And she asked Frédéric to go and see if Monsieur Arnoux was in the kitchen.

The floor was covered with row upon row of half-filled glasses; and the saucepans, the cooking pots, the turbot-kettle, and the frying-pan were trembling on the stove. Arnoux was gaily giving orders to the servants, stirring the gravy, tasting the sauces, and joking with the cook.

'Right,' he said. 'Tell her I'm going to dish up.'

The dancing had stopped, the women had just sat down, and the men were walking about. In the middle of the drawing-room one of the window-curtains was billowing in the wind; and the Sphinx, in spite of her neighbours' comments, was exposing her sweating arms to the draught. Where could Rosanette be? Frédéric looked for her farther afield, in the boudoir and the bedroom. Several of the guests had taken refuge in these rooms, so as to be alone or tête-à-tête. The darkness was full of whispers and laughs stifled by handker-chiefs; and fans could be glimpsed fluttering over the bosoms of dresses, slowly and gently, like the wing-beats of wounded birds.

Entering the conservatory, he saw, under the broad leaves of a caladium near the fountain, Delmar lying face down on the sofa; Rosanette, sitting beside him, was running her fingers through his hair, and they were gazing at one another. At the same moment Arnoux came in from the other end, by the aviary. Delmar jumped to his feet, then walked slowly out without turning round. He even stopped near the door to pick a hibiscus blossom which he put in his buttonhole. Rosanette bowed her head; Frédéric, who could see her in profile, noticed that she was crying.

'Hullo! What's the matter?' said Arnoux.

She shrugged her shoulders without answering.

'Is it because of him?' he went on.

She put her arms round his neck, and, kissing him on the forehead, said slowly:

'You know perfectly well that I'll always love you, darling. Don't let's think about it any more. Let's go and have supper.'

A brass chandelier with forty candles lit the dining-room, the walls of which were covered with old china plates; and this glaring light, shining straight down, intensified the pallor of an enormous turbot which occupied the middle of the table-cloth, among the hors-d'œuvre and the fruit. All the way round the table, dishes of shell-fish soup had been laid. With a rustling of dresses, the women sat down one after another, tucking in their skirts, their sleeves, and their stoles; the men stood in the corners. Pellerin and Monsieur Oudry were placed beside Rosanette; Arnoux was opposite. Palazot and his mistress had just left.

'Right!' said Rosanette. 'Into action!'

And the Choir-boy, who was a wit, made a grandiloquent sign of the cross and began reciting the *Benedicite*.

The women were shocked, especially the Fishwife, who had a daughter she wanted to bring up to be respectable. Arnoux also 'did not like that sort of thing', considering that religion ought to be treated with reverence.

A German clock struck two, giving rise to countless jokes about the cuckoo. Talk of every conceivable kind ensued: puns, anecdotes, boasts, wagers, plausible lies, improbable assertions – a torrent of words which soon split up into separate conversations. The wine went round; one course followed another; the doctor carved. Oranges and corks were thrown across the table; people left their places to talk to other guests. Rosanette kept turning round to Delmar, who stood motionless behind her; Pellerin gossiped away: Monsieur Oudry smiled. Mademoiselle Vatnaz emptied the dish of crayfish almost single-handed, the shells crackling between her long teeth. The Angel, perched on the piano-stool – the only place where her wings allowed her to sit – munched away stolidly, without stopping.

'What an appetite!' the Choir-boy kept saying in amazement. 'What an appetite!'

The Sphinx was drinking brandy, shouting at the top of her voice, and throwing herself around like a madwoman. Suddenly her cheeks puffed out, and, unable to hold back the blood which was choking her, she put her napkin to her lips, then threw it under the table.

Frédéric had seen her.

'It's nothing!'

And when he urged her to go home and take care of herself, she answered slowly:

'Oh, what's the use? If it wasn't this, it would be something else. Life isn't much fun.'

He shivered, seized with an icy melancholy, as if he had caught a glimpse of whole worlds of misery and despair, a charcoal stove beside a trestle-bed, and the corpses at the mortuary in their leather aprons, with the cold tap-water running over their hair.

Meanwhile Hussonnet, crouching at the feet of the Savage Woman, was bawling in a husky voice, in imitation of the actor Grassot:

'Do not be cruel, O Celuta! This little family party is so delightful! Intoxicate me with pleasure, my beloved ones! Let us frisk! Let us frolic!'

And he started kissing the women on the shoulder. They flinched, pricked by his moustache. Then he hit on the idea of breaking a plate against his head, by giving it a gentle tap. Others copied him; pieces of china flew about like tiles in a high wind, and the Stevedore shouted:

'Go ahead! It's all free! The fellow who makes them gives them to us.'

All eyes were turned on Arnoux. He replied:

'Ah, but payment is requested by return,' apparently wanting to give the impression that he was not, or was no longer, Rosanette's lover.

But then two voices were raised in anger.

'Idiot!'

'Swine!'

'I'm at your service!'

'And I'm at yours!'

The Medieval Knight and the Russian Postilion were quarrelling; the latter had asserted that a man in a suit of armour did not need to be brave, and the other had taken this as an insult. He wanted to fight, everybody intervened; and in the middle of the uproar the Captain tried to make himself heard:

'Gentlemen, listen to me! One word! I have plenty of experience of this sort of thing.'

Rosanette, striking a glass with her knife, finally managed to secure silence; and, turning first to the Knight, who had kept his helmet on, and then to the Postilion, who was wearing a shaggy fur bonnet, she said:

'First of all, take that saucepan off – it makes me hot just to look at it. And you over there, take off that wolf's head. Do what I tell you, dammit. Can't you see my epaulettes? I am your Marshal!'

They obeyed, and everybody applauded, laughing and shouting:

'Long live the Marshal! Long live the Marshal!'

Then she took a bottle of champagne which was standing on the stove and, lifting it high in the air, emptied it into the glasses which were held out to her. As the table was extremely wide, the guests, especially the women, leaned over towards her, standing on tiptoe or on the bars of the chairs, so for a moment they formed a pyramid of headdresses, bare shoulders, outstretched arms, and leaning bodies; and long jets of wine spurted through the air, for the Pierrot and Arnoux, in opposite corners of the room, had each opened a bottle and were splashing the company's faces. The door of the aviary had been left open, and the little birds invaded the room, fluttering in bewilderment around the chandelier, and beating their wings against the window-panes and the furniture; some of them settled on the heads of the women, so that the latter appeared to be wearing great flowers in their hair.

The orchestra had gone home. The piano was dragged from the entrance-hall into the drawing-room. Mademoiselle Vatnaz sat down at it, and, accompanied by the Choir-boy on the tambourine, she launched into a frenzied quadrille, striking the keys like a prancing horse, and swaying from side to side in time to the music. The Marshal seized Frédéric, Hussonnet turned cartwheels, the Stevedore did acrobatics like a clown, the Pierrot pretended to be an orang-outang, and the Savage Woman, her arms outstretched, imitated the rocking of a boat. Finally they all stopped, tired out; and somebody opened a window.

The daylight streamed in, together with the cool morning air. There was an exclamation of astonishment, then silence. The yellow flames flickered, cracking a drip-glass every now and then; the floor was strewn with ribbons, flowers, and pearls; sticky patches of punch and syrup stained the tables; the chair-covers were dirty, the guests' costumes crumpled and smeared with powder: the women's hair hung down over their shoulders; and their paint, running with their sweat, revealed livid faces with red, blinking eyelids.

The Marshal, looking as fresh as if she had just come out of her bath, had pink cheeks and sparkling eyes. She tossed her wig aside; and her hair fell around her like a fleece, covering the whole of her costume except the breeches. The effect was at once comic and charming.

The Sphinx, whose teeth were chattering with fever, asked for a shawl.

Rosanette ran into her bedroom to fetch one, and, when the other woman came after her, slammed the door in her face.

The Turk remarked for all to hear that Monsieur Oudry had not been seen to leave. The company were so tired that nobody took up this innuendo.

Then, waiting for their carriages, they pulled on their cloaks and coats. Seven o'clock struck. The Angel was still in the dining-room, tucking into a mixture of butter and sardines; and the Fishwife, sitting beside her, was smoking cigarettes and giving her advice about life.

At last the cabs arrived and the guests left. Hussonnet, who was the Paris correspondent of a provincial journal, had to read fifty-three newspapers before lunch; the Savage Woman had a rehearsal at her theatre, Pellerin a model, the Choir-boy three assignations. But the Angel, a prey to the first symptoms of indigestion, could not get up. The Medieval Knight carried her to the cab.

'Mind her wings!' shouted the Stevedore through the window.

On the landing Mademoiselle Vatnaz said to Rosanette:

'Good-bye, my dear! It was a lovely party!'

Then she whispered in her ear:

'Keep him!'

'Until better times,' replied Rosanette, slowly turning away.

Arnoux and Frédéric went home together, as they had come. The pottery dealer looked so gloomy that his companion thought he was ill.

'Me? Not a bit of it!'

He kept chewing his moustache and frowning. Frédéric asked him if it was his business affairs which were worrying him.

'Of course not!'

Then suddenly he said:

'You knew him, didn't you, old Oudry?'

And he added with a bitter look:

'He's rich, the old scoundrel!'

After that Arnoux talked about an important firing at his factory which was due to be finished that day. He wanted to watch it. The train left in an hour's time.

'But I really must go and give my wife a kiss.'

'His wife!' thought Frédéric.

Then he went to bed, with an unbearable pain in the back of his head; and he drank a decanter of water to quench his thirst.

Another thirst had come upon him: the thirst for women, for luxury, for everything that life in Paris implies. He felt slightly dazed, like a man disembarking from a ship; and in the hallucination of his first sleep he saw passing to and fro before him the Fishwife's shoulders, the Stevedore's back, the Polish girl's calves, and the Savage Woman's hair. Then two big dark eyes, which were not at the ball, appeared; and, light as butterflies, bright as torches, they darted here and there, quivered, flew up to the ceiling, then swooped down to his lips. Frédéric struggled to recognize these eyes, without success. But already a dream had taken hold of him; he thought he was harnessed side by side with Arnoux in the shafts of a cab, and the Marshal, sitting astride him, was tearing his belly open with her golden spurs.

II

ON the corner of the Rue Rumfort Frédéric found a small mansion, and at one and the same time he bought a brougham, a horse, some furniture, and two flower-stands from Arnoux's shop, to put on either side of the drawing-room door. Behind this room were a bedroom and a closet. The idea of lodging Deslauriers there occurred to him. But then how would he be able to receive *her*, his future mistress? The presence of a friend would be embarrassing. He had the partition knocked down to lengthen the drawing-room, and turned the closet into a smoking-room.

He bought the works of his favourite poets, travel books, atlases, and dictionaries, for he had countless plans for work. He urged the workmen to make haste, hurried round the shops, and in his impatience for possession, bought whatever he fancied without bargaining.

When the tradesmen's bills came in, Frédéric realized that he would soon have to pay out some forty thousand francs, quite apart from the legacy duties, which would come to over thirty-seven thousand; as his fortune was in land, he wrote to the lawyer at Le Havre to sell some of it so that he could pay his debts and have a certain sum of money in hand. Then, anxious to know at last that vague, glittering, indefinable thing called *society*, he sent a note to the Dambreuses asking if he might call on them. Madame replied that she looked forward to seeing him the following day.

It was her at-home day. Carriages were standing in the courtyard. Two footmen rushed out under the awning, and a third, at the top of the staircase, walked ahead of him.

He crossed a hall, a second room, and then a great drawing-room with tall windows. There was a spherical clock on the monumental mantelpiece, flanked by a pair of enormous porcelain vases from which two clusters of sconces sprouted like golden bushes. Pictures in the Ribera manner adorned the walls; the heavy tapestry door-curtains hung in majestic folds; and the armchairs, tables, consoles, and other pieces of furniture, which were all in the Empire style, had an imposing, ambassadorial air. Frédéric could not help smiling with pleasure.

Finally he reached an oval room, panelled in rosewood, filled with dainty pieces of furniture, and lit by a single window looking out on to a garden. Madame Dambreuse was by the fire, with about a dozen people grouped around her. With a few friendly words she motioned to him to sit down, showing no surprise at not having seen him for so long.

When he came in, the company were extolling the eloquence of the Abbé Cœur. Then they deplored the immorality of servants, in connexion with a theft committed by a valet; and after that, one item of gossip followed after another. Old Madame de Sommery had a cold; Mademoiselle de Turvisot was getting married; the Montcharrons were not coming back until the end of January; nor were the Bretancourts; people stayed longer in the country nowadays. The pettiness of the conversation seemed to be emphasized by the luxury of the setting; although the subject-matter was not as stupid as the manner of its delivery, which was aimless, lifeless, and inconsequential. There were men present with experience of life – a former minister, the curé of a large parish, two or three high government officials – yet they confined themselves to the most threadbare commonplaces. Some looked like tired old dowagers, others like crafty horse-dealers; and old men accompanied wives who might have been their granddaughters.

Madame Dambreuse treated them all with consummate grace. If somebody spoke of a sick person, she frowned anxiously, while she assumed a joyful expression if there was mention of balls or parties. She would soon be obliged to forgo such pleasures, for she was going to fetch a niece of her husband's, an orphan, from boarding-school. Everybody praised her self-abnegation; she was behaving like a true mother.

Frédéric looked closely at her. Her matt skin seemed to be stretched over her face; it had freshness but no bloom, like a preserved fruit. But her hair, dressed in corkscrew curls in the English style, was as fine as silk, her eyes a brilliant blue, her movements graceful. Sitting on the settee, at the far end of the room, she was stroking the red tassels of a Japanese screen, probably to show off her hands, long, rather thin hands with fingers which turned up at the ends. She was wearing a dress of grey watered silk with a high neck, like a Puritan.

Frédéric asked her if she was going to La Fortelle that year. Madame Dambreuse did not know. He could understand that perfectly well: she was bound to find Nogent boring. More people arrived. There was a continual rustling of dresses on the carpets; the ladies, perched on the edge of their chairs, gave a few little giggles, uttered two or three words, and, after five minutes, went off with their daughters. Soon it became impossible to follow the conversation, and Frédéric was just leaving when Madame Dambreuse said to him:

'Remember, Monsieur Moreau, every Wednesday.'

With this solitary sentence she made up for all the indifference she had shown.

He was pleased with himself. All the same, he breathed in a large mouthful of air in the street; and, feeling the need for a less artificial setting, he remembered that he owed a call to the Marshal.

The hall door was open. Two Havana lap-dogs ran up to him. A voice called out:

'Delphine! Delphine! Is that you, Félix?'

He stayed where he was; the two little dogs went on barking. At last Rosanette appeared, wrapped in a sort of white muslin dressing-gown trimmed with lace; her bare feet were in Turkish slippers.

'Oh! Forgive me, Monsieur. I thought you were the hairdresser. I'll be back in a moment.'

And he was left by himself in the dining-room.

The Venetian shutters were closed. Frédéric was glancing round the room, recalling the uproar of the other night, when he noticed, on the table in the middle, a man's hat, an old felt hat, battered, greasy, and filthy. Whose could it be? Insolently displaying its lining, which had come unstitched, it seemed to be saying: 'What do I care? I'm master here!'

The Marshal came in. She took the hat, opened the conservatory, threw it inside, shut the door – other doors were opening and shutting at the same time – and, after leading Frédéric through the kitchen, took him into her dressing-room.

It was obvious at a glance that this was the most lived-in part of the house, its focal point as it were. The walls, the armchairs, and a huge spring divan were covered in chintz with a bold leaf pattern; on a marble table there were two large china basins; some crystal shelves above were loaded with bottles, brushes, combs, sticks of make-up, and powder boxes; the fire was reflected in a tall cheval-glass; a cloth was draped over the edge of a bath, and the scents of almond paste and benzoin filled the air.

'I hope you don't mind the mess. I'm dining out this evening.'

Turning round, she nearly stepped on one of the little dogs. Frédéric said that he thought they were charming. She picked them both up and, lifting their black muzzles up to his face, she said:

'Come along, smile now! Kiss the gentleman.'

A man dressed in a dirty frock-coat with a fur collar came rushing in.

'Félix, my dear fellow,' she said, 'that little business of yours will be settled Sunday next, without fail.'

The man started dressing her hair. He gave her news of her friends: Madame de Rochegune, Madame de Saint-Florentin, Madame Lombard – all aristocrats, as at the Dambreuses'. Then he chatted about the theatre: they were giving a special performance at the Ambigu that evening.

'Are you going?'

'Good heavens, no! I'm staying at home.'

Delphine appeared. Rosanette scolded her for going out without permission. The other woman swore that she 'had just come back from the market'.

'Well then, bring me your book! – You'll excuse me, won't you?'

Reading the entries out in an undertone, Rosanette made remarks about every item. The total was wrong.

'Give me back four sous!'

Delphine gave them back, and, after dismissing her, Rosanette exclaimed:

'Mother of God! Those people will be the end of me!'

Frédéric was shocked by this complaint. It reminded him too much of the others he had heard, and thus established a sort of equality between the two houses which annoyed him.

Delphine, who had come back, went up to the Marshal and whispered something in her ear.

'No! I won't!'

Delphine reappeared.

'Madame, she insists.'

'Oh, what a nuisance! Chuck her out!'

At that very moment, an old lady in black pushed open the door. Frédéric heard nothing and saw nothing; Rosanette rushed into the bedroom to meet her.

When she returned, her cheeks were flushed and she sat down in one of the armchairs without speaking. A tear trickled down her cheek; then, turning to the young man, she asked gently:

'What's your Christian name?'

'Frédéric!'

'Ah! Frederico! You don't mind if I call you that?'

And she looked at him archly, almost amorously. Suddenly she gave an exclamation of joy at the sight of Mademoiselle Vatnaz.

The actress had not a minute to spare, since on the stroke of six she had to preside over her boarding-house table; and she was tired and breathless. To begin with, she took a watch-chain and a piece of paper out of her shopping-bag, then various things which she had bought.

'You know, there are some wonderful Swedish gloves for sale, in the Rue Joubert, at thirty-six sous a pair. Your cleaner wants another week. As for the lace, I told them we'd call again. Bugneaux has had his money on account. I think that's the lot. You owe me a hundred and eighty-five francs.'

Rosanette went and took ten napoleons out of a drawer. Neither of the women had any change, so Frédéric offered some.

'I'll pay you back,' said Mademoiselle Vatnaz, thrusting the fifteen francs into her bag. 'But you're a wicked man, and I don't like you any more. You didn't ask me to dance with you once, the other night! – Oh, my dear, I've found the most divine case of stuffed humming-birds in a shop on the Quai Voltaire. If I were you, I'd buy them straight away. And what do you think of this?'

She displayed a piece of old pink silk which she had bought in one of the Temple shops to make into a medieval doublet for Delmar.

'He came here today, didn't he?'

'No.'

'That's strange.'

And a minute later:

'Where are you going tonight?'

'To Alphonsine's,' said Rosanette.

This was the third version of the way in which she intended to spend the evening.

Mademoiselle Vatnaz went on:

'And what news of the Old Man of the Mountain?'

But with a rapid wink the Marshal told her to be quiet; and she accompanied Frédéric as far as the hall, to find out whether he was going to see Arnoux soon.

'Do ask him to come and see me; but not in front of his wife, of course!'

At the top of the stairs an umbrella was standing against the wall, next to a pair of overshoes.

'La Vatnaz's galoshes,' said Rosanette. 'What a size, eh? Oh, she's a big woman, my friend is.'

Then in a melodramatic tone, and rolling the *r*, she added:

'But not to be tr-r-rusted.'

Emboldened by this confidence, Frédéric tried to kiss her on the neck. She said coldly:

'Oh, go ahead. It doesn't cost anything.'

He left the house with a light step, convinced that the Marshal would soon become his mistress. This desire awoke another, and in spite of the kind of grudge he bore her, he felt an urge to see Madame Arnoux.

Besides, he had to go to her house to deliver Rosanette's message.

'But just now,' he thought, hearing six o'clock striking, 'Arnoux will probably be at home.'

He put off his call until the next day.

She was in the same position as on the first day, and was sewing a child's shirt. The little boy was playing with a wooden menagerie at her feet; a little way off, Marthe was busy writing.

He began by complimenting her on her children. She replied without any stupid maternal exaggeration.

The room had a peaceful look. Bright sunshine streamed through the window-panes, the corners of the furniture glittered, and, as Madame Arnoux was sitting by the window, a great sunbeam, falling on the curls at the nape of her neck, suffused her amber skin with liquid gold. Then he said:

'Here's a young lady who's grown a lot in the last three years!

Do you remember, Mademoiselle, the time when you slept on my knees in the carriage?'

Marthe did not remember.

'One evening, coming back from Saint-Cloud?'

Madame Arnoux gave him a look of singular sadness. Was it to forbid him any reference to the memory they shared?

Her lovely black eyes, with their brilliant sheen, moved gently under their somewhat heavy lids, and in the depths of her pupils there was an infinite kindness. He was seized once again by a feeling of immeasurable love, more powerful than ever; the sight of her dazed him, but he shook off his torpor. How could he impress her? By what means? After careful consideration, Frédéric could think of nothing better than money. He started talking about the weather, which was not as cold as at Le Havre.

'Why, have you been there?'

'Yes, on family business . . . a legacy.'

'Oh, I'm so glad,' she said, with so sincere a look of pleasure that it touched him as much as if it had been some great service.

Then she asked him what he planned to do, since a man had to have some occupation. He remembered his lie and said that he hoped to enter the service of the Council of State, with the help of Monsieur Dambreuse, the deputy.

'Perhaps you know him?'

'Only by name.'

Then, in a low voice, she asked:

'*He* took you to the ball the other evening, didn't he?'

Frédéric said nothing.

'Thank you. That is all I wanted to know.'

After that she asked him two or three discreet questions about his family and his home town. It was nice of him not to have forgotten them all the time he had been in the country.

'But . . . how could I?' he replied. 'Did you think I might?'

Madame Arnoux stood up.

'I think you are a good and loyal friend to both of us. Good-bye . . . for now.'

And she held out her hand to him, in a frank and manly gesture. Wasn't this a pledge, a promise? Frédéric felt glad to be alive; he could scarcely restrain himself from singing; he felt an urge to express himself, to perform some generous action, to give alms. He looked around to see if there was somebody he could help. No beggar happened to be passing, and his impulse of self-abnegation faded away, for he was not the man to go out of his way to look for such opportunities.

Then he remembered his friends. The first he thought of was Hussonnet, the second Pellerin. Dussardier's lowly position naturally called for consideration; as for Cisy, he looked forward to showing off his wealth a little to him. He therefore wrote to all four inviting them to a housewarming party the following Sunday, at eleven o'clock sharp, and he asked Deslauriers to bring along Sénécal.

The teacher had been dismissed from his third boarding-school for having stood out against the prize-giving ceremony, a practice which he regarded as fatal to equality. He was now working for a machine manufacturer, and he had stopped living with Deslauriers six months before.

There had been nothing painful about their parting. Recently Sénécal had been inviting men in smocks to his room; they were all patriots, all workers, all excellent fellows, but the lawyer found their company tedious. Besides, he disliked certain of his friend's ideas, however excellent they might be as munitions of war. He said nothing, out of ambition, humouring Sénécal in the hope of controlling him, for he looked forward impatiently to a great upheaval in which he confidently expected to make a niche for himself.

Sénécal's convictions were more disinterested. Every evening, when his work was over, he went home to his attic and searched in his books for a justification of his dreams. He had made notes on the *Contrat social*. He wolfed down the *Revue indépendante*. He was familiar with Mably, Morelly, Fourier, Saint-Simon, Comte, Cabet, Louis Blanc, the whole cartload of Socialist writers – those who wanted to reduce mankind to the level of the barrackroom, send it to the brothel for its amusement, and tie it to the counter or the bench; and out of this mixture he had evolved an ideal of a virtuous democracy, half farm and half factory, a sort of American Sparta in which the individual would exist only to serve the State, which would be more omnipotent, more absolute, more infallible, and more divine than any Grand Lama or Nebuchadnezzar. He had no doubt that this idea would soon be realized, and anything which he considered hostile to it he attacked with the logic of a mathematician and the faith of an inquisitor. Titles, decorations, plumes, liveries in particular, and even an excessive degree of fame shocked him; and every day his studies and his sufferings added fuel to his hatred of any sort of distinction or superiority.

'What has that fine gentleman done for me that I should toady to him? If he wanted to see me, he could come here.'

Deslauriers dragged him off.

They found their friend in his bedroom. Roller blinds, double curtains, Venetian mirror – there was nothing lacking; and Frédéric, dressed in a velvet jacket, was lolling in an easy-chair, smoking a Turkish cigarette.

Sénécal scowled, like a Puritan lured to a party. Deslauriers took everything in at a glance; then, bowing low to Frédéric, he said:

'My lord, I humbly present my respects.'

Dussardier threw his arms round his neck.

'So you're rich now! So much the better, darn it, so much the better!'

Cisy appeared with a crêpe ribbon round his hat. Now that his grandmother was dead, he enjoyed a considerable fortune, and he gave less thought to amusing himself than to distinguishing himself from other people, to being original, in short to 'having tone'. That was his expression.

It was now noon and everybody was yawning; Frédéric was waiting for somebody. At the mention of Arnoux's name, Pellerin pulled a face. He regarded him as a renegade since he had deserted the arts.

'Let's forget about him. What do you say?'

Everybody approved.

A servant in long leggings opened the door, revealing the dining-room with its lofty dado of oak decorated with gold and its two dressers loaded with crockery. The wine-bottles were warming on the stove; the blades of the new knives glittered beside the oysters; there was a delightful softness in the milky tint of the muslin glasses; and the table was practically hidden under game, fruit, and exotic delicacies. All this was lost on Sénécal.

He started by asking for some home-made bread – the crustier the better – and in this connexion spoke of the murders at Buzançais and the food crisis.[19]

None of this would have happened if agriculture were better protected, if everything were not abandoned to competition, to anarchy, to the deplorable theories of *laissez-faire* and non-inter-ference. This was how the feudalism of money, which was far worse than the old feudalism, came into being! But let them beware! In the end the people would lose patience and might well avenge their sufferings on the capitalists, either by sanguinary proscriptions or by the looting of their houses.

Frédéric had a sudden glimpse in imagination of a flood of men with bare arms invading Madame Dambreuse's great drawing-room, and breaking the mirrors with their pikes.

In view of the low level of wages, Sénécal went on, the worker was worse off than the helot, the Negro, and the pariah, especially if he had any children.

'Must he get rid of them by smothering them, as some English doctor of the Malthusian school recommends?'

And turning to Cisy, he asked:

'Are we to be reduced to following the advice of the infamous Malthus?'

Cisy, who knew nothing of the infamy, or even of the existence, of Malthus, replied that, all the same, a great deal was done for the needy, and that the upper classes . . .

'Oh, the upper classes!' sneered the Socialist. 'To begin with, there aren't any upper classes; only the heart can uplift a person. It isn't charity that we want, you see, it's equality, and a just division of goods.'

What he asked was that the worker should be able to become a capitalist, just as the private soldier could become a colonel. The old guilds, by limiting the number of apprentices, did at least prevent a surplus of workers, and the feeling of brotherhood was sustained by festivals and banners.

Hussonnet, speaking as a poet, regretted the banners of old, as did Pellerin, expressing a taste which had come to him at the Café Dagneaux while listening to the conversation of some Fourierists. He declared his conviction that Fourier was a great man.

'Oh, come now!' said Deslauriers. 'He's an old fool, who sees the effect of divine vengeance in the fall of empires! He's like old Saint-Simon and his precious church, with their hatred of the French Revolution: a lot of jokers who'd like to saddle us with Catholicism all over again.'

Monsieur de Cisy, presumably to clarify his ideas, or else to create a good impression, said gently:

'You mean to say that those two philosophers aren't of the same opinion as Voltaire?'

'Voltaire? You're welcome to him!' said Sénécal.

'What? But I thought . . .'

'Oh, no! He had no love for the people!'

Then the conversation came down to the events of the day: the Spanish marriages, the Rochefort peculations, and the reorganization of the chapter of Saint-Denis, which was going to mean an increase in taxation.[20] Yet taxation was high enough already, according to Sénécal.

'And what's it all for, anyway? To build palaces for the monkeys at the zoo, to send gaudy staff-officers parading about our squares, or to keep up a feudal etiquette among the lackeys at Court!'

'I read in *La Mode*,' said Cisy, 'that at the Tuileries ball on St Ferdinand's day everybody came in fancy dress.'

'How absolutely pitiful!' said the Socialist, shrugging his shoulders in disgust.

'And look at the Versailles Museum!' exclaimed Pellerin. 'What about that? Those idiots have cut off part of a Delacroix and lengthened a Gros! At the Louvre, they've done so much restoring, scraping, and messing about with all the pictures, that I doubt if there'll be a single one left in ten years' time. As for the mistakes in the catalogue, a German has written a whole book on the subject. Upon my word, foreigners regard us as a joke!'

'Yes, we're the laughing-stock of Europe,' said Sénécal.

'That's because Art is in the power of the Crown.'

'As long as you haven't got universal suffrage . . .'

'No, thank you!' said the artist, who, after being rejected at every Salon for twenty years, had a grudge against authority. 'I'd rather we were left in peace. I don't want anything for myself, but I think the Chambers ought to legislate in the interests of Art. A chair of aesthetics ought to be founded, with a professor who combined theory with practice, and who one day, I should hope, might succeed in educating the masses. It might be a good idea, Hussonnet, if you said something about it in your paper.'

'But do you imagine the press is free? Do you imagine we are free?' said Deslauriers passionately. 'When I think that you have to fill in anything up to twenty-eight forms just to keep a boat on the river, I feel like going off to live among the cannibals. The Government doesn't allow us any freedom at all! It controls everything

– philosophy, law, the arts, the very air we breathe; and France groans and suffers under the policeman's boot and the priest's cassock!'

The future Mirabeau went on venting his spleen freely in this fashion. Finally he took his glass, stood up, and with his hand on his hip and his eyes blazing, said:

'I drink to the total destruction of the existing order, in other words of everything known as Privilege, Monopoly, Control, Hierarchy, Authority, State' – and raising his voice – 'which I would like to break as I break this' – and he dashed the handsome wine-glass on the table, where it shattered into a thousand pieces.

Everybody applauded, especially Dussardier.

The sight of any injustice stirred him profoundly. He worried over the fate of Barbès,[21] and was the sort of man who would plunge under a carriage to help a fallen horse. His learning was confined to two works, one called *Royal Crimes* and the other *Mysteries of the Vatican*. He had listened to the lawyer with open-mouthed delight. At last, unable to keep silent any longer, he exclaimed:

'What I hold against Louis-Philippe is that he deserted the Poles!'

'One moment,' said Hussonnet. 'To begin with, Poland doesn't exist; it was an invention of Lafayette's. You can be quite sure that all the Poles you meet come from the Faubourg Saint-Marceau: the real ones were drowned with Poniatowski.'[22]

In short, 'he wasn't taken in any more'; he had 'got over all that'. It was like the sea-serpent, the revocation of the Edict of Nantes, and 'that old story about the massacre of St Bartholomew's Eve'.

Sénécal, without standing up for the Poles, took up Hussonnet's last words. People had been unfair to the Papacy, which, after all, defended the people; and he called the League 'the dawn of democracy, a great egalitarian movement against the individualism of the Protestants'.

Frédéric was somewhat startled by these views. They probably bored Cisy, for he turned the conversation to the *tableaux vivants* which were drawing big audiences to the Gymnase.

Sénécal deplored them. Spectacles of that sort, with their insolent display of luxury, corrupted the daughters of the proletariat. He therefore approved of the Bavarian students who had insulted Lola

Montez. Like Rousseau, he valued a charcoal-burner's wife more highly than a king's mistress.

'That's just sour grapes!' said Hussonnet scornfully.

And he spoke in defence of these ladies, with special reference to Rosanette. When he happened to mention her ball and Arnoux's costume, Pellerin remarked:

'They say he's pretty shaky, don't they?'

The picture-dealer had just been engaged in a lawsuit over his building-sites at Belleville, and he was at present tied up with a company dealing in porcelain-clay from Lower Brittany, together with some other fellows of his ilk.

Dussardier knew more about all this; for his employer, Monsieur Moussinot, had made inquiries about Arnoux from the banker Oscar Lefebvre, who, knowing about some of the bills he had renewed, considered him anything but sound.

Dessert was over; they moved into the drawing-room, which, like the Marshal's, was hung with yellow damask and furnished in the Louis Seize style.

Pellerin scolded Frédéric for not having chosen the neo-Grecian style instead; Sénécal struck matches on the hangings; Deslauriers said nothing. But he spoke up in the library, which he described as a little girl's library. It contained most contemporary writers. It proved impossible to discuss their work, for Hussonnet promptly began telling personal anecdotes about them, criticizing their faces, their habits, and their dress, extolling the fifteenth-rate, denigrating the first-class minds, and, of course, deploring the decadence of modern literature. Such-and-such a folk-song had more poetry in it than all the lyrics of the nineteenth century; Balzac was overrated, Byron discredited, Hugo knew nothing about the theatre, and so on, and so forth.

'Why,' said Sénécal, 'haven't you got the works of our worker-poets?'

And Monsieur de Cisy, who dabbled in literature, expressed surprise at not seeing on Frédéric's table 'some of those new "physiologies" – *The Physiology of the Smoker, of the Angler, of the Toll-keeper.*'

They eventually succeeded in irritating him to such an extent that he felt tempted to seize them by the shoulders and push them outside. 'But I'm being silly,' he reflected. And taking Dussardier aside, he asked him whether he could be of any service to him.

The good fellow was touched. But with his post as cashier he needed nothing.

Then Frédéric led Deslauriers into his room, and, taking two thousand francs from his desk, he said:

'There you are, old fellow, put that in your pocket. That settles the rest of my debts to you.'

'But . . . what about the newspaper?' said the lawyer. 'You know very well that I've spoken to Hussonnet about it.'

Frédéric replied that he was 'a little hard-up just now'. The other smiled bitterly.

After the liqueurs they drank beer; after the beer, punch; and they filled their pipes time and again. Finally, at five in the evening, they all went off; and they were walking along side by side, in silence, when Dussardier remarked that Frédéric had been a perfect host. Everybody agreed.

Hussonnet declared that the lunch had been a little too heavy. Sénécal criticized the triviality of the interior decoration. Cisy agreed with him. It was absolutely lacking in 'tone'.

'For my part,' said Pellerin, 'I think he might at least have commissioned a picture from me.'

Deslauriers said nothing, clutching the banknotes in his trouser-pocket.

Frédéric was left on his own. Thinking about his friends, he felt as if there were a great, dark gulf separating them from him. Yet he had held out his hand to them; it was they who had failed to respond to his generous gesture.

He remembered what Pellerin and Dussardier had said about Arnoux. It was all probably a slanderous fabrication. Or was it? He imagined Madame Arnoux ruined, in tears, selling her furniture. This idea tormented him all night; the next day he called to see her.

Not knowing how to set about telling her what he knew, he asked her casually whether Arnoux still had his building-sites at Belleville.

'Yes, he's still got them.'

'He's now with a company dealing in porcelain-clay from Brittany, I believe?'

'Yes, that's right.'

'His factory's doing very well, isn't it?'

'I . . . I suppose so.'

And, as he hesitated, she said:

'But what's the matter? You frighten me.'

He told her about the renewing of the bills of exchange. She bowed her head and said:

'I feared as much.'

Arnoux, as it happened, hoping to bring off a coup, had refused to sell his land, had borrowed heavily on it, and, finding no buyers, had tried to recover his losses by building a factory. Expenditure had exceeded income. That was all she knew about it; he evaded all her questions and invariably declared that 'things were going well'.

Frédéric tried to reassure her. Perhaps these were just temporary difficulties. In any case, if he heard anything, he would let her know.

'Oh, yes, please do,' she said, joining her hands with a charming look of entreaty.

So he could be useful to her. Here he was, entering into her existence, into her heart!

Arnoux came in.

'Ah, how nice of you to come and take me out to dinner!'

Frédéric was so taken aback that he said nothing.

Arnoux talked about indifferent matters, then warned his wife that he would be very late coming home, as he had an appointment with Monsieur Oudry.

'At his house?'

'Yes, of course, at his house.'

Going downstairs, he confessed that, as the Marshal was free that evening, they were going to have a little dinner together at the Moulin Rouge; and, since he always needed somebody to confide in, he allowed Frédéric to take him as far as her door.

Instead of going in, he walked up and down the pavement, eyeing the second-floor windows. Suddenly the curtains were drawn aside.

'Ah! Splendid! Old Oudry has left. Good night!'

So it was old Oudry who kept her? Frédéric did not know what to think now.

From that day onwards Arnoux was even friendlier than before; he invited him to dinner at his mistress's, and soon Frédéric was a regular visitor to both houses.

Rosanette's amused him. He went there after leaving the club or the theatre; he drank tea or played lotto; on Sunday there were charades; and Rosanette, wilder than the others, excelled in droll ideas, running around on all fours or putting on a cotton-nightcap. She wore a leather helmet to watch the passers-by from her window; she smoked long Turkish pipes and sang Tyrolean yodelling songs.

In the afternoon, to while away the time, she would cut flowers out of a piece of chintz and stick them to the window-panes, daub her two little dogs with rouge, burn incense, or tell her own fortune.

Incapable of resisting an impulse, she would fall in love with some knick-knack she had seen, lose sleep over it, rush to buy it, and then exchange it for another. She wasted dress material, lost her jewels, squandered her money, and would have sold her nightdress for a stage-box she wanted. Often she asked Frédéric the meaning of a word she had read, but did not listen to his answer, for she would chase after another idea and ply him with further questions. Bursts of gaiety were followed by childish rages; or she would sit dreaming on the floor in front of the fire, her head bowed and her hands clasped round her knees, as motionless as a torpid snake. Without paying any attention to him, she would dress in front of him, would slowly pull on her silk stockings, and then sluice her face with water, bending her body backwards like a shivering naiad; and her laughing white teeth, her sparkling eyes, her beauty, and her gaiety dazzled Frédéric and set his nerves tingling.

He nearly always found Madame Arnoux teaching her little boy to read, or standing behind Marthe's chair while she was practising scales on the piano. When she was sewing, it was a joy to him to be able to pick up her scissors now and then. All her movements had a tranquil dignity; her little hands seemed made to distribute alms or wipe away tears; and her voice, which was soft by nature, had tender intonations like the light murmurs of a breeze.

She did not wax enthusiastic about literature, but she made simple, penetrating remarks which showed a charming intelligence. She liked travelling, listening to the sound of the wind in the woods, and walking bare-headed in the rain. Frédéric listened to these confidences with delight, thinking that he could see in them the beginning of her surrender.

The company of these two women made as it were two melodies in his life: the one playful, wild, amusing; the other grave and almost religious. And the two melodies, sounding at the same time, swelled continually and gradually intermingled; for, if Madame Arnoux merely brushed him with her finger, his desire immediately conjured up the image of the other woman, since in her case his hopes were less remote; while if, in Rosanette's company, his heart happened to be stirred, he promptly remembered his great love.

This confusion was brought about by similarities between the two establishments. One of the chests which he used to see in the Boulevard Montmartre flat now adorned Rosanette's dining-room, while the other graced Madame Arnoux's drawing-room. The dinner-service was identical in both houses; in both the same velvet skull-cap was to be found lying on an easy-chair; and then a host of small gifts – screens, boxes, and fans – came and went between mistress and wife, for Arnoux, without the slightest embarrassment, often took back something he had given to one, in order to present it to the other.

The Marshal used to laugh with Frédéric at Arnoux's peculiar habits. One Sunday, after dinner, she took Frédéric behind the door and showed him a bag of cakes in his overcoat, which he had just scrounged from the table, presumably to offer as a treat to his children. Monsieur Arnoux indulged in all sorts of pranks which bordered on dishonesty. He regarded it as a duty to defraud the city dues, never paid for his seat at the theatre, always travelled first-class with a second-class ticket, and used to recount as an excellent joke how he was in the habit, at the swimming-baths, of dropping a trouser-button into the attendant's box instead of a fifty-centime piece. Yet this did not prevent the Marshal from loving him.

However, talking about him one day, she said:

'Oh, he makes me tired! I've had enough. Well, serve him right, I'll find somebody else!'

Frédéric remarked that he thought she had already found 'somebody else' and that his name was Monsieur Oudry.

'Well,' said Rosanette, 'and what of it?'

Then, with tears in her voice, she went on:

'After all, I ask him for next to nothing, and the beast won't even give me that! He just won't give it me! But when it comes to promises, that's a different kettle of fish!'

He had even promised her a quarter of his profits from those porcelain-clay pits he was always talking about; no profit appeared, and nor did the cashmere shawl which he had been dangling before her for the last six months.

Frédéric promptly thought of giving it to her as a present. Arnoux might think he was being taught a lesson and get angry.

Yet he was a kind-hearted man; even his wife said so. He was so crazy though! Instead of inviting people every day to dinner at his house, he now entertained his acquaintances at restaurants. He bought absolutely useless objects, such as gold chains, clocks, and household utensils. Madame Arnoux even showed Frédéric, in the corridor, a huge stock of kettles, foot-warmers, and samovars. Finally, one day, she confessed her uneasiness: Arnoux had made her sign a bill made out to the order of Monsieur Dambreuse.

In the meantime Frédéric kept his literary plans alive, as a sort of private point of honour. He decided to write a history of aesthetics – a result of his conversations with Pellerin – then, under the indirect influence of Deslauriers and Hussonnet, to dramatize various periods of the French Revolution and to compose a grand comedy. Often, in the midst of his work, the face of one or other of the two women passed before his eyes; he struggled against the desire to see her, but soon gave in to it; and he was more depressed when he came back from seeing Madame Arnoux.

One morning he was nursing his melancholy by the fire when Deslauriers came in. Sénécal's inflammatory talk had alarmed his employer; and once again he found himself penniless.

'What do you want me to do about it?' asked Frédéric.

'Nothing. I know you haven't any money. But surely it wouldn't be too much trouble for you to find him a job, either through Monsieur Dambreuse or Arnoux?'

The latter was bound to need engineers in his factory. Frédéric had an inspiration: Sénécal would be able to tell him of the husband's absences, carry letters, and help him to make the best of the countless opportunities which would arise. Men always rendered one another this sort of service. Moreover, he would find ways of using him without his suspecting it. Fate was offering him an ally; it was a good omen, and he must seize the chance. Assuming a casual air, he replied that it might be possible to arrange and that he would see about it.

He saw about it straight away. Arnoux was going to great pains over his factory. He was searching for the copper-red of the Chinese; but his colours evaporated in the firing process. In order to prevent flaws in his china, he mixed lime with his clay; but most of the pieces broke, the enamel of his paintings on unbaked clay came out in bubbles, and his large plates buckled. Attributing these mishaps to the faulty equipment of his factory, he wanted to order new grinding mills and new drying plant. Frédéric remembered some of these things; and he went to him with the announcement that he had found a highly skilled man for him, capable of discovering his famous red. Arnoux leapt up at the news, then, after listening to Frédéric, replied that he did not need anybody.

Frédéric extolled Sénécal's amazing knowledge, which combined engineering, chemistry, and book-keeping, for he was a first-rate mathematician.

The porcelain manufacturer agreed to see him.

The two of them quarrelled over terms. Frédéric intervened and at the end of the week succeeded in bringing about an agreement.

But as the factory was at Creil, Sénécal could not be of any assistance to him. This very simple reflection disheartened Frédéric as much as some serious misfortune. It occurred to him that the more Arnoux was separated from his wife, the better his chances with her would be. He therefore started constantly taking up the cudgels for Rosanette; he pointed out to Arnoux how badly he treated her, recounted the vague threats she had made a few days before, and even mentioned the cashmere shawl, not forgetting to add that she had accused him of meanness.

Stung by the word, and also beginning to feel a little uneasy, Arnoux took Rosanette the shawl but scolded her for having complained to Frédéric. When she said that she had reminded him of his promise a hundred times, he claimed that he had been so busy that he had forgotten about it.

The next day Frédéric called to see her. Although it was two o'clock, the Marshal was still in bed; and Delmar, sitting at a little table by her bedside, was finishing a slice of *foie gras*. She called out from a distance:

'I've got it! I've got it!'

Then, taking him by the ears, she kissed him on the forehead, thanked him again and again, spoke to him endearingly, and even asked him to sit on her bed. Her pretty, tender eyes sparkled, her moist lips smiled, her round arms emerged from her sleeveless nightdress; and now and then he felt the firm contours of her body through the batiste. In the meantime Delmar kept rolling his eyes.

'But really, my dear,' he said, 'my dear! . . .'

It was the same the following times. As soon as Frédéric came in, she stood on a cushion to kiss him more easily, called him a pet, a darling, put a flower in his buttonhole, and straightened his cravat; these attentions were always exaggerated when Delmar was there.

Were they advances? Frédéric thought so. Arnoux, in his place, would not have had any scruples about deceiving a friend, and he was entitled to take his pleasure with Arnoux's mistress, since he had always behaved correctly with his wife; for he believed that he had, or rather he wanted to make himself believe it, to justify his amazing cowardice. However, he considered his conduct with the Marshal stupid, and he decided to make a determined attack on her.

So one afternoon, as she was bending down in front of her chest of drawers, he went up to her and made a movement so eloquent and unequivocal that she straightened up, crimson in the face. He tried again straight away, whereupon she burst into tears, saying that she was very unhappy but that that was no reason for despising her.

He repeated his attempts. She adopted another line of defence, which was to laugh at him every time. He thought it clever to reply in the same way, only with exaggerated mirth. But this made him seem too gay to be sincere; and their comradeship prevented the expression of any serious emotion. Finally, one day, she said that she could not accept another woman's leavings.

'What other woman?'

'Oh, you know! Go back to Madame Arnoux!'

For Frédéric often spoke of her; Arnoux, for his part, had the same habit; Rosanette was getting tired of always hearing the praises of that woman, and this insinuation of hers was a sort of revenge.

Frédéric resented it. Moreover, he was beginning to find her intensely irritating. Sometimes, posing as a woman of experience, she spoke contemptuously of love with a cynical laugh which made him itch to slap her. A quarter of an hour later, it was the only thing in the world, and, folding her arms across her breast as if she were clasping a man in them, she would murmur: 'Oh, yes, it's wonderful! It's so wonderful!' with her eyes half closed and swooning in ecstasy. It was impossible to know what she was really like, to find out, for instance, whether she was in love with Arnoux, for she laughed at him and appeared to be jealous of him too. It was the same with Mademoiselle Vatnaz, whom she sometimes called a bitch, sometimes her best friend. Her whole person, down to the way in which she wore her chignon, contained something inexpressible, in the nature of a challenge; and he desired her, above all for the pleasure of conquering and dominating her.

What was he to do? For often she would dismiss him unceremoniously, appearing for a moment in the passage to whisper: 'I'm busy; I'll see you tonight!'; or else he would find her with a dozen people around her; and when they were alone there were so many interruptions that it was as if a wager had been laid against him. He invited her to dinner; she invariably refused; once she accepted, but did not come.

His brain conceived a Machiavellian plan.

Having heard from Dussardier about Pellerin's complaints against him, he hit on the idea of commissioning him to paint a portrait of the Marshal, a life-size portrait which would call for a good many sittings; he would not miss a single one, and the artist's habitual unpunctuality would ensure that they were often alone together. He accordingly urged Rosanette to have her portrait painted, so that she could present her likeness to her beloved Arnoux. She agreed, for she saw herself in the middle of the Grand Salon, in the place of honour, with a crowd in front of her and the newspapers talking about her, something which would immediately 'launch her'.

As for Pellerin, he seized on the proposal with avidity. This portrait would be a masterpiece, and would make a great man of him.

In his memory he went over all the portraits by old masters that he knew, and finally decided on a Titian, which would be set off with touches in the style of Veronese. This meant that he would execute his composition without any artificial shadows, in a bright light which would bring out a single flesh tone and make the accessories sparkle.

'Supposing,' he thought, 'I put her in a pink silk dress with an Oriental burnous? No — burnouses are vulgar! Then what if I dressed her in bright blue velvet against a grey background? Or I could give her a white lace collar, with a black fan and a scarlet curtain behind?'

Searching around like this, he expanded his concept every day, marvelling at it as it grew.

His heart beat fast when Rosanette, accompanied by Frédéric, arrived for the first sitting. He got her to stand on a sort of platform in the middle of the room; and, complaining all the time about the light and regretting having left his old studio, he first of all made her lean her elbows on a pedestal, and then sit down in an armchair. Alternately moving away from her and going up to her to adjust the folds of her dress with a flick of his fingers, he looked at her with his eyes half closed and briefly consulted Frédéric.

'Dammit, no!' he exclaimed. 'I'm going back to my first idea. You're going to be rigged out as a lady of Venice!'

She would wear a dress of flaming red velvet with a jewelled belt, and her broad sleeve, lined with ermine, would reveal her bare arm, which would touch the balustrade of a staircase going up behind her. On her left, a tall column would rise to the top of the canvas, where it would join a curving mass of architecture. Below, clumps of orange-trees, almost black in colour, would be dimly visible, framing a blue sky streaked with white clouds. On the carpeted balustrade there would be a silver dish containing a bunch of flowers, an amber rosary, a dagger, and a casket of old, yellowish ivory, overflowing with golden sequins; some of these sequins would have fallen on the floor and lie scattered in a series of shining drops, so as to lead the eye towards the tip of her foot – for she would be posed on the last step but one, in a natural attitude and full in the light.

He went to fetch a packing-case, which he placed on the platform to represent the step; then taking a stool to do duty as the balustrade, he laid on it, by way of accessories, his jacket, a shield, a tin of sardines, a packet of pens, and a knife; and after scattering a dozen ten-centime pieces in front of Rosanette, he made her take up her pose.

'Imagine that these things are splendid treasures, sumptuous gifts. The head a little to the right. Perfect! Don't move! That majestic attitude suits your type of beauty.'

She was wearing a tartan dress with a big muff and was trying her best not to laugh.

'For your head-dress, we'll have a string of pearls: that always looks well with red hair.'

The Marshal protested that her hair was not red.

'Nonsense! The artist's red isn't the same as the red of the common man!'

He started sketching in the main outlines, and he was so preoccupied with the great artists of the Renaissance that he began talking about them. For a whole hour he dreamt aloud of those wonderful lives, full of genius, glory, and luxury, with triumphal entries into cities and torchlight feasts among half-naked women as beautiful as goddesses.

'You were born to live in those days. A woman of your calibre would have merited a prince!'

Rosanette thought these compliments extremely charming. A day was fixed for the next sitting, and Frédéric undertook to bring along the accessories.

As the heat of the stove had dazed her slightly, they went home on foot along the Rue du Bac, stopping on the Pont Royal.

The weather was fine, sharp, and bright. The sun was sinking; some windows of houses in the Cité glittered in the distance like gold plaques, while behind, on the right, the towers of Notre-Dame stood out darkly against the blue sky, which on the horizon was bathed in soft grey mists. The wind rose; Rosanette declared that she was hungry, and they went into the Pâtisserie Anglaise.

Some young women with their children were standing eating by the marble counter, on which plates of cakes were stacked under glass cloches. Rosanette swallowed two cream tarts. The caster sugar made a moustache at the corners of her mouth. Every now and then she pulled a handkerchief out of her muff to wipe it off; and her face, under her green silk hood, looked like a rose in full bloom among its leaves.

They set off again; in the Rue de la Paix she stopped in front of a jeweller's shop to look at a bracelet; Frédéric wanted to make her a present of it.

'No,' she said. 'Keep your money.'

He was hurt at this remark.

'What's the matter with my pet? Isn't he happy?'

And when the conversation began again he proceeded, as usual, to make a declaration of love.

'You know perfectly well it's impossible.'

'Why?'

'Oh, because . . .'

They were walking side by side, with her leaning on his arm and the flounces of her dress flapping against his legs. He recalled a winter twilight when, on this same pavement, Madame Arnoux had walked like this beside him; and this memory absorbed his attention so completely that he no longer noticed Rosanette and did not think about her.

She was looking vaguely in front of her and allowing herself to be pulled along a little, like a lazy child. It was the time of day when people returned from their afternoon outing, and carriages were rolling past at a brisk pace along the dry road. Pellerin's compliments must have come back to her mind, for she gave a sigh.

'Ah, there are some lucky women in this world! There's no doubt about it: I was made for a rich man.'

He retorted brutally:

'But you've already got one!' For Monsieur Oudry was said to be a millionaire three times over.

She asked for nothing better than to get rid of him.

'What's preventing you?'

And he made some bitter jokes about that old fogey of a business-man, pointing out to her that a liaison of that sort was unworthy of her and she should break it off.

'Yes,' replied the Marshal, as if talking to herself. 'I'll probably end up by doing that.'

Frédéric was delighted by this expression of disinterestedness. She slowed down; he thought she was tired. But she insisted that she did not want a carriage, and she dismissed him at her door, blowing him a kiss.

'What a damned shame! And to think that some fools think I'm a rich man!'

He arrived home in a gloomy mood.

Hussonnet and Deslauriers were waiting for him.

The Bohemian was sitting at his table, drawing Turks' heads; and the lawyer, in muddy boots, was dozing on a divan.

'Ah, at last!' he exclaimed. 'But what a glum expression! Can you listen to what I have to say?'

His reputation as a coach was declining, for he crammed his pupils with theories which were unsuitable for their examinations. He had pleaded in court two or three times and had lost; and each fresh disappointment threw him back more violently on his old dream: a newspaper in which he could spread himself, take his revenge, vent his spleen and his ideas. Moreover, wealth and fame would come to him as a result. It was with this end in view that he had won over the Bohemian, for Hussonnet owned a periodical.

At the moment, he printed it on pink paper; he invented hoaxes, composed puzzles, tried to stir up controversies, and even – despite the unsuitability of the premises – attempted to put on concerts. A year's subscription 'entitled the subscriber to an orchestra stall in one of the principal theatres in Paris; and the management also undertook to furnish visitors from abroad with any information they might desire, artistic or otherwise.' But the printer was uttering threats, the rent was three quarters in arrears, all kinds of difficulties were arising; and Hussonnet would have allowed *L'Art* to die a natural death if it had not been for the lawyer, who exhorted and encouraged him every day. He had brought him along with him, to add weight to his argument.

'We've come about the paper,' he said.

'Oh, are you still thinking about that?' replied Frédéric absent-mindedly.

'Of course I'm still thinking about it!'

And he explained his plan once more. By means of articles on the Stock Exchange they would enter into relations with financiers, and they would thus obtain the indispensable hundred thousand francs of caution-money. But before they could turn the paper into a political journal, they would have to secure a large circulation, and to do this, they must accept the necessity for a certain outlay of money, for paper, printing, and administrative expenses, in short a sum of fifteen thousand francs.

'I haven't any money,' said Frédéric.

'We certainly haven't,' said Deslauriers, folding his arms.

Frédéric, offended by this gesture, retorted:

'Is that my fault?'

'Oh, I see! Some people have got logs in their fireplace, truffles on their table, a comfortable bed, a library, a carriage, every luxury. If somebody else has to shiver in a garret, dine for a franc, work like a black, and flounder in poverty – is that *their* fault?'

And he repeated: 'Is that *their* fault?' with a Ciceronian sarcasm which smacked of the law-court. Frédéric tried to answer, but was interrupted.

'Besides, I can see that *they* have certain aristocratic standards to keep up . . . some woman . . .'

'Well, what of it? I'm free to do as I please, aren't I?'

'Oh, yes, perfectly free!'

And after a moment's silence Deslauriers added:

'It's so easy to make promises!'

'Heavens,' said Frédéric, 'I'm not taking them back.'

The lawyer went on:

'At school we vow that we're going to form a phalanx in later life, like Balzac's *Thirteen*. Then, when we meet again, it's "Good night, old fellow, and be off with you!" Because the one who could help the other prefers to keep everything for himself.'

'What do you mean?'

'You know perfectly well. Why, you haven't even introduced us to the Dambreuses!'

Frédéric looked at him; with his shabby frock-coat, his dirty spectacles, and his pale face, the lawyer cut such a poor figure that he could not prevent a contemptuous smile from touching his lips. Deslauriers saw it and flushed.

He had already picked up his hat to go. Hussonnet was anxiously trying to calm him down with imploring glances; and, as Frédéric turned his back on him, he said:

'Come, my boy! Be my Maecenas! Give your patronage to the arts!'

With a sudden gesture of resignation, Frédéric took a sheet of paper, scrawled a few lines on it, and held it out to him. The Bohemian's face lit up. Then, passing the letter to Deslauriers, he said:

'Make your apologies, my lord.'

Their friend had written to his lawyer asking him to send him, as quickly as possible, fifteen thousand francs.

'Ah, that's the Frédéric I used to know,' said Deslauriers.

'Upon my word,' the Bohemian added, 'you're a splendid fellow. You'll be counted among the benefactors of society.'

The lawyer went on:

'You won't lose by it. It's an excellent investment.'

'I should think so!' exclaimed Hussonnet. 'I'd stake my head on it.'

And he said so many silly things and promised so many miracles (which he may have believed in) that Frédéric did not know whether he was laughing at the others or at himself.

That evening he received a letter from his mother.

She was surprised that he had not yet been appointed a cabinet minister, and teased him a little about this. Then she spoke about her health, and informed him that Monsieur Roque had taken to calling on her again. 'Now that he is a widower, I see no objection to receiving him. Louise has greatly improved.' And as a postscript she wrote: 'You tell me nothing about your fine acquaintance, Monsieur Dambreuse. In your place, I would make use of him.'

Why not? He had abandoned his intellectual ambitions, and he now realized that his fortune was inadequate; for, once he had paid his debts and handed over the agreed sum to his friends, his income would be diminished by four thousand francs at the very least. Besides, he felt an urge to escape from the life he was leading, and to attach himself to something. So the next day, dining at Madame Arnoux's, he said that his mother was pestering him to enter some profession.

'But I was under the impression,' she said, 'that Monsieur Dambreuse was going to get you into the Council of State? That would suit you splendidly.'

So that was her wish. He obeyed.

As on his first visit, the banker was sitting at his desk, and he motioned to Frédéric to wait for a few minutes, for a gentleman with his back to the door was discussing some important matters with him. It was a question of coal and a merger to be carried out between various companies.

Portraits of General Foy and Louis-Philippe hung on either side of the mirror; filing cabinets standing against the panelled walls rose to the ceiling; and there were half a dozen straw-bottomed chairs. Monsieur Dambreuse had no need of a more luxurious office for his business than this room, which resembled those gloomy kitchens in which great banquets are prepared. Frédéric particularly noticed two huge safes in the corners. He wondered how many millions they might contain. The banker opened one, and the iron door swung back, revealing nothing inside but some blue paper notebooks.

At last the visitor passed in front of Frédéric. It was old Oudry. The two men blushed and bowed to one another, which seemed to surprise Monsieur Dambreuse. For the rest, he was extremely pleasant. Nothing would be easier than to recommend his young friend to the Keeper of the Seals. They would be only too happy to take him on; and he concluded his courtesies by inviting him to a party he was giving in a few days' time.

Frédéric was getting into his brougham to go to this party when a note arrived from the Marshal. In the light of the carriage-lamps he read:

My dear, I have followed your advice. I have just got rid of my encumbrance. As from tomorrow night – freedom! What do you think of that for courage?

Nothing else. But this was an explicit invitation to him to fill the vacancy. He gave an exclamation, put the note in his pocket, and set off.

Two mounted policemen were on duty in the street. A string of lights was burning over the two gates; and servants were shouting in the courtyard to get the carriages to move up to the awning over the steps. Inside the entrance-hall, the noise was suddenly cut off.

Some tall trees filled the staircase well; the porcelain globes of the lamps shed a light which rippled over the walls like white watered silk. Frédéric went briskly up the stairs. An usher called out his name: Monsieur Dambreuse held out his hand to him; almost immediately Madame Dambreuse appeared.

She was in a mauve dress trimmed with lace; there were more ringlets than usual in her hair; and she was not wearing a single jewel.

She complained of the infrequency of his visits and added one or two nondescript remarks. The guests were arriving; by way of greeting, they twisted their bodies to one side, or bent double, or simply nodded their heads. Finally a married couple and a whole family went by, and everybody dispersed into the drawing-room, which was already crowded.

Under the chandelier in the middle of the room there was a huge tuffet supporting a flower-stand whose blossoms, nodding like plumes, hung down over the heads of the women sitting round it. Other women were occupying the easy-chairs which formed two straight lines broken at regular intervals by the long window-curtains of orange-red velvet and the high doorways with their gilded lintels.

The crowd of men standing around with their hats in their hands appeared from a distance as a single mass of black, relieved here and there by the red dots of the ribbons in their buttonholes, and made more sombre by the monotonous whiteness of their cravats. Except for some insignificant young men just beginning to grow beards, they all looked bored; a few dandies with peevish expressions were rocking on their heels. There were a great many grey heads and wigs; here and there a bald pate glistened; and the faces, which were either flushed or very pale, revealed in their degeneration the trace of immense weariness, for the men there were mostly in politics or business. Monsieur Dambreuse had also invited several men of learning, some magistrates, and two or three famous doctors; and with humble gestures he kept protesting at the compliments on his party and the allusions to his wealth which were made to him.

Everywhere footmen loaded with gold braid were moving about. The great candelabra, like fiery bouquets, spread their light over the hangings and were reflected in the mirrors; and at the far end of the dining-room, the walls of which were lined with a jasmine-covered trellis, the buffet looked like the high altar of a cathedral or a jeweller's window-display, there were so many dishes, dish-covers, knives, forks, and spoons, in silver and silver-gilt, in the midst of cut-glass flashing its iridescent light across the food. The other three drawing-rooms were overflowing with works of art: landscapes by old masters on the walls, ivory and porcelain on the tables, and Chinese curios on the consoles: lacquer screens stood in front of the windows, bouquets of camellias filled the fireplaces; and the soft strains of music could be heard in the distance, like the hum of bees.

There were not many quadrilles, and the dancers, judging by the listless way in which they dragged their feet, looked as if they were performing a duty. Frédéric heard snatches of conversation such as these:

'Were you at the last charity ball at the Hôtel Lambert, Mademoiselle?'

'No, Monsieur.'

'It's going to be terribly hot soon.'

'Yes, absolutely stifling.'

'Whom is this polka by?'

'I really don't know, Madame.'

Behind him, three old men, standing in a window-recess, were whispering obscene remarks; others were talking about railways and free trade; a sportsman was telling a hunting story; a Legitimist was arguing with an Orleanist.

Wandering from group to group, he came to the card-room, where, surrounded by grave-looking men, he recognized Martinon, who was now attached to the Public Prosecutor's office in Paris.

His fat, waxen face fitted snugly into the frame of his beard, which, with its evenly trimmed black hairs, was a positive marvel. Striking a careful balance between the elegance which his age called for and the dignity which his profession demanded, he would hook his thumb into his arm-pit in the style of the dandy, and then thrust his arm into his waistcoat after the fashion of the doctrinaire. Although he wore shiny patent-leather boots, he had had his hair shaved at the temples to give himself a thinker's forehead.

After a few chilly words to Frédéric, he went back to his confabulation. A landowner was saying:

'It's a class which dreams of a social revolution.'

'They're asking for the right to organize labour,' said another. 'Have you ever heard the like?'

'What can you expect,' said the third, 'when you see Monsieur de Genoude joining forces with the *Siècle*?'[23]

'And Conservatives calling themselves Progressives! Where do they want to take us? To a republic? As if it were possible in France!'

One and all declared that a republic was impossible in France.

'All the same,' a gentleman observed in a loud voice, 'people are paying far too much attention to the Revolution. They're publishing dozens of histories and books about it . . .'

'Not to mention the fact,' said Martinon, 'that there must be more serious subjects for study.'

A law official launched an attack on the scandals of the theatre.

'Take this new play, *La Reine Margot*, for instance. It really goes beyond all bounds! Who asked the author to talk about the Valois? That sort of thing shows the monarchy in an unfavourable light. It's the same with the Press. You can say what you like, it's my opinion that the September laws are far too mild. If I had my way, I'd have courts-martial set up to gag those journalists. Court-martial them for the slightest sign of impudence, and they'd soon shut up!'

'Oh, have a care, Monsieur, have a care!' said a professor. 'Don't attack our precious gains of 1830! Let us respect our liberties!'

A better solution would be to decentralize, to spread the surplus population of the towns over the countryside.

'But the towns are rotten to the core!' exclaimed a Catholic. 'Let us help to strengthen religion!'

Martinon was quick to say:

'Religion certainly is a restraining force.'

The whole trouble lay in the modern desire to rise above one's station, to enjoy luxury.

'All the same,' protested an industrialist, 'luxury fosters trade. So that I thoroughly approve of the Duc de Nemours insisting on knee-breeches at his parties.'

'Monsieur Thiers went in trousers. You know what he said?'

'Yes – a delightful joke. But he's turning into something of a demagogue, and his speech on the division of powers had quite a lot to do with the insurrection of the 12th of May.'[24]

'Oh, nonsense!'

'Come, now!'

The group was forced to divide to make way for a servant carrying a tray, who was trying to get into the card-room.

Under the green shades of the candelabra, rows of cards and gold coins covered the tables. Frédéric stopped at one of them, lost the fifteen napoleons which he had in his pocket, turned on his heel, and found himself in the doorway of the boudoir where Madame Dambreuse now happened to be.

This room was full of women sitting next to one another on backless seats. Their long skirts, puffed out around them, looked like waves from which their waists projected, and their low-cut bodices revealed their breasts. Nearly all of them were holding a bunch of violets. The dull colour of their gloves heightened the natural whiteness of their arms; fringes and flowers hung down over their shoulders, and sometimes, when one of them shivered, it seemed as if her gown was going to fall. But the respectability of their faces compensated for the daring of their dresses; several of them indeed wore expressions of almost animal calm, and this gathering of half-naked women suggested a scene in a harem; a cruder comparison came into the young man's mind. Every type of beauty was, in fact, to be found there – English girls with keepsake-book profiles; an Italian whose dark eyes blazed like Vesuvius; three sisters from Normandy, all in blue, and as fresh as apple-trees in April; and a tall redhead wearing an amethyst necklace – and the white sparkle of the diamonds trembling on sprays in their hair, the glow of the jewels displayed on their breasts, and the soft gleam of the pearls framing their faces mingled with the glitter of their gold rings, with their lace, powder, and feathers, with the vermilion of their little mouths and the mother-of-pearl of their teeth. The domed ceiling gave the boudoir the shape of a basket; and a scented breeze was wafted about by the fluttering fans.

Frédéric, standing behind the women with his monocle in his eye, did not consider all the shoulders faultless; he thought of the Marshal, and this banished his temptations, or else consoled him for them.

However, he looked at Madame Dambreuse and found her delightful, for all that her mouth was a little too long and her nostrils too wide. But her charm was of a distinctive nature. Her ringlets had a sort of passionate languour about them, while her agate forehead denoted a masterful temperament and looked as if it harboured a host of ideas.

She had placed her husband's niece, a rather ugly young thing, beside her. Now and then she got up to greet the women who came in; and the murmur of feminine voices, growing steadily louder, was like the twittering of birds.

They were talking about the Tunisian ambassadors and their costumes. One lady had attended the latest reception at the Academy; another mentioned Molière's *Don Juan*, which had recently been put on at the Français. Darting a glance at her niece, Madame Dambreuse put a finger to her lips, but she could not conceal a smile which gave the lie to this admonition.

Suddenly Martinon appeared in the doorway opposite. She rose. He offered her his arm. To watch him pursuing his courtesies, Frédéric threaded his way between the card-tables and joined them in the big drawing-room; Madame Dambreuse promptly left her cavalier and started a friendly conversation.

She understood that he did not play cards or dance.

'Young people are so sad!' she said.

Then, embracing the whole ball in a single glance, she added:

'Not that there's much pleasure in all this – for some people at any rate.'

She stopped in front of the row of armchairs, distributing a kindly remark here and there, while bespectacled old men came up to pay court to her. She introduced Frédéric to some of them. Monsieur Dambreuse touched him gently on the elbow and led him out on to the terrace.

He had seen the Minister. It was not an easy matter. Before becoming a Council of State official, a candidate had to sit for an examination; Frédéric, filled with inexplicable self-confidence, replied that he knew the subjects required.

The financier was not surprised, seeing how highly Monsieur Roque had spoken of him.

This name conjured up little Louise, his home, and his room for Frédéric; and he recalled similar nights when he had sat at his window, listening to the waggoners going by. This recollection of his melancholy brought Madame Arnoux to his mind; and he said nothing as he walked up and down the terrace. The windows formed tall patches of red in the darkness; the sound of the ball grew fainter; the carriages were beginning to leave.

'But why,' asked Monsieur Dambreuse, 'are you so set on the Council of State?'

And, speaking as a man of the world, he declared that public office led nowhere – he knew something about that – and that business was more profitable. Frédéric pointed out that business was hard to master.

'Nonsense! I could teach you all about it in no time.'

Did he plan to offer Frédéric a place in his enterprises?

The young man suddenly saw, as in a flash, a huge fortune coming to him.

'Let's go in,' said the banker. 'You'll have supper with us, I hope?'

It was three o'clock, and the guests were leaving. A table had been laid in the dining-room for the friends of the family.

Monsieur Dambreuse caught sight of Martinon, and, going over to his wife, he asked her in an undertone:

'Was it you who invited him?'

She answered curtly:

'Yes, of course.'

The niece had disappeared. There was a lot of drinking and loud laughter, and some broad jokes which shocked nobody, since they were all experiencing that sense of relief which follows a fairly long period of restraint. Martinon alone remained serious, and thought it good form to refuse champagne; but otherwise he was extremely ingratiating and polite, for when Monsieur Dambreuse, who was narrow-chested, complained of breathlessness, he inquired several times after his health, and then turned his bluish eyes in the direction of Madame Dambreuse.

She asked Frédéric to say which of the girls at the party had attracted him. He had not noticed any one in particular, and in any case he preferred women of thirty.

'There may be something in that,' she replied.

Later, when cloaks and overcoats were being put on, Monsieur Dambreuse said to him:

'Come and see me one morning, and we'll have a chat.'

At the foot of the stairs, Martinon lit a cigar; and as he pulled on it he displayed such a stupid profile that his companion could not help blurting out:

'Heavens, what a great lump of a head you've got!'

'It's turned a few in its time,' replied the young magistrate, with a mixture of conviction and annoyance.

As he was going to bed, Frédéric went over the party in his mind. To begin with, his appearance – he had studied himself in the mirrors several times – had left nothing to be desired, from the cut of his dress-coat down to the laces of his shoes; he had talked to important men and seen wealthy women from close to; Monsieur Dambreuse had been very friendly and Madame Dambreuse almost inviting. One by one he weighed her slightest words, her glances, a thousand indefinable yet significant details. It would be splendid to have a mistress like that. And after all, why not? He was as good as anybody else. Perhaps she was not so very inaccessible? Then he remembered Martinon; and he fell asleep with a pitying smile for the poor fellow.

The thought of the Marshal awoke him; the phrase in her note — 'as from tomorrow night' — was clearly an invitation for that very day. He waited until nine o'clock, and then hurried round to see her.

Somebody going up the stairs in front of him shut the door. He rang the bell; Delphine opened the door and stated that Madame was out.

Frédéric begged and insisted. He had something very important to tell her, just a few words. Finally the argument of the five-franc piece had its effect, and the maid left him alone in the hall.

Rosanette appeared. She was in her nightdress, with her hair down; she shook her head from a distance, made a sweeping gesture with both arms, to indicate that she could not see him.

Frédéric went slowly down the staircase. This last caprice of hers outdid all the rest. He could not understand it.

Outside the concierge's lodge Mademoiselle Vatnaz stopped him.

'Did she agree to see you?'

'No.'

'You were shown the door?'

'How do you know?'

'It's obvious! But come along; let's go! I'm choking with anger.'

She took him into the street. She was panting. He could feel her thin arm trembling on his. Suddenly she exploded.

'Oh, the swine!'

'What do you mean?'

'But it's him! Delmar!'

This revelation cut Frédéric to the quick, and he asked:

'Are you sure?'

'I tell you I followed him!' exclaimed Mademoiselle Vatnaz. 'I saw him go in! Do you understand now? But I got what was coming to me, because it was I who was fool enough to introduce him to her. Oh, if you only knew! I adopted him, I fed him, I dressed him.

And when I think of all the newspapers I've pestered to give him publicity! Why, I loved him like a mother!'

Then she went on with a laugh:

'But Monsieur had to have a bit of luxury in his life – as an investment, you understand! As for her – when I think that I knew her when she was making underclothes! If it hadn't been for me, she'd have been in the gutter a score of times. But I'll shove her into it yet, you see if I don't! I want her to peg out in the workhouse! And everybody'll know the truth!'

And like a torrent of dishwater sweeping refuse along with it, her anger drenched Frédéric with all her rival's shameful secrets.

'She's slept with Jumillac and Flacourt and little Allard and Bertinaux and Saint-Valéry – the pock-marked one. No, the other one – they're brothers, you know. But it doesn't matter. And when she was in a mess, I settled everything. What did I get out of it? She's so stingy. And then, you must admit that it was a kindness on my part, associating with her, because after all we don't belong to the same class. Am I a whore? Do I sell my body? Quite apart from the fact that she's as stupid as they come. Why, she even writes category with a *k*. When you come to think of it, they go well together; they're birds of a feather, for all that he calls himself an artist and thinks he's a genius. But dammit all, if he had any brains at all, he wouldn't have played a dirty trick like that. You don't leave a woman of intelligence for a trollop! But I don't care really. He's getting ugly. I loathe him. If I met him now, you know what I'd do? I'd spit in his face!'

She spat.

'Yes, that's what I think of him now. And what about Arnoux? Isn't it disgusting? He's forgiven her so many times. You can't imagine the sacrifices he's made. She ought to kiss his feet. He's so generous, so kind!'

Frédéric enjoyed hearing Delmer being attacked. He had resigned himself to having Arnoux as a rival. Rosanette's treachery struck him as abnormal and unfair; and stirred by the old maid's indignation, he began to feel something akin to affection for him. All of a sudden he found himself outside Arnoux's door; without his noticing, Mademoiselle Vatnaz had led him down the Faubourg Poissonnière.

'Here we are,' she said. 'I can't go up myself. But there's no reason why you shouldn't.'

'But what for?'

'Why, to tell him everything, of course!'

As if awakening with a start, Frédéric understood the infamous action into which he was being impelled.

'Well?' she said.

He looked up at the second-floor windows. Madame Arnoux's lamp was burning. It was perfectly true that there was nothing to stop him going up.

'I'll wait for you here. Go on!'

This order damped what sympathy he still felt, and he said:

'I'll be up there quite a time. You'd better go home. I'll come and see you tomorrow.'

'No, no!' said Mademoiselle Vatnaz, stamping her foot. 'Bring him down! Take him along there! Help him to catch them in the act!'

'But Delmar will have gone.'

She hung her head.

'Yes, perhaps you're right.'

And she stood silently in the middle of the street, with carriages passing on either side of her; then, fixing her wild-cat's eyes on him, she said:

'I can count on you, can't I? There's a sacred bond between us now. Go ahead. I'll see you tomorrow.'

Going along the corridor, Frédéric could hear two voices arguing. Madame Arnoux was saying:

'Don't lie to me! I tell you, don't lie to me!'

He went in. They fell silent.

Arnoux was walking up and down, and his wife was sitting on the little chair by the fire. She was extremely pale and her eyes were fixed in a stare. Frédéric made as if to leave. Arnoux seized him by the hand, delighted with the help which had come to him.

'But I'm afraid . . .' said Frédéric.

'Don't go away!' Arnoux whispered in his ear.

His wife went on:

'You must forgive us, Monsieur Moreau. This is one of those things you sometimes come across in a married couple.'

'That's because they've been put there,' said Arnoux gaily. 'Women have always got something against you. Take my wife, for instance. She isn't a bad sort – on the contrary. But she's been amusing herself for the last hour by pestering me with a lot of silly stories.'

'They're true!' retorted Madame Arnoux, losing patience. 'Because after all, you did buy it.'

'I?'

'Yes, you. At the Persian shop.'

'The cashmere shawl!' thought Frédéric.

He felt guilty and afraid.

She added straight away:

'It was last month, on a Saturday, the fourteenth.'

'Oh! Well, that particular day I was at Creil. You see!'

'Not a bit of it. We dined with the Bertins on the fourteenth.'

'The fourteenth?' said Arnoux, raising his eyes as if searching for a date.

'And the assistant who served you had fair hair.'

'As if I could remember a shop-assistant.'

'All the same, he wrote out the address at your dictation: 18, Rue de Laval.'

'How do you know?' said Arnoux in amazement.

'Oh, it's very simple. I went there to have my shawl mended, and the head of the department told me that they had just sent one like it to Madame Arnoux's house.'

'But it isn't my fault, is it, if there's another Madame Arnoux in the same street?'

'No, but not Jacques Arnoux,' she replied.

Then he started to digress, protesting his innocence. It was a mistake, a coincidence, one of those inexplicable things that sometimes happen. People ought not to be condemned on mere suspicion, on vague evidence; and he cited the example of the unfortunate Lesurques.[25]

'In short, I tell you that you're wrong. Do you want me to give you my word of honour?'

'No, don't bother.'

'Why not?'

She looked him straight in the eyes, without saying anything; then she stretched out her hand, took the silver casket which was on the mantelpiece, and held out an open bill to him.

Arnoux flushed to his ears and his distorted features puffed out.

'Well?'

'But . . .' he answered slowly, 'what does that prove?'

'Ah!' she said, with a peculiar intonation in which there was both pain and irony. 'Ah!'

Arnoux held the bill in his hands, turning it over and over and not taking his eyes off it, as if he expected to find the solution of some great problem in it.

'Oh, yes, yes, I remember,' he said at last. 'It was an errand for somebody else. You must know about it, don't you, Frédéric?'

Frédéric said nothing.

'It was . . . it was old Oudry who asked me to buy it.'

'And for whom?'

'For his mistress.'

'For yours!' exclaimed Madame Arnoux, jumping to her feet.

'I swear to you . . .'

'Don't start that again! I know all about it!'

'Oh, do you? So I'm spied on, am I?'

She retorted coldly:

'Does that wound your sense of delicacy?'

'Once people lose their tempers,' said Arnoux, looking for his hat, 'and it becomes impossible to discuss matters unemotionally . . .'

Then, with a deep sigh, he said:

'Never get married, my good friend. Take my advice.'

And he went off to get some fresh air.

After that there was a profound silence; and everything in the apartment seemed more motionless than before. There was a white circle of light on the ceiling above the oil-lamp, while in the corners of the room the shadows gathered like so many thicknesses of black gauze; the ticking of the clock could be heard together with the crackling of the fire.

Madame Arnoux had just sat down again in the armchair on the other side of the fireplace; she bit her lips and shivered; her hands went up to her face, and a sob escaped from her; she was crying.

He sat down on the little chair; and in a soothing voice, as if he were talking to a sick person, he said:

'You know that I don't share . . .'

She made no reply. Instead, speaking her thoughts aloud, she murmured:

'I leave him free enough! He had no need to lie!'

'Certainly not,' said Frédéric.

It was probably the result of his way of life, he had not thought about it, and perhaps in more important matters . . .

'What do you mean by more important matters?'

'Oh, nothing.'

Frédéric bowed his head, with an obedient smile. All the same, Arnoux possessed certain qualities: he loved his children.

'Oh, he does all he can to spoil them!'

That was due to his easy-going nature; because after all, he was a good fellow.

She exclaimed:

'But what do you mean by "a good fellow"?'

He went on defending Arnoux like that, with the vaguest excuses he could find, and, while he pitied her, he rejoiced and exulted in his heart of hearts. Out of revenge or a longing for affection, she would seek refuge with him. His hopes, enormously increased, gave added strength to his passion.

Never before had she appeared so fascinating to him, so profoundly beautiful. Now and then a deep breath lifted her breasts; her staring eyes seemed dilated by an inner vision, and her mouth remained half open, as if in order to exhale her soul. Occasionally she pressed her handkerchief hard against her lips; he would have liked to be that little piece of batiste, all soaked in tears. In spite of himself, he glanced at the bed in the depths of the alcove, imagining her head on the pillow; and he pictured the scene so clearly that he could scarcely refrain from clasping her in his arms. She closed her eyes, soothed, inert. Then he drew nearer, and, bending over her, gazed greedily into her face. The sound of boots echoed along the hall; it was Arnoux. They heard him shut the door of his room. Frédéric motioned to Madame Arnoux to ask if he should go to see him.

She answered 'yes' in the same way; and this mute exchange of thoughts was like an acquiescence, a first step towards adultery.

Arnoux was unbuttoning his frock-coat to go to bed.

'Well, how is she?'

'Oh, a lot better,' said Frédéric. 'She'll get over it.'

But Arnoux was worried.

'You don't know her. She gets into such a state these days . . . That fool of an assistant! That's what comes of being generous! If only I hadn't given Rosanette that damned shawl!'

'Oh, don't regret that. She's tremendously grateful to you.'

'You think so?'

Frédéric was certain. The proof of it was that she had just dismissed old Oudry.

'Oh, the poor darling!'

Arnoux was so overcome by emotion that he wanted to hurry round to see her.

'It isn't worth it. I've just been there. She's ill.'

'All the more reason why I should go.'

He put on his frock-coat again and picked up his candlestick. Frédéric cursed himself for his stupidity, and pointed out to him that in all decency he ought to stay with his wife that evening. He could not desert her: that would be too bad of him.

'Frankly, you'd be wrong to go now. There's no hurry. You can go tomorrow. Come now, stay here for my sake.'

Arnoux put down his candlestick, and, embracing Frédéric, said: 'What a good fellow you are!'

III

A WRETCHED existence now began for Frédéric. He was the parasite of the house.

If anybody in the family was ill, he would call three times a day for news, go to see the piano tuner, and devise a thousand little services. With every sign of delight he endured the sulks of Mademoiselle Marthe and the caresses of little Eugène, who invariably passed his dirty hands over his face. He was present at dinners during which Monsieur and Madame sat opposite each other without exchanging a single word; or else Arnoux would infuriate his wife with his jocular remarks. After dinner he would play with his son in the drawing-room, hiding behind the furniture or crawling about on all fours with the boy on his back, like Henri IV. Finally he would go out; and she would promptly start on the eternal subject of complaint: Arnoux.

It was not his misconduct which annoyed her. But she seemed to be wounded in her pride, and she made no secret of her repugnance for this man who had no delicacy, dignity or honour.

'Or rather he's mad,' she would say.

Frédéric artfully persuaded her to confide in him. Soon he knew the whole story of her life.

Her parents were small shopkeepers at Chartres. One day, Arnoux had been sketching by the river – he fancied himself as an artist in those days – when he had caught sight of her coming out of church and had asked for her hand in marriage. On account of his wealth there had been no objection. Besides, he had been madly in love with her. She added:

'Heavens, he still loves me, after his fashion.'

They had spent the first months of their married life travelling in Italy.

In spite of his enthusiasm for the scenery and the masterpieces of Italian art, Arnoux had done nothing but complain about the wine, and he had got up picnics with English tourists to while away the time. A few pictures which he had bought and sold at a profit had encouraged him to become an art-dealer. Then he had set his heart on a china factory. Other speculations were tempting him now; and, as he grew increasingly vulgar, he was falling into coarse, extravagant habits. It was not so much his vices that she held against him as his whole way of life. There was no likelihood of any improvement, and her unhappiness was irreparable.

Frédéric declared that his life too was a failure.

But he was a young man. Why should he despair? And she gave him some good advice: 'Work! Get married!' He replied with a bitter smile; for instead of giving the real reason of his despondency he invented another, nobler motive, posing as an ill-starred Antony[26] – an attitude which was not entirely at variance with his ideas.

For some men, the stronger their desire, the more difficult it is for them to act. They are hampered by mistrust of themselves, daunted by the fear of causing offence; besides, deep feelings of affection are like respectable women; they are afraid of being found out and go through life with downcast eyes.

Although he now knew Madame Arnoux better – or perhaps because of that – he was even more cowardly than before. Every morning he swore that he was going to be bold. An invincible sense of decency restrained him; and he could not find any example to follow, since she was different from other women. His dreams had raised her to a position outside the human condition. Beside her, he felt less important on earth than the scraps of silk which fell from her scissors.

Then he would think of absurd, monstrous things such as assaults at night, with drugs and skeleton keys, for anything seemed easier than braving her scorn.

Besides, the children, the two maids, and the arrangement of the rooms raised insuperable difficulties. He therefore resolved to make her his alone and to go far away with her to live in some remote region; he even wondered what lake would be blue enough, what beach pleasant enough, and whether it should be Spain, Switzerland, or the East. Deliberately choosing the days on which she seemed most irritated, he would tell her that she must make an end of it all and find some solution, and that he could think of none except a separation. However, for the children's sake, she would never take such an extreme step. This virtuous resolution increased his respect for her.

His afternoons were spent in recalling the previous day's visit and looking forward to the one he was going to pay that evening. When he was not dining with them he would station himself about nine o'clock at the corner of the street; and as soon as Arnoux had closed the outer door, Frédéric would hurry up to the second floor and innocently ask the maid:

'Is Monsieur at home?'

Then he would pretend to be surprised at not finding him in.

Arnoux often came home unexpectedly. Then he would have to accompany him to a little café in the Rue Sainte-Anne which was now a haunt of Regimbart's.

The Citizen would begin by airing some new grievance against the monarchy. Then they would chat away, exchanging friendly insults; for the manufacturer considered Regimbart to be a great thinker, and, annoyed at seeing such a waste of talent, he would tease him about his laziness. For his part, the Citizen thought Arnoux full of feeling and imagination, but far too immoral; he therefore treated him without the slightest indulgence and even refused to dine at his house, declaring that 'formality annoyed him'.

Sometimes, as they were taking leave of one another, Arnoux would suddenly feel hungry. He 'simply had to have' an omelette or some baked apples and, as the food was never to be found on the premises, he sent out for it. They waited. Regimbart did not go off and ended up by grumpily agreeing to have something.

He was a gloomy fellow all the same, for he would sit for hours in front of the same half-empty glass. Because Providence would not arrange things to suit his ideas, he was turning into a hypochondriac, would not even read the papers any more, and roared with anger at the mere mention of England. Once, when a waiter served him badly, he exclaimed:

'Don't we get enough insults from abroad?'

Apart from outbursts like that, he remained silent, thinking out 'an infallible plan to send the whole works sky-high'.

While he was lost in his thoughts, Arnoux, in a monotonous voice and with a slightly drunken look in his eyes, would reel off incredible stories in which he was always the cool-headed hero; and Frédéric – probably because of some hidden resemblance between them – felt a certain attraction towards him. He blamed himself for this weakness, considering that on the contrary he ought to hate the man.

Arnoux complained to him about his wife's moods, her stubbornness, her unfair prejudices. She did not use to be like that.

'If I were in your place,' said Frédéric, 'I'd make her an allowance and live on my own.'

Arnoux made no reply, and a moment later started singing her praises. She was kind, devoted, intelligent, virtuous; and going on to her physical qualities, he was prodigal in his revelations, like those careless folk who display their valuables in inns.

A catastrophe upset his balance.

He had gone into a porcelain clay company as a member of the board of trustees. But, believing everything he was told, he had signed some inaccurate reports and had approved, without an audit, the annual balance-sheets which had been fraudulently drawn up by the manager. The company had collapsed, and Arnoux, who was legally liable, had just been condemned, with the other trustees, to pay damages amounting in his case to some thirty thousand francs – a loss aggravated by the grounds upon which the judgement had been delivered.

Frédéric read this in a newspaper and hurried over to the Rue de Paradis.

He was shown into Madame's room. It was breakfast time. A little table by the fire was covered with bowls of coffee. Slippers were lying about on the carpet, clothes on the armchairs. Arnoux, in underpants and a knitted waistcoat, was red-eyed and tousle-haired; little Eugène, on account of his mumps, was crying as he nibbled his bread and butter; his sister was eating quietly; Madame Arnoux, a little paler than usual, was waiting on all three of them.

'Well,' said Arnoux, giving a deep sigh, 'I see you've heard the news.'

And when Frédéric made a gesture of sympathy, he went on:

'There you are! I've been a victim of my trust in others!'

Then he fell silent; and he was so depressed that he pushed his breakfast away. Madame Arnoux raised her eyes and shrugged her shoulders. He passed his hands over his forehead.

'After all, it isn't my fault. I've got nothing on my conscience. It's just a piece of bad luck. I'll get over it. It can't be helped.'

And he bit into a roll, in obedience to his wife's entreaties.

That evening he wanted to dine alone with her in a private room at the Maison d'Or. Madame Arnoux did not understand this tender impulse and even took offence at being treated like a woman of easy virtue, when in fact, coming from Arnoux, such treatment was a proof of affection. Then, as he was bored, he went off to the Marshal's house in search of amusement.

Until now, people had forgiven him a great many things, on account of his good-natured character. His lawsuit classed him as a person with a shady reputation. People shunned his house.

Frédéric made it a point of honour to see more of them than ever. He booked a box at the Italiens and took them there every week. However, they had reached that stage in an ill-assorted marriage when the mutual concessions of the past result in an invincible weariness which makes life unbearable. Madame Arnoux struggled to keep her feelings under control, Arnoux was sunk in gloom, and the sight of these two unhappy creatures saddened Frédéric.

As he enjoyed Arnoux's confidence, she had asked him to inquire into his affairs. But he was ashamed of eating Arnoux's dinners while coveting his wife. He continued all the same, excusing himself on the grounds that it was his duty to protect her, and that an opportunity might occur to be useful to her.

A week after the ball he had called on Monsieur Dambreuse. The financier had offered him twenty shares in his coal company; Frédéric had not gone there again. Deslauriers kept writing to him; he left his letters unanswered. Pellerin had urged him to come and see the portrait; he put him off. However, he gave in to Cisy, who had been pestering him to introduce him to Rosanette.

She gave Frédéric a friendly reception, but without throwing her arms around his neck as she used to do. His companion was delighted at finding himself in a light woman's house, and above all at talking to an actor, for Delmar was there.

A play in which he had taken the part of a peasant who sermonizes Louis XVI and prophesies 1789 had made him so famous that the same part was constantly being reproduced for him; and his occupa-

tion now consisted in insulting the monarchs of every country
under the sun. As an English brewer, he railed against Charles I; as
a student of Salamanca, he cursed Philip II; or as a heartbroken
father, he denounced the Pompadour – and that was his finest part.
Street-urchins waited at the stage-door to see him; and his bio-
graphy, which was on sale in the intervals, depicted him as caring
for his aged mother, reading the Bible, and helping the poor, in fact
as a combination of St Vincent de Paul, Brutus, and Mirabeau.
People spoke of 'our Delmar'. He had a mission; he was turning
into a Messiah.

All this had fascinated Rosanette; and she had got rid of old
Oudry, without worrying about the future, for she was not grasping
by nature.

Arnoux, knowing this, had taken advantage of the fact for
a long time to keep her at small expense to himself; the old man
had come on the scene, and the three of them had been careful to
avoid any straightforward explanations. Then, imagining that she
had dismissed Oudry for his sake alone, Arnoux had increased her
allowance. But she renewed her demands with a frequency hard
to understand, seeing that she was now living on a reduced scale;
she had even sold her cashmere shawl, explaining that she wanted
to settle her old debts; and he paid up every time, for she bewitched
him and imposed on him without mercy. Bills and writs inundated
the house. Frédéric felt that a crisis was imminent.

One day he called to see Madame Arnoux. She was out. Monsieur
was working downstairs in the shop.

Arnoux, surrounded by his vases, was in fact trying to 'put one
over' on a young middle-class couple from the country. He spoke
of turning and throwing, of crackling and glazing; the others, not
wanting to show their ignorance, made signs of approval and bought
his wares.

When the customers had gone, he told Frédéric that he had had
a slight quarrel with his wife that morning. To forestall any comments on his expenditure, he had declared that the Marshal was no
longer his mistress.

'I even told her she was yours.'

Frédéric was furious; but as reproaches might betray him, he
simply stammered:

'Oh, you shouldn't have done that, you really shouldn't.'

'Why not?' asked Arnoux. 'What's the disgrace in passing for her lover? I *am* her lover, and proud of it. Wouldn't you be delighted to be in my place?'

Had she talked? Was this an allusion? Frédéric hastily replied:

'No! Not at all! On the contrary!'

'Well then?'

'Yes, you're right. It doesn't matter.'

Arnoux went on:

'Why don't you come along there any more?'

Frédéric promised to go there soon.

'Oh, I was forgetting . . . When you're talking to my wife about Rosanette . . . you might blurt something out . . . I don't know what, but you'll find something . . . to convince her that you're her lover. You'll do that for me, won't you?'

The young man's only reply was an equivocal smile. This slander was going to spoil everything for him. He went to see her that evening and swore that Arnoux's allegation was false.

'Really and truly?'

He seemed to be speaking the truth; and after drawing a deep breath she said: 'I believe you', with a beautiful smile. Then she bent her head and, without looking at him, said:

'In any case, nobody has any rights over you.'

So she did not suspect anything, and she despised him, since she did not think that he loved her enough to be faithful to her. Forgetting his attempts to seduce the other woman, Frédéric considered this indulgence insulting.

Then she asked him to go and see 'that woman' now and then to find out how things stood.

Arnoux arrived, and five minutes later wanted to take him along to Rosanette's.

The situation was becoming unbearable.

His mind was taken off it by a letter from his solicitor saying that he was going to send him fifteen thousand francs the following day; and to make up for his neglect of Deslauriers, he went to give him this good news straight away.

The lawyer lived in the Rue des Trois-Maries, on the fifth floor, looking on to a courtyard. His office was a small, cold room with a tiled floor and greenish wallpaper, in which the chief ornament was a gold medal, the prize for his doctorate, set in an ebony frame next to the mirror. There was a mahogany bookcase containing about a hundred volumes behind glass. A leather-topped desk occupied the middle of the room; four old green velvet armchairs stood in the corners; and a fire of wood shavings was blazing in the fireplace, where there was always a log waiting to be lit as soon as the bell rang. It was his consulting hour; the lawyer was wearing a white cravat.

At the news of the fifteen thousand francs – he was probably no longer counting on them – he gave a chuckle of pleasure.

'That's good, old fellow; that's good, that's very good!'

He threw some wood on the fire, sat down again, and promptly started talking about the newspaper. The first thing was to get rid of Hussonnet.

'That idiot gets on my nerves. As for the paper's point of view, my opinion is that the cleverest and fairest thing to do is to have no point of view at all.'

Frédéric looked surprised.

'Why yes! It's high time that politics were treated scientifically. The old boys of the eighteenth century were making a start when Rousseau and the men of letters brought in philanthropy and poetry and all that, to the great delight of the Catholics – a natural alliance, incidentally, because our present-day reformers, as I can prove to you, all believe in revealed religion. But if you celebrate Masses for Poland; if you replace the God of the Dominicans, who was a butcher, with the God of the Romantics, who is an upholsterer; if, in fact, your concept of the Absolute is no wider than that of your forefathers, then the monarchy will push its way through your republican forms, and your red bonnet will never be anything but a priest's calotte. The only difference will be that solitary confinement will have replaced torture, offences against religion will have replaced sacrilege, and the concert of Europe will have replaced the Holy Alliance. And in this magnificent, much admired society, made up of Louis Quatorze relics and Voltairian ruins with a coat of Imperial paint and fragments of the English constitution, we'll see the municipal councils trying to annoy the mayor, the general councils their prefect, the chambers the king, the Press the powers that be, and the government everybody. There are good people who actually go into ecstasies over the Civil Code, a piece of work manufactured, whatever you may say, in a mean, tyrannical spirit; for the legislator, instead of doing his job, which was to regularize tradition, had the presumption to mould society as he thought fit, like another Lycurgus. Why does the law interfere with a father's rights when it comes to making a will? Why does it hinder the compulsory sale of buildings? Why does it punish vagrancy as a crime, when it shouldn't even be a misdemeanour? And there are plenty other examples. I know them all. So I'm going to write a little novel entitled *A History of the Idea of Justice*, which will be terribly funny. But I'm absolutely parched. What about you?'

He leant out of the window and shouted to the concierge to go and fetch some grog from the tavern.

'To sum up, I see three parties ... no, three groups, none of which interests me: those who have, those who used to have, and those who are trying to have. But they are all united in their imbecile worship of Authority. Let me give you a few examples: Mably recommends preventing philosophers from publishing their doctrines; Monsieur Wronski, the geometrician, calls the censorship, in his own language, "the critical repression of speculative spontaneity"; Père Enfantin gives the Habsburgs his blessing for "having stretched a firm hand across the Alps to restrain Italy"; Pierre Leroux wants to force us to listen to an orator, and Louis Blanc favours a state religion, this nation of serfs has such a mania for being governed. But not a single form of government is legitimate, for all their eternal principles. You see, since *principle* means *origin*, you must always go back to a revolution, an act of violence, some transient event. Thus the principle of our state is national sovereignty, expressed in the form of parliamentary government, although our parliament doesn't agree! But why should the sovereignty of the people be more sacred than the divine right of kings? They're both of them fictions! Let's have no more metaphysics, no more ghosts. You don't need dogmas to keep the streets clean! I suppose I'll be told that I'm trying to overthrow society. Well, what of it? Where would be the harm? Because it's a pretty sight, your society is.'

Frédéric could have found a good many arguments in reply. But seeing how far Deslauriers had come from Sénécal's theories, he was full of indulgence. He contented himself with pointing out that a system like that would make them universally hated.

'On the contrary, since we shall have given every party reason to hate its neighbours, they'll all give us their support. You'll lend us a hand too, and write some transcendental criticism for us.'

They must attack all accepted ideas, the Academy, the École Normale, the Conservatoire, the Comédie française, anything which bore any resemblance to an institution. In this way they could provide their review with an overall doctrine. Then, once it was solidly established, it would suddenly turn into a daily paper; and after that they could start attacking individuals.

'And people will have a healthy respect for us, you can be sure of that!'

Deslauriers was about to fulfil his old dream: an editor's chair, in other words the ineffable joy of controlling other people, of carving up their articles, of commissioning copy and turning it down. His eyes sparkled behind his spectacles, and as he grew more and more excited he automatically emptied one glass after another.

'You must give a dinner once a week. That's absolutely indispensable, even if it costs you half your income. People will want to be invited; it will be a meeting-place for others, a lever for you; and using the two handles of literature and politics to manipulate public opinion, we'll have Paris at our feet within six months, you'll see!'

Listening to him, Frédéric had a feeling of rejuvenation, like a man who, after a long period of confinement in a bedroom, is taken out into the open air. He was caught up in this enthusiasm.

'Yes, you're right. I've been a lazy fool.'

'Capital!' exclaimed Deslauriers. 'That's more like my old Frédéric!'

And putting his fist under Frédéric's chin, he added:

'Ah, you've made me suffer! Never mind! I'm fond of you in spite of everything.'

They stood looking at each other, both of them moved and on the point of embracing.

A woman's bonnet appeared in the hall doorway.

'What brings you here?' asked Deslauriers.

It was Mademoiselle Clémence, his mistress.

She replied that she had happened to be passing his house and had been unable to resist the desire to see him; she had brought him some cakes, which she put on the table, for them to eat together.

'Mind my papers!' snapped the lawyer. 'In any case, I've told you twice already not to come here during my consulting-hours.'

She tried to kiss him.

'That's enough! Be off with you! Make yourself scarce!'

He pushed her away, and she gave a great sob.

'Oh, you make me tired!'

'It's because I love you!'

'I don't want to be loved, I want to be obliged.'

This harsh remark stopped Clémence's tears. She planted herself in front of the window and stood there motionless, with her forehead pressed against the glass.

Her attitude and her silence exasperated Deslauriers.

'When you've finished, you'll order your carriage, won't you?' She swung round to face him.

'You're turning me out!'

'Right first time!'

She fixed her big blue eyes on him, presumably in a final entreaty, then crossed the two ends of her plaid, waited a moment longer, and went off.

'You ought to call her back,' said Frédéric.

'Get along with you!'

As he had to go out, Deslauriers went into the kitchen, which served as his dressing-room. On the stone flags there was a pair of boots, the remains of a meagre luncheon, and a mattress with a blanket rolled up in a corner.

'As you can see,' he said, 'I don't entertain many marquises here. I can get along perfectly well without them, and the others too. Those who don't cost you anything take up your time; that's another form of money, and I'm not a rich man. And then they're all so stupid, so stupid! Can you bear to talk to a woman?'

They parted at the corner of the Pont-Neuf.

'It's agreed then? You'll bring me the money tomorrow, as soon as you get it.'

'Agreed!' said Frédéric.

The next morning, when he awoke, the post brought him a bank bond for fifteen thousand francs.

This scrap of paper represented fifteen great bags of money; and he reflected that with this sum he could either keep his carriage for three years, instead of selling it as he would soon be forced to do, or else buy himself two beautiful suits of inlaid armour which he had seen on the Quai Voltaire, and also a great many other things – paintings, books, and countless bouquets and presents for Madame Arnoux. Anything, in fact, would have been better than risking, or rather losing, so much money on that newspaper. Deslauriers struck him as insufferably conceited, and his cruel behaviour the day before had cast a chill over Frédéric's feelings for him. He was abandoning himself to these regrets when he was surprised to see

Arnoux come in and sit down heavily on the edge of his bed, like a man bowed down by grief or fatigue.

'What's the matter?'

'I'm ruined!'

That very day he had to repay the sum of eighteen thousand francs, lent him by a certain Vanneroy, at the office of Maître Beauminet, a lawyer in the Rue Sainte-Anne.

'It's an inexplicable disaster. I've already given him a mortgage which ought to have calmed him down. But he's threatening me with a writ if he isn't paid this very afternoon.'

'And then?'

'Then it's all very simple. He'll have my house seized. The first notice that goes up will be the end of me, that's all. Oh, if only I could find somebody to advance me that cursed sum, he could take Vanneroy's place and I should be saved. You wouldn't happen to have it, by any chance?'

The bond was still on the bedside table, next to a book. Frédéric picked up the volume and placed it on top of it.

'Good heavens, no, my dear fellow.'

But it hurt him to turn Arnoux away.

'You mean you can't find anybody who's willing . . .'

'Not a soul! And to think that I shall have some money coming in within a week. There's how much . . . perhaps fifty thousand francs due to me at the end of the month.'

'Couldn't you ask your debtors to advance . . .?'

'You can see me doing that, can't you?'

'But haven't you any securities or bills?'

'Not a thing.'

'Then what are you going to do?' said Frédéric.

'That's what I'm wondering,' replied Arnoux.

He fell silent and paced up and down the room.

'I'm not worried about myself, heaven knows, but about my children, my poor wife!'

Then, pronouncing each word separately, he said:

'Well . . . I'll show them . . . I'll sell everything up . . . and go seek my fortune . . . somewhere or other.'

'You can't possibly do that!' exclaimed Frédéric.

Arnoux replied calmly:

'How do you expect me to go on living in Paris, after all this?'

There was a long silence.

Frédéric blurted out:

'When would you pay this money back?'

Not that he had it – far from it! But there was nothing to prevent him from asking his friends and seeing what could be done. And he rang for his servant to get dressed. Arnoux thanked him.

'It's eighteen thousand francs you need, is it?'

'Oh, sixteen thousand would do. Because I can raise two thousand five hundred or three thousand with my silver plate, provided Vanneroy gives me till tomorrow. And, as I said before, you can tell the lender – swear to him, indeed – that the money will be repaid within a week, perhaps even in five or six days. In any case, the mortgage is there as security. So there's no risk, you understand?'

Frédéric assured him that he understood and that he would go out straight away.

He stayed at home, cursing Deslauriers, for he wanted to keep his promise and yet help Arnoux at the same time.

'What if I approached Monsieur Dambreuse? But under what pretext could I ask him for money? On the contrary, I ought to be taking him some money for his coal shares! Oh, to hell with him and his shares! I don't owe him anything for them!'

And Frédéric congratulated himself on his independence, as if he had refused Monsieur Dambreuse a favour.

'Well,' he said to himself, 'seeing that I'm losing money there – for with fifteen thousand francs I could make a hundred thousand: that sometimes happens on the Stock Exchange – and seeing that I'm breaking my word to Dambreuse, surely that leaves me free? . . . Besides, what would it matter if Deslauriers had to wait? . . . No, no, that's wrong! Let's be off!'

He looked at his clock.

'Oh, there's no hurry. The bank doesn't shut until five.'

And at half past four, when he had drawn his money, he said to himself:

'It's no use going now. He'd be out; I'll go tonight.'

In this way he gave himself an opportunity to go back on his decision, for every conscience retains some trace of the sophisms which have been poured into it; they leave an after-taste in it, like a bad liqueur.

He took a stroll along the boulevards and dined on his own in a restaurant. Then, to amuse himself, he dropped into the Vaudeville for one act. But he felt uneasy about his banknotes, as if he had stolen them. He would not have been sorry to lose them.

Returning home, he found a letter containing these words:

> What news?
> My wife joins with me, dear friend, in hope, etc.
> Yours,

followed by initials.

'His wife is asking me for help!'

At that very moment Arnoux appeared, to find out if he had found the required sum.

'Yes, here it is!' said Frédéric.

And twenty-four hours later he told Deslauriers:

'It hasn't arrived.'

The lawyer came back three days running. He urged him to write to the solicitor. He even offered to go to Le Havre.

'No, there's no point in doing that. I'll go there myself.'

At the end of the week Frédéric timidly asked Arnoux for his fifteen thousand francs.

Arnoux put him off to the next day, and then to the day after that. Frédéric ventured out only after dark, for fear that Deslauriers should catch him.

One evening somebody bumped into him at the corner of the Madeleine. It was Deslauriers.

'I'm on my way to get the money,' he said.

Deslauriers accompanied him to the door of a house in the Faubourg Poissonnière.

'Wait for me.'

He waited. At last, after forty-three minutes had elapsed, Frédéric came out with Arnoux, and motioned to him to be patient a little longer. The porcelain-manufacturer and his companion went up the Rue Hauteville arm in arm, and then turned into the Rue de Chabrol.

It was a dark night, with warm gusts of wind. Arnoux walked along slowly, talking about the Galeries du Commerce, a series of arcades planned to lead from the Boulevard Saint-Denis to the Châtelet – a splendid enterprise in which he was strongly tempted to take part. Every now and then he stopped, to look at the young milliners' faces in the shop-windows, then went on with his conversation.

Frédéric could hear Deslauriers' footsteps behind him, like so many reproaches, like blows striking his conscience. But he did not dare to ask for the money, partly out of false shame, and partly because he was afraid it would be useless. Deslauriers drew nearer. He made up his mind.

In a very casual voice Arnoux replied that, as debts owing to him had not been paid, he was unable to return the fifteen thousand francs for the time being.

'You don't need the money, I suppose?'

Just at that moment Deslauriers accosted Frédéric, and, drawing him aside, asked:

'Tell me the truth. Have you got the money, or haven't you?'

'Well, no,' said Frédéric. 'I've lost it.'

'Oh! And how?'

'Gambling!'

Deslauriers did not say a word, but made a deep bow and went off. Arnoux had taken the opportunity to light a cigar in a tobacconist's shop. Joining Frédéric again, he asked who the young man was.

'Nobody. A friend.'

Then, three minutes later, outside Rosanette's door, Arnoux said:

'Come upstairs with me. She'll be delighted to see you. What a bear you are nowadays!'

A street-lamp opposite lit up his face; and with his cigar between his white teeth, and his complacent expression, there was something insufferable about him.

'Oh, by the way, my solicitor went to see yours this morning, about registering that mortgage. It was my wife who reminded me about it.'

'A capable woman,' said Frédéric mechanically.

'She is indeed!'

And once again Arnoux started singing her praises. She had no equal for intelligence, feeling, and thrift; then he added in an undertone, rolling his eyes:

'And physically too!'

'Good-bye,' said Frédéric.

Arnoux gave a start.

'Why, what's the matter?'

And with his hand half stretched towards Frédéric, he gazed at him, quite disconcerted by the anger in his face.

Frédéric answered curtly:

'Good-bye.'

He went down the Rue de Bréda like a rolling stone, furious with Arnoux, swearing never to see him again – or her either – heart-broken and despairing. Instead of the break which he had been expecting, here was Arnoux, on the contrary, beginning to love his wife, and what was more, beginning to love her completely, from the hair on her head to the depths of her soul. The man's vulgarity infuriated Frédéric. And the fellow had everything he wanted! He pictured him again on the courtesan's doorstep, and the mortification of a quarrel added to his impotent rage. Besides, Arnoux's honesty in offering sureties for his money humiliated him; he would willingly have strangled him; and over and above his misery, there hung like a fog in his conscience the awareness of his cowardly behaviour to his friend. Tears choked him.

Deslauriers was hurrying down the Rue des Martyrs, swearing out loud in his indignation; for his project, like a fallen obelisk, now struck him as possessing an extraordinary grandeur. He considered himself robbed, as if he had suffered a grievous injury. His friendship for Frédéric was dead, and he was glad of it; that was some sort of compensation! He was filled with a hatred of the rich. Sénécal's opinions appealed to him, and he vowed to give them his support.

In the meantime, Arnoux, comfortably ensconced in an easy chair by the fire, was savouring the aroma of his cup of tea, with the Marshal on his knee.

Frédéric did not go to see them again; and, to take his mind off his disastrous passion, he took up the first subject which occurred to him, and decided to write a history of the Renaissance. He heaped his desk pell-mell with humanists, philosophers, and poets; he went to the Print Room to see engravings of Marcantonio; and he tried to understand Machiavelli. Gradually his work exerted a soothing influence on him. He forgot his own personality by immersing it in that of others – which is perhaps the only way to avoid suffering from it.

One day, when he was quietly taking notes, the door opened and the servant announced Madame Arnoux.

It was really she! Alone? No! For she was holding little Eugène by the hand, and behind her was her maid in a white apron. She sat down, and after giving a cough, said:

'You haven't been to see us for a long time.'

As Frédéric could not think of an excuse, she added:

'It's very tactful of you.'

'Tactful?' he said. 'Why?'

'Because of what you did for Arnoux,' she replied.

Frédéric made a gesture signifying: 'Not a bit of it. I did it for you.'

She sent her child into the drawing-room, to play with the maid. They exchanged two or three words about their health; then the conversation dropped.

She was wearing a brown silk dress, the colour of Spanish wine, with a black velvet coat edged with sable; he felt a longing to stroke this fur, and his lips were drawn towards her long bandeaux. But something was troubling her, and turning her eyes towards the door, she said:

'It's rather warm here.'

Frédéric guessed the discreet meaning of her glance.

'I beg your pardon. The door has been left ajar.'

'Oh, so it has.'

And she smiled, as if to say: 'I'm not afraid of anything.'

He immediately asked her the purpose of her visit.

'My husband,' she said, making an obvious effort, 'asked me to come and see you, since he did not dare to approach you himself.'

'And why?'

'You know Monsieur Dambreuse, don't you?'

'Yes, slightly.'

'Oh, only slightly.'

She fell silent.

'Never mind. Go on.'

Then she told him that, two days before, Arnoux had been unable to meet four bills for a thousand francs written to a banker's order, and to which he had made her put her signature. She regretted having compromised her children's fortune. But anything was better than dishonour, and if Monsieur Dambreuse stopped his legal proceedings, he would certainly be paid soon; for she was going to sell a little house she owned at Chartres.

'Poor woman!' murmured Frédéric. 'I'll go and see him. Count on me.'

'Thank you.'

And she rose to go.

'Oh, there's no hurry!'

She remained standing, examining the trophy of Mongolian arrows hanging from the ceiling, the bookcase, the bindings, all the writing materials; she picked up the bronze bowl containing his pens; her heels rested in various places on the carpet. She had called to see Frédéric several times, but always with Arnoux. They were alone this time, alone in his own house; it was an extraordinary event, almost a stroke of luck.

She asked to see his little garden; he offered her his arm to show her his estate, thirty feet of ground surrounded by houses, with shrubs in the corners and a flower-bed in the middle.

It was early in April. The leaves of the lilac bushes were already turning green, a fresh breeze was stirring the air, and little birds were chirping, mingling their song with the distant noise of a coach-builder's forge.

Frédéric went to fetch a shovel, and while they strolled along side by side the child built sand castles on the path.

Madame Arnoux did not think he would have much imagination later on, but he had an affectionate character. His sister, on the other hand, had an innate coldness which occasionally hurt her.

'That will change,' said Frédéric. 'One must never despair.'

She replied:

'One must never despair.'

This mechanical repetition of his phrase struck him as a kind of encouragement; he picked a rose, the only one in the garden.

'Do you remember . . . a certain bunch of roses, one evening in a carriage?'

She blushed slightly, and answered with an expression of compassionate mockery:

'Oh, I was very young at the time.'

'And will this rose suffer the same fate?' said Frédéric in a low voice.

She twirled the stem round between her fingers, like the thread on a spindle, and replied:

'No. I shall keep it.'

She beckoned to the maid, who took the child in her arms; then, outside the door, in the street, Madame Arnoux smelt the flower, bending her head towards one shoulder, with a glance as gentle as a kiss.

Back in his study, he gazed at the armchair in which she had sat, and at all the things she had touched. Something of her hovered in the air around him. The soft caress of her presence lingered on.

'So she has been here!' he said to himself.

And waves of infinite tenderness engulfed him.

The next day at eleven o'clock he called to see Monsieur Dambreuse. He was shown into the dining-room. The banker was lunching opposite his wife. Her niece was sitting beside her, and on the other side was the governess, an Englishwoman with a heavily pock-marked face.

Monsieur Dambreuse invited his young friend to join them, and when he refused, asked:

'What can I do for you?'

With assumed indifference Frédéric confessed that he had come to ask a favour for a certain Arnoux.

'Ha! The former picture dealer,' said the banker, showing his gums in a silent laugh. 'Oudry used to act as his guarantor, but they fell out.'

And he started looking through the letters and newspapers which had been placed beside his plate.

Two servants were waiting on the family, moving silently over the parquet floor; and the high-ceilinged room, with its three tapestry door-curtains and its two white marble fountains, the gleaming dish-warmers, the carefully arranged hors-d'œuvre, even the stiffly folded napkins – all this luxurious comfort reminded Frédéric by contrast of another meal he had seen at Arnoux's house. He did not dare to interrupt Monsieur Dambreuse.

Madame noticed his embarrassment.

'Do you ever see our friend Martinon?'

'He's coming tonight,' the girl said quickly.

'Oh, are you sure?' replied her aunt, giving her an icy look.

One of the servants whispered in her ear.

'Your dressmaker, my child! . . . Miss John!'

The governess obediently disappeared with her charge.

Monsieur Dambreuse, disturbed by the moving of the chairs, asked what was happening.

'It's Madame Regimbart.'

'Well, well! Regimbart! I know that name. I've come across his signature.'

Frédéric finally broached the question. Arnoux deserved some consideration; with the sole purpose of fulfilling his obligations, he was even going to sell a house belonging to his wife.

'People say she's very pretty,' said Madame Dambreuse.

The banker added in a good-natured manner:

'Are you a . . . close friend of theirs?'

Without making a definite reply Frédéric said that he would be greatly obliged if Monsieur Dambreuse would take into consideration. . .

'Well, just to please you, so be it. I shall wait. I have a few moments to spare. Suppose we went down to my office?'

Luncheon was over; Madame Dambreuse gave a slight bow, with a strange smile which was full of both irony and politeness. Frédéric had no time to think about it, for, as soon as they were on their own, Monsieur Dambreuse said:

'You didn't come for your shares.'

And, without allowing him to apologize, he went on:

'Never mind. It's only right that you should know a little more about the business.'

He offered him a cigarette and began.

The General Coal Company of France had already been constituted; they were only waiting for the official decree. The mere fact of the merger of different firms, by reducing administrative and labour costs, would increase the profits. What is more, the Company had devised a novel idea, which was to give the workers an interest in the enterprise. It would build them houses and hygienic hostels and in addition it would become its employees' general purveyor, supplying them with everything they needed at cost price.

'And they will gain by it, Monsieur. There's real progress for you – a triumphant reply to the grousing and grumbling of the Republicans. On our board' – he displayed the prospectus – 'we have a peer of France, a member of the Institut, a retired general of the Engineers, all well-known names. A board like that will reassure the timid investor and attract the intelligent. The Company will obtain orders from the State, and also from the railways, the steamship lines, the ironworks, the gas companies, and the kitchens of the middle classes. Like that we shall give heat and light, reaching the hearths of the humblest homes. But you'll ask me how we are going to make sure of sales. The answer, my dear sir, is by means of import duties; and we'll get those, you can be sure of that! In any case, I'm frankly a prohibitionist. The country comes first, that's my motto!'

He had been appointed a director, but he had not the time to attend to certain details, such as the writing of reports.

'I'm not as well up in the classics as I used to be; I've forgotten my Greek! I should need somebody to . . . interpret my ideas.'

And all of a sudden he said:

'Would you like to be that man, with the title of general secretary?'

Frédéric did not know what to reply.

'Well, what's to prevent you?'

His duties would be confined to writing a report once a year for the shareholders. He would find himself in daily contact with the most important men in Paris. As the Company's representative among the workers, he would naturally win their affection, and that would enable him later on to become a departmental councillor and then a deputy.

Frédéric's ears were buzzing. What could be the reason for this benevolence? He thanked the banker profusely.

But it was essential, said Monsieur Dambreuse, that he should not be dependent on anybody. The surest method was to buy some shares, 'an excellent investment in any case, for your capital guarantees your position, and your position your capital'.

'Roughly how much ought I to invest?' said Frédéric.

'Heavens, as much as you like. Between forty and sixty thousand francs, I suppose.'

This sum was so infinitesimal in the eyes of Monsieur Dambreuse, and his authority was so great, that the young man promptly decided to sell a farm. He accepted. Monsieur Dambreuse would fix an appointment one of these days to conclude their arrangements.

'So I can tell Jacques Arnoux . . .'

'Anything you like! Poor chap! Anything you like.'

Frédéric wrote to Arnoux and his wife, telling them to set their minds at rest. He sent the letter by his servant, who came back with the reply:

'Good!'

His efforts deserved better than this. He expected a call, or a letter at the very least. He received no call. No letter arrived.

Was this forgetfulness on their part, or was it deliberate? Seeing that Madame Arnoux had come to see him once, what prevented her from coming again? Was the sort of hint, of admission she had made to him nothing but a selfish manoeuvre? 'Are they making a fool of me? Is she Arnoux's accomplice?' In spite of his longing to return to their house, a kind of timidity restrained him.

One morning, three weeks after their conversation, Monsieur Dambreuse wrote to say that he expected him that very day, in an hour's time.

While he was on his way, the thought of Arnoux and his wife assailed him once more; and, unable to think of any explanation for their conduct, he was seized with a pang of fear, an ominous presentiment. To get rid of it, he hailed a cab and drove to the Rue de Paradis.

Arnoux was away on a journey.

'And Madame?'

'Madame is in the country at the factory.'

'When is Monsieur coming back?'

'Tomorrow, without fail.'

He would find her alone; this was his moment. An imperious voice within him cried: 'Go ahead!'

But what about Monsieur Dambreuse? 'Oh, never mind! I'll say that I was ill.' He ran to the station; then, in the railway carriage, he thought:

'Perhaps I was wrong. Oh, what does it matter?'

Green fields stretched away to right and left; the train rolled along; the little station houses glided by like stage sets; and the big, fleecy puffs of smoke from the engine, always falling to the same side, danced on the grass for a moment, then melted away.

Frédéric, alone on his seat, looked at all this out of boredom, sunk in that lethargy which comes from the very excess of impatience. Finally cranes and warehouses appeared. It was Creil.

The town, built on the slope of two low hills, one bare and the other wooded, with its church tower, its houses of different sizes, and its stone bridge, struck him as gay, unassuming, and wholesome. A big barge was floating down the river, which the wind was lashing into waves; hens were pecking about in the straw at the foot of the calvary; a woman went by, carrying a basket of damp washing on her head.

Beyond the bridge he found himself on an island, with a ruined abbey on the right. A mill-wheel was turning, blocking the entire width of the second arm of the Oise, which was overlooked by the factory. The size of this building astonished Frédéric. His respect for Arnoux increased. A few yards further on he turned down an alley-way which was closed at the end by an iron gate.

He went in. The concierge called him back, shouting:

'Have you got a pass?'

'What for?'

'For visiting the factory.'

Frédéric curtly stated that he had come to see Monsieur Arnoux.

'Who's Monsieur Arnoux?'

'But the chief, the master, the owner, dammit!'

'No, Monsieur, this is the factory of Messieurs Lebœuf and Milliet.'

No doubt the good woman was joking. Some workmen were arriving; he stopped two or three of them; their reply was the same.

Frédéric left the yard, staggering like a drunken man. He looked so bewildered that a man smoking a pipe on the Pont de la Boucherie asked him if he was looking for something. He knew Arnoux's factory. It was at Montataire.

Frédéric asked about a carriage. They were only to be found at the station. He went back there. A broken-down fly, drawn by an old horse whose dilapidated harness was dangling between the shafts, was standing on its own in front of the luggage office.

A street-urchin offered to find 'old Pilon'. He came back after ten minutes: old Pilon was having lunch. Frédéric, losing patience, set off. But the gates of the level crossing were closed. He had to wait until two trains had gone by. At last he rushed out into the countryside.

The monotonous green expanse was like a huge billiard table. Heaps of iron dross lined both sides of the road, like piles of pebbles. A little further on, some factory chimneys built close to one another were smoking. Facing him, on a round hill, there was a little turreted château and the square tower of a church. Some long walls, below, formed uneven lines among the trees; and right at the bottom stretched the houses of the village.

These houses had only two stories, with staircases of three steps, made of dry blocks of stone. Every now and then a grocer's bell could be heard. Heavy footsteps sank into the black mud, and a fine drizzle was falling, cutting the pale sky with a thousand lines.

Frédéric kept to the middle of the paved road, and eventually, on his left, at the turning of a lane, he saw a big wooden arch which bore in letters of gold the word: FAIENCES.

It was not for nothing that Jacques Arnoux had picked on the neighbourhood of Creil; by placing his factory as close as possible to the other one, which had an established reputation, he created a confusion in the public's mind which was favourable to his interests.

The main building stood on the very edge of a river which crossed the meadow. The master's house, which was surrounded by a garden, was distinguished by its flight of steps adorned with four vases bristling with cactus plants. Heaps of white clay were drying in sheds; there were others out in the open; and in the middle of the yard stood Sénécal, in his everlasting blue overcoat with the red lining.

The sometime tutor held out his cold hand.

'You've come to see the master? He isn't here.'

Frédéric, caught off his guard, stupidly replied:

'I know.'

But recovering himself immediately, he added:

'I've come on a matter concerning Madame Arnoux. Can she see me?'

'Oh, I haven't set eyes on her for three days,' said Sénécal.

And he launched out on a whole string of complaints. When he had accepted the manufacturer's terms, he had expected to stay in Paris, not bury himself in the country, away from his friends and deprived of newspapers. Never mind! He had risen above all that! But Arnoux seemed to pay no attention to his merits. Moreover he was unimaginative, old-fashioned, and incredibly ignorant. Instead of searching for artistic improvements, it would have been better to introduce heating by coal and gas. The master was 'going under'; Sénécal stressed these words. In short he disliked his job; and he practically ordered Frédéric to put in a word for him, so that his pay should be raised.

'Don't worry!' said the other.

He met nobody on the stairs. On the first floor he put his head into an empty room; it was the drawing-room. He called out at the top of his voice. Nobody replied; the cook and the maid were probably out; finally, reaching the second floor, he pushed open a door. Madame Arnoux was alone in front of a wardrobe mirror. Her dressing-gown was half-open, with the cord hanging down her hips. The whole of one side of her hair was spread in a black wave over her right shoulder; and she had her arms raised, holding her chignon with one hand while she was thrusting a pin into it with the other. She gave a cry, and vanished.

Then she came back fully dressed. Her figure, her eyes, the rustle of her dress, everything delighted him. Frédéric could scarcely restrain himself from covering her with kisses.

'I beg your pardon,' she said, 'but I couldn't . . .'

He ventured to interrupt her:

'All the same . . . you looked wonderful . . . just now.'

She probably found the compliment a little coarse, for her cheeks coloured. He was afraid he had offended her. She went on:

'What happy chance brings you here?'

He did not know what to reply; and after a little chuckle which gave him time to think, he said:

'If I told you, would you believe me?'

'Why not?'

Frédéric explained that a few nights before he had had a horrible dream:

'I dreamt that you were seriously ill, at the point of death.'

'Oh, neither my husband nor I are ever ill.'

'I only dreamt of you,' he said.

She looked at him calmly.

'Dreams don't always come true.'

Frédéric stammered, searched for words, and finally embarked on a long discourse on the affinity of souls. There was a force which put two people in contact across space, informed them of each other's feelings, and brought them together.

She listened to him with bowed head, smiling her beautiful smile. He watched her delightedly out of the corner of his eye, and poured out his love more freely through the medium of commonplaces. She offered to show him over the factory; and as she insisted, he agreed.

To begin with something entertaining, she showed him the sort of museum which decorated the staircase. The specimens hanging on the walls or standing on shelves bore witness to Arnoux's successive efforts and infatuations. After searching for the copper red of the Chinese, he had tried his hand at majolica, faenza, Etruscan and Oriental china, and had finally attempted some of the refinements achieved in later times. Thus the series included big vases covered with mandarins, bowls of an iridescent bronze, pots decorated with Arabic script, flagons in the Renaissance manner, and large plates adorned with two figures which looked as if they had been drawn with red chalk, in a vapid, cloying style. He was now making signboards and wine labels; but his mind was not lofty enough to attain to art, nor pedestrian enough to aim exclusively at profit, with the result that he was ruining himself without satisfying anybody. The two of them were looking at these things when Mademoiselle Marthe went by.

'Don't you recognize him?' her mother asked her.

'Yes, I do!' she replied, giving him her hand, while her clear, suspicious gaze, her virgin gaze, seemed to be murmuring: 'What are you doing here?' She went up the steps, turning her head slightly over her shoulder.

Madame Arnoux took Frédéric into the yard, and then solemnly explained to him how the clay was crushed, cleaned and sifted.

'The important thing is the preparation of the pastes.'

And she took him into a room full of vats, in which a vertical axis fitted with horizontal arms was revolving. Frédéric felt sorry that he had not declined her offer straight out.

'These are the drabblers,' she said.

He considered the word grotesque, and almost unseemly on her lips.

Wide belts were rolling from one end of the ceiling to the other, to wind themselves round drums, and everything was moving with a rhythm which was continuous, mathematical, and irritating.

They went out, and passed close to a derelict hut which had previously served as a toolshed.

'It's no use for anything now,' said Madame Arnoux.

He answered in a trembling voice:

'There's room for happiness inside!'

The din of the fire pump drowned his words, and the two of them went into the roughing shop.

Men sitting at a narrow table were placing lumps of paste on revolving disks in front of them; their left hand scraped out the inside while their right stroked the surface, and vases could be seen rising like flowers blossoming out.

Madame Arnoux showed Frédéric the moulds for the more difficult pieces of work.

In another room the pots were being decorated with fillets, grooves, and projecting lines. On the upper storey the seams were being removed, and the little holes which had been left by the previous processes were being filled with plaster.

There were pots lined up everywhere: on gratings, in corners, in the middle of the corridors.

Frédéric was beginning to be bored.

'Perhaps all this is tiring you?' she said.

For fear that he might have to end his visit there, he replied with a show of considerable enthusiasm. He even expressed regret that he had not devoted himself to this industry.

She looked surprised:

'Why yes! Because then I could have lived close to you!'

He tried to catch her eye, and to avoid looking at him, Madame Arnoux picked up from a table some little balls of paste which came from the unsuccessful repairs, flattened them into a cake, and imprinted her hand on it.

'May I take that away with me?' asked Frédéric.

'Heavens, what a child you are!'

He was about to reply when Sénécal came in.

As soon as he set foot in the room, the deputy manager noticed a breach of the regulations. The workshops were supposed to be swept out every week; as it was Saturday and the workers had failed to do anything of the sort, Sénécal told them that they would have to stay behind an extra hour.

'Serve you right,' he said.

They bent over their work without a murmur; but their anger could be guessed from the hoarse sound of their breathing. In any case they were anything but easy to manage, since they had all been dismissed from the big factory. The Republican governed them harshly. A man of theory, he respected only the masses and was merciless towards individuals.

Embarrassed by his presence, Frédéric asked Madame Arnoux in a whisper if it would be possible to see the ovens. They went down to the ground floor; and she was explaining the use of the cases when Sénécal, who had followed them, pushed his way between them.

He went on with the demonstration himself, dwelling on the different sorts of fuel, on the charging of ovens, pyroscopes, hovel hearths, types of slip, glazes, and metals, with a wealth of chemical terms such as chloride, sulphur, borax, and carbonate. Frédéric could not make head or tail of it, and kept turning towards Madame Arnoux.

'You're not listening,' she said. 'Yet Monsieur Sénécal is perfectly clear. He knows all these things much better than I do.'

Flattered by this eulogy, the mathematician suggested a visit to the colouring shop. Frédéric threw Madame Arnoux an anxious glance of inquiry. She remained impassive, presumably unwilling either to be alone with him or to leave him. He offered her his arm.

'No, thank you. The staircase is too narrow.'

When they got to the top, Sénécal opened the door of a room full of women.

They were busy with paint-brushes, bottles, shells, and glass slides. Along the cornice, against the wall, there were rows of engraved blocks; scraps of thin paper were flying about, and an iron stove was throwing out a sickening heat, mingled with the smell of turpentine.

The women were nearly all dressed in dirty clothes. But there was one who was wearing a Madras kerchief and long ear-rings. Slim and plump at the same time, she had big dark eyes and the thick lips of a negress. Her ample bosom pushed out her blouse, which was fastened round her waist by the belt of her skirt; with one elbow resting on the work-bench and the other arm hanging down, she was gazing vacantly at the distant countryside. Beside her was a bottle of wine and some cold meat.

The regulations forbade eating in the workshops, to safeguard the cleanliness of the work and the health of the workers.

Out of a sense of duty or a desire to play the tyrant, Sénécal pointed to a framed notice and called out from a distance:

'Hey! You there – the woman from Bordeaux! Read Article 9 out aloud to me.'

'Well, what of it?'

'What of it, Mademoiselle? You'll pay a fine of three francs, that's what!'

She looked him insolently in the eye.

'What do I care? When the master gets back, he'll cancel your fine! You can go to the devil, you silly little man.'

Sénécal, who was walking up and down with his hands behind his back, like an usher in a classroom, just smiled.

'Article 13, insubordination, ten francs!'

The woman from Bordeaux went back to her work. Out of a sense of propriety, Madame Arnoux said nothing, but her forehead puckered up. Frédéric murmured:

'You're very harsh, for a democrat.'

The other replied pontifically:

'Democracy doesn't mean licence for the individual to do as he pleases. It means equality before the law, the division of labour, good order.'

'You're forgetting humanity,' said Frédéric.

Madame Arnoux took his arm; and Sénécal, who may have been offended by this tacit approval, went away.

Frédéric felt immensely relieved. He had been looking all day for an opportunity to declare his love; now it had come. Moreover Madame Arnoux's spontaneous gesture seemed to him to contain a promise; and he asked if he might go up to her room, as he wanted to warm his feet. But as soon as he was seated beside her he found himself in difficulties: he did not know how to begin. Luckily he thought of Sénécal.

'Nothing could be more absurd,' he said, 'than that punishment.'

Madame Arnoux replied:

'Sometimes severity is essential.'

'How can you say that, you who are so kind? Oh, I was forgetting! You sometimes enjoy making others suffer.'

'I don't understand riddles, my friend.'

And her stern glance, even more than her words, checked him. Frédéric was determined to go on. A volume of Musset happened to be lying on a chest of drawers. He turned a few pages, and then started talking about love, its despairs and its transports.

According to Madame Arnoux, that sort of thing was criminal or artificial.

The young man felt hurt by this rebuttal; and to counter it he cited as proof the suicides reported in the papers, and extolled the great lovers of literature – Phèdre, Dido, Romeo, Des Grieux. He began to be carried away by his own eloquence.

The fire in the hearth had gone out; the rain lashed against the window-panes. Madame Arnoux sat motionless with her hands on the arms of her chair; the ribbons of her cap hung down like the head-bands of a sphinx; her clear-cut profile stood out in pale relief in the dusk.

He longed to throw himself on his knees. There was a creaking noise in the corridor; he did not dare.

Besides, he was restrained by a sort of religious awe. That dress of hers, merging into the shadows, struck him as enormous, infinite, impossible to lift; and precisely because of that his desire increased. But the fear of going too far, and that of not going far enough, robbed him of all power of judgement.

'If she doesn't want me,' he thought, 'let her throw me out! If she wants me, let her give me some encouragement!'

He said with a sigh:

'Then you don't agree that a man may love . . . a woman?'

Madame Arnoux replied:

'If she is free, he marries her; if she belongs to another, he leaves her alone.'

'Then happiness is unattainable?'

'No. But it is never to be found in falsehood, anxiety, and remorse.'

'What does that matter, if it affords sublime joys?'

'The price of the experience is too high.'

He tried irony as a weapon.

'So virtue is nothing but cowardice?'

'I should prefer to call it perspicacity. Even for women who forget duty or religion, mere common sense may be enough. Selfishness makes a solid foundation for good behaviour.'

'Oh, what a collection of middle-class maxims!'

'But I don't claim to be a great lady.'

At that moment the little boy ran into the room.

'Mamma, are you coming down to dinner?'

'Yes, in a minute.'

Frédéric got up; at the same time Marthe appeared.

He could not make up his mind to go; and with a gaze full of entreaty he said:

'Then those women you were speaking of are utterly heartless?'

'No, but they are deaf when necessary.'

And she stood there, in the doorway of her room, with her two children at her sides. He bowed without a word. She acknowledged his bow in silence.

His first reaction was one of infinite stupefaction. This method of making him understand the futility of his hopes completely crushed him. He felt as doomed as a man who has fallen into a chasm where he knows that no help will come and he is going to die.

He went on walking, at random, seeing nothing; he tripped over stones, he lost his way. A noise of clogs sounded close by; it was the workers leaving the foundry. Then he realized where he was.

On the horizon the lamps of the railway drew a line of fire. He arrived just as a train was leaving, allowed himself to be pushed into a carriage, and fell asleep.

An hour later, on the boulevards, the gaiety of Paris in the evening suddenly banished his journey into a past which was already remote. He decided to be strong-minded, and soothed his wounded heart by finding insulting descriptions for Madame Arnoux.

'She's a fool, a goose, a beast, let's forget about her.'

When he returned home he found in his study an eight-page letter on glossy blue paper, signed with the initials 'R.A.'

It began with some friendly reproaches:

'What has become of you, my dear? I'm bored.'

But the handwriting was so abominable that Frédéric was going to throw the whole letter away when he caught sight of a postscript:

'I'm counting on you tomorrow to take me to the races.'

What was the meaning of this? Was it another of the Marshal's tricks? But a woman doesn't make a fool of the same man twice for no reason at all; and, his curiosity aroused, he read the letter again carefully.

Frédéric made out the words: 'Misunderstanding . . . taken the wrong turning . . . disillusionment . . . Poor children that we are! . . . Like two rivers meeting . . .' and so on.

This style differed from the courtesan's usual language. What change could have occurred?

He held the pages between his fingers for a long time. They smelt of iris; and there was something about the shape of the letters and the uneven spacing of the lines that disturbed him, like an irregularity of dress.

'Why, shouldn't I go?' he said to himself at last. 'But what if Madame Arnoux found out? Oh, let her find out! So much the better! And I hope it makes her jealous – that will be my revenge!'

IV

THE Marshal was ready and waiting for him.

'You're a darling!' she said, gazing at him with her pretty eyes, which looked at once gay and tender.

When she had tied the ribbons of her hood, she sat down on the divan and remained silent.

'Shall we go?' asked Frédéric.

She looked at the clock.

'Oh, no! Not before half past one!' she said, as if she had inwardly fixed this limit to her indecision.

At last the half-hour struck.

'Well, *andiamo, caro mio*!'

She gave a final touch to her hair, and left instructions with Delphine.

'Is Madame coming back for dinner?'

'Why should we? We'll have dinner together somewhere – at the Café Anglais, or anywhere you like.'

'All right.'

Her little dogs were yelping around her.

'We can take them with us, can't we?'

Frédéric carried them himself to the carriage, which was a hired berlin with two horses and a postilion; he had placed his own servant on the seat behind. The Marshal seemed satisfied with his attentions; then, as soon as she had taken her seat, she asked him if he had been to see Arnoux lately.

'Not for a month,' said Frédéric.

'I met him the day before yesterday, and he was going to come today. But he's in all sorts of difficulties, another lawsuit, I don't know what. He's such an odd man!'

'Yes, very odd.'

Frédéric added casually:

'Incidentally, do you still see anything of . . . what's his name? . . . that fellow who used to be a singer . . . Delmar?'

She replied curtly:

'No! That's finished!'

So there was no doubt about their estrangement. This gave hope to Frédéric.

They drove down through the Bréda district at a walking-pace; as it was Sunday, the streets were empty, and householders' faces could be seen behind the windows. The carriage began to move faster; the noise of the wheels made the passers-by turn round; the folded leather hood shone, the servant drew himself up, and the two dogs sitting next to one another looked like two ermine muffs on the cushions. Frédéric gave himself up to the rocking of the springs. The Marshal smilingly turned her head right and left.

Her hat of pearly straw was trimmed with black lace. The hood of her burnous fluttered in the breeze; and she sheltered from the sun under a parasol of lilac satin, rising to a point in the middle like a pagoda.

'What sweet little fingers!' said Frédéric, gently taking her free hand, the left hand, which wore a gold bracelet in the form of a curb-chain.

'Why, that's pretty. Where did you get it?'

'Oh, I've had it a long time,' said the Marshal.

The young man made no comment on this hypocritical reply. He preferred to 'make the most of the opportunity'. And, keeping hold of her wrist, he pressed his lips to it, between the glove and the sleeve.

'Stop it, or somebody'll see us!'

'Well, what does it matter?'

After the Place de la Concorde they drove along the Quai de la Conférence and the Quai de Billy, where there was a cedar in a garden. Rosanette thought that Lebanon was in China; she laughed at her own ignorance and asked Frédéric to give her some lessons in geography. Then, leaving the Trocadéro on their right, they crossed the Pont d'Iéna, and finally came to a stop in the middle of the Champ de Mars, near some other carriages which were already drawn up in the Hippodrome.

The grassy slopes were crowded with humble folk. Some on-lookers could be seen on the balcony of the École Militaire; and the two pavilions outside the paddock, the two stands inside, and a third in front of the royal box, were filled with a smartly dressed crowd whose behaviour bore witness to the reverence they felt for this novel amusement. The racing set was more select at that time and less vulgar in appearance; it was the period of trouser-straps, velvet collars, and white gloves. The women wore brightly coloured dresses with long waists, and, sitting on the tiered seats in the stands, they looked like great banks of flowers, flecked with black here and there by the dark clothes of the men. But all eyes were turned towards the famous Algerian, Bou-Maza,[27] who was sitting im-passively between two staff officers in one of the private stands. The Jockey Club's stand was exclusively occupied by solemn-faced gentlemen.

The more enthusiastic spectators had stationed themselves down below, next to the course, which was protected by two lines of posts linked by ropes. Inside the huge oval formed by this track, liquorice-water vendors were shaking their rattles, while other hawkers were selling programmes and cigars; there was a vast buzz of noise, and policemen kept walking to and fro. Then a bell hanging from a post covered with numbers suddenly rang. Five horses appeared, and everybody went back to the stands.

In the meantime, some big clouds came rolling up, touching the tops of the elm-trees opposite. Rosanette was afraid it was going to rain.

'I've got some umbrellas,' said Frédéric, 'and everything we need to keep us happy,' he added, opening the boot, which contained a hamper of food.

'Bravo! We understand each other.'

'And we're going to understand each other, even better, aren't we?'

'Perhaps,' she said, blushing.

The jockeys, in silk jackets, were trying to keep their horses in line, reining them in with both hands. Somebody dropped a red flag. Then all five, bending over their horses' manes, shot away. At first they remained bunched together in a single mass, but this soon spread out, and then broke up; half-way round the first lap, the jockey in the yellow jacket nearly fell; for a long time Filly and Tibi were neck and neck; then Tom Thumb took the lead; but Clubstick, who had been behind ever since the start, caught them up and came in first, beating Sir Charles by two lengths. This was a surprise; the crowd shouted and the wooden stands shook with their stamping.

'What fun this is!' said the Marshal. 'I adore you, darling!'

Frédéric no longer had any doubts about his good fortune; Rosanette's last words confirmed it.

A hundred yards away, a lady appeared in a victoria. She leant out of the window, then drew back quickly; this happened several times, but Frédéric could not make out her face. A suspicion took hold of him: it seemed to him that it was Madame Arnoux. But that was impossible! Why should she have come?

He got out of the carriage, under the pretext of strolling round the paddock.

'You're not very gallant,' said Rosanette.

He took no notice and went forward. The victoria, wheeling round, moved off at a trot.

At the very same moment Frédéric was buttonholed by Cisy.

'Hullo, my dear fellow! How are you? Hussonnet's over there. I say, listen here!'

Frédéric tried to get away to catch up with the victoria. The Marshal beckoned him to come back to her. Cisy caught sight of her, and insisted on going to greet her.

Since he had come out of mourning for his grandmother, he had begun to fulfil his ideal, and was succeeding in 'acquiring tone'. With his tartan waistcoat, his short coat, the big tassels on his shoes, and the admission ticket in his hat-band, nothing, in fact, was missing from what he himself called his *chic*, the *chic* of an Anglomaniac and a musketeer. He began by complaining of the Champ de Mars, which he described as an execrable race-course, then spoke of the Chantilly races and the tricks people got up to there, swore that he could drink twelve glasses of champagne during the twelve strokes of midnight, suggested a bet on it with the Marshal, and gently stroked her two dogs. Leaning on the carriage door with his other elbow, he went on talking nonsense, with the knob of his stick pressed against his mouth, his legs apart, and his bottom sticking out. Frédéric stood beside him, smoking and trying to find out what had become of the victoria.

The bell rang and Cisy made off, much to the relief of Rosanette, who said that she found him a bore.

There was nothing remarkable about the second race, nor about the third, apart from a man who was carried off on a stretcher. The fourth, in which eight horses competed for the City Stakes, was more interesting.

The spectators in the stands had climbed on to the benches. The others, standing in their carriages, followed the jockeys' manoeuvres through field-glasses; they could be seen as red, yellow, blue, and white dots moving past the crowd which lined the whole circuit of the Hippodrome. At a distance their speed did not appear to be exceptional; at the far end of the Champ de Mars, they even seemed to slow down, so that they advanced only by a sort of gliding motion in which the horses touched the ground with their bellies without bending their outstretched legs. However, coming back quickly, they increased in size; they cut the air as they passed; the earth shook; pebbles flew; the wind, blowing into the jockeys' jackets, puffed them out like sails; and they lashed their horses with their whips as they strained towards the winning-post. The numbers were taken down; another went up; and, to the sound of applause, the winning horse dragged itself to the paddock, covered in sweat, with its knees rigid and its head down, while its rider held his sides as if he were dying in his saddle.

A dispute held up the start of the last race. The crowd grew bored and broke up. Groups of men chatted together at the foot of the stands. The conversation was broad; and a few society ladies went off, scandalized by the proximity of light women.

There were also some dance-hall stars and boulevard actresses there; and it was not the most beautiful among them who received the greatest homage. Old Georgine Aubert, whom some vaude-villist once called the Louis XI of prostitution, horribly painted, and uttering a sort of grumbling laugh every now and then, lay stretched out in her long barouche, covered with a sable tippet as if it were mid-winter. Madame de Remoussot, whose lawsuit had put her in the public eye, sat in state on the box of a break, in the company of a party of Americans. And Thérèse Bachelu, looking as she always did like a Gothic virgin, occupied, together with her twelve flounces, the whole interior of a carriage, whose apron had been replaced by a flowerholder full of roses. The Marshal was jealous of these notabilities; in order to attract attention, she started making grandiloquent gestures and talking very loud.

Some gentlemen recognized her and waved to her. She acknowledged their greetings and told Frédéric their names. They were all counts, viscounts, dukes, and marquesses; and he puffed himself up, for every man's eyes expressed a certain respect for his good fortune.

Cisy, who was surrounded by a circle of elderly men, looked just as pleased with himself. They were smiling above their cravats, as if they regarded him as a joke; finally he shook hands with the oldest of them and came towards the Marshal.

She was eating a slice of *foie gras* with a great show of hunger. Frédéric, who had a bottle of wine on his knees, was dutifully imitating her.

The victoria reappeared; it was Madame Arnoux. She turned extraordinarily pale.

'Give me some champagne!' said Rosanette.

And, raising her glass as high as she could, she shouted:

'Hi there! Here's a health to decent women, and my protector's wife!'

There were roars of laughter all round her; the victoria disappeared. Frédéric pulled at her dress, on the point of losing his temper. But Cisy was there, in the same position as before; and with extraordinary self-assurance he invited Rosanette to dinner that very evening.

'Out of the question!' she replied. 'We're going to the Café Anglais together.'

Frédéric remained silent, as if he had heard nothing, and Cisy left the Marshal looking disappointed.

While he had been leaning against the right-hand door, talking to her, Hussonnet had come up on the left, and, catching the words 'Café Anglais', said:

'That's a nice place! What if we went there for a bite?'

'Just as you like,' said Frédéric, who, slumped in a corner of the berlin, was watching the victoria disappear over the horizon. He felt that something irreparable had just happened, and that he had lost his great love. And the other was there beside him, the gay, easy love! Tired out, full of contradictory desires, and no longer even knowing what he wanted, he felt an infinite melancholy, a longing to die.

A loud din of footsteps and voices made him raise his head; some street-urchins, climbing over the ropes lining the track, were coming to have a look at the stands; the crowd was moving away. A few drops of rain fell. The block of carriages grew bigger. Hussonnet had disappeared.

'Ah! Well, so much the better,' said Frédéric.

'You mean you'd rather be alone?' said the Marshal, putting her hand on his.

Then, with a flashing of brass and steel, there passed before them a splendid landau drawn by four horses, and driven by a couple of jockeys in velvet jackets with gold fringes. Madame Dambreuse was sitting beside her husband, and Martinon on the seat opposite; all three looked astonished.

'They've recognized me!' said Frédéric to himself.

Rosanette wanted to stop, to get a better view of the parade. But Madame Arnoux might reappear. He shouted to the postilion:

'Hurry up! Hurry up! Drive off!'

And the berlin made off in the direction of the Champs-Élysées in the midst of the other carriages – barouches, britzkas, wurts, tandems, tilburies, dog-carts, covered waggonettes with leather curtains full of singing workmen out on the spree, and go-carts carefully driven by fathers of families. There were crowded victorias in which some young man would be sitting on the feet of other passengers, with his legs dangling over the side. Big broughams with cloth-covered seats carried dozing dowagers; and occasionally a magnificent high-stepper went by, drawing a post-chaise as simple and smart as a dandy's tail-coat. In the meantime the downpour grew heavier. Umbrellas, parasols, and mackintoshes were brought out; shouts of 'Good afternoon!' – 'How are you keeping?' – 'Fine!' – 'Not so bad!' – 'See you later!' were exchanged from a distance; and face followed face with the rapidity of magic-lantern slides. Frédéric and Rosanette said nothing to each other, dazed as it were by the sight of all these carriage wheels continually revolving beside them.

Now and then the files of carriages, packed too closely together, would all stop at the same time in several lines. Forced to remain for a while side by side, everybody stared at his neighbour. From above emblazoned door-panels indifferent glances were cast at the crowd; eyes full of envy gleamed in the depths of cabs; sneering smiles replied to heads held arrogantly high; gaping mouths expressed stupid admiration; and here and there some pedestrian in the middle of the road would suddenly leap backwards to avoid a rider galloping between the carriages before succeeding in making his escape. Then everything moved off again; the coachmen slack-ened the reins and lowered their whips; the frisky horses, shaking their bits, scattered foam around them, while their damp cruppers and harness steamed in the watery mist. Piercing this haze, the setting sun cast through the Arc de Triomphe, a few feet above the ground, a ray of reddish light which sparkled on the wheel-hubs, the door-handles, the tips of the shafts, and the rings of the axle-trees; and on either side of the great avenue, which resembled a river carrying manes, clothes, and human heads, the trees stood glistening with rain, like two green walls. The blue sky above, reappearing here and there, was as soft as satin.

Then Frédéric remembered those days, already distant, when he had longed for the ineffable joy of sitting in one of these carriages, next to one of these women. He now possessed that joy, and he was none the happier.

The rain had stopped. The passers-by who had taken refuge

between the pillars of the Garde-Meuble went on their way. Strollers in the Rue Royale returned towards the boulevard. In front of the Foreign Ministry a row of idlers stood on the steps.

Opposite the Chinese Baths, the berlin slowed down on account of some holes in the road. A man in a nut-brown overcoat was walking along the edge of the pavement. A splash of mud, spurting up from under the springs, plastered itself across his back. The man swung round in a fury. Frédéric turned pale; he had recognized Deslauriers.

At the door of the Café Anglais he dismissed the carriage. Rosanette went upstairs ahead of him while he paid the postilion.

He caught up with her on the stairs, talking to a gentleman. Frédéric took her arm. But in the middle of the corridor a second lordling stopped her.

'Go on,' she said. 'I'll be with you in a minute.'

And he went into the private room by himself. Through the two open windows he could see people in the windows of the houses opposite. Broad puddles quivered like watered silk on the drying asphalt, and a magnolia on the edge of the balcony filled the room with its perfume. This scent and the cool of the evening soothed his nerves; and he sank on to the red divan under the mirror.

Rosanette came in; and, kissing him on the forehead, she said:

'Is my poor darling upset?'

'Perhaps,' he replied.

'You aren't the only one, you know!'

This meant: 'Let's both forget our troubles in a common happiness!'

Then she put a flower petal between her lips, and held it out for him to nibble. There was a lascivious grace, and almost gentleness, about this movement which touched Frédéric.

'Why do you make me unhappy?' he asked, thinking of Madame Arnoux.

'I, make you unhappy?'

And, standing in front of him, she gazed at him, with her eyes half shut and her hands on his shoulders.

All his virtuous wrath sank in a sea of cowardice.

He went on:

'Because you refuse to love me,' and pulled her on to his knee.

She offered no resistance; he put his arms round her waist; the rustling of her silk dress set his senses on fire.

'Where are they?' said Hussonnet's voice in the corridor.

The Marshal rose abruptly and went and stood at the other end of the room, with her back to the door.

She asked for some oysters, and they sat down to table.

Hussonnet was not at all amusing. Forced to write every day on all sorts of subjects, to read countless newspapers, to listen to a great many arguments, and to produce startling paradoxes, he had ended up by losing all sense of reality, blinding himself with his own damp squibs. The difficulties of what had once been an easy life kept him in a state of perpetual agitation; and his literary impotence, which he refused to acknowledge to himself, made him peevish and sarcastic. Talking about a new ballet called *Ozaï*, he made a violent attack on dancing, and, talking about dancing, on the Opéra; then, talking about the Opéra, on the actors of the Italiens, who had now been replaced by a company of Spanish players, 'as if we hadn't had our fill of the Castiles!' Frédéric, with his romantic love of Spain, was shocked by this remark; and to change the subject he asked about the Collège de France, from which Edgar Quinet and Mickiewicz had just been dismissed.[28] But Hussonnet, who admired Monsieur de Maistre, declared himself in favour of Authority and Idealism. He kept on expressing doubt of the best-proved facts, denying history, and disputing the most obvious truths – even exclaiming at the mention of geometry: 'What utter nonsense that is!' All this was interlarded with imitations of actors, Sainville being his chief model.

These absurdities bored Frédéric. He made an impatient movement and caught one of the dogs under the table with his foot.

They both started barking in an odious manner.

'You ought to have them taken home,' he said sharply.

Rosanette did not trust anybody.

He turned to the Bohemian:

'Come along, Hussonnet, be a good fellow!'

'Oh, yes,' she said. 'That would be sweet of you!'

Hussonnet went off without waiting to be pressed.

How was he going to be rewarded for this service? The question did not occur to Frédéric. He was even beginning to congratulate himself on their *tête-à-tête* when a waiter came in.

'Madame, somebody's asking for you.'

'What! Again?'

'All the same, I must go and see,' said Rosanette.

He needed her, longed for her. Her disappearance struck him as a breach of faith, almost an outrage. What was she after? Was it not enough for her that she had insulted Madame Arnoux? So much the worse for the latter, in any case! He hated all women now; and tears choked him, for his love had been misunderstood and his lust cheated.

The Marshal came in again, accompanied by Cisy.

'I've invited this gentleman,' she said. 'That was right, wasn't it?'

'Why, of course.'

With an agonized smile Frédéric motioned to Cisy to sit down.

The Marshal started looking through the menu, stopping at all the peculiar names.

'What if we had a dish of rabbit *à la Richelieu* and a pudding *à la d'Orléans*?'

'Oh, no Orléans!' exclaimed Cisy, who was a Legitimist and thought he was making a joke.

'Would you prefer a turbot *à la Chambord*?' she went on.

These courtesies irritated Frédéric.

The Marshal decided on a plain steak, crayfish, truffles, a pineapple salad, and vanilla ices.

'After that, we'll see. In the meantime, get on with it. Oh, I was forgetting – bring me a sausage, but without garlic!'

And she called the waiter 'young man', struck her glass with her knife, and threw pellets of bread up to the ceiling. She wanted to drink some burgundy straight away.

'You don't drink burgundy at the beginning of a meal,' said Frédéric.

According to the viscount this was sometimes done.

'Oh, no! Never!'

'Yes, it is, I assure you!'

'There, you see?'

The look with which she accompanied this phrase signified: 'He's a rich man: you should listen to him.'

Meanwhile the door kept opening every minute, the waiters yelped, and somebody strummed a waltz on a dreadful piano in the next room. After talking about the races, they went on to discuss riding and the two rival systems. Cisy supported Baucher, Frédéric the Comte d'Aure, until Rosanette shrugged her shoulders and said:

'Oh, that's enough! He knows more about it than you do.'

She was biting into a pomegranate, with her elbow on the table; the flames of the candelabra in front of her flickered in the draught, and this white light steeped her skin with mother-of-pearl hues, tinged her eyelids with pink, and made her eyeballs glow; the redness of the fruit blended with the crimson of her lips; her slender nostrils quivered; and there was something insolent, intoxicated, and indefinable about her whole person which exasperated Frédéric, and yet filled his heart with mad desires.

Then she asked in a calm voice who owned that big landau with the men in brown livery.

'The Comtesse Dambreuse,' replied Cisy.

'They're very rich, aren't they?'

'Oh, very! Although Madame Dambreuse, who used to be just plain Mademoiselle Boutron, a prefect's daughter, has only a moderate fortune.'

Her husband, on the other hand, was likely to inherit from several quarters, which Cisy enumerated; seeing a great deal of the Dambreuses, he knew their family history.

To annoy her, Frédéric insisted on contradicting him. He maintained that Madame Dambreuse was a de Boutron, and swore that she was of noble birth.

'I don't care what she is! I'd like to have her carriage!' said the Marshal, leaning back in the armchair.

And the sleeve of her dress, slipping slightly, revealed a bracelet set with three opals on her left wrist.

Frédéric caught sight of it.

'Why, isn't that . . .'

All three looked at one another and blushed.

The door was discreetly opened a little way, and the brim of a hat appeared, followed by Hussonnet's profile.

'Forgive me if I'm disturbing you love-birds!'

Then he stopped in astonishment when he saw that Cisy was there and had taken his place.

Another place was laid; and, as he was ravenously hungry, he picked food at random from the remains of the meal, some meat from a dish, some fruit from a basket, drinking with one hand and helping himself with the other, at the same time telling the story of his mission. He had taken the two bow-wows home. Everything was all right there. He had found the cook with a soldier – an untrue story, invented simply for effect.

The Marshal took her bonnet off the peg. Frédéric rushed over to the bell and called out to the waiter from a distance:

'A carriage!'

'I have mine here,' said the viscount.

'But, Monsieur . . .'

'Really, Monsieur . . .'

And they looked each other in the eye, with pale faces and trembling hands.

Finally the Marshal took Cisy's arm, and pointing to the Bohemian, who was still tucking in, she said:

'Take care of him! He's choking himself. I wouldn't want him to die on account of his kindness to my little dogs.'

The door closed.

'Well?' said Hussonnet.

'Well, what?'

'I thought . . .'

'What did you think?'

'Weren't you . . . ?'

He completed his sentence with a gesture.

'Oh, no! Not on your life!'

Hussonnet did not press the point.

He had a purpose in inviting himself to dinner. His paper, which had changed its name from *L'Art* to *Le Flambard*, with the motto: 'Gunners to your cannon!' was in financial straits; and he wanted to turn it into a weekly review, on his own, without Deslaurier's help. He mentioned the old project once more, and expounded his new plan.

Frédéric, who apparently failed to understand, replied with a few vague remarks. Hussonnet grabbed some cigars from the table, said: 'Good-bye, old fellow', and disappeared.

Frédéric asked for the bill. It was a long one; and the waiter, his napkin tucked under his arm, was waiting for his money when another waiter, a pallid individual who looked like Martinon, came and said to him:

'Beg pardon, but the cashier forgot to charge for the cab.'

'What cab?'

'The one that gentleman took earlier on for the little dogs.'

And the waiter's face grew longer, as if he pitied the poor young man. Frédéric felt like slapping him. He gave the man his twenty francs change as a tip.

'Thank you, my lord!' said the man with the napkin, bowing very low.

Frédéric spent the next day nursing his anger and humiliation. He blamed himself for not having slapped Cisy. As for the Marshal, he swore never to see her again; there were plenty of women just as beautiful; and since money was necessary to possess these women, he would gamble on the Stock Exchange with the price he got for his farm, he would become rich, and he would crush the Marshal and everybody else with his opulence. When evening came he was astonished to find that he had not given a thought to Madame Arnoux.

'So much the better! What's the use?'

Two days later Pellerin came to see him at eight o'clock. He began by admiring the furniture and flattering Frédéric in other ways. Then, all of a sudden, he asked:

'Were you at the races on Sunday?'

'Alas, yes.'

The painter promptly started railing against the anatomy of English horses, and extolling Géricault's horses and the horses of the Parthenon.

'Was Rosanette with you?'

And he skilfully sang her praises.

Frédéric's coldness disconcerted him. He did not know how to bring up the subject of the portrait.

His original intention had been to produce a Titian. But little by little his model's varied colouring had fascinated him; he had worked boldly, piling brushstroke on brushstroke and light on light. Rosanette was delighted at first; then her rendezvous with Delmar had interrupted the sittings and left Pellerin plenty of time to be dazzled by his art. Eventually, as his admiration cooled, he had begun to wonder if his painting was not lacking in grandeur. He had gone to look at the Titians again, seen the distance which separated them from his work, recognized his mistake, and started simplifying his outlines. Next, by blurring them, he had tried to blend the tones of the head with those of the background; this had given solidity to the face, vigour to the shadows; everything seemed firmer. At last the Marshal had come back. She had even permitted herself a few criticisms; the artist had of course persevered. After some angry outbursts against her stupidity, he had admitted to himself that she might be right. Then had begun the period of doubts, of those pangs of uncertainty which result in stomach-ache, insomnia, fever, and self-contempt; he had plucked up the courage to retouch the painting, but his heart was not in it and he felt that his work was bad.

He merely complained that he had been rejected by the Salon and then reproached Frédéric for not coming to see the Marshal's portrait.

'I don't care a damn about the Marshal!'

This declaration emboldened Pellerin.

'Would you believe it, that wretched woman doesn't want the picture now!'

What he failed to say was that he had asked her for three thousand francs. Now the Marshal had not given much thought to the problem of who was going to pay for the portrait, and she had not even mentioned it to Arnoux, preferring to use his money for more urgent things.

'Well, what about Arnoux?' asked Frédéric.

She had referred Pellerin to him. The former picture-dealer had refused to have anything to do with the portrait.

'He maintains that it belongs to Rosanette.'

'He is right, it is hers.'

'What! But she's sent me round to see you!' replied Pellerin.

If he had believed in the excellence of his work, he might not have thought of exploiting it. But a price – especially if it were a large price – would be a rebuff for the critics and an encouragement for himself. To get rid of him, Frédéric politely asked how much he wanted.

The exorbitance of the sum shocked him, and he replied:

'No! Oh, no!'

'But you're her lover, and it was you who commissioned the portrait!'

'I beg your pardon! I merely acted as go-between.'

'But you can't leave me with that on my hands!'

The artist lost his temper.

'I must say, I didn't think you were so grasping.'

'Nor you so mean! Good-bye!'

He had just gone when Sénécal appeared.

Frédéric was startled and felt a twinge of anxiety.

'What's the matter?'

Sénécal told his story.

'On Saturday, about nine o'clock, Madame Arnoux received a

letter summoning her to Paris. As it happened there was nobody there to go and fetch her a carriage from Creil, so she tried to get me to go myself. I refused, because that isn't part of my duties. She went off, and came back on Sunday evening. Yesterday morning Arnoux showed up at the factory. The girl from Bordeaux complained to him. I don't know what there is between them, but he cancelled her fine in front of everybody. We exchanged a few sharp words. To cut a long story short, he paid me off, and here I am!'

Then, pronouncing each word separately, he added:

'For my part, I've no regrets: I've done my duty. All the same, it's all your fault.'

'What do you mean?' exclaimed Frédéric, fearing that Sénécal had guessed his secret.

'I mean that, if it hadn't been for you, I might have done better for myself.'

Frédéric was afflicted with a sort of remorse.

'What can I do for you now?'

Sénécal wanted a job of some sort, a position.

'That's a simple matter, for you. You know so many people, including Monsieur Dambreuse, according to what Deslauriers told me.'

This reminder of Deslauriers annoyed his friend. He was in no hurry to go back to the Dambreuses' house after the encounter on the Champ de Mars.

'I'm not on sufficiently good terms with him to recommend anybody.'

The democrat took this refusal stoically, and, after a moment's silence, remarked:

'I'm sure that all this is due to that girl from Bordeaux and your Madame Arnoux too.'

This word 'your' destroyed what little good-will Frédéric still felt towards him. However, out of courtesy he reached for the key to his desk.

Sénécal forestalled him.

'No, thank you.'

Then, forgetting his own troubles, he started talking about national affairs, the lavish award of decorations on the King's birthday, a change of ministers, contemporary scandals such as the Drouillard and Bénier cases,[29] inveighed against the middle classes, and predicted a revolution.

A Japanese kris hanging on the wall caught his eye. He took it down, tried the handle, and then tossed it on to the sofa with a look of disgust.

'Well, good-bye! I've got to go to Notre-Dame de Lorette.'

'Whatever for?'

'It's the annual memorial service for Godefroy Cavaignac today.[30] There you had a man who died in harness! But everything isn't over yet ... Who knows?'

And Sénécal thrust out his hand.

'We may never see each other again. Good-bye!'

The repetition of his farewell, the frown he gave as he glanced at the dagger, and above all his look of solemn resignation, made Frédéric wonder; but he soon forgot about it.

The same week, his solicitor at Le Havre sent him the price of his farm: a hundred and seventy-four thousand francs. He divided it into two parts, placing one in government securities, and taking the other to a stockbroker to gamble with on the Stock Exchange.

He dined at fashionable restaurants, went to the theatre, and generally tried to amuse himself. Then one day Hussonnet sent him a letter in which he gaily related that the Marshal had dismissed Cisy the day after the races. Frédéric was pleased to hear it, and did not stop to wonder why the Bohemian should have given him this piece of news.

It so happened that he met Cisy three days later. The nobleman put up a bold front, and even invited him to dinner the following Wednesday.

On the morning of that day Frédéric received an official notification in which Monsieur Charles-Jean-Baptiste Oudry informed him that, by virtue of the judgement of the court, he had become the purchaser of a property situated at Belleville belonging to Monsieur Jacques Arnoux, and that he was prepared to pay the price of the sale, amounting to two hundred and twenty-three thousand francs. But the same document revealed that, since the mortgages with which the building was encumbered exceeded the purchase price, Frédéric's claim was null and void.

The whole trouble was that the registration of the mortgage had not been renewed at the right time. Arnoux had undertaken to see to this, and then had forgotten all about it. Frédéric flew into a rage against him, but soon his anger cooled, and he said to himself:

'After all, what of it? If it will help to save him, so much the better! It won't kill me. Let's forget about it.'

But, moving his papers about on his table, he came across Hussonnet's letter, and noticed a postscript which he had overlooked the first time. The Bohemian asked him for five thousand francs, no more and no less, to start his newspaper.

'Oh, that fellow gets on my nerves!'

And he brusquely rejected his request in a laconic note. After that, he got dressed to go to the Maison d'Or.

Cisy introduced his guests, beginning with the most respectable, a portly gentleman with white hair:

'The Marquis Gilbert des Aulnays, my godfather. Monsieur Anselme de Forchambeaux,' he went on: this was a slim, fair-haired young man who was already going bald. Then, pointing to an unpretentious-looking man of about forty, he continued:

'My cousin, Joseph Boffreu; and this is my old tutor Monsieur Vezou.' The latter was a cross between a carter and a seminarist, with bushy sidewhiskers and a long frock-coat fastened at the bottom with a single button, so that it crossed his chest like a shawl.

Cisy was expecting another guest, the Baron de Comaing, 'who may be coming, though it isn't certain.' He kept going out and seemed uneasy; finally, at eight o'clock, they moved into a splendidly lit room which was too big for the number of guests. Cisy had chosen it on purpose, out of ostentation.

A silver-gilt centre-piece, loaded with flowers and fruit, occupied the middle of the table, which was covered with silver dishes in the old French style, surrounded by hors-d'œuvre dishes containing spices and seasoning; at regular intervals there stood pitchers of iced *vin rosé*; and five glasses of different heights were lined up in front of every plate, together with a variety of ingenious eating utensils whose precise purpose was a mystery. For the first course alone, there was a sturgeon's head drenched in champagne, a York ham cooked in tokay, thrushes *au gratin*, roast quail, a *vol-au-vent Béchamel*, a *sauté* of red-legged partridges, and, flanking all this, stringed potatoes mixed with truffles. The room, which was hung with red damask, was lit by a chandelier and some candelabra. Four servants in tail-coats stood behind the morocco-leather armchairs. This sight drew cries of admiration from the guests, particularly from the tutor.

'Upon my word, our host has done us proud! This is too magnificent for words!'

'This?' said the Vicomte de Cisy. 'Oh, come now!'

And after the first spoonful he said:

'Well, old des Aulnays, have you been to see *Père et Portier* at the Palais-Royal?'

'You know perfectly well I haven't the time!' replied the marquis.

His mornings were taken up by a course in forestry, his evenings by the Agricultural Club, and his afternoons by visits to factories which manufactured farming implements. Spending three quarters of the year in Saintonge, he took advantage of his stays in the capital to improve his knowledge; and his broad-brimmed hat, which he put on a side-table, was full of pamphlets.

Then Cisy, noticing that Monsieur Forchambeaux was refusing wine, said:

'Drink up, dammit! You're not showing much spirit for your last meal as a bachelor!'

At these words everybody bowed and congratulated him.

'The young lady,' said the tutor, 'is charming, I'm sure.'

'She is indeed,' exclaimed Cisy. 'All the same, he's making a mistake; marriage is just stupid.'

'You speak lightly, my friend,' replied Monsieur des Aulnays, while his eyes filled with tears at the memory of his deceased spouse.

And Forchambeaux repeated several times with a chuckle:

'You'll come to it yourself, you'll come to it.'

Cisy denied it. He preferred to enjoy himself, 'to be Regency'. He said that he intended to learn foot-boxing, so as to visit the low haunts of the Cité like Prince Rodolphe in *Les Mystères de Paris*, pulled a short clay pipe out of his pocket, bullied the servants, drank to excess, and, in order to impress the company, criticized all the dishes. He even sent back the truffles, and the tutor, who had been enjoying them, said cravenly:

'They're not as good as your grandmother's *œufs à la neige*.'

Then he went back to his conversation with his neighbour the agriculturist, who remarked that living in the country offered many advantages, not the least of which was the opportunity to bring up one's daughters with simple tastes. The tutor applauded his opinions and flattered him, for he imagined that the marquis had some

221

influence on his former pupil, whose financial adviser he secretly aspired to become.

Frédéric had arrived full of ill-feeling towards Cisy; then his stupidity had disarmed him. But his gestures, his face, the whole of his person reminded him of the Café Anglais dinner and annoyed him more and more; and he lent a ready ear to the disrespectful remarks whispered by Cousin Joseph, a good fellow without any money, who liked hunting and speculated on the Stock Exchange. Cisy, by way of a joke, called him 'swindler' several times, then suddenly exclaimed:

'Ah! The baron!'

There entered a fellow of thirty with a somewhat coarse face, an athletic build, his hat over one ear, and a flower in his buttonhole. He was the viscount's ideal. Cisy was delighted that he had come; and, inspired by his presence, he even attempted a pun, for as a *coq de bruyère* was being passed round he remarked:

'This is the best of La Bruyère's characters!'

After that he put a whole series of questions to Monsieur de Comaing about people unknown to the company; then, as if an idea had suddenly occurred to him, he blurted out:

'I say! Did you remember me?'

The other shrugged his shoulders.

'You're not old enough, my boy! It's out of the question.'

Cisy had asked him to put him up for his club. The baron, presumably taking pity on his wounded pride, added:

'Oh, I was forgetting. Congratulations on your bet, my dear fellow!'

'What bet?'

'The one you made at the races, that you'd spend that very night with that lady.'

Frédéric felt as if he had been struck with a whip. But he was promptly calmed by the sight of Cisy's crestfallen face.

The fact was that the following morning the Marshal had been regretting the whole affair when Arnoux, her first lover, her man, had called to see her. The two of them had made it clear to the viscount that he was 'in the way', and he had been unceremoniously turned out of the house.

He pretended not to have heard. The baron added:

'How is dear Rose keeping, anyway? Are her legs still as pretty as ever?' – thus showing that he knew her intimately.

Frédéric was annoyed by this revelation.

'There's nothing to blush about,' the baron went on. 'She's a good catch.'

Cisy clicked his tongue.

'Pooh! Not as good as all that.'

'Oh?'

'Good heavens, no! In the first place, I personally don't see anything remarkable in her; and then you can pick up any number of women just like her, because after all . . . she's for sale.'

'Not to everybody,' snapped Frédéric.

'He thinks he's different from the others!' exclaimed Cisy. 'What a joke!'

A ripple of laughter went round the table.

Frédéric felt stifled by the pounding of his heart. He swallowed two glasses of water, one after the other.

The baron had retained pleasant memories of Rosanette.

'Is she still with that fellow Arnoux?'

'I haven't the faintest idea,' said Cisy. 'I don't know that gentleman.'

All the same, he expressed the opinion that he was a swindler of sorts.

'Wait a moment!' exclaimed Frédéric.

'But everybody knows that. He's even been taken to court.'

'That's a lie!'

Frédéric started defending Arnoux. He guaranteed his honesty, ended up by believing in it, and invented facts and figures to prove it. The viscount, full of resentment and drunk into the bargain, stuck to his assertions so obstinately that Frédéric asked him solemnly:

'Are you trying to offend me, Monsieur?'

And he looked at him with his eyes glowing as fiercely as his cigar.

'Oh, not in the least. I'll even grant you that he's got one good thing: his wife.'

'Do you know her?'

'Good Lord, yes! Everybody knows Sophie Arnoux!'

'What did you say?'

Cisy, who had got to his feet, repeated in a stammering voice:

'Everybody knows Sophie Arnoux!'

'Shut up! She isn't like the women you go around with!'

'I should hope not! I've got better taste.'

Frédéric threw his plate at his face.

It flew across the table like a flash of lightning, knocked over two bottles, smashed a fruit-dish, broke into three pieces against the centre-piece, and hit the viscount in the stomach.

Everybody stood up to hold Frédéric back. He struggled and shouted in a sort of frenzy; Monsieur des Aulnays kept saying:

'Calm yourself! Come now, my dear boy!'

'But this is awful!' exclaimed the tutor.

Forchambeaux, as yellow as the plums, was trembling; Joseph was roaring with laughter; the waiters were mopping up the wine and picking up the broken crockery from the floor; and the baron went and shut the window, for in spite of the noise of the traffic, the din might have been heard on the boulevard.

As everybody had been talking at once when the plate had been thrown, it was impossible to discover the cause of the attack, whether it was in connexion with Arnoux, Madame Arnoux, Rosanette, or somebody else. What was indisputable was Frédéric's unspeakable savagery; he positively refused to express the slightest regret for his behaviour.

Monsieur des Aulnays tried to calm him down, as did Cousin Joseph, the tutor, and even Forchambeaux. Meanwhile the baron was comforting Cisy, who, giving way to a nervous weakness, had burst into tears. Frédéric, on the other hand, was growing angrier; and things would probably have remained like that until morning if the baron, to put an end to it all, had not said:

'The viscount, Monsieur, will send you his seconds tomorrow.'

'At what time?'

'At midday, if that suits you.'

'Perfectly, Monsieur.'

Out in the street, Frédéric took a deep breath. He had held his emotions in check far too long. Now at last he had given free rein to them; and he felt a sort of manly pride, a surge of inner strength which intoxicated him. He needed two seconds. The first he thought of was Regimbart; and he promptly made his way towards a tavern in the Rue Saint-Denis. The shutters were down, but there was a light shining through a pane of glass above the door. It opened, and he went in, bending very low under the porch.

A candle on the edge of the bar lit up the deserted room. All the stools had been placed on the tables, with their legs in the air. The proprietor and his wife were having supper with the waiter in the corner by the kitchen; and Regimbart, with his hat on, was sharing their meal, and indeed getting in the way of the waiter, who was forced to turn slightly to one side at every mouthful. Frédéric gave him a brief account of the affair and asked for his help. The Citizen made no reply at first; he rolled his eyes, looked as if he were thinking, walked up and down the room several times, and finally said:

'Yes, gladly!'

And his face lit up with a murderous smile when he learnt that Frédéric's opponent was a nobleman.

'We'll give him something to remember us by, never fear! First of all . . . with your sword . . .'

'But perhaps,' protested Frédéric, 'I'm not entitled . . .'

'I tell you you've got to choose swords!' snapped the Citizen. 'Do you know how to use one?'

'A little.'

'Oh, a little! That's what they all say! And they've all got this passion for fencing! What's the use of a fencing-school, I'd like to know? Listen to me: keep your distance, enclose yourself in circles, and give ground, give ground! It's perfectly permissible. Tire him out! Then lunge straight at him. And above all, no tricks, no Fougère thrusts. No, just ordinary lunges: one, two, and disengage. Look, like this, turning your wrist as if you were opening a lock. Père Vauthier, give me your stick. No, this will do.'

He seized the rod which was used for lighting the gas, curved his left arm, bent his right, and started thrusting at the partition. He stamped his feet, getting more and more excited, and even pretended to be encountering difficulties. All the time he kept on shouting: 'You understand? You follow?' while his huge shadow moved across the wall so that his hat seemed to touch the ceiling. Every now and then the proprietor said: 'Bravo! Jolly good!' His wife too, although somewhat nervous, was equally impressed; while Théodore, who was an old soldier and a fervent admirer of Monsieur Regimbart, was rooted to his seat in awe.

Early the next day, Frédéric hurried round to Dussardier's shop. After going through a succession of rooms, all full of materials arranged on shelves or stretched across tables, with shawls draped over mushroom-shaped stands, he caught sight of Dussardier standing writing at a desk, surrounded by ledgers, in a sort of cage. The good fellow immediately dropped his work.

The seconds arrived at noon. Frédéric considered it good form not to be present at the discussion.

The baron and Monsieur Joseph declared that they would be satisfied with the most perfunctory apology. But Regimbart, who had made it a principle of his never to give way, and who was determined to defend Arnoux's honour – for Frédéric had not mentioned anything else – insisted on an apology from the viscount. Monsieur de Comaing was shocked by this presumptuous demand. The Citizen would not give an inch. All conciliation becoming impossible, it was decided that the duel should take place.

Further difficulties arose, for Cisy, who was the insulted party, was legally entitled to the choice of weapons. But Regimbart maintained that by sending the challenge he automatically became the aggressor. Cisy's seconds protested that a slap was the most offensive insult there could be. The Citizen quibbled over their words, arguing that a blow with a plate was not a slap. Finally they decided to refer the problem to the military; and they went out to consult the officers at some barracks or other.

They stopped at the barracks on the Quai d'Orsay. Monsieur de Comaing accosted a couple of captains and explained the dispute to them.

The captains could not make head or tail of the story, especially as it was complicated by incidental remarks from the Citizen. In short, they advised the gentlemen to draw up a statement of the facts; after that they would make their decision. The seconds accordingly moved to a café; and, for the sake of greater discretion, they even referred to Cisy as H. and Frédéric as K.

Then they returned to the barracks, The officers had gone out. When they reappeared they declared that the choice of weapons clearly belonged to Monsieur H. They all went back to Cisy's house. Regimbart and Dussardier stayed outside in the street.

On hearing the seconds' report, Cisy was so upset that he had it repeated to him several times; and when Monsieur de Comaing came to Regimbart's demands he murmured: 'All the same', feeling secretly tempted to grant them. Then he sank into an armchair and declared that he would not fight.

'Eh? What's that?' said the baron.

Then Cisy launched out into an incoherent flood of words. He wanted to fight with blunderbusses, at point-blank range, or with a single pistol.

'Or else we could put arsenic in a glass, and draw lots for it. That's done sometimes; I've read about it.'

The baron, who was not a patient man, cut him short.

'Those gentlemen are waiting for your answer. Dammit all, this is indecent. Come along now, what do you choose? Swords?'

The viscount answered yes with a nod of the head, and the encounter was fixed for the following day, at the Porte Maillot, at seven o'clock sharp.

Dussardier had to return to his shop, so Regimbart went to tell Frédéric.

He had been left all day without news, and his impatience had become unbearable.

'So much the better!' he exclaimed.

The Citizen was pleased with this show of spirit.

'Would you believe it? They wanted us to apologize! Nothing much, just one word. But I sent them off with a flea in their ear! That was right, wasn't it?'

'Yes, of course,' said Frédéric, thinking to himself that he would have done better to choose a different second.

Then, when he was alone, he said to himself several times aloud:

'I'm going to fight. I'm actually going to fight. How peculiar!'

Walking up and down his room, he noticed as he passed his mirror that he was pale.

'Does that mean that I'm afraid?'

A dreadful anguish gripped him at the thought that he might lose his nerve on the duelling-ground.

'But what if I were killed? My father died in the same way. Yes, I'm going to be killed.'

And suddenly he pictured his mother in a black dress; a succession of confused images unfolded in his mind. His own cowardice infuriated him. He was seized with a fit of bravado, a thirst for blood. He would have held his ground against a whole battalion. When this fever had left him he discovered to his joy that he was unshakable. To distract his mind he went to the Opéra, where they were giving a ballet. He listened to the music, quizzed the dancers, and drank a glass of punch in the interval. But when he returned home, and saw his study and his furniture, possibly for the last time, he felt a momentary weakness.

He went down into his garden. The stars were shining. He gazed at them. The thought of fighting for a woman magnified him and elevated him in his own eyes. Then he went calmly to bed.

This was not the case with Cisy. After the baron's departure, Joseph had tried to raise his spirits, and, as this had no effect on the viscount, he remarked:

'You know, old fellow, if you want to drop the whole thing, I could go and say so.'

Cisy did not dare to reply 'Please do,' but he felt annoyed with his cousin for not doing him this service without talking about it.

He hoped that Frédéric would die of a stroke during the night, or that an insurrection might break out and that there would be enough barricades in the streets the next day to block all the approaches to the Bois de Boulogne; or that some accident would prevent one of the seconds from turning up, for without seconds the duel could not take place. He longed to escape by taking an express train in no matter what direction. He was sorry that he had not studied medicine, so that he could take something which, without endangering his life, would make people think he was dead. He even got to the point of wanting to be seriously ill.

To obtain help and advice he sent for Monsieur des Aulnays. The good man had gone to Saintonge, in response to a message that one of his daughters was ill. This struck Cisy as a bad omen. Luckily Monsieur Vezou, his old tutor, came to see him, and he promptly opened his heart to him.

'What am I to do, in heaven's name? What am I to do?'

'If I were you, Monsieur le Comte, I should hire a market porter to give him a thrashing.'

'But he would still know who was behind it,' replied Cisy.

From time to time he uttered a groan, and then said:

'But has anybody any right to fight a duel?'

'It's a relic of barbarism, and there's nothing to be done about it.'

Out of kindness the tutor invited himself to dinner. His pupil ate nothing, and after the meal felt the need to go for a stroll.

As they were passing a church he said:

'Supposing we went in for a moment . . . just to have a look?'

Monsieur Vezou asked for nothing better, and even offered him some holy water.

It was the month of May; the altar was covered with flowers; voices were singing and the organ thundering. But Cisy found it impossible to pray; the pomp of religion made him think of funerals; he imagined he could hear the strains of the *De Profundis*.

'Let's go! I don't feel well.'

They spent the whole night playing cards. The viscount did his best to lose, in order to keep away bad luck – a policy which Monsieur Vezou turned to good advantage. At last, towards dawn, Cisy, utterly exhausted, let his head sink on to the card-table and fell into a sleep full of unpleasant dreams.

However, if courage consists in trying to overcome one's weakness, then the viscount was courageous. For when he saw his seconds coming to fetch him, he braced himself as hard as he could, his vanity telling him that any climbing-down would spell his ruin. Monsieur de Comaing congratulated him on looking so well.

But on the way, the rocking of the cab and the heat of the morning sun unnerved him. His energy disappeared. He could not even recognize where they were.

The baron amused himself by adding to his fears, by talking about the 'corpse' and how it had to be smuggled secretly back to town. Joseph played up to him; both of them considered the whole affair ridiculous and were convinced that it would be settled peacefully.

Cisy remained with his head sunk on his chest; he raised it gently and remarked that they had not brought a doctor.

'That's unnecessary,' said the baron.

'Then there's isn't any danger?'

Joseph replied solemnly:

'Let us hope not!'

And nobody in the carriage said another word.

At ten past seven they arrived at the Porte Maillot. Frédéric and his seconds were there, all three dressed in black. Instead of a cravat, Regimbart was wearing a horse-hair collar like a soldier; and he was carrying a sort of long violin-case, specially designed for this kind of occasion. Cold greetings were exchanged. Then they all plunged into the Bois de Boulogne, along the Route de Madrid, to look for a suitable spot.

Regimbart said to Frédéric, who was walking between him and Dussardier:

'Well, what are you going to do about the funk you're in? If you need anything, don't hesitate to say so. I know all about it. Fear is natural to man.'

Then he added in an undertone:

'Don't smoke any more. It's weakening!'

Frédéric threw away his cigar, which was bothering him, and walked on with a firm step. The viscount followed, leaning on the arms of his two seconds.

They met an occasional passer-by. The sky was blue, and now and then rabbits could be heard scuttling about. At the corner of a path a woman in a madras kerchief was talking to a man in a smock, and in the main avenue, under the chestnut-trees, grooms in linen jackets were exercising their horses. Cisy recalled the happy days when, mounted on his sorrel, with a monocle in his eye, he had ridden along beside carriage doors; these memories intensified his anguish; an unbearable thirst scorched his throat; the buzzing of the flies blended with the throbbing of his arteries; his feet sank into the sand; it seemed to him that he had been walking for eternities.

The seconds, without stopping, scanned both sides of the road. They debated whether to go to the Croix Catelan or to stop beneath the walls of Bagatelle. Finally they turned to the right and came to a halt in a sort of clearing between some pine-trees.

The place was chosen so as to divide the level of the ground evenly. The two spots where the opponents had to stand were marked. Then Regimbart opened his box. It was padded with red leather and contained four exquisite swords, with grooved blades and bound hilts. A ray of sunlight, passing through the leaves, fell upon them; and to Cisy's eyes they seemed to shine like silver vipers in a pool of blood.

The Citizen demonstrated that they were of equal length; he took the third sword himself, to separate the combatants in case of need. Monsieur de Comaing had a stick in his hand. There was a silence. They looked at one another. There was fear and cruelty in every face.

Frédéric had taken off his frock-coat and waistcoat. Joseph helped Cisy to do the same; when his cravat was removed, it was seen that he was wearing a religious medal round his neck. This brought a pitying smile to Regimbart's lips.

Then, in order to give Frédéric time for reflection, Monsieur de Comaing tried to raise some points of detail. He claimed the right to wear a glove, and the right to seize one's opponent's sword with the left hand; Regimbart who was in a hurry, raised no objection. Finally the baron said to Frédéric:

'It all depends on you, Monsieur. There's nothing dishonourable about admitting one's faults.'

Dussardier nodded his approval. Regimbart was indignant.

'Dammit, do you think we've come here to pluck chickens? . . .
On guard!'

The combatants were facing each other, with their seconds on
each side. Regimbart shouted the signal:

'Go!'

Cisy turned horribly pale. The end of his sword quivered like a
riding-crop. His head tilted backwards, his arms spread out, and he
fell on his back in a faint. Joseph picked him up, and, holding a
bottle of smelling-salts to his nostrils, shook him hard. The viscount
opened his eyes, and then, all of a sudden, threw himself on his
sword like a madman. Frédéric was still holding his; and he waited
for him, steady-eyed, with his guard high.

'Stop! Stop!' shouted a voice from the road, accompanied by the
sound of galloping hooves; and the hood of a gig broke through the
branches. A man leant out, waving a handkerchief and shouting all
the time: 'Stop! Stop!'

Monsieur de Comaing, thinking that the police were intervening,
raised his stick.

'Enough! The viscount's bleeding!'

'Me?' said Cisy.

True enough, he had grazed his left thumb in his swoon.

'But that was in falling,' protested the Citizen.

The baron pretended not to hear.

Arnoux had jumped out of the gig.

'I've got here too late! No! God be praised!'

He hugged Frédéric to him, felt him all over, covered his face
with kisses.

'I know why you did it; you wanted to defend your old friend.
That's splendid, splendid! I'll never forget it! How good you are!
Oh, my dear boy!'

He gazed at him and began to cry, chuckling with joy at the same
time. The baron turned to Joseph.

'I think we're out of place in this family reunion. It's all over,
isn't it, gentlemen? Viscount, put your arm in a sling; look, take
my handkerchief.'

Then, with an authoritative gesture, he added:

'Come now! No hard feelings! That's only right and
proper.'

The two combatants grudgingly shook hands. The viscount,

Monsieur de Comaing, and Joseph disappeared in one direction, and Frédéric went off the other way, with his friends.

The Restaurant de Madrid being close by, Arnoux suggested going there for a glass of beer.

'We could even have breakfast,' said Regimbart.

But as Dussardier did not have time for a meal, they confined themselves to a drink in the garden. They were all in that blissful state which follows a happy ending. The Citizen, however, was annoyed that the duel had been broken off at the critical moment.

Arnoux had heard about it from a friend of Regimbart's called Compain; and on an emotional impulse he had hurried over to stop it, believing, moreover, that he was the cause of the quarrel. He begged Frédéric to give him a few details of the affair. Frédéric, touched by the proof Arnoux had given of his affection, was unwilling to add to his illusions.

'Please,' he said, 'don't let's talk about it any more.'

Arnoux thought this reserve of his very tactful. Then, with his usual volatility, he turned to another subject.

'What news, Citizen?'

And they started talking about bills and dates of maturity. For convenience's sake they even went off to another table to whisper together.

Frédéric caught the words: 'You'll apply for shares for me.' 'Yes, but of course you for your part ...' 'I finally fixed it for three hundred!' 'A nice commission, I must say!' In short, it was obvious that Arnoux did a goodly amount of shady business with the Citizen.

Frédéric thought of reminding him of his fifteen thousand francs. But his recent action made even the mildest reproaches impossible. Besides, he felt tired. The place was not suitable. He put it off to another day.

Arnoux, sitting in the shade of a privet, was smoking happily. He glanced up at the doors of the private rooms, which all opened on to the garden, and said that he had often come here in the old days.

'And not alone, I'll be bound,' said the Citizen.

'I should think not!'

'What a rascal you are! A married man, too!'

'Well, and what about you?' said Arnoux.

And with an indulgent smile he added:

'I'd even go so far as to wager that that rogue has got a room somewhere, where he entertains little girls!'

By merely raising his eyebrows the Citizen admitted that this was true. The two men then proceeded to compare their tastes. Arnoux's preference was now for youth, for working girls. Regimbart hated women who were 'stuck-up', and favoured the matter-of-fact sort. The conclusion put forward by the porcelain manufacturer was that women ought not to be taken seriously.

'Yet he loves his wife,' thought Frédéric on his way home; and he decided that Arnoux was a blackguard. He bore him a grudge for this duel, as if it had been for his sake that he had just risked his life.

But he was grateful to Dussardier for his devotion; at his suggestion, the clerk soon took to calling on him every day.

Frédéric lent him books: Thiers, Dulaure, Barante, Lamartine's *Girondins*. The good fellow listened to him with rapt attention and accepted his opinions as if they were those of a master.

One evening he arrived in a state of panic.

That morning, on the boulevard, a man running along at full speed had bumped into him, and, recognizing him as a friend of Sénécal's, had said to him:

'They've just arrested him, and I'm running for it!'

It was perfectly true. Dussardier had spent the day finding out what had happened. Sénécal was under lock and key, charged with political conspiracy.

Born in Lyons, the son of a foreman, and taught by a former disciple of Chalier's,[31] he had joined the Société des Familles as soon as he arrived in Paris. His way of life was known, and the police kept him under observation. He had fought in the insurrection of May 1839; and since then he had lain low; but he had become more and more fanatical, worshipped Alibaud, confused his own grievances against society with those of the people against the monarchy, and awoke every morning hoping for a revolution which would change the world within a fortnight or a month. At last, disgusted by his colleagues' lethargy, infuriated by the obstructions put in the way of his dreams, and despairing of his country, he had placed his knowledge as a chemist at the service of the incendiary bomb conspiracy; and he had been caught carrying some gunpowder which he was going to try out at Montmartre, in a supreme attempt to establish the Republic.

The Republic was just as dear to Dussardier's heart, for he believed that it meant emancipation and universal happiness. One day, at the age of fifteen, outside a grocer's shop in the Rue Trans-nonain,[32] he had seen some soldiers with their bayonets red with blood, and hair sticking to their rifle butts; and from that time on, he had loathed the Government as being the very incarnation of Injustice. He tended to confuse murderers with policemen; in his eyes a police informer was as bad as a parricide. He naïvely attributed all the evil in the world to Authority, which he hated with a funda-mental, undying hatred that filled his soul and refined his sensibility. Sénécal's rhetoric had dazzled him. However guilty he might be, and however horrifying his plot, it did not matter. Once he had fallen a victim to Authority, it was their duty to help him.

'The Peers are sure to condemn him. Then he'll be taken away in a prison van like a convict and shut up at Mont Saint-Michel, where the Government kills off its prisoners. Austen went mad there! Steuben committed suicide! When they were transferring Barbès to a dun-geon, they dragged him by his legs and his hair. They stamped on his body, and his head bumped on every step on the staircase.[33] What cruelty! The fiends!'

Sobs of anger shook him, and he walked up and down the room as if he were in the grip of some dreadful anguish.

'All the same, we ought to do something. Let's think! I don't know what. Supposing we tried to rescue him? What do you think of that? While they're taking him to the Luxembourg,[34] we could hurl ourselves on the escort in the corridor. A dozen determined men can do anything.'

There was such a glow in his eyes that Frédéric trembled.

Sénécal struck him as a greater man than he had imagined. He remembered his sufferings, his life of austerity; without sharing Dussardier's enthusiasm for him, he none the less felt the admiration inspired by any man who sacrifices himself to an idea. He told him-self that if he had helped him, Sénécal would not be in his present plight; and the two friends racked their brains to find some way of saving him.

It was impossible for them to get to him.

Frédéric hunted for news of his fate in the papers, and for three weeks haunted the reading-rooms.

One day he came across a few numbers of *Le Flambard*. The leading article was invariably devoted to an attack on some famous man. After that came the society news and gossip. Then there were jokes about the Odéon, Carpentras, fish-breeding, and any prisoners there might be who had been condemned to death. The disappearance of a steamer provided humorous material for a whole year. The third column contained a chronicle of the arts which, in the form of an anecdote or a piece of advice, furnished sales publicity or book reviews, treating a book of poems and a pair of boots in exactly the same style. The only serious part of the paper was given up to criticism of the smaller theatres, in which two or three managers were savagely pilloried and the interests of Art were invoked in connexion with the scenery at the Funambules or an actress at the Délassements.

Frédéric was going to toss them all aside when his eye fell on an article entitled 'A Pullet with Three Roosters'. It was an account of his duel, related in a coarse, flippant style. He had no difficulty in recognizing himself, for he was referred to by his pun, which recurred several times: 'A young man from the college of Sens who hasn't any.' He was even depicted as a poor country bumpkin, an obscure simpleton trying to mix with the aristocracy. As for the viscount, he was given the hero's part, first at the supper-party, where he forced his way in, then in the affair of the wager, since he walked off with the lady, and finally on the duelling-ground, where he acquitted himself like a true nobleman. Frédéric's courage was not exactly denied, but the reader was given to understand that an intermediary, the 'protector' in person, had arrived just in time. The whole thing was rounded off with this query, full of possible innuendoes:

'What is the reason for their affection for each other? Who knows? As Don Basilio says, who the devil is deceiving whom here?'

There was not the slightest doubt that this was Hussonnet's revenge on Frédéric for refusing the five thousand francs.

What was he to do? If he called him to account for the article, the Bohemian would protest his innocence, and he would be no better off. The best course was to swallow the insult in silence. After all, nobody read *Le Flambard*.

Coming out of the reading-room, he caught sight of some people in front of a picture-dealer's shop. They were looking at the portrait of a woman with these words underneath in black letters:

'Mademoiselle Rose-Annette Bron, the property of Monsieur Frédéric Moreau of Nogent.'

It was her all right, or something like her, with her breasts bare, her hair down, and holding a red velvet purse in her hands, while a peacock poked its beak over her shoulder from behind, covering the wall with its great fan-like feathers.

Pellerin had arranged this display to force Frédéric to pay up, for he was convinced that he was famous and that the whole of Paris, rising to his defence, would take an interest in his plight.

Was it a plot? Had the painter and the journalist planned their attacks together?

His duel had done nothing to help him. He was becoming ridiculous, and everybody was laughing at him.

Three days later, at the end of June, there was a rise of fifteen francs in Northern Railway shares; and as he had bought two thousand the month before, he found that he had made thirty thousand francs. This stroke of luck restored his confidence. He told himself that he had no need of other people, and that all his difficulties were due to his timidity and irresolution. He ought to have been brutal to Rosanette from the start, to have refused Hussonnet's request on the spot, and to have avoided compromising himself with Pellerin. To show that he felt no embarrassment, he went to Madame Dambreuse's house for one of her regular evening receptions.

Martinon, who arrived at the same time as he did, turned round in the middle of the hall.

'What – *you* here?' he said, looking surprised and even annoyed at seeing him.

'Why not?'

And wondering what could be the reason for a greeting of that sort, Frédéric went on into the drawing-room.

In spite of the lamps standing in the corners, the light was dim; for the three windows were wide open, and formed three broad rectangles of darkness side by side. The spaces in between, under the pictures, were occupied by flower-stands five or six feet high; and a silver tea-pot with a samovar was reflected in a mirror in the distance. There was a discreet murmur of voices, and shoes could be heard squeaking on the carpet.

He made out a few tail-coats, then a round table lit by a big shaded lamp, seven or eight women in summer dresses, and, a little farther on, Madame Dambreuse in a rocking-chair. Her lilac taffeta dress had slashed sleeves with puffed muslin linings; the soft shade of the material harmonized with the colour of her hair; and she was leaning back a little, with the tip of her foot on a cushion, as calm as some delicate work of art or rare flower.

Monsieur Dambreuse and an old man with white hair were walking up and down the whole length of the drawing-room. Some of the men were talking together, sitting on the edge of the little divans; the others were standing in a circle in the middle of the room.

They were chatting about votes, amendments, counter-amendments, Monsieur Grandin's speech and Monsieur Benoist's reply. The Third Party was really going too far! The Left Centre ought to have been a little more mindful of its origins! The Minister had taken some hard blows. However, it was reassuring that nobody could think of any possible successor to him. In short, the situation was absolutely analagous to that of 1834[35].

As all this bored Frédéric, he went over to the women. Martinon was standing near them, his hat under his arm and his face in half-profile, so elegant that he looked like a piece of Sèvres porcelain. He picked up a *Revue des Deux Mondes* which was lying on the table, between an *Imitation of Christ* and an *Annuaire de Gotha*, spoke scathingly of a famous poet, said that he was going to Saint-François's lectures, complained about his larynx, and swallowed a lozenge every now and then; in the intervals he spoke about music and made small talk. Mademoiselle Cécile, Monsieur Dambreuse's niece, who was embroidering a pair of cuffs, gazed at him furtively with her pale blue eyes; and Miss John, the snub-nosed governess, had put down her tapestry-work to look at him. Both of them seemed to be exclaiming inwardly: 'How handsome he is!'

Madame Dambreuse turned towards him.

'Hand me my fan, will you; it's on that table over there. No, not that one – the other!'

She stood up, and, as he was coming back, they met in the middle of the room; she said a few rapid words to him, in reproach, it seemed, to judge by the haughty expression on her face. Martinon tried to smile, then went to join the group of solemn-looking men. Madame Dambreuse sat down again, and, leaning on the arm of her chair, said to Frédéric:

'I saw somebody the day before yesterday who spoke to me about you: Monsieur de Cisy. You know him, don't you?'

'Yes ... slightly.'

Suddenly Madame Dambreuse exclaimed:

'Duchess! Oh, how wonderful!'

And she went over to the door to meet a little old lady in a pale brown taffeta dress and a lace bonnet with long ribbons. The daughter of a companion in exile of the Comte d'Artois, and the widow of a marshal of the Empire who had been created a peer of France in 1830, she had connexions with both the old court and the new, and wielded considerable influence. The men who were standing and talking moved aside, then resumed their conversation.

It had now turned to pauperism, the accounts of which, according to these gentlemen, were all greatly exaggerated.

'All the same,' protested Martinon, 'poverty exists, and we have to admit it. But neither Science nor Authority can be expected to apply the remedy. It is purely a matter for the individual. When the lower classes make up their minds to rid themselves of their vices, they will free themselves from their wants. Let the common people be more moral and they will be less poor!'

According to Monsieur Dambreuse, nothing useful could be done without enormous capital. So the only possible policy was to entrust, 'as was suggested, incidentally, by Saint-Simon's disciples (oh, yes, there was some good in them! Give the devil his due), to entrust, I say, the cause of Progress to those who can increase the national wealth'. Imperceptibly the conversation moved on to the great industrial undertakings, the railways and the mines. And Monsieur Dambreuse, turning to Frédéric, said to him in an undertone:

'You didn't come about that business of ours.'

Frédéric said that he had been ill; but, feeling that this excuse was too lame, he added:

'Besides, I needed my money.'

'To buy a carriage?' asked Madame Dambreuse, who was passing near him with a cup of tea in her hand; and she gazed at him for a moment, turning her head slightly over her shoulder.

She thought that he was Rosanette's lover; the reference was obvious. Frédéric even had the impression that all the ladies were looking at him from a distance and whispering. To find out what they thought, he went over to them again.

On the other side of the table Martinon was sitting beside Mademoiselle Cécile and turning the pages of an album. It contained lithographs of Spanish costumes. He was reading out the captions: 'Woman of Seville ... Gardener of Valencia ... Andalusian Picador'; and once, going down to the bottom of the page, he continued in the same breath:

'Jacques Arnoux, publisher . . . A friend of yours, eh?'

'That's correct,' said Frédéric annoyed by his tone.

Madame Dambreuse went on:

'Why, yes, you came here one morning about . . . a house, wasn't it? . . . Yes, a house belonging to his wife.'

This meant: 'She is your mistress.'

He blushed scarlet; and Monsieur Dambreuse, coming up just then, added:

'You even seemed to be very interested in them.'

These last words completed Frédéric's discomfiture. He was thinking that his embarrassment, which he imagined everybody could see, was going to confirm their suspicions, when Monsieur Dambreuse came closer and said to him in a serious tone of voice:

'You don't do business together, I trust?'

He shook his head vigorously, not understanding the financier's intention, which was to give him a warning.

He wanted to leave. The fear of appearing a coward held him back. A servant was clearing away the tea-cups; Madame Dambreuse was talking to a diplomat in a blue coat; two girls, their heads close together, were looking at a ring; the others, sitting in armchairs in a semi-circle, were gently moving their white faces, fringed with dark or fair hair, this way or that; nobody in fact was paying any attention to him. Frédéric turned on his heel; and, by a series of long zigzags, he had almost reached the door, when, passing a small table, he noticed a newspaper on it, folded in two, between a Chinese vase and the panelling. He pulled it out a little way and read the words: *Le Flambard*.

Who had brought it? Cisy! It could not be anybody else. Anyway, what did it matter? They would believe the article; indeed, perhaps they believed it already. Why this determined persecution? An ironic silence surrounded him. He felt as if he were lost in a desert. But then Martinon raised his voice:

'Talking of Arnoux, I noticed the name of one of his employees, Sénécal, among the accused in the incendiary bomb case. Is that our Sénécal?'

'The same,' said Frédéric.

Martinon repeated at the top of his voice:

'What? Our Sénécal! Our Sénécal!'

He was promptly questioned about the plot. Being connected

with the Public Prosecutor's office, he was bound to have some information.

He admitted that he had none. Besides, he scarcely knew the man in question, having seen him only two or three times; but he believed he was something of a scoundrel. Frédéric indignantly exclaimed:

'Not a bit of it! He's a thoroughly good sort!'

'All the same, Monsieur,' said a landowner, 'a fellow who takes part in a plot can't be a good sort!'

Most of the men there had served at least four governments; and they would have sold France or the whole human race to safeguard their fortune, to spare themselves the slightest feeling of discomfort or embarrassment, or even out of mere servility and instinctive worship of strength. They all declared that political crimes were unpardonable. It would be far better to forgive those crimes which were caused by want. And they did not fail to cite the classic example of the family man who steals the classic piece of bread from the classic baker.

One high official even exclaimed:

'For my part, Monsieur, if I found out that my brother was involved in a plot, I should denounce him!'

Frédéric invoked the right of resistance; and, remembering a few phrases Deslauriers had used in conversation with him, he cited Desolmes, Blackstone, the Bill of Rights in England, and Article 2 of the Constitution of 1791. It was by virtue of that right that Napoleon had been dethroned; it had been recognized in 1830 and inscribed at the head of the Charter.

'Besides, when the sovereign fails to fulfil his part of the social contract, justice demands that he be overthrown.'

'But that's dreadful!' exclaimed the wife of a prefect.

All the other women remained silent, vaguely alarmed, as if they had heard the noise of bullets. Madame Dambreuse rocked in her chair and listened to him with a smile on her lips.

An industrialist, a former *carbonaro*,[36] tried to convince him that the Orléans were a splendid family; admittedly there were abuses ...

'Well, then?'

'But people shouldn't talk about them, my dear sir! If you only knew how much harm all these Opposition complaints do to business!'

'I don't care a damn about business!' retorted Frédéric.

The corruption of these old men infuriated him, and, carried away by the courage which sometimes takes hold of the most timid, he attacked the financiers, the deputies, the Government, and the King, defended the Arabs, and said a great many foolish things. Some of the men encouraged him sarcastically, saying: 'Go on! Pile it on!' while others murmured: 'Heavens, what a fanatical spirit!' At last he thought it best to withdraw; and, as he was leaving, Monsieur Dambreuse said to him with reference to the secretarial post:

'Nothing has been settled yet. But hurry up.'

And Madame Dambreuse said:

'We'll see you soon, shan't we?'

Frédéric interpreted their farewells as a final mockery. He was determined never to set foot again in that house, never to see any more of all those people. He thought that he had offended them, failing to realize what vast reserves of indifference high society possesses. The women in particular aroused his indignation. Not one of them had supported him, even with a glance. He bore them a grudge because he had not managed to move them. As for Madame Dambreuse, he found in her a mixture of languor and hardness which prevented him from attaching any specific label to her. Had she a lover? What lover? Was it the diplomat or somebody else? Martinon perhaps? Impossible! All the same, he felt a sort of jealousy towards him, and towards her an inexplicable ill-will.

Dussardier, who had come round that evening as usual, was waiting for him. Frédéric's heart was full; he opened it to Dussardier, and his grievances, although vague and difficult to understand, saddened the kindly shop-assistant; he even complained of his loneliness. After a certain hesitation, Dussardier suggested calling on Deslauriers.

On hearing the lawyer's name, Frédéric was seized with a keen desire to see him again. He was intellectually isolated, and Dussardier's company was insufficient to satisfy him. He told him to make whatever arrangements he thought fit.

Deslauriers too had felt a gap in his life ever since their quarrel. He responded promptly to Frédéric's friendly advances.

The two of them embraced, and then started talking about unimportant matters.

Deslauriers's reserved manner touched Frédéric; and, as a sort of atonement, he told him the next day all about his loss of fifteen thousand francs, without saying that these fifteen thousand francs had been originally intended for him. The lawyer none the less guessed the truth. This misadventure, which justified his prejudices against Arnoux, completely dispelled his resentment, and he said nothing about the old promise.

Frédéric, deceived by his silence, thought that he had forgotten it. A few days later he asked Deslauriers if there was any way of recovering his money.

They could dispute the previous mortgages, attack Arnoux for fraudulent misrepresentation, or take proceedings against the wife at her house.

'No, no! Not against her!' exclaimed Frédéric.

And, yielding to the former clerk's questions, he admitted the truth. Deslauriers was convinced that he was concealing something, probably out of tact. This lack of trust hurt him.

However they were as closely attached as in the old days, and they even enjoyed each other's company so much that Dussardier's presence irked them. By pretending to have appointments they gradually managed to shake him off. There are some men whose only function in life is to act as intermediaries; one crosses them as if they were bridges, and leaves them behind.

Frédéric kept nothing back from his old friend. He told him about the coal company, and Monsieur Dambreuse's proposal.

The lawyer looked thoughtful.

'That's odd! For that position they'd need somebody who's fairly well up in law.'

'But you'll be able to help me,' said Frédéric.

'Yes . . . why . . . dammit, of course!'

The same week he showed him a letter from his mother.

Madame Moreau accused herself of having misjudged Monsieur Roque, who had given her a satisfactory explanation of his behaviour. Then she spoke of his fortune, and the possibility of his marrying Louise later on.

'That might not be a bad idea,' said Deslauriers.

Frédéric dismissed it out of hand; besides, Roque was an old swindler. That did not matter, according to the lawyer.

At the end of July an inexplicable slump occurred in Northern Railway shares. Frédéric had not sold his, and he lost sixty thousand francs at one blow. His income was considerably reduced as a result. He must either cut down his expenditure, or adopt a profession, or make a rich marriage.

Deslauriers then spoke to him about Mademoiselle Roque. There was nothing to prevent him from going to see for himself how things stood. Frédéric was rather tired; the country and his mother's house would restore his energy. He set off.

The sight of the streets of Nogent, through which he drove by moonlight, brought back old memories; and he felt a sort of anguish, like somebody coming home after a long journey.

At his mother's house there were all the usual visitors: Monsieur Gamblin, Monsieur Heudras, Monsieur Chambrion, the Lebrun family, and 'the Auger girls'; and in addition there was old Roque and, sitting at a card-table opposite Madame Moreau, Mademoiselle Louise. She was a woman now. She stood up with a cry. There was a general commotion. She stood motionless, with the light from the four silver candlesticks on the table heightening her pallor. When she started playing again her hand was trembling. Frédéric, whose pride was ailing, found this emotion immensely flattering. He said to himself: 'You at least will love me!' and, in revenge for the slights he had suffered in the capital, he began to play the Parisian and the social celebrity, giving news of the theatres, telling anecdotes about society culled from the gossip-sheets, and generally succeeding in dazzling his fellow townsmen.

The next day Madame Moreau expatiated on Louise's virtues, and then listed the woods and farms which would eventually be hers. Monsieur Roque's fortune was considerable.

He had made it by making investments for Monsieur Dambreuse; for he lent money to people who could offer good mortgage securities, and this enabled him to ask for extras or commissions. Thanks to his active supervision, the capital was never in any danger. Besides, old Roque never hesitated to foreclose; then he would buy back the mortgage property at a low price, and Monsieur Dambreuse, seeing his money repaid like this, thought that his business affairs were very well conducted.

But these extra-legal operations compromised him with his agent. He could refuse him nothing. It was at Monsieur Roque's request that he had given Frédéric such a friendly welcome.

The fact was that old Roque nursed a single ambition in the depths of his heart. He wanted his daughter to be a countess; and he knew no other young man but Frédéric through whom he might achieve this without endangering the happiness of his child.

Through Monsieur Dambreuse's influence his grandfather's title would be obtained for him, for Madame Moreau was the daughter of a Comte de Fouvens, and was also related to the oldest families in Champagne, the Lavernades and the d'Étrignys. As for the Moreau side of the family, a Gothic inscription near the mills at Villeneuve-l'Archevêque mentioned a certain Jacob Moreau who had rebuilt them in 1576; and the tomb of his son, who was master of the horse to Louis XIV, could be seen in the chapel of Saint-Nicolas.

All these noble connexions fascinated Monsieur Roque, who was the son of a former footman. If a count's coronet proved impossible to obtain, he would console himself with something else; for Frédéric might manage to become a deputy when Monsieur Dambreuse was raised to the peerage, and then he would be able to help him in his business, getting him orders and concessions. He liked the young man as a person. Finally, he wanted him as his son-in-law because he had been attracted by the idea for a long time, and its appeal was constantly growing.

He was now a regular churchgoer; and he had won over Madame Moreau, chiefly with the bait of the title. However, she had refrained from giving any definite reply.

So, a week later, although no undertaking had been given, Frédéric was generally regarded as Mademoiselle Louise's 'intended'; and old Roque, who was not over-scrupulous, sometimes left them alone together.

V

DESLAURIERS had taken home from Frédéric's house a copy of the deed of subrogation together with a power of attorney in proper form giving him full authority. But when he had climbed his five flights of stairs, and was alone in the middle of his dismal study, sitting in his leather armchair, the sight of the stamped documents sickened him.

He was tired of that sort of thing, and tired too of cheap restaurants, omnibus rides, his poverty, his struggles. He picked up the papers again; there were others with them – the prospectus of the coal company with the list of the mines and details of their capacity. Frédéric had left him all this so that he could give him his opinion on it.

An idea occurred to him: to go and see Monsieur Dambreuse and ask for the secretary's post for himself. But the post was sure to be conditional on the purchase of a certain number of shares. He realized the folly of his plan and said to himself:

'Oh, no! That would be wrong of me.'

Then he racked his brains to find a way of recovering the fifteen thousand francs. A sum like that was nothing for Frédéric. But if he had had it, what a lever it would have been! And the former clerk waxed indignant that the other's fortune was so large.

'The use he makes of it is pitiful. He's selfish to the core. Oh, what do I care about his fifteen thousand francs?'

Why had he lent them? For love of Madame Arnoux. She was his mistress: Deslauriers had no doubt about that. 'That's another thing for which money comes in useful.' Hatred flooded into his mind.

Then his thoughts turned to Frédéric's physical appearance, which had always exerted an almost feminine charm on him; and soon he came to admire him for a success of which he knew himself to be incapable.

But was not resolution the essential factor in every undertaking? And since, given sufficient resolution, one could overcome any obstacle . . .

'Ah, that would be a lark!'

He felt ashamed of this treacherous idea, but a minute later he said to himself:

'Bah! Why should I be afraid?'

He had heard so much about Madame Arnoux that she had ended up by assuming an extraordinary life in his imagination. The long duration of this love irritated him like a problem. His somewhat theatrical asceticism bored him now. Besides, the society woman – or what he imagined as such – dazzled the lawyer as the symbol and the epitome of countless pleasures he had never known. A poor man, he hankered after luxury in its most obvious form.

'After all, even if he were annoyed, it would serve him right. He's behaved too badly to me for me to bother about him. I've no proof that she's his mistress. He's denied it to me. So I'm free to do as I please!'

The desire to make this attempt haunted him. It was a test of his powers that he wanted to make; with the result that one day, all of a sudden, he polished his boots himself, bought a pair of white gloves, and set off, putting himself in Frédéric's place and almost imagining that he was the other, by a strange mental process which combined resentment and sympathy, imitation and audacity.

He had himself announced as Doctor Deslauriers.

Madame Arnoux was surprised, as she had not sent for a doctor.

'Oh, I beg your pardon. I am a Doctor of Law. I have come on some business of Monsieur Moreau.'

This name appeared to disturb her.

'So much the better,' thought the former clerk. 'Since she was willing to have him, she will want me.' And he drew encouragement from the old idea that it is easier to supplant a lover than a husband.

He had had the pleasure of meeting her once at the Palais de Justice; he even recalled the date. Madame Arnoux was astonished by his memory. He went on in an ingratiating voice:

'You were already ... in difficulties ... with your business affairs.'

She made no reply; so it was true.

He began talking about this and that, his rooms, the factory; then, seeing some miniatures round the mirror, he said:

'Ah, family portraits, I suppose!'

He noticed one of an old woman, Madame Arnoux's mother.

'She looks a most worthy person, very much the southern type.'

And, when it was pointed out that she was a native of Chartres, he went on:

'Chartres! Now that's a pretty town.'

He praised its cathedral and its pies; then, returning to the portrait, he found points of resemblance with Madame Arnoux in it, and paid her a few devious compliments. She did not take offence. Feeling more confident, he said that he had known Arnoux a long time.

'He's a good fellow, but he keeps compromising himself. Take this mortgage, for instance; for sheer thoughtlessness . . .'

'Yes, I know,' she said, shrugging her shoulders.

This involuntary display of contempt encouraged Deslauriers to go on.

'You may not know it, but that porcelain-clay business nearly turned out very badly, and even his reputation . . .'

A frown stopped him.

Then, falling back on generalities, he expressed pity for those unfortunate women whose husbands squandered their fortunes ...

'But it's his, Monsieur! I have no money of my own.'

No matter! One could never tell ... A man of experience might be of some use. He offered his devoted services, extolled his own merits; and he looked her straight in the eyes, through his gleaming spectacles.

A vague languor came over her, but then she suddenly said:

'Let's to business, please.'

He displayed the dossier.

'This is Frédéric's power of attorney. If a document of this sort were placed in the hands of a court officer and he issued a writ, then nothing could be simpler: within twenty-four hours ...'

She remained impassive, and he changed his tactics.

'For my part, I really don't understand why he's trying to recover this money; because after all, he doesn't need it!'

'What! Monsieur Moreau was kind enough ...'

'Oh, I agree!'

And Deslauriers started singing his praises, then went on to disparage him, very gently, describing him as forgetful, selfish, and mean.

'I thought he was your friend, Monsieur?'

'That doesn't prevent me from seeing his faults. For instance, he doesn't show much appreciation of – how shall I put it? – sympathy ...'

Madame Arnoux was turning the pages of the big notebook. She interrupted him to ask the meaning of a word.

He bent over her shoulder, so close to her that he brushed against her cheek. She blushed; this blush excited Deslauriers; he avidly kissed her hand.

'What are you doing, Monsieur?'

And, standing with her back to the wall, she kept him rooted to the spot under the angry glare of her great dark eyes.

'Listen to me! I love you!'

She gave vent to a burst of laughter: shrill, heart-rending, terrible laughter. Deslauriers felt so furious he could have strangled her. He held himself back; and, with the expression of a victim begging for mercy, he said:

'Oh, you are making a mistake! I wouldn't go like him and ...'

'Whom are you talking about?'

'Frédéric.'

'But I've already told you that I'm not worried about Monsieur Moreau.'

'Oh, I beg your pardon . . . I beg your pardon.'

Then, in a cutting voice, he drawled:

'I did think you were sufficiently interested in him to be pleased to hear . . .'

She turned very pale. The former clerk added:

'He's going to get married.'

'He!'

'In a month's time, at the latest, to Mademoiselle Roque, the daughter of Monsieur Dambreuse's agent. He has even left for Nogent, simply on account of that.'

She put her hand to her heart, as if she had suffered a great shock; but immediately afterwards she rang the bell. Deslauriers did not wait to be thrown out of the house. When she turned round he had disappeared.

Madame Arnoux felt stifled. She went to the window to get some air.

On the pavement on the other side of the street, a packer in shirt sleeves was nailing up a crate. Some cabs went by. She closed the window and sat down again. The tall houses opposite shut out the sun, so that a cold light entered the room. Her children were out; nothing stirred around her. She felt completely deserted.

'He's going to get married! Is it possible?'

And a fit of nervous trembling seized her.

'Why am I doing that? Do I love him?'

Then all of a sudden.

'Why, yes! I love him! . . . I love him!'

She felt as if she were falling endlessly from a great height. The clock struck three. She listened to the vibrations of the sound dying away. And she remained sitting on the edge of her armchair, staring in front of her, and smiling all the time.

The same afternoon, at the same time, Frédéric and Mademoiselle Louise were strolling in the garden which Monsieur Roque owned at the end of the island. Old Catherine was watching them from a distance as they walked side by side; and Frédéric was saying:

'Do you remember when I used to take you into the country?'

'How kind you were to me!' she replied. 'You helped me to make sand-castles, to fill my watering-can, to hold on to my swing.'

'What's become of all those dolls of yours that were called after queens or marquises?'

'I've really no idea.'

'And your little dog Darky?'

'He got drowned, the poor dear!'

'And the *Don Quixote* with the illustrations we coloured together?'

'I've still got it!'

He reminded her of the day of her first communion, and how sweet she looked at Vespers, with her white veil and her long taper, while all the girls were filing round the choir and the bell was tolling.

These memories presumably held little charm for Mademoiselle Roque; she made no answer, and a minute later said:

'It was naughty of you not to write even once to send me your news.'

Frédéric excused himself on the ground of all his work.

'But what exactly do you do?'

He found the question embarrassing, then said he was studying politics.

'I see.'

And without inquiring any further, she said:

'That keeps you busy, but as for me . . .'

Then she told him of the dreariness of her life, with nobody to see, not the smallest pleasure, not the slightest distraction. She wanted to go riding.

'The curate says it isn't seemly for a young girl: aren't the proprieties silly! In the old days they used to let me do whatever I liked; but now, nothing!'

'All the same, your father loves you.'

'Yes, but . . .'

She gave a sigh which meant: 'That isn't enough to make me happy.'

Then there was a silence. They could hear nothing but the crunch of the sand under their feet and the murmur of the weir; for the Seine is divided into two above Nogent. The stream which turned the water-mills disgorged its overflow at this point, to meet the main current of the river farther down; and coming from the bridges, one could see a grassy mound on the right, on the other bank, dominated by a white house. On the left, in the meadows, there stretched a line of poplars, while the horizon opposite was bounded by a bend in the river; the water was as smooth as a mirror, and large insects skimmed over its unbroken surface. Clumps of reeds and rushes lined it unevenly; all sorts of plants which had taken root there were flaunting golden buds, trailing yellow clusters, pointing spindly purple flowers or darting out random spikes of green. Water-lilies were floating in an inlet; and on this side of the island a row of old willows concealing spring-traps constituted the only defence the garden possessed.

Inside, four walls with a slate coping enclosed the kitchen garden, where the squares of newly dug earth formed a pattern of brown patches. The cloches over the melons gleamed in a line along their narrow bed; artichokes, beans, spinach, carrots, and tomatoes grew alternately as far as a bed of asparagus, which looked like a little forest of feathers.

Under the Directory the whole of this ground had been what was known as a 'folly'. Since then the trees had grown enormously. Clematis choked the arbours, the paths were covered with moss, and brambles abounded everywhere. Plaster flaked off fragments of statues lying under the weeds; and one caught one's feet in the remains of old wire ornaments. Of the pavilion nothing was left but two rooms on the ground floor with some shreds of blue wallpaper. Along the front of the building stretched a pergola whose wooden trellis-work, standing on brick pillars, supported a vine.

The two of them walked beneath it; the light filtered through the foliage here and there, and Frédéric, turning to talk to Louise, watched the shadow of the leaves playing over her face.

In the chignon at the back of her red hair she had a pin with a glass head coloured to look like an emerald; and despite the fact that she was in mourning, her bad taste was so ingenuous that she was wearing straw slippers trimmed with pink satin, vulgar curios which she had probably bought at some fair.

He noticed them and ironically complimented her on them.

'Don't poke fun at me,' she said.

Then, looking him up and down, from his grey felt hat to his silk socks, she said:

'How smart you are!'

Then she asked him to tell her some books to read. He mentioned a few, and she said:

'Oh, what a lot you know!'

When she had been a little girl, she had conceived one of those childish passions which combine both the purity of a religion and the violence of a desire. He had been her companion, her brother, her master; he had entertained her mind, made her heart beat, and unconsciously filled the depths of her being with a perpetual latent intoxication. Then he had left her at a moment of tragic crisis, when her mother had just died, so that the two sorrows had been confused in her mind. Absence had idealized him in her memory; he had come back wearing a kind of halo; and now she artlessly gave herself up to the pleasure of looking at him.

For the first time in his life Frédéric felt himself to be loved; and this novel pleasure, which was little more than an agreeable sensation, gave him a sort of inner satisfaction, so that he stretched out his arms and threw his head back.

A big cloud was moving just then across the sky.

'It's going towards Paris,' said Louise. 'You'd like to follow it, wouldn't you?'

'Me! What for?'

'Who knows?'

And, with a sharp glance, she added:

'Perhaps you've got some . . .' – she searched for the word – 'some attachment there.'

'Oh, I've no attachments!'

'You're sure?'

'Why yes, Mademoiselle, quite sure!'

In less than a year an extraordinary transformation had taken place in the girl which Frédéric found astonishing. After a moment's silence he added:

'We ought to call each other by our Christian names, as we used to do. Would you like to?'

'No.'

'Why not?'

'Because.'

He insisted. She lowered her head and answered:

'I don't dare.'

They had reached the end of the garden and were standing on the Livon beach. Frédéric boyishly started playing ducks and drakes with the pebbles. She ordered him to sit down. He obeyed; then, looking at the weir, he said:

'It's like Niagara.'

He went on to talk about distant countries and long voyages. The idea of travelling appealed to her. Nothing would frighten her, neither storms nor lions.

Sitting beside one another, they picked up handfuls of sand in front of them and let it trickle through their fingers while they talked; and the warm breeze from the plains brought whiffs of lavender together with the smell of tar from a boat behind the lock. The sun shone on the cascade, and the greenish stones of the little wall over which the water was flowing seemed to be covered by a never-ending ribbon of silver gauze. Down below, a long bar of foam spurted up in rhythm, before forming bubbling whirlpools and innumerable cross-currents which ended up by merging into a single limpid sheet of water.

Louise murmured that she envied the life of fishes.

'It must be so nice to roll about in the water and feel yourself being stroked all over.'

And she shivered with a movement of voluptuous delight.

Then a voice called out:

'Where are you?'

'Your maid's calling you,' said Frédéric.

'All right! All right!'

Louise gave no sign of moving.

'She's going to be angry,' he went on.

'I don't care! And anyhow . . .'

Mademoiselle Roque made a gesture indicating that she could do what she liked with her.

All the same, she got up, and then complained of a headache. And, as they were passing a huge shed containing piles of faggots, she said:

'What if we went inside, in the *égaud*?'

He pretended not to understand this dialect word, and even teased her about her accent. Gradually the corners of her mouth turned down and she bit her lips; she turned away to sulk.

Frédéric went over to her and swore that he had not meant to hurt her, that he was really very fond of her.

'Do you mean it?' she exclaimed, looking at him with a smile which lit up the whole of her freckled face.

He could not resist this frank expression of feeling or the freshness of her youth, and he went on:

'Why should I lie to you? . . . You mean you don't believe me?' And he put his left arm round her waist.

A cry, as soft as the coo of a dove, came from her throat; her head fell back; she nearly fainted; he held her up. Then he gently helped her to take a few steps. His endearments had ceased, and, determined to speak nothing but trivialities, he started talking about Nogent society.

All of a sudden, she pushed him away, saying in a bitter voice:

'You wouldn't have the courage to take me away from here!'

He stood motionless, looking utterly bewildered. She burst out sobbing, and, pressing her head against his chest, said:

'How can I possibly live without you?'

He tried to calm her. She put her hands on his shoulders so that she could look straight at him, and, with something almost fierce in her moist gaze, she fixed her green eyes on his and asked:

'Will you be my husband?'

'But . . .' replied Frédéric, searching for a reply, 'probably . . . I should like nothing better.'

At that moment Monsieur Roque's cap appeared behind a lilac-bush.

He took his 'young friend' off for a couple of days, on a little tour of his estates in the neighbourhood; and when Frédéric returned he found three letters waiting for him at his mother's house.

The first was a note from Monsieur Dambreuse inviting him to dinner the following Tuesday. What was the reason for this civility? Did it mean that he had been forgiven for his tirade?

The second letter was from Rosanette. She thanked him for having risked his life for her; Frédéric did not understand at first what she meant; finally, after a great many digressions, invoking his friendship, trusting in his discretion, going down on her knees, she said, her need was so urgent, she asked him, as if she were begging for bread, for a little loan of five hundred francs. He immediately decided to let her have this money.

The third letter, which came from Deslauriers, spoke of the subrogation, and was long and obscure. The lawyer had not yet come to any decision. He urged Frédéric to stay where he was: 'There's no point in your coming back.' Indeed he stressed this point with a curious insistence.

Frédéric gave himself up to all sorts of conjectures. He felt tempted to return to Paris; this attempt to dictate his behaviour annoyed him.

Besides, he was beginning to feel a certain nostalgia for the boulevards; and then his mother was so pressing, Monsieur Roque so full of attentions, and Mademoiselle Louise so deeply in love with him, that he could not stay at home any longer without declaring himself. He needed time to think; he would be able to judge matters better at a distance.

To explain his departure, Frédéric made up a story; and off he went, telling everybody, and believing himself, that he would be back soon.

VI

His return to Paris gave him no pleasure. It was an evening towards the end of August; the boulevards looked empty, and the few people he saw went by with scowling faces; here and there a cauldron of tar was smoking; a good many houses had all their shutters closed. He arrived at his own house: there was dust all over the hangings. Dining all by himself, Frédéric was overcome by a strange feeling of loneliness; then he thought of Mademoiselle Roque.

The idea of marriage no longer struck him as fantastic. They would travel, they would go to Italy, to the East! And he imagined her standing on a little hill, gazing at a landscape, or else leaning on his arm in a Florentine gallery, and pausing in front of the pictures. What a joy it would be to see that dear little thing blossoming out at the sight of the splendours of Art and Nature! Once she had been removed from her present environment, she would soon become a charming companion. Besides, Monsieur Roque's fortune tempted him. However, he found a decision of this kind repugnant, as if it were a weakness or a degradation.

But whatever he did in the end, he was determined to change his way of life, in other words to stop wasting his emotions on fruitless passions; and he even hesitated to carry out the commission with which Louise had entrusted him. This was to buy for her, from Jacques Arnoux's, two big coloured statuettes of negroes, like the ones in the prefecture at Troyes. She knew the manufacturer's trademark, and refused to have them from anybody else. Frédéric was afraid that if he went back to see *them* he would be caught up again in his old love.

These reflections preoccupied him throughout the evening; and he was just going to bed when a woman came in.

'It's me,' said Mademoiselle Vatnaz laughingly. 'I've come from Rosanette.'

So they had made it up?

'Good heavens, yes! I'm not one to bear a grudge, you know. Besides, the poor girl ... But it would take too long to tell the whole story.'

In short, the Marshal wanted to see him, and was waiting for a reply to her letter, which had been forwarded from Paris to Nogent; Mademoiselle Vatnaz had no idea what was in it. Then Frédéric asked after the Marshal.

She was now 'with' a very rich man, a Russian, Prince Tzernou-koff, who had seen her at the races at the Champ de Mars the previous summer.

'She's got three carriages, a saddle-horse, livery of her own, an English-style groom, a country house, a box at the Italiens, and heaven knows what else besides. So there you are, my dear.'

Mademoiselle Vatnaz looked gayer and happier, as if she had profited by this change of fortune. She removed her gloves and examined the furniture and ornaments in the bedroom. She put a price on every one of them, like a dealer. He ought to have consulted her to have got them cheaper; and she congratulated him on his good taste.

'Oh, it's sweet, perfectly charming. Nobody has such good ideas as you.'

Then, noticing a door by the bed in the alcove, she said:

'So that's where you let your little women out, eh?'

And she playfully took him by the chin. He shivered at the touch of her long hands, which were at once thin and soft. She had lace at her wrists, and the bodice of her green dress was trimmed with braid like a hussar's uniform. Her black tulle hat had a drooping brim, which partly concealed her forehead; beneath it, her eyes were glittering; and her hair gave off a scent of patchouli. The oil-lamp, which was standing on the table, lit up her face from below, like the footlights of a theatre, throwing her jaw into relief; and suddenly, in the presence of this ugly woman with the lithe body of a panther, Frédéric felt an overwhelming lust, a longing for sensual pleasure.

Taking three squares of paper from her purse, she said to him in an unctuous voice:

'You're going to take these!'

They were three tickets for a benefit performance for Delmar.

'What! Him?'

'Why, of course!'

Without further explanation, Mademoiselle Vatnaz added that she was more in love with him than ever. According to her, the actor undoubtedly occupied a place among 'the giants of the age'. And he did not just interpret this character or that, but the very genius of France, the Common People. He had 'a humanitarian soul; he understood the priestly role of the artist'. To bring these eulogies to an end, Frédéric gave her the money for the three seats.

'There's no point in your saying anything about this to her ... Good heavens, how late it is! I must be going. Oh, I was forgetting the address: it's 14, Rue Grange-Batelière.'

And on the doorstep she added:

'Good-bye, you breaker of hearts!'

'Whose heart?' Frédéric asked himself. 'What a peculiar creature!'

And he remembered that Dussardier had once said to him, speaking of her:

'Oh, she's no better than she should be,' as if referring to business.

The next day he went to see the Marshal. She was living in a new house with awnings which overhung the street. There was a wall-mirror on every landing, rustic flower-holders in front of the windows, and canvas carpeting on the stairs; the coolness of the staircase was refreshing to anybody coming into the house.

It was a manservant who opened the door: a footman in a red waistcoat. A woman and two men, presumably tradespeople, were waiting on a bench in the hall, as if they were in a minister's ante-room. On the left, the half-open door of the dining-room revealed some empty bottles on the side-boards and napkins on the backs of the chairs; running parallel was a gallery in which gilded sticks supported an espalier of roses. Down below, in the courtyard, two boys with bare arms were polishing a landau. Their voices rose up to the hall, together with the intermittent sound of a curry-comb being banged against the stone.

The footman came back. 'Madame would receive Monsieur'; and he led him across a second hall, and then a large drawing-room hung with yellow brocade, with rope-mouldings in the corners which met in the middle of the ceiling and seemed to be continued in the cable-shaped loops of the chandelier. There appeared to have been a party the night before. There was still some cigar ash on the tables.

Finally he entered a sort of boudoir which was unevenly lit by stained-glass windows. The wood above the doors had been carved in a clover design; behind a balustrade, three purple mattresses formed a divan, on which there lay the tube of a platinum hookah. Instead of a mirror, there was a pyramid of little shelves over the mantelpiece, bearing a whole collection of curios: old silver watches, Bohemian vases, jewelled brooches, jade buttons, enamels, Chinese porcelain figures, and a little Byzantine Virgin with a silver-gilt cope. All this merged together in a kind of golden twilight, with the bluish colour of the carpet, the mother-of-pearl gleam of the stools, and the fawn tint of the walls lined with brown leather. On pedestals in the corners of the room there were bronze vases containing bunches of flowers whose scent hung heavy in the air.

Rosanette appeared, dressed in a pink satin jacket, white cashmere trousers, a necklace of piastres, and a red skull-cap with a spray of jasmine twined round it.

Frédéric gave a start of surprise; then he said that he had brought 'the thing in question', and held out the bank-note.

She looked at him in utter bewilderment, and, as he still had the note in his hand and did not know where to put it, he said:

'But take it!'

She seized it and threw it on the divan.

'You're very kind,' she said.

It was to help buy a plot of land at Belleville, which she was paying for like this by annual instalments. Her casual manner offended Frédéric. Apart from that, so much the better! This was his revenge for the past.

'Sit down,' she said, 'there, nearer to me.'

And in a serious voice she went on:

'First of all, I must thank you, my dear, for having risked your life for me.'

'Oh, it was nothing really.'

'What do you mean? It was magnificent!'

And the Marshal expressed a gratitude which he found embarrassing; for he was convinced that she believed he had fought for Arnoux alone, since the latter, who thought that was the case, could not have resisted the temptation to tell her so.

'Perhaps she's making fun of me,' thought Frédéric.

He had nothing more to do, and he stood up, pleading an appointment.

'No! Do stay.'

He sat down again and complimented her on her costume.

She pulled a face and replied:

'The prince likes me like this. And I have to smoke that sort of thing,' she added, pointing to the hookah. 'Shall we have a puff? Would you like to?'

A light was brought; the tombac proved difficult to kindle and she started stamping with impatience. Then she suddenly grew languid and lay motionless on the divan, with a cushion under her armpit, her body slightly twisted, one knee bent, and the other leg outstretched. The long snake of red morocco formed loops on the floor and coiled round her arm. She pressed the amber mouthpiece to her lips and gazed at Frédéric with half-closed eyes, through the spirals of smoke which enveloped her. Every breath she drew made the water gurgle, and now and then she murmured:

'The poor dear! The poor darling!'

He tried to find a pleasant subject of conversation, and remembered Mademoiselle Vatnaz.

He said that she had struck him as very smart.

'I don't doubt it,' said the Marshal. 'She's lucky to have me, I can tell you that!' And she said no more, it was so difficult for them to make conversation.

They both felt a certain constraint, a barrier separating them. The fact was that the duel, of which Rosanette believed herself to be the cause, had flattered her vanity. Afterwards she had been very surprised that he had not hurried round to turn his action to good account; and she had invented her need for five hundred francs to compel him to come back. How was it that Frédéric did not demand a little affection in return? She marvelled at his delicacy, and in a burst of emotion she said to him:

'Would you like to come to the seaside with us?'

'Who is *us*?'

'Me and my friend, I'll say that you're my cousin, like they do in the old comedies.'

'No thank you!'

'Well, then, you can arrange to stay near us.'

He found the idea of hiding from a rich man humiliating.

'No, that's out of the question.'

'Just as you please.'

Rosanette turned away with tears in her eyes. Frédéric caught sight of them; and to show that he cared for her, he said how glad he was to see her so well off at last.

She shrugged her shoulders. What was the trouble, then? Was it, by any chance, that nobody loved her?

'Oh, people always love me!'

She added:

'The only thing is, how they do it.'

Complaining that 'the heat was stifling', the Marshal undid her jacket; and with nothing on her back but her silk chemise, she leant her head on his shoulder, with the provocative expression of a slave-girl.

The idea that the viscount, Monsieur de Comaing, or somebody else might come in would never have occurred to a man less obsessively preoccupied with himself. But Frédéric had been taken in too often by these very glances to risk a fresh humiliation.

She wanted to know about his friends and his pastimes; she even went so far as to ask about his business affairs and to offer to lend him money if he needed any. Frédéric could not stand it any longer and picked up his hat.

'Well, my dear, enjoy yourself at the seaside. Good-bye.'

She opened her eyes wide, then answered curtly:

'Good-bye!'

He went again through the yellow drawing-room and the second hall. On the table, between a bowl full of visiting-cards and an inkstand, there was a chased silver casket. It was Madame Arnoux's! He felt deeply moved, and at the same time horrified, as if by sacrilege. He longed to touch it, to open it; but he was afraid of being seen, and he went away.

Frédéric was virtuous. He did not go back to Arnoux's house.

He sent his manservant to buy the two Negroes, after giving him all the necessary instructions; and the packing-case went off to Nogent that very evening. The next day, he was on his way to see Deslauriers when, on the corner of the Rue Vivienne and the boulevard, he met Madame Arnoux face to face.

Their first impulse was to draw back; then the same smile came to the lips of both, and they went up to one another. For a moment neither of them said a word.

The sunshine surrounded her; and her oval face, her long

eyebrows, her black lace shawl moulding her shoulders, her dove-coloured shot-silk dress, the bunch of violets at one corner of her bonnet, all struck him as full of an extraordinary splendour. An infinite sweetness flowed from her lovely eyes; and, stammering at random the first words which occurred to him, he said:

'How is Arnoux keeping?'

'Very well, thank you.'

'And your children?'

'They are very well.'

'Ah . . . ah . . . Lovely weather we're having, isn't it?'

'Yes, it's splendid.'

'You're shopping?'

'Yes.'

And with a slight inclination of her head she said:

'Good-bye!'

She had not held out her hand to him, had not said a single affectionate word, had not even invited him to come and see her; but in spite of all that, he would not have exchanged this meeting for the most wonderful of adventures, and he savoured its sweetness as he continued on his way.

Deslauriers was surprised to see him, but concealed his annoyance, for out of stubbornness he had not given up all hope of conquering Madame Arnoux; and he had written to Frédéric to stay at Nogent so as to have more freedom for his own manoeuvres.

All the same, he mentioned that he had been to see her, to find out if their marriage contract stipulated a joint estate; for if it had done, they could have taken proceedings against the wife.

'And she looked very peculiar when I told her you were getting married.'

'Good heavens, why make up a story like that?'

'I had to, to show that you needed your money. If she didn't care about you, she wouldn't have had the sort of heart attack that affected her.'

'Really?' exclaimed Frédéric.

'Oh, you old rogue, you're giving yourself away. Come along now, own up!'

An immense cowardice overcame Madame Arnoux's admirer.

'No, no! . . . I assure you! . . . On my word of honour!'

These feeble denials convinced Deslauriers that he was right. He congratulated his friend. He asked him for 'details'. Frédéric did not give him any, and even resisted the temptation to invent some.

As for the mortgage, he told him to do nothing, to wait. Deslauriers thought he was wrong and was cutting in his remonstrances.

Altogether he was more gloomy, malevolent, and irascible than ever. In a year's time, unless his luck changed, he was going to sail for America or blow out his brains. In short, he seemed so angry about everything and so uncompromising in his radicalism that Frédéric could not help saying:

'You're just like Sénécal.'

In this connexion Deslauriers told him that Sénécal had been released from Sainte-Pélagie, presumably because the preliminary investigation had not produced enough evidence to bring him to trial.

To celebrate this deliverance, Dussardier was going to give a punch-party, and he invited Frédéric to 'come along', at the same time warning him that he would meet Hussonnet, who had behaved very well towards Sénécal.

It so happened that *Le Flambard* had just opened an agency office which described itself in its prospectus as a 'wine bureau, advertising agency, debt-collecting, and information office, etc.'. But the Bohemian was afraid that his commercial activities might injure his literary reputation, so he had taken on the mathematician to keep his accounts. Though the post was anything but remunerative, Sénécal would have starved to death without it. Not wanting to offend the kindly clerk, Frédéric accepted his invitation.

Three days before the party, Dussardier had waxed the red tiles of his attic floor himself, beaten the armchair, and dusted the mantelpiece, on which there stood an alabaster clock in a glass case between a stalactite and a coconut. As his nightlight and two candlesticks were insufficient, he had borrowed a pair of sconces from the concierge; and these five lights shone on the chest of drawers, which had been spread with three napkins, to provide a decent setting for some macaroons, some biscuits, a scone, and a dozen bottles of beer. Opposite, standing against the yellow-paper wall, there was a mahogany bookcase containing Lachambeaudie's *Fables*, *Les Mystères de Paris*, and Norvin's *Napoléon*, while in the middle of the bed-alcove Béranger's smiling face looked out from an ebony frame.[37]

Besides Deslauriers and Sénécal, the guests consisted of a chemist who had just qualified but lacked the necessary capital to set up in business; a young man from the host's firm; a traveller in wines; an architect; and a gentleman who was in the insurance business. Regimbart had been unable to come. Everybody expressed regret at his absence.

They gave Frédéric an extremely cordial welcome, for they all knew, through Dussardier, how he had spoken at Monsieur Dambreuse's house. Sénécal simply held out his hand to him in a dignified manner.

He was standing against the mantelpiece. The others sat smoking their pipes and listened to him talking about universal suffrage, which would result in the victory of Democracy and the application of the principles of the Gospel. Besides, the decisive moment was drawing near; more and more Reform banquets were being held in the provinces, while Piedmont, Naples, Tuscany . . .[38]

'You're right,' said Deslauriers, cutting him short. 'Things can't go on like that much longer.'

And he started to give a summary of the situation.

Holland had been sacrificed to obtain the recognition of Louis-Philippe by England; and now this vaunted English alliance had been lost, thanks to the Spanish marriages. In Switzerland, Monsieur Guizot, towed along by the Austrian, was supporting the treaties of 1815. Prussia, with its Customs Union, was going to be troublesome in the future. And the Eastern question was no nearer a solution.[39]

'Just because the Grand Duke Constantine sends presents to Monsieur d'Aumale, that's no reason for trusting Russia. As for home affairs, nobody has ever seen such blindness and stupidity before. They can't even keep their majority together. Everywhere in fact, as somebody said, there's nothing, nothing, nothing.[40] And in the face of this disgraceful state of affairs,' the lawyer continued, putting his hands on his hips, 'they declare themselves satisfied.'

This reference to a famous vote aroused applause. Dussardier opened a bottle of beer; the froth splashed the curtains, but he took no notice; he filled the pipes, cut the scone, went down several times to see if the punch was coming; and soon everybody was in a state of excitement, for they all shared the same loathing of authority. It was a violent loathing, with no other cause than the hatred of injustice; and they mingled legitimate grievances with the most ludicrous grumbles.

The chemist complained about the pitiful condition of the fleet. The insurance broker found Marshal Soult's two sentries more than he could bear. Deslauriers denounced the Jesuits, who had just installed themselves publicly at Lille.[41] Sénécal detested Monsieur Cousin much more, for eclecticism, which taught how to use reason to attain truth, encouraged selfishness and destroyed solidarity. The traveller in wines, finding these topics a little beyond his comprehension, remarked loudly that Sénécal was forgetting a lot of scandals.

'The royal coach on the Northern Railways is going to cost eighty thousand francs! Who's going to pay for it?'

'Yes, who's going to pay for it?' echoed the clerk, who was as angry as if the money had been taken out of his own pocket.

There followed recriminations against the crooks of the Stock Exchange and the corruption of the Civil Service. According to Sénécal, one ought to go higher up, and start by accusing the princes, who were reviving the manners and morals of the Regency.

'Did you know that, not so long ago, the Duc de Monpensier's friends, coming home from Vincennes and probably drunk, disturbed the workers of the Faubourg Saint-Antoine with their singing?'

'People even shouted: "Down with the robbers!"' said the chemist.

'I was there, and I shouted!'

'Splendid! At last the people are waking up after the Teste-Cubières case.'[42]

'That case upset me,' said Dussardier, 'because it resulted in the disgrace of an old soldier.'

'Do you know,' Sénécal went on, 'that at the Duchesse de Praslin's[43] they found ...'

Just then the door was kicked open. Hussonnet came in.

'Greetings, my lords!' he said, sitting down on the bed.

No mention was made of his article, which he regretted writing anyway, for the Marshal had given him a thorough scolding for it.

He had just seen *Le Chevalier de Maison-Rouge* at Dumas's theatre, and considered it 'a dreadful bore'.

This judgement surprised the democrats, since the play's tendencies, or rather its setting, flattered their ideas. They protested. To settle the matter, Sénécal asked if the play advanced the cause of democracy.

'Yes ... I suppose so; but the style ...'

'Well then, it's a good play. What does the style matter? It's the idea that counts.'

And without allowing Frédéric to speak, he went on:

'I was just saying that in the Praslin case . . .'

Hussonnet interrupted him.

'Oh, that's another old story. I'm sick of hearing it.'

'You aren't the only one,' retorted Deslauriers. 'It's been responsible for the suppression of a mere five papers. Listen to this note.'

And taking out his notebook, he read:

'Since "the best of republics" was established, we have had 1,229 prosecutions of the press, as the result of which our journalists have been sentenced to 3,141 years' imprisonment and fined the trifling sum of 7,110,500 francs. It makes a pretty story, doesn't it?'

They all laughed bitterly. Frédéric, as indignant as the rest, said:

'The *Démocratie pacifique* has been prosecuted on account of its serial, a novel called *The Share of Women*.'

'Oh, come now,' said Hussonnet. 'Surely they aren't going to forbid us our share of women!'

'But what's left that isn't forbidden?' exclaimed Deslauriers. 'We're forbidden to smoke in the Luxembourg, and forbidden to sing the hymn to Pius IX.'[44]

'And the printers' banquet has been banned!' remarked a hollow voice.

It was the architect, who was hidden in the shadows of the alcove, and who had remained silent until then. He added that, the week before, a man called Rouge had been convicted for insulting the King.

'I bet his face was red!' said Hussonnet.

Sénécal considered this joke in such bad taste that he accused Hussonnet of sticking up for 'the conjurer of the Hôtel de Ville', the friend of the traitor Dumouriez.[45]

'What — me? Not a bit of it!'

He regarded Louis-Philippe as the epitome of all that was dull and commonplace, a grocer in a cotton nightcap. And, putting his hand on his heart, the Bohemian recited the sacramental phrases: 'It is always with renewed pleasure . . . The Polish nation shall not perish . . . Our great enterprises will go on . . . Give me some money for my little family . . .' Everybody laughed uproariously and pronounced him a great wit; their joy increased at the sight of a bowl of punch which was brought in by a bar-keeper.

The flames of the punch and those of the candles rapidly warmed the room; and the light from the attic window, crossing the yard, lit up the edge of the roof opposite, together with a chimney-pot, which stood out black against the night. They talked at the tops of their voices, all at the same time; they took off their jackets; they bumped into the furniture and clinked glasses.

Hussonnet cried:

'Bring up the great ladies! 'Od's blood, let's have a bit more Tour de Nesle,[46] local colour, and Rembrandt.'

And the chemist, who was tirelessly stirring the punch, started bellowing:

'I have two great oxen in my stable.
Two white oxen . . . '[47]

Sénécal put his hand over his mouth, for he hated any sort of rowdiness; and the tenants appeared at their windows, surprised at the unusual din coming from Dussardier's room.

The good fellow was in high spirits, and said that this reminded him of their little parties they used to have on the Quai Napoléon; several faces were missing though – Pellerin for instance . . .

'We can do without him,' said Frédéric.

Then Deslauriers asked after Martinon.

'What's become of that interesting gentleman?'

Frédéric promptly gave vent to the grudge he bore him and attacked his mind, his character, his fake elegance, and everything about him. He was a perfect specimen of the self-made man. The new aristocracy, the middle class, was not a patch on the old aristocracy, the nobility. He put forward this opinion, and the democrats expressed their approval, just as if they had belonged to the one aristocracy and rubbed shoulders with the other. They were delighted with him. The chemist even likened him to Monsieur d'Alton-Shée, who, although he was a peer of France, spoke up for the common people.[48]

The time had come to go home. They all took leave of one another with warm handshakes; out of affection, Dussardier decided to walk home with Frédéric and Deslauriers. As soon as they were out in the street, the lawyer assumed a pensive look and, after a moment's silence asked:

'So you're still very angry with Pellerin?'

Frédéric made no secret of his rancour.

All the same, the painter had withdrawn the notorious picture from display. People ought not to fall out over trifles. What was the use of making enemies?

'He gave way to an angry impulse, which is pardonable in a man who hasn't a penny to his name. *You* can't understand that sort of thing.'

And after Deslauriers had gone up to his rooms, the clerk stayed with Frédéric; he even urged him to buy the portrait. In point of fact, Pellerin, having given up hope of intimidating Frédéric, had asked the two of them to try to persuade him to take the thing.

Deslauriers brought up the subject again and pressed the point. The artist's demands were reasonable, he said.

'I'm sure that for, say, five hundred francs . . .'

'Oh, let him have them!' said Frédéric. 'Look, here you are.'

The picture was delivered the same evening. It struck him as even more appalling than the first time. An excessive amount of retouching had given a leaden hue to the half-tints and shadows, so that they looked darker in comparison with the highlights, which, shining here and there, contrasted violently with the overall effect.

Having paid for the picture, Frédéric took his revenge by subjecting it to scathing criticism. Deslauriers believed everything he said and approved of his conduct, for it was still his ambition to form a group of which he should be the leader; some men enjoy making their friends do things which they find disagreeable.

In the meantime Frédéric had not gone back to the Dambreuses' house. He lacked the necessary capital. There would have to be no end of explanations, and he could not make up his mind. Perhaps he was right to stay away? Nothing was safe nowadays, the coal business no more than any other; he ought to give up mixing in that sort of society; finally Deslauriers succeeded in turning him against the enterprise. Hatred was changing him into a man of principle; besides he preferred Frédéric to stay mediocre. Like that he remained his equal and at the same time closer to him.

Mademoiselle Roque's commission had been very badly executed. So her father wrote, giving Frédéric the most detailed explanations, and finishing his letter with this witticism: 'I trust that you won't have to work like a black to get those Negroes.'

Frédéric had no choice but to go back to Arnoux's factory. He went upstairs to the shop but could not find anybody there. The business was on its last legs, and the employees were imitating their master's slackness.

He walked past the long display-stand, loaded with pottery, which stretched along the middle of the room from one end to the other; then, reaching the counter at the far end, he stamped his feet to attract attention.

The door-curtain was lifted and Madame Arnoux appeared.

'What! You here! You!'

'Yes,' she stammered, somewhat embarrassed. 'I was looking for ...'

He caught sight of her handkerchief beside the desk, and guessed that she had come down to her husband's office to see how things stood, to get to the bottom of something that was worrying her.

'But ... perhaps there's something you want?' she said.

'Nothing important, Madame.'

'These assistants are impossible. They're never here.'

They were not to be blamed. On the contrary he was delighted to find her alone.

She gave him an ironical look.

'Well, and what about that marriage?'

'What marriage?'

'Why, yours!'

'Mine? Not likely!'

She brushed aside his denial.

'What difference would it make anyway? A man falls back on the second-rate when he has given up hope of the ideal he has dreamt of.'

'Yet your dreams weren't all so ... innocent.'

'What do you mean?'

'When you go to the races with ... certain creatures.'

He inwardly cursed the Marshal. Then he remembered something.

'But it was you that used to beg me to see her for Arnoux's sake!'

She tossed her head and retorted:

'And you took advantage of that to amuse yourself.'

'Good heavens, let's forget all that nonsense.'

'Very well, since you're going to get married.'

And she bit her lips to hold back a sigh.

Then he exclaimed:

'But I tell you again it isn't true. How can you possibly imagine that somebody with my habits and my intellectual needs could bury himself in the country to play cards, supervise builders, and walk about in clogs? Whatever for? You've been told that she's rich, I suppose? But I don't care a fig about money. Do you think that when I've always longed for the ultimate in beauty, tenderness, and charm, and when I've finally found this ideal, when this vision prevents me from seeing any other . . .'

And, taking her head in his hands, he began kissing her eyelids, saying over and over again:

'No, no, no, I shall never marry! Never! Never!'

She accepted his caresses, transfixed by surprise and delight.

The door between the shop and the staircase slammed to. She gave a start and stood with one hand outstretched, as if ordering him to keep quiet. Footsteps drew near. Then somebody said outside:

'Is Madame there?'

'Come in!'

Madame Arnoux had one elbow on the counter and was calmly rolling a pen between her fingers when the accountant drew aside the door-curtain.

Frédéric stood up.

'My respects, Madame. The service will be ready, I trust? I can count on it?'

She made no reply. But this silent complicity of hers made her face glow with all the blushes of adulterous love.

The next day he called on her again and was admitted. To follow up his advantage, without beating about the bush, he promptly began by explaining the encounter on the Champ de Mars. A sheer accident had brought him together with that woman. Even admitting that she was pretty – which was not the case – how could she occupy his thoughts, even for a moment, seeing that he loved another?

'You know that perfectly well. I have told you so.'

Madame Arnoux bowed her head.

'I am sorry that you told me.'

'Why?'

'The most elementary proprieties now require that I should never see you again.'

He insisted on the innocence of his love. The past should reassure her about the future; he had promised himself not to disturb her life, nor to importune her with his complaints.

'But yesterday my heart brimmed over.'

'We must forget all about that moment.'

Yet what would be the harm in two unhappy creatures sharing their sadness?

'For you are not happy either! Oh, I know you! You have nobody to satisfy your need for affection and devotion; I will do everything you want, I shall not offend you, I swear I shan't.'

And he fell on his knees, despite himself, sinking under an inner weight which was too heavy for him.

'Stand up!' she said. 'I insist.'

And she imperiously declared that if he did not obey he would never see her again.

'Ah! I defy you to prevent me!' replied Frédéric. 'What is there for me to do in the world? Others strain after wealth, fame, power. I have no profession; you are my exclusive occupation, my entire fortune, the aim and centre of my life and thoughts. I can no more live without you than without the air of heaven. Can't you feel my soul yearning for yours? Don't you feel that they are destined to mingle, and that I am dying of impatience?'

Madame Arnoux began trembling all over.

'Oh, go away, please.'

The anguished expression on her face stopped him. Then he took a step forward. But she drew back, putting her hands together.

'Leave me! In heaven's name! For pity's sake!'

And Frédéric loved her so much that he went out.

Soon he was filled with anger against himself, cursing himself for a fool, and twenty-four hours later he returned.

Madame was not there. He remained on the landing, numb with fury and indignation. Arnoux appeared, and informed him that his wife had gone off that very morning to move into a little country house they were renting at Auteuil, since they no longer had the one at Saint-Cloud.

'It's another of her caprices. Still, so much the better, if it suits her; it suits me anyway. Shall we dine together tonight?'

Frédéric pleaded an urgent engagement, then hurried to Auteuil.

Madame Arnoux gave a cry of joy. Immediately all his anger vanished.

He said nothing about his love. To give her more confidence, he even exaggerated his reserve; and when he asked if he might come again, she answered: 'Of course,' giving him her hand, which she drew back almost immediately.

From then on Frédéric called to see her often. He used to promise the cab-driver large tips. But often he lost patience with the slowness of the horse and got out of the cab; then, panting for breath, he would clamber on to an omnibus; and how scornfully he examined the faces of the people sitting opposite him, who were not going to see her!

He recognized her house from a distance by a huge honeysuckle which covered the planks of the roof on one side; it was a sort of Swiss chalet, painted red, with an outside balcony. There were three old chestnut-trees in the garden, and on a mound in the middle, a thatched sunshade supported by a tree-trunk. Under the slate coping of the walls, a large vine had come loose and was hanging down here and there like a rotten rope. The gate bell, which was somewhat hard to pull, gave a prolonged peal, and there was always a long wait before anybody came. Every time he felt a pang of anxiety, an indefinable fear.

Then he would hear the maid's slippers flapping along the sandy path, or else Madame Arnoux herself would appear. One day he came up behind her when she was crouching on the lawn, looking for violets.

Her daughter's temper had forced her to send her to a convent. Her little boy spent the afternoon at school while Arnoux lingered over lunch at the Palais-Royal, with Regimbart and his friend Compain. No intruder could surprise them.

It was clearly understood that they were not to give themselves to one another. This agreement, which preserved them from danger, made it easier for them to open up their hearts.

She told him about her life in the old days at Chartres, at her mother's house; about her piety at the age of twelve; and then about her passion for music, when she used to sing until nightfall in her little bedroom, which looked out on to the ramparts. He told her about his fits of melancholy at school, and how a woman's face used to shine in his poetic paradise, so that, the first time he had seen her, he had promptly recognized her.

These conversations usually referred only to the years they had known each other. He reminded her of insignificant details, the colour of her dress at a certain time, who had come along one day, what she had said on another occasion; and she would answer in astonishment:

'Yes, I remember!'

Their tastes and opinions were identical. Often the one who was listening would exclaim:

'So do I!'

And the other in his turn would say:

'So do I!'

Then there would follow endless complaints about Fate:

'Why didn't heaven allow it? If only we had met . . .'

'Ah, if I had been younger!' she would sigh.

'No! If I had been a little older!'

And they imagined a life which would have been entirely devoted to love, rich enough to fill the widest deserts, surpassing all joys, and defying all sorrows; a life in which the hours would have gone by in a continuous exchange of confidences; a life which would have become something splendid and sublime like the shimmering of the stars.

They nearly always stayed out of doors at the top of the stairs, with the tops of trees yellowed by the autumn rising in uneven curves up to the pale horizon in front of them; or else they went to the far end of the avenue, to a summer-house whose only furniture was a sofa covered in grey linen. The mirror was stained with black spots; the walls gave off a musty smell; and they stayed there talking about themselves, about others, about anything and everything, in an ecstasy of delight. Sometimes the sunbeams, coming through the Venetian blind, would stretch what looked like the strings of a lyre from ceiling to floor, and specks of dust would whirl about in these luminous bars. She amused herself by breaking them with her hand; Frédéric would gently seize it and gaze at the tracery of her veins, the grain of her skin, the shape of her fingers. For him, each of her fingers was something more than a thing, almost a person.

She gave him her gloves, and a week later her handkerchief. She called him Frédéric and he called her Marie, worshipping that name, which he said was made specially to be breathed in ecstasy, and which seemed to contain clouds of incense and trails of roses.

Eventually they took to fixing the days of his visits in advance; and, going out as if by chance, she would come to meet him on the road.

She did nothing to stimulate his love, for she was in that carefree mood which is characteristic of great happiness. During the whole season she wore a dressing-gown of brown silk edged with velvet in the same colour, a loose-fitting garment which suited her languid attitudes and her serious face. Besides, she was approaching the August of a woman's life, a period which combines reflection and tenderness, when the maturity which is beginning kindles a warmer flame in the eyes, when strength of heart mingles with experience of life, and when, in the fullness of its development, the whole being overflows with a wealth of harmony and beauty. She had never been gentler or more indulgent. Sure that she was not going to falter, she gave herself up to a feeling which struck her as a right she had earned by her sorrows. Moreover it was so wonderful and so new! What a gulf there was between Arnoux's coarseness and Frédéric's adoration!

He was terrified in case a slip of the tongue might lose him everything he thought he had gained, telling himself that a missed opportunity could be recovered, but not a blunder. He wanted her to give herself, and not to take her. The certainty of her love delighted him like a foretaste of possession, and then her physical charms disturbed his heart more than his senses. It was an indefinable bliss, an intoxication so profound that it made him forget even the possibility of an absolute happiness. Away from her, raging lusts devoured him.

Soon there were long intervals of silence in their conversations. Sometimes a kind of sexual modesty made them blush in one another's presence. All the precautions they took to hide their love only uncovered it; the stronger it became, the more reserved was their behaviour. Living a lie like this acerbated their sensibility. They obtained a delicious pleasure from the smell of wet leaves; the east wind caused them pain; they suffered inexplicable irritations and gloomy presentiments; the sound of footsteps or the creaking of a panel caused them as much terror as if they had done wrong; they felt themselves being driven towards an abyss; a stormy atmosphere enveloped them; and when Frédéric blurted out some words of complaint she blamed herself.

'Yes, it's my fault! I'm behaving like a coquette! You mustn't come again!'

Then he would repeat the same promises, to which she listened with pleasure every time.

His return to Paris and the hustle and bustle of New Year's Day interrupted their meetings somewhat. When he returned there was something bolder about his manner. She kept going out of the room to give orders, and, despite his entreaties, received all the neighbours who called to see her. There were conversations about Léotade, Monsieur Guizot, the Pope, the rising at Palermo, and the Twelfth Arrondissement banquet, which was arousing a certain anxiety.[49] Frédéric consoled himself by railing against authority, for like Deslauriers he longed for a general upheaval, he had become so embittered. Madame Arnoux, for her part, became increasingly gloomy.

Her husband, piling one extravagance on another, was keeping a working-girl from his factory, the one they called the girl from Bordeaux. Madame Arnoux herself told Frédéric about it. He tried to use this as an argument, 'since she was being deceived'.

'Oh, I don't care!' she said.

This declaration seemed to him to put their intimacy on a firm footing. Did Arnoux suspect anything?

'No, not now.'

She told him how one evening he had left them alone together, and then had come back and listened at the door. And as they had both been talking of indifferent matters, he had not felt the slightest anxiety from then on.

'He has no reason to feel anxious, has he?' said Frédéric bitterly.

'No, of course not.'

She would have done better not to venture a remark like this.

One day she was not at home at the time he usually called. To him this was a sort of betrayal.

Then he showed his annoyance at seeing the flowers he brought her always thrust into a glass of water.

'But where do you want me to put them?'

'Oh, not there! Though they are not as cold there as they would be on your heart.'

Some time later he reproached her with having been to the Italiens the night before without telling him. Others had seen her, admired her, loved her perhaps; Frédéric clung to his suspicions just to be able to quarrel with her and torment her; for he was beginning to hate her, and it was only right that she should share his sufferings.

One afternoon towards the middle of February he found her

profoundly disturbed. Eugène was complaining that his throat hurt. The doctor, however, had said that it was nothing serious, a heavy cold or influenza. Frédéric was astonished at the child's feverish appearance. Nevertheless he reassured the mother, quoting instances of several children of the same age who had recently had illnesses of the same sort and had soon recovered.

'Really?'

'Why, yes, of course!'

'Oh, how kind you are!'

And she took his hand. He squeezed it in his own.

'Oh, let me go!'

'Why should I? You give me your hand when I comfort you, because you think I'm useful for that sort of thing, but you doubt me . . . when I speak to you about my love.'

'I have no doubts about that, my poor dear.'

'Why do you distrust me, as if I were a blackguard capable of taking advantage of you?'

'But I don't.'

'If only I had proof of that!'

'What proof?'

'The proof you would give anybody, the proof you once granted me.'

And he reminded her that one foggy winter evening they had gone out together. That was a long time ago now. What was to prevent her, then, from appearing in public on his arm, in front of everybody, without any fear on her part or ulterior motive on his, since there was nobody around to trouble them?

'So be it,' she said, with an air of determined bravado which astonished Frédéric for a moment.

But then he went on quickly:

'Shall I wait for you at the corner of the Rue Tronchet and the Rue de la Ferme?'

'Good heavens, but . . .' stammered Madame Arnoux.

Without giving her time to think, he added:

'Tuesday next, I suppose?'

'Tuesday?'

'Yes, between two o'clock and three.'

'I shall be there.'

And she turned her face away in a movement of shame. Frédéric pressed his lips against the nape of her neck.

'Oh, you mustn't do that,' she said. 'You'll make me change my mind.'

He drew back, fearing the usual changeability of women. Then, at the door, he murmured softly, as if they were both agreed about it: 'I shall see you on Tuesday, then.'

She lowered her eyes discreetly with an air of resignation.

Frédéric had a plan.

He hoped that he might be able to persuade her to stop in a doorway, to shelter from the rain or the sun, and that once in the doorway, she would go into the house. The difficulty was to find a suitable one.

He accordingly started searching, and near the middle of the Rue Tronchet he saw from a distance a sign which read: 'Furnished rooms'.

The servant, realizing what he wanted, promptly showed him a bedroom and dressing-room on the first floor, with two entrances. Frédéric took the apartment for a month and paid in advance.

Then he went to three shops to buy the rarest of scents; he bought a piece of imitation lace to replace the horrible red cotton counter-pane; and he chose a pair of blue satin slippers. Only the fear of seeming vulgar put a limit to his purchases. He brought them back, and, more reverently than somebody decking out an altar of repose, he moved the furniture about, hung the curtains himself, and put heather on the mantelpiece and violets on the chest of drawers. He would have liked to pave the whole room with gold. 'It's tomorrow,' he kept telling himself. 'Yes, tomorrow! I'm not dreaming.' And he felt his heart beating wildly in delirious hope; when everything was ready, he carried off the key in his pocket, as if the happiness which was sleeping there might have flown away.

A letter from his mother was waiting for him at home.

Why are you staying away so long? Your behaviour is beginning to look ridiculous. I can understand your hesitating at first about this marriage, up to a point; but now think it over.

And she listed the relevant details: an income of forty-five thousand francs a year. Moreover, 'people were beginning to talk', and Monsieur Roque was waiting for a firm reply. As for the young person, her position was really embarrassing. 'She is very much in love with you.'

Frédéric tossed the letter aside without finishing it, and opened another, a note from Deslauriers:

Dear Frédéric; the 'pear' is ripe.[50] We are counting on you, in accordance with your promise. There is a meeting at dawn tomorrow in the Place du Panthéon. Go into the Café Soufflot. I must have a word with you before the demonstration.

'Oh, I know their demonstrations. No, thank you! I have an appointment of a pleasanter nature!'

And the next day Frédéric was out before eleven o'clock. He wanted to have a last look at his arrangements; and then – who could tell? – she might by some chance come along early. Emerging from the Rue Tronchet, he heard a great din behind the Madeleine; he went forward, and at the far end of the square, on the left, he saw some men in smocks and others in street clothes.

The fact was that a manifesto published in the newspapers had summoned all the subscribers to the Reform banquet to this spot. The Ministry had almost immediately issued a proclamation banning the banquet. The previous evening the parliamentary opposition had given up the idea; but the patriots, knowing nothing of their leaders' decision, had come to the meeting-place, followed by a great many spectators. A deputation from the Schools had just been to Odilon Barrot's house. It was now at the Foreign Office; and nobody knew if the banquet would be held, if the Government would carry out its threat, or if the National Guards would appear. There was as much ill-feeling against the deputies as against the authorities. The crowd was growing steadily when all of a sudden the strains of the *Marseillaise* filled the air.

It was the column of students arriving. They were marching slowly, in two lines, and in good order. They were not carrying any arms, but they looked angry, and they all shouted at intervals:

'Reform for ever! Down with Guizot!'

Frédéric's friends were sure to be there. They would catch sight of him and carry him off. He quickly took refuge in the Rue de l'Arcade.

When the students had gone round the Madeleine twice they went down towards the Place de la Concorde. It was packed with people, and from a distance the dense crowd looked like a field of black corn swaying to and fro.

At the same moment some infantrymen lined up in battle order on the left of the church.

The groups of people stayed where they were, however. To put an end to it all, some plain-clothes policemen started seizing the rowdiest demonstrators and brutally dragging them off to the guard-house. Despite his indignation, Frédéric kept quiet; he might have been arrested with the others, and he would have missed Madame Arnoux.

A little later the helmets of the municipal guards appeared. They struck out about them with the flat of their swords. A horse fell to the ground; people hurried to its aid; and, as soon as the rider was in the saddle, everybody fled.

Then there was a great silence. The drizzle which had wet the asphalt had stopped falling. Some clouds drifted overhead, gently driven along by the west wind.

Frédéric started to walk up and down the Rue Tronchet, looking in front and behind.

Finally two o'clock struck.

'Ah, it's now!' he said to himself. 'She's leaving her house, she's drawing near.' And a minute later: 'She could have got here by now.' Until three o'clock he tried to reassure himself. 'No, she isn't late. A little patience!'

And, to kill time, he inspected the few shops in the street, a bookseller's, a saddler's, and an undertaker's. Soon he knew all the titles of the books, all the pieces of harness, all the mourning material. The shopkeepers, seeing him go by again and again, were first of all astonished and then frightened, and they put up their shutters.

Doubtless something was delaying her, and she was as upset as he was. But what joy would be theirs in a little while! For she was going to come; that was certain. 'She promised me she would!' All the same, an unbearable anxiety was beginning to come over him.

On a stupid impulse he went back into the house, as if she might have been there. At that very moment perhaps she was coming down the street. He rushed out again. There was nobody there! And he started pacing the pavement again.

He gazed at the cracks between the paving-stones, the mouths of the drain-pipes, the street-lamps, and the numbers over the doors. The tiniest objects became companions for him, or rather ironic spectators; and the regular fronts of the houses struck him as pitiless. His feet were cold. He felt as if he were melting away with despair. The echo of his footsteps jarred his brain.

When he saw that his watch said four o'clock he felt a sort of dizziness and panic. He tried to recite some poetry to himself, to do a sum at random, to make up a story. It was impossible, for he was haunted by the picture of Madame Arnoux. He longed to run and meet her. But which way should he go so as not to miss her?

He stopped a messenger, put five francs in his hand, and told him to go to Jacques Arnoux's house in the Rue Paradis and ask the concierge 'if Madame was at home'. Then he stationed himself on the corner of the Rue de la Ferme and the Rue Tronchet, so that he could see down both streets at the same time. At the far end of the vista, on the boulevard, vague masses of people were moving about. Now and then he made out the plume of a dragoon's helmet or a woman's hat, and he strained his eyes in an attempt to recognize it. A ragamuffin who was exhibiting a marmot in a cage asked him with a smile for some money.

The man in the velvet jacket reappeared. 'The concierge had not seen her go out.' What was keeping her? If she was ill, the concierge would have said so. Had somebody called to see her? She could easily have put any visitor off. He slapped his forehead.

'Oh, what a fool I am! It's the riot!' This obvious explanation comforted him. Then all of a sudden he thought: 'But everything is quiet in her district.' And an appalling suspicion occurred to him. 'What if she isn't coming? What if her promise was just a trick to get rid of me? No, no!' What was keeping her was probably an unexpected accident, one of those occurrences which cannot be foreseen. In that case she would have written. And he sent the manservant to his home in the Rue Rumfort to see if there was a letter for him there.

No letter had been delivered. This lack of news reassured him.

He looked for omens in the number of coins grasped at random in his hand, in the expressions of passers-by, in the colour of horses; and, when the augury was unfavourable, he refused to believe it. In his outbursts of anger against Madame Arnoux, he cursed her under his breath. Now and then he felt so weak that he thought he was going to faint, but then all of a sudden hope would surge within him once more. She was going to appear. She was there behind him. He turned round: nothing! Once, about thirty yards away, he caught sight of a woman of the same height, wearing the same dress. He went up to her; it was not she! Five o'clock came. Half past five. Six o'clock. The gas-lamps were lit. Madame Arnoux had not come.

The night before, she had dreamt that she had been standing for a long time on the pavement in the Rue Tronchet. She was waiting there for something indefinite yet important, and without knowing why, she was afraid of being seen. But a horrible little dog which had taken a dislike to her was worrying at the hem of her dress. It kept coming back to her and barked louder and louder. Madame Arnoux awoke. The dog's barking went on. She strained her ears. The noise was coming from her son's bedroom. She rushed into the room in her bare feet. It was the child himself who was coughing. His hands were burning hot, his face red and his voice strangely hoarse. His breathing became more laboured with every minute that passed. She stayed there until dawn, bending over his bed, watching him.

At eight o'clock the drum of the National Guard warned Monsieur Arnoux that his comrades were waiting for him. He dressed hurriedly and went off, promising to call straight away at the house of their doctor, Monsieur Colot. At ten o'clock Monsieur Colot had not come, and Madame Arnoux sent round her maid. The doctor was away in the country, and the young man who was standing in for him was out on his rounds.

Eugène had his head cocked to one side on the bolster, and he kept frowning and dilating his nostrils; his poor little face had grown paler than his sheets; and his breathing became shorter and shorter, dry and metallic, producing a whistling sound with every intake of breath. His coughing was like the barking noise made by the crude devices inside toy dogs.

Madame Arnoux was filled with panic. She rang all the bells, calling for help and shouting:

'A doctor! A doctor!'

Ten minutes later there arrived an old gentleman with a white cravat and neatly trimmed grey side-whiskers. He asked a great many questions about the young patient's habits, then examined his throat, applied his ear to his back, and wrote out a prescription. The man's unruffled calm was detestable. He gave the impression of being at an embalmment. She would willingly have struck him. He said he would come back in the evening.

Soon the horrible fits of coughing started again. Now and then the child would sit up all of a sudden. Convulsive movements shook his chest-muscles, and as he breathed in and out his stomach contracted as if he were choking for breath after a race. Then he would sink on to the bed again, with his head thrown back and his mouth wide open. With infinite precautions Madame Arnoux tried to make him swallow the contents of the medicine bottles, some ipecacuanha syrup and an antimony potion. But he pushed away the spoon, groaning in a weak voice. He seemed to be puffing out his words.

From time to time she re-read the prescription. The formula frightened her; perhaps the chemist had made a mistake. Her helplessness filled her with despair. Monsieur Colot's pupil arrived.

He was a young man with an unassuming manner, who was new to his profession and did not conceal his impressions. To begin with he remained undecided, for fear of committing himself, and finally prescribed the application of pieces of ice. It took a long time to find some ice. The bladder holding the pieces burst. The child's night-shirt had to be changed. All this disturbance brought on another, more violent paroxysm.

The child started pulling away the bandages round his neck, as if he were trying to remove the obstruction which was choking him, and he clawed at the wall and grabbed the curtains of his bed, looking for some point of support to help his breathing. His face was now a bluish colour, and his whole body, which was soaked in a cold sweat, seemed to be growing thinner. His haggard eyes gazed in terror at his mother. He threw his arms round her neck, clinging to her in desperation, and, choking back her sobs, she stammered out endearments:

'Yes, my love, my angel, my precious!'

She went to fetch some toys, a doll, a picture-book, and spread them out on his bed to amuse him. She even tried to sing.

She started a song which she used to sing to him when she was dandling him on her knees and dressing him in his baby-clothes in that very same little tapestry chair. But he shivered along the whole length of his body, like a wave in a gust of wind; his eyeballs stood out; she thought he was going to die, and turned away to avoid seeing him.

A moment later she felt strong enough to look at him. He was still alive. The hours went by, heavy, dreary, interminable, heartbreak-ing; and she counted the minutes only by the progress of this death-agony. The spasms of his chest threw him forward as if they were going to break him up; finally he vomited something peculiar which looked like a tube of parchment. What could it be? She supposed that he had thrown up a piece of his bowels. But he was breathing freely and regularly. This apparent improvement frightened her more than anything else; and she was standing there petrified, her arms dangling and her eyes fixed in a stare, when Monsieur Colot arrived. According to him, the child was out of danger.[51]

She did not understand at first, and asked him to repeat what he had said. Was this not just one of those comforting remarks medical men always made? The doctor went off looking perfectly calm. Then she felt as if the cords binding her heart had come loose.

'He's out of danger! Can it be true?'

Suddenly the thought of Frédéric entered her mind, clearly and inexorably. This was a warning from Heaven. But the Lord in his mercy had not wished to punish her completely. What dreadful punishment she would suffer later on if she persisted in this love of hers! Probably somebody would insult her son because of her; and Madame Arnoux pictured him as a young man, wounded in a duel, and brought home on a stretcher, dying. Jumping to her feet, she flung herself on the little chair; and, sending up her soul with all her strength, she offered God, as a sacrifice, her first love, her only weakness.

Frédéric had gone home. He sat in his armchair, without even the strength to curse her. He sank into a kind of sleep; through his nightmare he heard the rain falling, and imagined all the time that he was still out there on the pavement.

The next day, in a final access of cowardice, he sent another messenger to Madame Arnoux's house.

Either because the man failed to run the errand, or because she had too much to say to be able to express it in a brief message, the same answer was brought back as before. This was pushing insolence too far! He was filled with angry pride. He swore to himself that he would never again feel the slightest desire for her; and, like a leaf carried away by a hurricane, his love disappeared. He felt a sense of relief, a stoic joy, and then a longing to indulge in violent action; and he went out to roam the streets.

Some men from the suburbs were passing by, armed with muskets and old swords; some of them were wearing red caps and they were all singing the *Marseillaise* or the *Girondins*. Here and there a National Guard was hurrying to his local town hall. Drums were beating in the distance. Fighting was going on at the Porte Saint-Martin. There was a gay, warlike feeling in the air. Frédéric went on walking. The excitement of the big city raised his spirits.

Opposite Frascati's he caught sight of the Marshal's windows; a mad idea occurred to him, a youthful reaction. He crossed the boulevard.

The main gate was being closed, and Delphine the maid was writing on it with a piece of charcoal: 'Arms handed over'. She gabbled at him:

'Oh, Madame's in such a state. She sacked her groom this morning for insulting her. She thinks there's going to be looting all over the place. She's scared to death, and all the more so because Monsieur has gone.'

'What Monsieur?'

'The Prince!'

Frédéric went into the boudoir. The Marshal appeared, in her petticoat, with her hair hanging down her back, and looking distracted.

'Oh, thank you! You've come to save me! That's the second time! And *you* never ask to be paid!'

'Forgive me!' said Frédéric, seizing her by the waist.

'Hey! What are you doing?' stammered the Marshal, at once surprised and amused by this behaviour.

He replied:

'I'm following the fashion. I've reformed.'

She allowed herself to be pushed back on to the divan, and went on laughing under his kisses.

They spent the afternoon watching the mob in the street from their window. Then he took her to dinner at the Trois-Frères-Provençaux. The meal was lengthy and exquisite. They returned on foot, since there were no carriages.

The news of a change of government had transformed Paris. Everybody was in high spirits; people were strolling about, and the fairy-lights on every floor made it as bright as day. The soldiers were slowly returning to their barracks, looking harassed and unhappy. They were greeted with shouts of: 'Long live the infantry!' They went on their way without answering. The officers of the National Guard, on the other hand, flushed with enthusiasm, kept brandishing their swords and shouting: 'Reform for ever!' Every repetition of the word 'reform' set the two lovers laughing. Frédéric made jokes and was extremely gay.

Going by way of the Rue Duphot, they arrived at the boulevards. Chinese lanterns were hanging from the houses, looking like garlands of fire. A vague mass of people was swarming about below;

here and there in its midst bayonets gleamed white against the dark background. A great din arose. The crowd was too thick for them to make their way straight back; and they were turning into the Rue Caumartin when, all of a sudden, there was a crackling noise behind them like the sound of a huge piece of silk being ripped in two. It was the fusillade on the Boulevard des Capucines.

'Ah! They're killing off a few bourgeois,' said Frédéric calmly.

For there are situations in which the kindest of men is so detached from his fellows that he would watch the whole human race perish without batting an eyelid.

The Marshal clung tightly to his arm. Her teeth were chattering, and she declared herself incapable of walking another twenty yards. Then, as a refinement of hatred, in order to degrade Madame Arnoux more completely in his mind, he took Rosanette to the house in the Rue Tronchet, and into the room prepared for the other woman.

The flowers had not faded. The lace was spread across the bed. He took the little slippers out of the wardrobe. Rosanette considered these little attentions very delicate.

About one o'clock she was awoken by distant rumblings; and she saw him sobbing with his head buried in his pillow.

'What's the matter, dearest?'

'I'm just too happy,' said Frédéric. 'I've been wanting you too long!'

PART THREE

I

THE rattle of musket-fire roused him suddenly from his sleep; and despite Rosanette's entreaties, Frédéric insisted on going out to see what was happening. He went down the Champs-Élysées, where the firing had taken place. On the corner of the Rue Saint-Honoré he met some men in smocks who shouted to him:

'No! Not this way! To the Palais-Royal!'

Frédéric followed them. The railings of the Church of the Assumption had been torn down. Further on he noticed three paving-stones in the middle of the roadway, presumably the beginnings of a barricade, and then some broken bottles and coils of wire intended to obstruct the cavalry. Suddenly, out of an alley, there rushed a tall, pale young man, with black hair hanging down over his shoulders, and wearing a sort of singlet with coloured dots. He was carrying a long infantry musket and running along on tiptoe, looking as tense as a sleepwalker and as lithe as a tiger. Every now and then an explosion could be heard.

The previous evening the sight of a cart containing five of the corpses collected from the Boulevard des Capucines had altered the mood of the common people; and while aides-de-camp came and went at the Tuileries, while Monsieur Molé, who was constructing a new cabinet, failed to reappear, while Monsieur Thiers tried to form another, and while the King dillied and dallied, giving Bugeaud complete authority only to prevent him from using it, the insurrection grew in strength, as if it were directed by a single hand. Men harangued the mob at street corners with frenzied eloquence; others set all the bells ringing in the churches; lead was melted down, cartridges rolled; on the boulevards the trees, public urinals, benches, railings, and gas-lamps were all pulled down or overturned; by the morning, Paris was covered with barricades. Resistance did not last long; everywhere the National Guard intervened, so that by eight o'clock, by force or consent, the people had taken possession of five barracks, nearly all the town halls, and the strongest strategic positions. Quietly and rapidly, the monarchy was disintegrating all by itself. Now the mob was attacking the guard-house at the

Château-d'Eau, to liberate fifty prisoners who were not there.

Frédéric was obliged to stop at the entrance to the square, which was full of groups of men carrying arms. Infantry companies occupied the Rue Saint-Thomas and the Rue Fromanteau. A huge barricade blocked the Rue de Valois. The smoke hanging over it broke up; men rushed at it with wild gestures and disappeared; then the firing started again. The guard-house replied, although nobody could be seen inside; its windows were protected by oak shutters, pierced with loop-holes; and the monument, with its two storeys and two wings, its fountain on the first floor and its little door in the middle, was beginning to show white pock-marks where the bullets had struck. Its flight of three steps remained empty.

Next to Frédéric a man in a fez, with a cartridge-pouch slung over his woollen jacket, was arguing with a woman with a kerchief round her hair. She was saying:

'Come back! Come back, I say!'

'Leave me alone!' the husband replied. 'You can easily look after the lodge by yourself. I ask you, Citizen, is it fair? I've done my duty every time, in 1830, in '32, in '34, in '39. Today they're fighting again, and I've got to fight with them! Go away!'

The concierge's wife finally gave in to his protests and those of a National Guard beside them, a man in his forties whose kindly face was fringed with a fair beard. He was loading his gun and firing it while talking to Frédéric, as calm in the midst of the riot as a gardener among his flowers. A boy wearing a tradesman's apron was trying to coax him into giving him some firing caps, so that he could use his gun, a fine sporting carbine which 'a gentleman' had given him.

'Grab some of those I've got behind me,' said the man, 'and make yourself scarce! You're going to get yourself killed!'

The drums beat the charge. Shrill cries arose, and shouts of triumph. The crowd surged backwards and forwards. Frédéric, caught between two dense masses, did not budge; in any case, he was fascinated and enjoying himself tremendously. The wounded falling to the ground, and the dead lying stretched out, did not look as if they were really wounded or dead. He felt as if he were watching a play.

In the middle of the crowd, above the swaying heads, an old man in a black coat could be seen on a white horse with a velvet saddle. He was holding a green branch in one hand and a piece of paper in the other, and he kept waving them stubbornly. Finally, giving up hope of making himself heard, he withdrew.

The troops had disappeared, and only the municipal guards remained to defend the guard-house. A wave of fearless men surged up the steps; they fell, only to be followed by others; the door echoed with the sound of iron bars battering at it; the guards would not give in. But then a carriage stuffed with hay and burning like a giant torch was dragged up against the walls. Faggots were hurriedly brought up, together with straw and a barrel of alcohol. The fire licked the stone wall; the building began smoking all over like a sulphur spring; and great roaring flames burst out through the balustrade round the roof terrace. The first floor of the Palais-Royal was crowded with National Guards. There was firing from every window overlooking the square; bullets whistled through the air; the fountain had been pierced, and the water, mingling with blood, spread in puddles on the ground. People slipped in the mud on clothes, shakos, and weapons; Frédéric felt something soft under his foot; it was the hand of a sergeant in a grey overcoat who was lying face down in the gutter. Fresh groups of workers kept coming up, driving the fighters towards the guard-house. The firing became more rapid. The wine-merchants' shops were open, and every now and then somebody would go in to smoke a pipe or drink a glass of beer, before returning to the fight. A stray dog started howling. This raised a laugh.

Frédéric was suddenly shaken by a man who fell groaning against his shoulder, with a bullet in his back. This shot, which for all he knew might have been aimed at him, infuriated him; and he was rushing forward when a National Guard stopped him.

'There's no point in it. The King has just left. Well, if you don't believe me, go and see for yourself!'

This assertion calmed Frédéric down. The Place du Carrousel looked peaceful enough. The Hôtel de Nantes still stood there on its own; and the houses behind, the dome of the Louvre in front, the long wooden gallery on the right, and the uneven waste land stretching as far as the shopkeepers' booths, appeared to be steeped in the greyish air, in which distant murmurs seemed to merge into the mist. But at the other end of the square a harsh light, falling through a gap in the clouds on to the façade of the Tuileries, made all its windows stand out in glaring white. Near the Arc de Triomphe a dead horse was stretched out on the ground. Behind the railings people were chatting in groups of five or six. The doors of the palace were open, and the servants on the threshold were letting people go in.

Downstairs, bowls of coffee were being served in a little room. Some of the spectators sat down to table jokingly; the others remained standing, including a cabman who seized a jar full of caster sugar, darted a worried glance to right and left, and then started eating greedily, plunging his nose right into the neck of the jar. At the foot of the main staircase a man was writing his name in a register. Frédéric recognized him from behind.

'Well, if it isn't Hussonnet!'

'Himself,' replied the Bohemian. 'I'm presenting myself at Court. This is great fun, isn't it?'

'Shall we go upstairs?'

And they went up to the Hall of the Marshals. The portraits of these great men were all intact, except for Bugeaud, who had been pierced through the stomach. They stood there, leaning on their swords, with gun-carriages behind them, in awe-inspiring postures ill suited to the present circumstances. A bulky clock showed that it was twenty past one.

Suddenly the *Marseillaise* rang out. Hussonnet and Frédéric leaned over the banisters. It was the mob. It swept up the staircase in a bewildering flood of bare heads, helmets, red caps, bayonets, and shoulders, surging forward so violently that people disappeared in the swarming mass as it went up and up, like a spring-tide pushing back a river, driven by an irresistible impulse and giving a continuous roar. At the top of the stairs it broke up and the singing stopped.

Nothing more could be heard but the shuffling of shoes and the babble of voices. The mob was content to stare inoffensively. But now and then an elbow, cramped for room, smashed a window-pane, or else a vase or a statuette rolled off a table on to the floor. The wainscoting creaked under the pressure of the crowd. Every face was red, with sweat dripping off it in large drops. Hussonnet remarked:

'Heroes don't smell very nice!'

'Oh, you're impossible,' retorted Frédéric.

Pushed along in spite of themselves, they entered a room in which a red velvet canopy was stretched across the ceiling. On the throne underneath sat a worker with a black beard, his shirt half-open, grinning like a stupid ape. Others clambered on to the platform to sit in his place.

'What a myth!' said Hussonnet. 'There's the sovereign people for you!'

The throne was picked up and passed unsteadily from hand to hand across the room.

'Good Lord! Look how it's pitching! The ship of state is being tossed on a stormy sea! It's dancing a can-can! It's dancing a can-can!'

It was taken to a window and thrown out, to the accompaniment of hisses and boos.

'Poor old thing!' said Hussonnet, as he watched it fall into the garden, where it was quickly picked up to be taken to the Bastille and then burnt.

An explosion of frenzied joy followed, as if, in place of the throne, a future of boundless joy had appeared; and the mob, less out of vengeance than from a desire to assert its supremacy, smashed or tore up mirrors, curtains, chandeliers, sconces, tables, chairs, stools – everything that was movable, in fact, down to albums of drawings and needlework baskets. They were the victors, so surely they were entitled to enjoy themselves. The rabble draped themselves mockingly in lace and cashmere. Gold fringes were twined round the sleeves of smocks, hats with ostrich plumes adorned the heads of blacksmiths, and ribbons of the Legion of Honour served as sashes for prostitutes. Everybody satisfied his whims; some danced, others drank. In the Queen's bedroom a woman was greasing her hair with pomade; behind a screen, a couple of keen gamblers were playing cards; Hussonnet pointed out to Frédéric a man leaning on a balcony and smoking his clay pipe; and in the mounting fury the continuous din was swollen by the sound of broken china and crystal, which tinkled as it fell like the keys of a harmonica.

Then the frenzy took on a darker note. An obscene curiosity impelled the mob to ransack all the closets, search all the alcoves, and turn out all the drawers. Jailbirds thrust their arms into the princesses' bed, and rolled about on it as a consolation for not being able to rape them. Others with more sinister faces wandered silently about, looking for something to steal; but there was too much of a crowd. Looking through the doorways across the long string of rooms, one could see nothing but the dark mass of people in a cloud of dust between the gilded carvings. Everybody was gasping for breath, the heat was becoming more and more stifling; and the two friends went out for fear of being suffocated.

In the entrance-hall, standing on a pile of clothes, a prostitute was posing as a statue of Liberty, motionless and terrifying, with her eyes wide open.

They had just got outside when a squad of municipal guards in overcoats came towards them. Taking off their policemen's caps, and revealing their somewhat bald heads, they bowed low to the mob. The ragged victors were delighted at this mark of respect. Hussonnet and Frédéric could not help deriving a certain pleasure from it either.

Full of high spirits, they went back to the Palais-Royal. At the end of the Rue Fromanteau the corpses of some soldiers were piled up on a heap of straw. They walked past without batting an eyelid, and even felt proud of the knowledge that they were showing no emotion.

The palace was overflowing with people. Seven bonfires were blazing in the inner courtyard. Pianos, chests of drawers, and clocks were being thrown out of the windows. Fire-engines were squirting water right up to the roofs. Some hooligans were trying to cut the hosepipes with their swords, and Frédéric urged a military cadet to intervene. The cadet did not understand, and indeed seemed to be half-witted. All round, in the two arcades, the mob, after raiding the wine-cellars, was abandoning itself to a horrifying orgy. Wine was flowing in torrents, wetting the people's feet, and ragamuffins were drinking out of the bottoms of broken bottles, shouting as they staggered about.

'Let's go,' said Hussonnet, 'I find the common people revolting.'

All along the Orléans gallery wounded men were lying on mattresses on the ground, with crimson curtains as blankets; and the wives of the local shopkeepers were bringing them soup and linen.

'I don't care what you think,' said Frédéric. 'I think the people are sublime.'

The great hall was filled with a swirling mass of angry people. Some were trying to gain access to the upper storeys to complete their work of destruction; some National Guards on the steps were trying to hold them back. The bravest of the guards was a bare-headed rifleman with his hair all tousled and his leather equipment in tatters. His shirt was bulging out between his trousers and his coat, and he was struggling desperately in the midst of the other guards. Hussonnet, who was very keen-sighted, recognized Arnoux from a distance.

Then they went into the Tuileries garden to breathe more freely.

They sat down on a bench, and stayed for a few minutes with their eyes shut, so exhausted that they had not the strength to speak. The passers-by around them were stopping one another to talk. The Duchesse d'Orléans had been appointed regent; it was all over; and everybody was savouring that pleasurable feeling which follows the swift solution of a crisis, when servants suddenly appeared at all the attic windows of the palace, tearing up their livery. They tossed it down into the garden as a mark of renunciation. The mob booed them. They withdrew.

The two men's attention was distracted by the sight of a big fellow walking briskly along between the trees with a musket on his shoulder. A cartridge-belt was strapped round his red tunic, and a kerchief was wound round his forehead, under his cap. He turned his head. It was Dussardier. Throwing himself into their arms, he cried:

'Oh, how happy I am, my dear fellows!'

He was incapable of saying another word, he was so breathless with joy and fatigue. He had been on his feet for the past forty-eight hours. He had worked on the barricades in the Latin Quarter, fought in the Rue Rambuteau, saved the lives of three dragoons, entered the Tuileries with Dunoyer's column, and then gone first to the Chamber and afterwards to the Hôtel de Ville.

'I've just come from there. All is well! The people have won! Workers and bourgeois are embracing! Oh, if only you'd seen what I've seen! What wonderful people! How splendid everything is!'

And without noticing that they were unarmed, he went on:

'I knew I'd find you in the thick of it! Things looked pretty bad for a moment, but it's all over now!'

A drop of blood was trickling down his cheek, and in answer to his two friends' inquiries he said:

'Oh, it's nothing. A scratch from a bayonet.'

'All the same you ought to have it seen to.'

'Nonsense! I'm no weakling. And what does it matter? The Republic has been proclaimed! We shall all be happy now! I heard some journalists saying just now that we're going to liberate Poland and Italy. No more kings! You understand what that means? The whole world free! The whole world free!'

And sweeping the horizon with a single glance, he stretched out his arms in a triumphant gesture. But then he saw a long file of men running along the terrace beside the water.

'Dammit, I was forgetting! The forts are still occupied. I must go over there. Good-bye!'

He turned round, brandishing his musket, to shout to them:

'Long live the Republic!'

Great clouds of smoke were pouring out of the chimneys of the palace, carrying sparks with them. The sound of bells in the distance was like the terrified bleating of sheep. Everywhere, to right and left, the victors were letting off their firearms. Frédéric, for all that he was no fighting man, felt his Gallic blood stirring. The ardour of the crowds had infected him. He greedily breathed in the stormy air, full of the smell of gunpowder; and at the same time he trembled with the consciousness of a vast love, a sublime, all-embracing tenderness, as if the heart of all mankind were beating in his breast.

Hussonnet gave a yawn and said:

'I suppose it's time I went off to educate the masses.'

Frédéric accompanied him to his office on the Place de la Bourse; and there he set to work and wrote a lyrical account of the recent events for the newspaper at Troyes, a real masterpiece to which he signed his name. Then they dined together in a tavern. Hussonnet was in a thoughtful mood: the eccentricities of the Revolution surpassed his own.

After coffee they went to the Hôtel de Ville in search of news, and by that time his playful nature had reasserted itself. He climbed the barricades like a chamois, and answered the sentries' challenges with patriotic quips.

They heard the Provisional Government proclaimed by torch-light. Finally, at midnight, Frédéric returned home, utterly exhausted.

'Well,' he said to his manservant while the latter was undressing him, 'are you pleased?'

'Yes, of course, Monsieur. But what I don't like is seeing the mob all marching together.'

The next morning, when he woke up, Frédéric thought of Deslauriers. He hurried round to see him. The lawyer had just left, having been appointed a provincial commissioner. The previous evening he had managed to see Ledru-Rollin, and, by pestering him in the name of the law schools, had wrung a post and a mission from him. In any case, said the concierge, he would be writing the following week to give his address.

After this, Frédéric went off to see the Marshal. She gave him a frosty welcome, for she was still annoyed with him for deserting her.

Her resentment vanished in response to his repeated assurances that peace had returned. Everything was quiet now; there was no cause for alarm; he kissed her; and she declared herself in favour of the Republic, a position which had already been taken up by His Grace the Archbishop of Paris, and which was to be adopted with remarkable alacrity by the Magistrature, the Council of State, the Institut, the Marshals of France, Changarnier, Monsieur de Falloux, all the Bonapartists, all the Legitimists, and a considerable number of Orleanists.

The fall of the monarchy had been so swift that, once the first moment of stupefaction had passed, the middle classes felt a sort of astonishment at finding that they were still alive. The summary execution of a few thieves, who were shot without trial, was regarded as an admirable act of justice. For a month everybody repeated Lamartine's remark about the red flag,[52] 'which had merely been carried round the Champ de Mars, whereas the tricolour . . .' and so on; and everybody paid lip-service to the tricolour, each party seeing only one colour in the flag – its own – and resolving to remove the other two as soon as it had the upper hand.

As business was at a standstill, anxiety and curiosity brought everybody out into the streets. The general casualness of dress blurred the distinction between the various social classes, hatred was concealed, high hopes were expressed, and the mob was in a gentle mood. Pride in a hard-won right was written on every face. There was a carnival gaiety in the air, a sort of camp-fire mood; nothing could have been more enchanting than Paris in those first days.

Frédéric gave the Marshal his arm, and they strolled through the streets together. She enthused over the rosettes decorating every buttonhole, the flags hanging from every window, and the bills of every colour posted up on the walls; and here and there she tossed a few coins into a collection-box for the wounded, placed on a chair in the middle of the road. Then she would stop to look at caricatures depicting Louis-Philippe as a pastrycook, an acrobat, a dog or a leech. But Caussidière's men[53] with their swords and sashes frightened her a little. Sometimes they came across a tree of liberty being planted. The clergy, escorted by uniformed acolytes, took part in this ceremony, giving their blessing to the Republic; and the crowd expressed its approval. The commonest sight was that of deputations of everything under the sun going to present a petition at the Hôtel de Ville, for every trade and every industry expected the Government to put an immediate end to its problems. Some people, it is true, went to offer advice or congratulations, or simply to pay a call on the Government and see the machine at work.

About the middle of March, one day when he was crossing the Pont d'Arcole on his way to run an errand for Rosanette in the Latin Quarter, Frédéric saw a column of men with weird hats and long beards coming towards him. At their head, beating a drum, marched a negro, a former artist's model, and their banner, which floated in the wind, bearing the inscription 'Pictorial artists', was carried by none other than Pellerin.

He motioned to Frédéric to wait for him, then reappeared five minutes later saying that he had plenty of time, for at the moment the Government was seeing a deputation of stonemasons. He and his colleagues were going to demand the creation of a Forum of Art, a sort of Stock Exchange handling aesthetic interests; sublime works of art would be produced because all the artists would pool their genius. Soon Paris would be covered with gigantic monuments which he would decorate; he had already started work on a picture of the Republic. One of his comrades came to fetch him, for a deputation from the poultry trade was hard on their heels.

'What nonsense!' grumbled a voice in the crowd. 'Always a lot of fancy ideas! Nothing significant!'

It was Regimbart. He did not greet Frédéric, but took the opportunity to vent his spleen.

The Citizen spent his days roaming the streets, tugging at his moustache, rolling his eyes, and collecting and passing on gloomy pieces of news. He had only two phrases: 'Look out, we're going to be outflanked!' and: 'Dammit all, they're pinching the Republic!' He was dissatisfied with everything, and particularly with the fact that France had not taken back her natural frontiers. The mere mention of Lamartine's name made him shrug his shoulders. He did not consider that Ledru-Rollin was 'up to dealing with the problem'; and he regarded Dupont (of the Eure) as an old fogey, Albert as an idiot, Louis Blancas a Utopian, and Blanqui as a thoroughly dangerous character.[54] When Frédéric asked him what they ought to have done, he took his arm in an iron grip and replied:

'Take the Rhine, that's what! Take the Rhine, dammit!'

Then he inveighed against the reactionaries.

They were beginning to show their hand. The sack of the castles of Neuilly and Suresnes, the fire at Les Batignolles, the riots in Lyons – every excess and every grievance was now exaggerated; and the reactionaries threw in Ledru-Rollin's circular, the forced issue of banknotes, the drop in Government stock to sixty francs, and lastly, as the final iniquity, the last straw, the supreme horror, the forty-five-centime tax.[55] And on top of all this there was Socialism too! Although these theories were about as new as love and war, and although in the past forty years they had been discussed in enough books to fill several libraries, they still terrified the middle classes as much as a shower of meteorites, arousing the hatred which any idea produces just because it is an idea, a detestation which later redounds to its glory and ensures its superiority over its enemies, however mediocre the idea itself may be.

Now property was raised to the level of Religion and became indistinguishable from God. The attacks being made on it took on the appearance of sacrilege, almost of cannibalism. In spite of the most humanitarian legislation ever passed in France, the spectre of '93 reappeared, and the sound of the guillotine made itself heard in every syllable of the word 'Republic' – although this did not prevent people from despising it for its weakness. Conscious of no longer having a master, France began to cry out in terror, like a blind man without a stick, or a child who has lost its nurse.

Of all Frenchmen, the one who trembled the most was Monsieur Dambreuse. The new state of affairs not only threatened his fortune but, far worse, contradicted his experience. Such a splendid system! Such a wise king! What could have happened? The world was coming to an end! The very day after the Revolution he dismissed three servants, sold his horses, bought a soft hat to wear in the street, and even thought of letting his beard grow; and he stayed at home, bitterly perusing those newspapers which were most hostile to his views, and so depressed that even the jokes about Flocon's pipe[56] could not bring a smile to his lips.

As a supporter of the late monarchy, he was terrified that the people would wreak their vengeance on his property in Champagne. Then Frédéric's journalistic effusion came to his notice, and he jumped to the conclusion that his young friend was a person of great influence who, if he could not help him, could at least defend him.

The result was that one morning Monsieur Dambreuse called at Frédéric's house, accompanied by Martinon.

The sole purpose of his visit, he said, was to have a little chat with Frédéric. All things considered, he was delighted with what had happened, and had enthusiastically adopted 'our sublime motto: Liberty, Equality, Fraternity', for he had always been a Republican at heart. If he had voted with the Government under the monarchy, that had simply been in order to hasten its inevitable downfall. He even inveighed against Monsieur Guizot, 'who – you can't deny it – has landed us in a fine mess!' On the other hand he greatly admired Lamartine, who had been 'absolutely splendid, upon my word, when he said that the red flag . . .'

'Yes, I know,' said Frédéric.

After that he declared his sympathy for the workers.

'For after all, we are all workers, more or less.'

And he carried his impartiality to the point of admitting that there was some logic in Proudhon.[57] 'Oh, a great deal of logic, dammit!' Then, with the detachment of a superior mind, he talked about the exhibition at which he had seen Pellerin's picture. He considered it an original work, which had come off very well.

Martinon supported all his remarks with approving comments; he too thought everybody should 'rally openly to the Republic'; he talked of his ploughman father and played the peasant, the man of the people. Soon they got on to the subject of the elections for the National Assembly, and the candidates in the La Fortelle district. The Opposition candidate did not stand a chance.

'You ought to take his place,' said Monsieur Dambreuse.

Frédéric pooh-poohed the idea.

'But why not?' He would obtain the votes of the extremists on account of his personal opinions, and those of the Conservatives because of his family.

'And perhaps,' the banker added with a smile, 'my influence might also help a little.'

Frédéric protested that he would not know how to set about it. Nothing could be easier: he simply had to get himself recommended to the patriots of the Aube by a Paris club. The important thing was to see that his speech was not one of the usual professions of faith, but a serious statement of principle.

'Bring it along to show me; I know the sort of thing they like down there. And, as I said before, you might well be able to render services to your country, to us all, and to me.'

In times like these people ought to help each other, and if Frédéric needed anything for himself or his friends . . .

'Oh, that's terribly kind of you!'

'On the understanding that you'll do the same for me one day, of course!'

The banker was definitely a splendid fellow.

Frédéric could not help thinking of his advice; and soon he was dazzled by a vision which made his head swim.

The great figures of the Convention passed before his eyes. It seemed to him that a magnificent dawn was about to break. Rome, Vienna, and Berlin were in revolt; the Austrians had been driven out of Venice; the whole of Europe was in a ferment. Now was the time for him to throw himself into the movement, perhaps to help it forward; and then he was attracted by the uniform which people said the deputies were going to wear. He already saw himself in a waistcoat with lapels and a tricolour sash; and this longing, this hallucination became so strong that he confessed it to Dussardier.

'Why, of course! By all means stand as a candidate.'

All the same, Frédéric consulted Deslauriers, too. The stupid opposition which was hindering the commissioner in his department had increased his liberalism. He promptly sent his friend some violent exhortations.

However Frédéric needed the approval of more people; and he told Rosanette all about it, one day when Mademoiselle Vatnaz was there.

She was one of those Parisian spinsters who, every evening, when they have given their lessons, or tried to sell their little drawings or place their pitiful manuscripts, go home with mud on their petti-coats, cook their dinner, eat it all alone, and then, with their feet on a foot-warmer, by the light of a smoking lamp, dream of a love-affair, a family, a home, a fortune – everything they have not got. Consequently, like many others, she had greeted the Revolution as the harbinger of revenge; she was devoting herself passionately to Socialist propaganda.

According to Mademoiselle Vatnaz, the emancipation of the proletariat was possible only through the emancipation of women. She wanted the admission of women to all types of employment, investigation into the paternity of illegitimate children, a new legal code, and either the abolition of marriage or at the very least 'a more intelligent regulation of the institution'. In her opinion, every Frenchwoman should be obliged to marry a Frenchman or to adopt an old man. Wet-nurses and midwives should become civil servants; and there should be a jury to examine books by women, special publishers for women, a polytechnic school for women, a National Guard for women, everything for women! And seeing that the Government did not recognize their rights, they would have to conquer force by force. Ten thousand citizenesses, armed with good muskets, could make the Hôtel de Ville tremble.

Frédéric's candidature seemed to promise well for her ideas. She encouraged him, showing him fame on the horizon. Rosanette was delighted to have a lover who was going to speak in the Chamber.

'And then perhaps they'll give you a good post.'

Frédéric, the weakest of men, was infected by the general madness. He wrote a speech and went to show it to Monsieur Dambreuse.

At the sound of the main gate closing, a curtain behind one window opened a little way and a woman appeared. He had not time to see who it was. In the hall a picture caught his eye and halted him in his tracks. It was Pellerin's picture, which had been placed on a chair, temporarily no doubt.

It showed the Republic, or Progress, or Civilization, in the form of Christ driving a locomotive through a virgin forest. After looking at it for a moment, Frédéric exclaimed:

'How utterly appalling!'

'Isn't it!' said Monsieur Dambreuse, who had heard this remark as he came in and assumed that it referred, not to the painting, but to the doctrine which the picture glorified.

Martinon arrived at the same time. They went into the study; and Frédéric was taking a piece of paper out of his pocket when Mademoiselle Cécile came in suddenly and asked with an innocent air:

'Is my aunt here?'

'You know perfectly well she isn't,' retorted the banker. 'Never mind! Make yourself at home, Mademoiselle.'

'Oh, no, thank you. I'm going.'

She had scarcely gone out before Martinon pretended to be looking for his handkerchief.

'I've left it in my overcoat. Will you excuse me?'

'Of course,' said Monsieur Dambreuse.

He was obviously not taken in by this trick, and even seemed to be encouraging it. Why? But soon Martinon reappeared, and Frédéric launched into his speech. When he got to the second page, which stigmatized the preponderance of financial interests, the banker pulled a face. Then, starting on the reforms he advocated, Frédéric called for free trade.

'What? . . . But if you'll allow me to say so . . .'

Frédéric went on without hearing him. He demanded a tax on income, graduated taxation, a European federation, education for the masses, and the greatest possible encouragement for fine arts.

'If the country paid men like Delacroix and Hugo a hundred thousand francs a year, what would be the harm in that?'

The whole thing concluded with some advice to the upper classes.

'Spare nothing, you rich men! Give! Give!'

He came to a stop and remained on his feet. His two listeners, who were seated, did not speak; Martinon's eyes were wide open and Monsieur Dambreuse was ghastly pale. Finally, concealing his emotion behind a sour smile, he said:

'Your speech is absolutely perfect!'

And he praised its form to the skies, so as to avoid expressing any opinion on its contents.

This virulence on the part of an inoffensive young man frightened him, above all as a symptom. Martinon tried to reassure him. Before long the Conservative Party would be sure to take its revenge; the commissioners of the Provisional Government had already been driven out of several towns; the elections were not due to be held until 23 April, so that there was plenty of time; in short, Monsieur Dambreuse himself ought to stand for the Aube. From that day on, Martinon stayed at his side, acting as his secretary and surrounding him with filial attentions.

Frédéric arrived at Rosanette's extremely pleased with himself. Delmar was there and informed him that he was definitely standing as a candidate for the Seine elections. In a poster addressed 'to the People', in which he spoke to them in familiar terms, the actor boasted that he really understood them, and that for their sake he had allowed himself to be 'crucified by Art', with the result that he had become their incarnation, their ideal. He was in fact convinced that he had an enormous influence on the masses, so that at a later date, in a Ministry office, he went so far as to offer to quell a riot single-handed; when asked what means he would employ, he replied:

'Have no fear! I shall show them my face!'

To annoy him, Frédéric informed him of his own candidature. As soon as the actor realized that his future colleague meant to stand for a country district, he put himself at Frédéric's service and offered to show him round the clubs.

They visited them all, or nearly all – the red clubs, the blue, the wild, the peaceful, the puritanical, the Bohemian, the mystical, the alcoholic, the clubs where the kings of the world were condemned to death, and those where the swindling tricks of the grocery trade were denounced. Everywhere tenants cursed landlords, smocks attacked tail-coats, and rich conspired against poor. Some wanted compensation for the ill-treatment they had suffered at the hands of the police, while others clamoured for money to develop inventions; there were plans for Fourierist communities, schemes for village bazaars, systems for universal happiness. Here and there a lightning-flash of wit appeared among these clouds of stupidity, an impassioned declaration was made with explosive suddenness, a point of law was formulated in an oath, and flowers of eloquence blossomed on the lips of a workman wearing a sword-belt across his bare chest. Sometimes, too, a gentleman would appear, an aristocrat affecting a humble manner, talking the language of the plebs, and leaving his hands unwashed to make them look horny. A patriot would recognize him, the more fanatical members of the company would insult him, and he would go out with rage in his heart. To obtain a reputation for common sense, it was necessary to criticize the lawyers all the time, and to use the following expressions as often as possible: 'Contribute one's stone to the building . . . social problem . . . workshop.'

Delmar never missed an opportunity to take the floor; and when he could not think of anything to say, he had a trick of putting his hand on his hip, thrusting his other arm inside his waistcoat, and turning his head sharply to one side, so as to show off his profile. Then there would be a burst of applause – from Mademoiselle Vatnaz at the back of the hall.

In spite of the poor quality of the oratory, Frédéric did not dare to try his hand. All these people seemed too uncultured and too hostile.

But Dussardier made inquiries and eventually informed Frédéric that there was a club in the Rue Saint-Jacques called the Club de l'Intelligence. A name like that promised well. Besides, he would take his friends with him.

He took along the people he had invited to his punch-party; the accountant, the traveller in wines, and the architect. Even Pellerin came; Hussonnet had said that he might; and on the pavement outside the door stood Regimbart with two men, one his faithful Compain, a rather thick-set individual, red-eyed and pock-marked, and the other a sort of negroid ape, an extremely hairy creature about whom he knew nothing except that he was 'a patriot from Barcelona'.

They went down a passage, and then were shown into a big room which was apparently used as a carpenter's workshop, with new walls which smelt of plaster. Four oil-lamps hanging in a row shed an unpleasant light. On a platform at the far end there was a desk with a bell, a table below which did duty as a rostrum, and on either side of it two lower tables for the secretaries. The audience which occupied the benches consisted of elderly painters, school ushers, and writers who had never been published. Among these rows of overcoats with greasy collars could be seen an occasional woman's hat or workman's overall. Indeed the back of the hall was full of workmen, who were probably there for want of anything better to do, or had been brought along by some of the speakers to applaud them.

Frédéric took care to place himself between Dussardier and Regimbart, who, as soon as he had sat down, put his hands on the knob of his stick, rested his chin on his hands, and closed his eyes. At the other end of the hall stood Delmar, towering over the assembled company.

Sénécal appeared at the chairman's desk.

Dussardier had thought that this surprise would please Frédéric. It annoyed him.

The audience showed great respect for its chairman. He was one of those who, on 25 February, had called for the immediate organization of labour; the next day, at the Prado, he had spoken in favour of an attack on the Hôtel de Ville; and as it was customary for every person in the public eye to model himself on some famous figure, one copying Saint-Just, another Danton, and yet another Marat, he himself tried to resemble Blanqui, who in his turn imitated Robespierre. His black gloves and his close-cropped hair gave him a severe look which was extremely becoming.

He opened the meeting with a declaration of the Rights of Man and the Rights of the Citizen, the customary act of faith. Then a loud voice broke into Béranger's *Memories of the People*.

'No! No! Not that!'

'*The Cap!*' the patriots at the back started shouting.

And they sang in unison the poem which was then in vogue:

> 'Hats off before the cap!
> On your knees before the workman!'

At a word from the chairman the audience fell silent. One of the secretaries started opening the letters.

'Some young men inform us that every evening they burn a copy of *L'Assemblée Nationale*[58] in front of the Panthéon, and they urge all patriots to follow their example.'

'Bravo! Carried!' the audience replied.

'Citizen Jean-Jacques Langreneux, printer, of the Rue Dauphine, would like a monument to be erected to the memory of the Thermidor martyrs.'

'Michel-Évariste-Népomucène Vincent, sometime professor, expresses the hope that European democracy will adopt a common language. A dead language might be used, such as Latin of the best period.'

'No! No Latin!' cried the architect.

'Why not?' retorted a schoolmaster.

And the two men launched into an argument in which others joined, each person trying to show off with some witty remark. Soon the discussion became so tedious that a good many people walked out.

But then a little old man, wearing a pair of green spectacles under a remarkably high forehead, asked permission to read out an urgent communication.

This was a memorandum on the assessment of taxation. The figures came pouring out; there was no end of them. The audience showed its impatience by muttering and talking, but nothing put him off his stride. Then people started hissing and calling out: 'Fido!' Sénécal chided them; the speaker went on like a machine. The only way of stopping him was to take him by the elbow. The good fellow looked as if he were coming out of a dream, and, calmly raising his spectacles, he said:

'Forgive me, citizens, forgive me! I'll withdraw! I beg your pardon!'

The failure of this reading disconcerted Frédéric. He had his speech in his pocket, but an impromptu address would have been better.

At last the chairman announced that they were going to pass on to the main business of the evening, the question of the elections. They were not going to argue about the main lists of Republican candidates. All the same, the Club de l'Intelligence, like any other club, was entitled – 'with all due respect to the tin gods of the Hôtel de Ville' – to draw up a list of its own, and those citizens who sought the people's mandate were invited to state their qualifications.

'Go on!' Dussardier said to Frédéric.

A man in a cassock, with crinkly hair and a peevish expression, had already put up his hand. He mumbled that his name was Ducretot, and that he was a priest and agronomist, the author of a work entitled *Manure*. He was advised to join a horticultural society.

Then a patriot in a smock climbed on to the platform. He was a man of the people, with broad shoulders, a plump, gentle face, and long black hair. He cast an almost voluptuous glance round the audience, flung back his head, and finally, stretching out his arms, said:

'Brethren, you have rejected Ducretot, and you have done well; but you did not do this out of impiety, for we are all pious men.'

Several members of the audience were listening open-mouthed, like children in a catechism class, in ecstatic attitudes.

'Nor did you do it because he is a priest, for we too are priests! The workman is a priest, like the founder of Socialism, the Master of us all, Jesus Christ!'

The time had come to inaugurate the reign of God. The Gospel led straight to 1789. After the abolition of slavery would come the abolition of the proletariat. The age of hatred was past; the age of love was about to begin.

'Christianity is the keystone and the foundation of the new edifice . . .'

'Are you making fun of us?' cried the traveller in wines. 'Who's landed us with this blasted priest?'

This interruption shocked the audience to the core. Nearly all of them climbed on to the benches, and, shaking their fists, yelled: 'Atheist! Aristocrat! Swine!' while the chairman's bell rang without stopping and there were shouts of 'Order! Order!' But the traveller, completely unabashed, and also fortified by three laced coffees which he had drunk before coming along, went on struggling in the midst of the mob.

'What, me an aristocrat? Get along with you!'

When in the end he was allowed to explain himself, he declared that there would never be any peace as long as there were priests around, and, seeing that they had just been talking about economy measures, a really good one would be to suppress the churches, sacred vessels, and finally all forms of worship.

Somebody protested that he was going to extremes.

'Yes! I'm going to extremes all right! But when a ship is caught in a storm . . .'

Without waiting for the end of the comparison, somebody else retorted:

'I agree! But you'd destroy everything at one fell blow, like a stupid builder . . .'

'That's an insult to us masons!' yelled a citizen covered with plaster.

And, stubbornly insisting that he had been provoked, he swore and cursed, trying to fight, and clinging to his bench. It took three men to throw him out.

In the meantime the workman was still standing on the platform. The two secretaries told him to get down. He protested at the injustice which was being done to him.

'You will never stop me from swearing eternal love to our beloved France, eternal love to the Republic!'

'Citizens!' said Compain. 'Citizens!'

By saying 'Citizens!' over and over again, he obtained comparative silence, whereupon he placed his two red stump-like hands on the table, leant forward, half-closed his eyes, and declared:

'I believe the scope of the calf's head ought to be extended.'[59]

All were silent, thinking they had misheard.

'Yes! The calf's head!'

Three hundred simultaneous guffaws came from the audience. The ceiling trembled. At the sight of all these faces convulsed with laughter, Compain drew back, and then went on angrily:

'What! You've never heard of the calf's head?'

The audience went into a paroxysm of delirious laughter. They held their sides. Some even rolled on the floor under the benches. Compain could not stand it any longer; he took refuge beside Regimbart and tried to drag him away.

'No!' said the Citizen. 'I'm staying here to the end!'

This reply decided Frédéric. Looking to right and left for support from his friends, he suddenly saw Pellerin on the platform in front of him. The artist treated the mob disdainfully.

'I'd like to know where the candidate for Art is to be found. I myself have painted a picture . . .'

'We don't want any pictures!' retorted a thin man with red spots on his cheekbones.

Pellerin protested that he was being interrupted.

But the other man went on in a tragic voice:

'The Government ought to have issued a decree by now, abolishing prostitution and poverty.'

This remark promptly won him the audience's sympathy, and he proceeded to thunder against the corruption of the great cities.

'Shame and infamy! We ought to grab hold of the rich as they're coming out of the Maison d'Or and spit in their faces! It wouldn't be so bad if the Government didn't encourage debauchery. But the city revenue officers get up to some filthy tricks with our daughters and sisters . . .'

A voice in the audience remarked:

'That's a good one!'

'Throw him out!'

'They bleed us white to pay for their debauchery. Look at all the money an actor gets, for instance . . .'

'I can't let that pass!' cried Delmar.

He jumped on to the platform, pushed everybody aside, and struck his usual attitude. Declaring that he felt nothing but contempt for such trivial accusations, he dilated on the civilizing mission of the actor. Seeing that the theatre was the focal point of national education, he was all for reforming it. To begin with, there should be no more managers and no more privileges.

'He's right there! No more privileges of any sort!'

The actor's performance inflamed the audience, and subversive proposals came from all parts of the hall.

'No more academies! Away with the Institut!'

'No more missions!'

'No more matriculation!'

'Down with university degrees!'

'No,' said Sénécal. 'Let us keep them, but let them be conferred by universal suffrage, by the People, the only true judge!'

In any case, this was not the most urgent thing to do. To begin with, the rich had to be levelled down. And he depicted them wallowing in crime under their gilded ceilings, while the poor, writhing with hunger in their garrets, practised all the virtues. The applause became so loud that he broke off. He stood for a few minutes with his eyes shut and his head thrown back, as if he were rocking himself to sleep on the wave of anger he had aroused.

Then he started speaking dogmatically, in phrases as imperious as laws. The State must seize the banks and the insurance companies. Legacies would be abolished. A public fund would be set up for the workers. A great many other measures would be necessary later on. For the time being, these were enough; and, returning to the subject of the elections, he said:

'We need upright citizens, men who are new to politics! Will anybody here come forward?'

Frédéric stood up. There was a buzz of approval created by his friends. But Sénécal, putting on the expression of a Fouquier-Tinville,[60] started questioning him about his surname, Christian names, antecedents, life, and morals.

Frédéric answered him briefly, biting his lips. Sénécal asked if anybody had any objection to this candidature.

'No! No!'

But Sénécal had. The whole audience leant forward, straining their ears. The candidate had failed to pay a certain sum which he had promised towards the foundation of a democratic newspaper. What is more, on 22 February, although adequately informed, he had failed to keep the rendezvous on the Place du Panthéon.

'I swear he was at the Tuileries!' cried Dussardier.

'Can you swear you saw him at the Panthéon?'

Dussardier bowed his head. Frédéric said nothing; his friends, shocked by this revelation, looked at him anxiously.

'At the very least,' Sénécal went on, 'do you know a patriot who can answer for your principles?'

'I can,' said Dussardier.

'Oh, that won't do. Somebody else!'

Frédéric turned towards Pellerin. The artist replied with a flourish of gestures as if to say:

'Oh, my dear fellow, they've rejected me. Dammit all, what can you expect?'

Then Frédéric gave Regimbart a nudge.

'Yes, you're right, it's time. I'm on my way!'

And Regimbart climbed on to the platform; then, pointing to the Spaniard who had followed him, he said:

'Citizens, allow me to present you a patriot from Barcelona.'

The patriot bowed low, rolled his silvery eyes like a clockwork doll, and, placing his hand on his heart, declared:

'*Ciudadanos! Mucho aprecio el honor que me dispensáis, y si grande es vuestra bondad mayor es vuestra atención.*'

'I demand a hearing!' cried Frédéric.

'*Desde que se proclamó la constitución de Cadiz, ese pacto fundamental de las libertades españolas, hasta la última revolución, nuestra patria cuenta numerosos y heroicos martires.*'

Once again Fréderic tried to make himself heard:

'But, citizens . . .'

The Spaniard went on:

'*El martes próximo tendrá lugar en la iglesia de la Magdalena un servicio funebre.*'

'But this is absurd. Nobody can understand a word.'

This remark infuriated the audience.

'Throw him out! Throw him out!'

'Who? Me?' asked Frédéric.

'Yes, you!' said Sénécal majestically. 'Get out!'

He got up to go, and the Spaniard's voice followed him:

'*Y todos los Españoles desearían ver alli reundidas las deputaciones de los clubs y de la milicia nacional. Una oración funebre, en honor de la libertad española y del mundo entero, será pronunciada por un miembro del clero de Paris en la sala Bonne-Nouvelle. Honor al pueblo francés, que llamaría yo el primero pueblo del mundo, sino fuese ciudadano de otra nación!*'[61]

'Aristo!' shouted a guttersnipe, shaking his fist at Frédéric, who rushed indignantly out into the courtyard.

He reproached himself with his devotion to the Republic, forgetting that the accusations levelled at him were, after all, perfectly just. What a mad idea it had been to put up for election! But what fools they were, what cretins! He compared himself to these men, and soothed his wounded pride with the thought of their stupidity.

Then he felt an urge to see Rosanette. After all that ugliness and bombast, her prettiness would be a relief. She knew that he had been due to offer himself for adoption at a club that evening. However, when he came in, she did not even ask him a single question.

She was sitting by the fire, unpicking the lining of a dress. This occupation surprised him.

'Hullo! What are you doing?'

'You can see for yourself,' she answered curtly. 'I'm patching up my old clothes. All because of your Republic.'

'What do you mean, my Republic?'

'I suppose it's mine, then?'

And she started blaming him for everything that had happened in France during the last months, accusing him of having started the Revolution; it was his fault if everybody was ruined, if the rich were leaving Paris, and if she died later on in the workhouse.

'You're all right with your private income. Though the way things are going, you won't have that very much longer.'

'You may be right,' said Frédéric. 'The more public-spirited you are, the less you are appreciated; and if you hadn't your conscience to support you, the boors you have to deal with would soon make you sick of self-sacrifice.'

Rosanette looked at him with half-closed eyes.

'Eh? What's that? What self-sacrifice? It looks as though the evening hasn't been such a great success. Serve you right! That'll teach you to go playing the generous patriot. Oh, don't deny it! I know you've given them three hundred francs, for she's an expensive mistress, your precious Republic. Well, go and enjoy yourself with her, my lad!'

Under this avalanche of stupidity, Frédéric forgot his other disappointment in a more painful disillusionment.

He had withdrawn to the far end of the room. She came over to him.

'Come on! Use your noddle! A country has to have a master, just like a house; otherwise everybody does what he likes with the housekeeping money. To begin with, everybody knows that Ledru-Rollin is up to his ears in debt. As for Lamartine, how can you expect a poet to know anything about politics? Oh, it's no use shaking your head and thinking you're cleverer than other people; that's the truth, whether you like it or not. But you're always splitting hairs; nobody else can get a word in edgeways. Take Fournier-Fontaine, for instance, who owns the Saint-Roch shops: do you know how much he lost? Eight hundred thousand francs! And look at Gomer, the carrier across the road. Broke the tongs over his wife's head, he did, and he's drunk so much absinthe they're going to put him in the madhouse. That's what they're like, your Republicans! A Republic on the cheap! Oh, yes, you can be proud of yourself!'

Frédéric went off. The woman's stupidity, suddenly revealed in this guttersnipe language, disgusted him. He even felt some of his patriotic fervour returning to him.

Rosanette's ill-humour grew steadily worse. Mademoiselle Vatnaz's enthusiasm irritated her. Convinced that she had a mission, the other woman insisted on lecturing and catechizing Rosanette; and with her superior knowledge she overwhelmed her friend with her arguments.

One day she arrived full of indignation against Hussonnet, who had just been indulging in ribald jokes at the women's club. Rosanette expressed approval of his behaviour, and even declared that she would put on men's clothes to be able to go and 'tell them what I think of them and give them a whipping'. Frédéric came in just at that moment.

'You'll come with me, won't you?'

And despite his being there, they began squabbling together, one adopting the housewife's point of view and the other the philosopher's.

Women, according to Rosanette, were born simply and solely to make love or else to bring up children and run a home.

Mademoiselle Vatnaz maintained that woman ought to have her place in the State. The women of ancient Gaul made laws, as did the Anglo-Saxon women, while the wives of the Hurons belonged to the tribal council. The work of civilization was common to both sexes. All women should contribute to it, so as to be able eventually to replace selfishness by fraternity, individualism by association, and the small-holdings system by collective farming.

'Oh, so you're an expert on agriculture now!'

'Why not? Besides, it's a question of humanity and its future.'

'Take care of your own!'

'That's my business!'

They were beginning to lose their tempers. Frédéric intervened. Mademoiselle Vatnaz was so excited that she went so far as to speak in favour of Communism.

'What nonsense!' said Rosanette. 'As if it could ever happen!'

As proof that it could, the other woman cited the Essenes, the Moravian Friars, the Jesuits in Paraguay, and the Pingon family near

Thiers in Auvergne, with such a wealth of gesture that her watch-chain got caught on a little gold sheep hanging in her bunch of charms.

All of a sudden Rosanette turned extraordinarily pale.

Mademoiselle Vatnaz went on trying to disentangle the charm.

'Don't take so much trouble,' said Rosanette. 'Now I know all about your political opinions.'

'What?' said Mademoiselle Vatnaz, blushing like a virgin.

'Oh, you know what I mean.'

Frédéric did not. Obviously something had come up between them which was more important and more personal than Social-ism.

'Well, what of it?' retorted Mademoiselle Vatnaz, drawing her-self up boldly. 'It's a loan, my dear, a debt for a debt!'

'Dammit, I'm not denying my debts. But you're not going to persuade me that you were lent that for a few thousand francs. At least I borrow; I'm not a thief!'

Mademoiselle Vatnaz gave a forced laugh.

'It's the truth – I'd put my hand in the fire to prove it!'

'Take care! It's dry enough to burn!'

The old maid held out her right hand, just in front of Rosanette's face.

'There are some friends of yours who find my hand attractive enough.'

'Andalusians, I suppose, who use it instead of castanets!'

'Whore!'

The Marshal bowed low.

'You couldn't be more ravishing.'

Mademoiselle Vatnaz made no reply. Beads of sweat appeared on her temples. Her eyes were fixed on the carpet. She was breathing hard. Finally she went to the door, and, before slamming it to, said:

'Good night! You'll be hearing from me!'

'Delighted, I'm sure,' said Rosanette.

Her self-control had exhausted her. She dropped on to the divan, weeping, trembling all over, and stammering out insults. Was it Mademoiselle Vatnaz's parting threat which was upsetting her? No, that didn't worry her at all. Then perhaps the other woman owed her some money? No, it was the gold sheep, a present; and in the midst of her tears she blurted out the name of Delmar. So she was in love with the actor!

'Then why has she accepted me?' Frédéric asked himself. 'How has he managed to come back into her life? What's obliging her to keep me? What's the meaning of it all?'

Rosanette's little sobs continued. She was still lying on her side, on the edge of the divan, with her right cheek resting on her hands and she seemed such a delicate, helpless, unhappy creature that he went over to her and kissed her gently on the forehead.

Then she assured him of the love she felt for him; the Prince had just gone away; henceforth they would be free. But for the moment she found herself . . . in financial difficulties. 'You could see that for yourself the other day, when I was using up my old linings.' She had no more carriages now! And that was not all; the upholsterers were threatening to take back the furniture in the bedroom and the big drawing-room. She did not know what to do.

Frédéric felt tempted to reply: 'Don't worry! I'll pay!' But the lady might be lying. Experience had taught him to be cautious. He contented himself with merely comforting her.

Rosanette's fears were well founded; she had to return the furniture and leave the fine apartment in the Rue Drouot. She took another, a fourth-floor apartment on the Boulevard Poissonnière. The knick-knacks from her old boudoir sufficed to give an elegant air to the three rooms. She had Chinese blinds, an awning over the terrace, and a brand-new card-table and pink silk tuffets in the drawing-room. Frédéric had contributed generously to these acquisitions; he experienced the joy of a newly married man who at last possesses a house of his own and a wife of his own. Feeling thoroughly at home at Rosanette's, he came and slept there almost every night.

One morning, as he was coming out of the hall, he saw on the third floor the shako of a National Guard who was climbing the stairs. Where was he going? Frédéric waited. The man kept on climbing, with his head slightly bowed. He looked up. It was Arnoux. The situation was obvious. They both blushed at the same time, feeling the same embarrassment.

Arnoux was the first to find a way out.

'She's getting better, isn't she?' he said, as if Rosanette were ill and he had come to ask how she was.

Frédéric took advantage of this opening.

'Yes, indeed! At least, that's what her maid told me,' he replied, in order to give the impression that he had not been admitted.

Then they stood there, face to face, both irresolute, watching one another. Which of the two was going to stay? Once again, Arnoux solved the problem.

'Oh, well, I'll come back another time! Where were you going? I'll come along with you.'

And when they were out in the street he chatted as naturally as ever. Obviously there was no jealousy in him, or else he was too good-natured to be angry.

Besides, he was preoccupied with the state of the country. He never took off his uniform these days. On 29 March he had defended the offices of the *Presse*. When the Chamber was invaded he distinguished himself by his courage, and he was present at the banquet offered to the National Guard of Amiens.[62]

Hussonnet, who was always on duty with him, drank his brandy and smoked his cigars more than anybody else; but, irreverent by nature, he amused himself by contradicting him. He poked fun at the ungrammatical style of the Government's decrees, the Luxembourg conferences, the Vesuvian legionaries, the Tyroleans, and everything else, down to the Chariot of Agriculture, which was drawn by horses instead of oxen and escorted by ugly girls.[63] Arnoux, on the other hand, defended the authorities and dreamt of a union of all the parties. In the meantime his business affairs were going from bad to worse. He did not let this worry him overmuch.

The discovery of the liaison between Frédéric and Rosanette had not upset him, since it enabled him, with a clear conscience, to cut off the allowance which he had begun paying her again after the Prince's departure. He pleaded financial difficulties and loudly bewailed his fate; Rosanette was generous. The result was that Monsieur Arnoux regarded himself as her true lover, which tickled his vanity and made him feel years younger. Convinced that Frédéric was keeping the Marshal, he imagined that he was 'playing a jolly good trick on him'; he even managed to make a secret of it, and left Frédéric a clear field when they met.

Sharing Rosanette with Arnoux hurt Frédéric's pride, and his rival's civilities struck him as a joke which was rapidly wearing thin. But a quarrel would rob him of any chance of returning to Madame Arnoux, and keeping in with Arnoux was the only way he could get news of her. After his usual custom, or possibly in a spirit of mischief, the china manufacturer often mentioned her in conversation, and even asked Frédéric why he no longer came to see her.

After exhausting all his excuses, Frédéric asserted that he had called to see Madame Arnoux several times, without ever finding her at home. Arnoux believed him, for he often told her how delighted he was at their friend's absence, and she always replied that she had missed his visit; so that these two lies, instead of contradicting one another, bore each other out.

The young man's meekness and the pleasure of duping him increased Arnoux's affection for him. He pushed familiarity beyond all bounds, not out of contempt for Frédéric, but because he trusted him. One day he wrote to him that he had to leave Paris for twenty-four hours on urgent business, and begged him to take his place on guard-duty. Frédéric did not dare to refuse and duly went to the guard-post on the Place du Carrousel.

Here he had to put up with the company of the National Guards. Apart from a refiner, a facetious individual with an enormous capacity for drink, they all seemed to him as brainless as their knapsacks. The chief topic of conversation was the replacement of their leather equipment by waistbelts. Some of them railed against the National Workshops. Somebody would ask: 'What are things coming to?' His neighbour would open his eyes wide, as if he had suddenly realized that he was standing on the edge of a precipice, and reply: 'What are things coming to?' Then a bolder spirit would cry: 'It can't go on like this! It's got to stop!' 'And as the same remarks were repeated over and over again until evening, Frédéric was bored to tears.

He was extremely surprised when, at eleven o'clock, Arnoux appeared. The latter explained straight away that his business had been concluded and that he had hurried round to relieve him.

There had been no business. He had made it up so as to be able to spend twenty-four hours alone with Rosanette. But the good fellow had overtaxed his strength and, in his exhausted condition, had been overcome with remorse. He had come to thank Frédéric and invite him to supper.

'Thank you, but I'm not hungry. All I want is my bed.'

'All the more reason why we should lunch together tomorrow! What a lazy fellow you are! You can't go home now. It's too late. It would be dangerous.'

Once again Frédéric gave way. Arnoux, whom nobody had expected to see, was given a warm welcome by his comrades in arms, especially the refiner. They all loved him, and he was so good-natured that he even regretted Hussonnet's absence. But he felt the need for a little nap, just forty winks.

'Sit down here beside me,' he said to Frédéric, as he stretched himself out on the camp-bed, without taking off his equipment.

For fear of an alarm, he even kept his musket with him, although this was against regulations. He stammered out a few words – 'My darling! My little angel!' and soon dropped off to sleep.

The conversation died away, and silence gradually descended on the guard-post. Frédéric, tormented by fleas, looked around him. Half-way up the yellow wall there was a long shelf, on which the knapsacks formed a row of little humps, while underneath, the lead-coloured muskets stood side by side. Snores came from the National Guards, whose stomachs were dimly silhouetted in the darkness. The stove was littered with plates and an empty bottle. There were three straw-bottomed chairs round the table, on which a pack of cards was spread out. In the middle of the bench there was a drum with its strap dangling. The warm breeze blowing in through the door was making the oil-lamp smoke. Arnoux was sleeping with his arms outstretched; and as his musket was resting at a slight angle, with its butt on the floor, the muzzle was under his armpit. Frédéric noticed it and took fright.

'But no! I'm a fool. There's nothing to be afraid of. All the same, if he happened to die . . .'

And straight away an endless succession of pictures passed through his mind. He saw himself in a postchaise with her at night; then beside a river on a summer evening; and in the lamplight at home, in their own house. He even dwelt on domestic details and household arrangements, seeing and savouring his happiness already, and all that was needed to bring it about was the cocking of the musket's hammer. He could push it with the tip of his big toe; the gun would go off; it would be an accident, nothing more.

Frédéric brooded over this idea, like a dramatist writing a play. Suddenly he felt that it was going to be put into action, that he was going to play his part in it, that he wanted to; and then panic seized him. In the midst of his anguish he felt a certain pleasure, into which he sank deeper and deeper, with a horrified awareness that his scruples were vanishing; in his wild reverie the rest of the world grew dim; and he was no longer conscious of himself except through an unbearable tightness in his chest.

'Shall we have a drop of white wine?' said the refiner, waking up.

Arnoux jumped off the bed, and after the white wine had been drunk, insisted on taking over Frédéric's guard-duty.

Then he carried him off to lunch at Parly's in the Rue de Chartres; and as he needed to restore his strength, he ordered two meat dishes, a lobster, a rum omelette, a salad, and so on, washing all this down with an 1819 Sauterne and a '42 Romanée, not to mention the champagne at dessert and the liqueurs.

Frédéric did nothing to thwart his wishes. He felt embarrassed, as if the other man could have found traces of his thoughts on his face.

Leaning right forward, with his elbows on the edge of the table, Arnoux gazed into Frédéric's eyes and confided his ideas to him.

He wanted to take a lease on all the embankments on the Northern Railway, to plant them with potatoes; or else to organize a gigantic procession along the boulevards in which the 'celebrities of the day' would take part. He planned to let all the windows on the route, which at an average fee of three francs would produce a splendid profit. In short, he hoped to obtain some sort of monopoly which would make his fortune. He had his principles, however, condemned excesses and misconduct, spoke of his 'poor father', and said that he examined his conscience every evening before confiding his soul to God.

'How about a drop of curaçao?'

'Just as you like.'

As for the Republic, everything would work out all right; all considered, he was the happiest man on earth; and, forgetting himself, he extolled Rosanette's qualities, even contrasting her with his wife. There was really no comparison. It was impossible to imagine lovelier thighs.

'Your health!'

Frédéric clinked glasses. Out of politeness he had drunk rather too much; besides, the bright sunshine was dazzling him; and when they walked back up the Rue Vivienne together, their epaulettes touched in a brotherly way.

Once he was home again, Frédéric slept until seven o'clock. Then he went to call on the Marshal. She had gone out with somebody. With Arnoux perhaps? Not knowing what to do with himself, he went on walking along the boulevard, but could not get past the Porte Saint-Martin, the crowd was so thick.

Poverty had condemned a considerable number of workmen to idleness; and they used to come here every evening, to go on parade, so to speak, while they waited for some signal. In spite of the law against unlawful assemblies, these 'clubs of despair' were growing in an alarming way; and a great many prosperous citizens came along every day to see them, out of bravado or because it was the fashion.

All of a sudden Frédéric caught sight of Monsieur Dambreuse with Martinon a couple of yards away; he turned his head aside, for he bore a grudge against Monsieur Dambreuse on account of his election to the Assembly. But the banker stopped him.

'Just a moment, my dear sir. I owe you an explanation.'

'I don't want one.'

'Please listen to me.'

It was not his fault at all. He had been begged, almost forced, to stand for election. Martinon promptly confirmed what he said: a deputation of people from Nogent had come to see him.

'Besides, I assumed that I was free to act, seeing that . . .'

A surge of people on the pavement forced Monsieur Dambreuse to move aside. A moment later he reappeared, saying to Martinon:

'That was a good turn you did me then! You won't have cause to regret it . . .'

All three stood with their backs against a shop, so as to be able to talk more easily.

Now and then there were shouts of 'Long live Napoleon! Long live Barbès! Down with Marie!'[64] Everybody in the vast crowd was talking very loud; and all these voices, thrown back by the houses, made a noise like the never-ending sound of the waves in a harbour. At certain moments they would fall silent, and then the *Marseillaise* would ring out. In the carriage gateways mysterious-looking men offered sword-sticks for sale. Sometimes two people would wink as they passed one another, and then hurry on their separate ways. Groups of idlers occupied the pavements; a dense throng swarmed in the roadway. Whole squads of policemen disappeared into the crowd as soon as they came out of the side-streets. Little red flags fluttered here and there like flames; the coachmen up on their boxes waved their arms about and then turned away. All this movement made a fascinating sight.

'How Mademoiselle Cécile would have enjoyed seeing this!' said Martinon.

'You know very well that my wife doesn't like my niece to accompany us,' Monsieur Dambreuse answered with a smile.

He had changed beyond recognition. For the past three months he had been shouting: 'Long live the Republic!' and he had even voted for the banishment of the Orléans family. But there must be no more concessions. He had become so fanatical on this subject that he carried a life-preserver in his pocket.

Martinon had one too. Since judicial posts had ceased to be life-long appointments he had resigned from the Public Prosecutor's office, so that he was even more violent in his opinions than Monsieur Dambreuse.

The banker felt a particular hatred for Lamartine, for having sup-ported Ledru-Rollin, and he also loathed Pierre Leroux, Proudhon, Considérant, Lamennais, all the hot-heads, all the Socialists.

'Because when all's said and done, what do they want? The tax on meat has been abolished, and so has imprisonment for debt; plans are being worked out for a mortgage bank; the other day it was a national bank! And there's five million on the budget for the work-men! But luckily that's all over, thanks to Monsieur Falloux![65] Good riddance, I say! Let them take themselves off!'

That very day, in fact, at a loss how to feed the 130,000 men in the National Workshops, the Minister for Public Works had signed a decree calling on all citizens between the ages of eighteen and twenty to enlist in the army, or else to go and till the land in the country.

This alternative infuriated the young men of Paris, who were con-vinced that it was an attempt to destroy the Republic. Life away from the capital struck them as an exile; they saw themselves dying of fever in desolate regions. Many of them, too, were accustomed to skilled work and regarded farming as a degrading occupation; in short, this was a trap, an insult, an outright refutation of all the promises which had been made to them. If they resisted, force would be used against them; they had no doubts on this score and got ready to forestall it.

About nine o'clock the crowds which had gathered at the Bastille and the Châtelet streamed back along the boulevard. From the Porte Saint-Denis to the Porte Saint-Martin they formed a swarming multitude, a solid mass of dark blue verging on black. All the men one saw had burning eyes, pale complexions, faces drawn with hunger and excited by the thought of injustice. In the meantime clouds were piling up; the stormy sky electrified the crowd and it swirled about irresolutely, surging backwards and forwards; in its depths one could sense an incalculable strength, an elemental force.

Then everybody started chanting: 'Lights! Lights!' Several windows failed to light up; stones were flung at them. Monsieur Dambreuse thought it prudent to withdraw. The two young men walked him home.

He foresaw terrible catastrophes. The mob might invade the Chamber again, and in this connexion he told how he would have been killed on 15 May, but for the devotion of the National Guard.

'But I was forgetting – it was your friend! Your friend the china manufacturer, Jacques Arnoux!'

He had been suffocating in the throng of rioters; and this worthy citizen had picked him up and carried him to safety. Since then a sort of bond had been established between them.

'We must all dine together one of these days. Since you see a lot of him, do tell him I'm very fond of him. He's an excellent fellow, unfairly criticized in my opinion; and he's got a ready wit too, the rascal! Once again, my respects, and a very good evening to you!'

After leaving Monsieur Dambreuse, Frédéric returned to the Marshal's apartment, and solemnly told her that she must choose between him and Arnoux. She gently answered that she did not understand 'that sort of talk'; she was not in love with Arnoux and was not in any way attached to him. Frédéric felt an urge to leave Paris. She said nothing to discourage this whim; and they set off for Fontainebleau the very next day.

The hotel where they stayed was distinguished from the others by a fountain splashing in the middle of its courtyard. The doors of the rooms opened on to a corridor, as in a monastery. The room they were given was spacious, well furnished, and hung with chintz; it was quiet too, as there were so few visitors. Prosperous citizens with time on their hands strolled along the street, while at dusk children played prisoners' base under their windows; and after the turmoil and confusion of Paris they found this tranquillity both surprising and refreshing.

Early in the morning they went to visit the palace. Going through the main gate, they saw the whole façade in front of them: the five towers with their pointed roofs and the horseshoe staircase at the far end of the courtyard, which was flanked on left and right by two lower buildings. In the distance, the moss-covered paving-stones blended with the fawn tint of the bricks; and the whole palace, rust-coloured like an old suit of armour, gave an impression of royal dignity, of sombre military splendour.

At last a servant appeared carrying a bunch of keys. To begin with, he showed them the apartments of the queens, the Pope's oratory, the François I gallery, the little mahogany table on which the Emperor signed his abdication, and, in one of the rooms into which the old Hunting Gallery had been divided, the spot where Christina had Monaldeschi murdered. Rosanette listened closely to this story; then, turning to Frédéric, she said:

'I suppose it was jealousy that drove her to it? You'd better look out for yourself!'

Next they crossed the Council Chamber, the Hall of the Guards, the Throne Room, and the saloon of Louis XIII. A pale light streamed in through the high, uncurtained windows; a film of dust dimmed the brightness of the window hasps and the brass feet of the tables; everywhere, armchairs were hidden under coarse linen sheets; over the doors there were Louis Quinze hunting scenes and, here and there, tapestries depicting the gods of Olympus, Psyche, or Alexander's battles.

Whenever she passed in front of a mirror, Rosanette would stop for a moment to smooth her hair.

After going through the Turret Court and the Chapel of Saint-Saturnin, they came to the Banqueting Hall.

They were dazzled by the magnificence of the ceiling, which was divided into octagonal sections, decorated in gold and silver, and more exquisitely worked than any jewel, and by the countless pictures which covered the walls, from the gigantic fireplace, over which crescents and quivers surrounded the arms of France, to the musicians' gallery stretching right across the other end of the hall. The ten arched windows were wide open; the sunshine made the paintings gleam; the blue sky extended to infinity the ultramarine of the arches; and from the depths of the forest, whose misty tree-tops filled the horizon, there seemed to come an echo of the morts sounded on ivory hunting-horns, an echo of the mythological ballets which had brought together under the trees princesses and noblemen disguised as nymphs and satyrs, an echo of an age of primitive science, violent passions, and sumptuous art, when mankind sought to transform the world into a dream of the Hesperides, and when the mistresses of kings vied with the constellations. The most beautiful of these legendary creatures was shown in a painting on the right, in the character of Diana the huntress, and indeed of Diana of the Underworld, no doubt to indicate the power she wielded even beyond the grave. All these symbols confirmed her fame; and something of her still remained there, a faint voice, a lingering splendour.

Frédéric was seized with an indescribable feeling of retrospective lust. To distract his desire, he gazed tenderly at Rosanette and asked if she would have liked to be that woman.

'What woman?'

'Diane de Poitiers.'

He repeated:

'Diane de Poitiers, the mistress of Henri II.'

She murmured: 'Ah!' That was all.

Her silence clearly proved that she knew nothing and did not understand, so that out of kindness he said to her:

'Perhaps you are getting bored?'

'No, no! On the contrary!'

And with her chin in the air, gazing vacantly around her, Rosanette pronounced this remark:

'All this brings back memories!'

Yet her face revealed a genuine effort to show respect; and as this serious expression made her look prettier, Frédéric forgave her.

She found the carp pond more amusing. For a quarter of an hour she threw pieces of bread into the water, to see the fishes jump.

Frédéric had sat down beside her, under the lime-trees. He thought of all the people who had walked within these walls, Charles V, the Valois, Henri IV, Peter the Great, Jean-Jacques Rousseau and 'the lovely ladies who wept in the stage-boxes',[66] Voltaire, Napoleon, Pius VII, and Louis-Philippe. He felt the dead crowding round him and jostling him; and all these pictures thronging his imagination dazed him, for all the pleasure he took in them.

At last they went down to the flower-garden. This was a huge rectangle, where in a single glance the eye could take in the broad yellow paths, the squares of turf, the ribbons of box, the conical yews, the low shrubs, and the narrow beds in which scattered flowers stood out brightly against the grey earth. Beyond the garden there was a park, with a long canal stretching the whole length of it.

Royal residences have a melancholy all their own, which is probably due to the disproportion between their immensity and the tiny number of inhabitants, to their silence, which seems surprising after so many fanfares have been sounded there, and to their unchanging luxury, which proves by its antiquity the transience of dynasties, the inevitable impermanence of all things; and this emanation of the past, as overpowering and funereal as the scent of a mummy, affects even the simplest mind. Rosanette started yawning hugely. They went back to the hotel.

After lunch an open carriage was brought round for them. They left Fontainebleau by a broad crossroads, then drove slowly up a sandy road through a wood of small pines. Soon the trees became taller; and every now and then the coachman said: 'Here are the Siamese Twins, the Pharamond, the King's Bouquet', omitting none of the famous beauty-spots, and sometimes even stopping to show them off.

They entered the Forest of Franchard. The carriage glided over the turf like a sledge; invisible pigeons cooed; suddenly a waiter appeared and they got down outside the gate of a garden full of round tables. Then, passing the walls of a ruined abbey on the left, they walked over some big rocks and soon came to the bottom of the gorge.

One side was covered with a jumble of sandstone rocks and junipers, while the other side, which was practically bare, sloped down to the trough of the valley, where a path drew a pale line across the purple of the heather; and far away in the distance a hilltop like a flattened cone could be seen, with a telegraph tower behind.

Half an hour later they got out of the carriage again to climb the Aspremont heights.

The road zigzagged between dwarf pines under rocks with rugged outlines; all this part of the forest had something muffled, quiet, and solitary about it. It conjured up thoughts of the hermits of old, the companions of the great stags with fiery crosses between their horns, who used to receive with fatherly smiles the good kings of France as they knelt in front of their grottoes. The warm air was full of the smell of resin; tree-roots interlaced on the ground like veins. Rosanette stumbled over them, felt miserable, and wanted to cry.

But when they reached the summit her spirits were revived by the discovery of a sort of tavern with a roof made of branches, where there were woodcarvings for sale. She drank a bottle of lemonade, bought herself a holly stick, and, without even glancing at the view to be seen from the plateau, went into the Brigands' Cave, preceded by a boy carrying a torch.

Their carriage was waiting for them in the Bas-Bréau.

A painter in a blue smock was working at the foot of an oak, with his paint-box on his knees. He looked up and watched them pass.

When they were in the middle of the Chailly slope a sudden cloudburst forced them to put up the hood. The rain stopped almost immediately; and the paving-stones in the streets were gleaming in the sun as they came back into the town.

Some travellers who had just arrived told them that a terrible and bloody battle was raging in Paris. Rosanette and her lover were not surprised. Then everybody went away, peace returned to the hotel, the gas was turned out, and they went to sleep to the murmur of the fountain in the courtyard.

The next day they went to see the Wolf's Gorge, the Fairies' Pool, the Long Rock, and the Marlotte; the day after, they set off again at random, going wherever their coachman took them, without asking where they were, and often indeed missing the better known beauty-spots.

They were wonderfully comfortable in their old landau, as low-slung as a sofa and covered with faded striped linen. The ditches full of brushwood glided past them with a gentle, continuous motion. White sunbeams pierced the tall bracken like arrows; occasionally a disused road appeared straight in front of them, with drooping plants growing on it here and there. At the centre of every cross-roads a signpost stretched out its four arms; elsewhere, stakes leaned to one side like dead trees, and little twisting paths, disappearing into the leaves, made them long to follow them; at that very moment the horse would turn and they would plunge into the wood, sinking into the mud; farther on, moss was growing on the edges of the deep ruts.

They thought that they were far from other people, completely alone. But all of a sudden a gamekeeper would go by with his gun, or a band of women in rags dragging along great bundles of faggots on their backs.

When the carriage stopped there was complete silence; all that could be heard was the breathing of the horse in the shafts, and the faint, repeated cry of a bird.

The sunshine, lighting up the skirt of the woods here and there, left the depths in shadow; or else, dimmed in the foreground by a sort of dusk, it created a purple mist, a pale brightness in the distance. At midday, blazing straight down on the spreading verdure, the sun splashed it with light, hung silvery drops on the tips of the branches, streaked the grass with trails of emeralds, and cast patches of gold on the banks of dead leaves. Throwing back one's head, one could see the sky between the tops of the trees. Some of these were astonishingly tall and bore themselves like patriarchs or emperors; some linked branches and with their long trunks looked like triumphal arches; while others grew obliquely from the ground like pillars about to fall.

Occasionally these ranks of thick vertical lines would open up, to reveal huge green waves rolling away in uneven curves to the bottom of valleys; and there other hills crowded forward, overlooking yellow plains which eventually disappeared in a misty pallor.

Standing side by side on some hillock, and breathing in the wind, they felt their souls filling with a sort of pride in a freer life, a surge of strength, an inexplicable joy.

The different trees afforded a changing spectacle. The beeches, with their smooth white bark, mingled their foliage; ashes gently curved their grey-green boughs; in the hornbeam coppices bristled holly-bushes which seemed to be made of bronze; then came a line of slender birches, bent in elegiac attitudes; and the pines, as symmetrical as organ-pipes, seemed to sing as they swayed continuously to and fro. Huge gnarled oaks rose convulsively out of the ground, embraced one another, and, solidly established on their torso-like trunks, threw out their bare arms in desperate appeals and furious threats, like a group of Titans struck motionless in their anger. An oppressive atmosphere, a feverish languor hung over the pools, whose still waters were hemmed in by thorn-bushes; the moss on their banks, where the wolves came to drink, was sulphur-coloured, as if it had been burnt by witches' footsteps; and the uninterrupted croaking of the frogs echoed the cawing of the wheeling crows. Then they crossed monotonous clearings, planted with saplings here and there. The sound of iron, a succession of hard blows, rang through the air; it was some quarrymen striking the rocks on a hillside. These rocks became more and more numerous, finally filling the whole landscape; cube-shaped like houses, or flat like paving-stones, they propped each other up, overhung one another, and merged together like the monstrous, unrecognizable ruins of some vanished city. But the frenzied chaos in which they lay conjured up rather thoughts of volcanoes, floods, great unknown cataclysms. Frédéric said that they had been there since the beginning of the world and would stay like that until its end; Rosanette turned her head away, saying that 'it would drive her mad', and went off to pick some heather. The little purple flowers, packed close together, grew in irregular patches, and the soil which came away from their roots formed a sort of black fringe to the quartz-spangled sand.

One day they climbed half-way up a sand-hill. Its untrodden surface was grooved with symmetrical undulations; here and there, like promontories on the dried-up bed of an ocean, rose rocks which bore a vague resemblance to animals, tortoises thrusting their heads forward, seals crawling along, hippopotamuses, and bears. Not a soul. Not a sound. The sand was dazzling in the sunshine; and all of a sudden, in the quivering light, the animals seemed to move. They hurried away, threatened by giddiness, almost panic-stricken.

The solemnity of the forest took hold of them; and there were hours of silence when, abandoning themselves to the gentle rocking of the springs, they lay sunk in a calm intoxication. With his arm round her waist, he listened to her talking while the birds twittered, taking in almost in the same glance the black grapes on her bonnet and the berries on the junipers, the folds of her veil and the wisps of the clouds; and when he bent over her, the freshness of her skin mingled with the all-pervading scent of the forest. They took pleasure in everything, pointing out to each other gossamer threads hanging from bushes, holes full of water in the middle of stones, a squirrel on a branch, a couple of butterflies flying after each other, or else, twenty yards away, under the trees, a doe walking placidly along, with a noble, gentle air, her fawn at her side. Rosanette felt like running after it to give it a kiss.

She had a fright once when a man suddenly appeared in front of her and showed her three adders in a box. She promptly threw herself into Frédéric's arms, and he was happy to feel that she was weak and that he was strong enough to protect her.

That evening they dined in an inn on the banks of the Seine. The table was next to the window; and he sat opposite Rosanette, gazing at her delicate little white nose, her pouting lips, her bright eyes, her loosely combed chestnut hair, her pretty oval face. Her dress of raw silk clung to her slightly sloping shoulders, while her hands, emerging from their plain cuffs, cut up her food, poured out her wine, moved over the tablecloth. They were given a spreadeagled chicken, an eel stew in a pipe-clay compote-dish, harsh wine, hard bread, and jagged knives. All this increased their pleasure, added to the illusion. They almost came to believe that they were travelling in Italy on their honeymoon.

Before going back to the hotel they went for a walk along the river-bank.

The soft blue sky, rounded like a dome, rested along the horizon on the jagged outline of the woods. Facing them, at the end of the meadow, there was a village steeple; and farther off, on the left, the roof of a house formed a red spot on the river, which seemed motionless along the whole of its winding course. Reeds were bending, however, and the water was gently shaking the sticks which had been driven into the bank to hold the nets; there was a wicker eel-pot there, and two or three longboats. Near the inn a girl in a straw hat was drawing buckets of water out of a well; every time the bucket came up Frédéric listened to the creaking of the chain with indescribable pleasure.

He felt certain that he was going to be happy for the rest of his days, his contentment struck him as so natural, so inseparably linked with his life and this woman. He felt an urge to murmur endearments to her. She responded with affectionate words, little taps on the shoulder, and gentle caresses whose unexpectedness delighted him. Altogether he discovered an unsuspected beauty in her, a beauty which was perhaps only a reflection of their surroundings, unless their secret potentialities had brought it to the surface.

When they were resting in the open country, he would stretch himself out with his head on her knees, in the shade of her parasol; or else they would lie face to face in the grass, gazing deep into each other's eyes, slaking the constant thirst they had for one another, and then remaining silent with half-closed eyelids.

Sometimes they heard the roll of drums far away in the distance. It was the call to arms being beaten in the villages for the defence of Paris.[67]

'Why, of course! It's the insurrection!' Frédéric would say with a disdainful pity, for all that excitement struck him as trivial in comparison with their love and eternal Nature.

They talked about nothing in particular, about things they knew thoroughly, about people who did not interest them in the slightest, about a thousand and one stupid trifles. She told him about her maid and her hairdresser. One day she forgot herself so far as to tell him her age – twenty-nine; she was growing old.

And several times, without meaning to, she provided him with details about herself. She had been a 'young lady in a shop', had travelled to England, had begun training to be an actress; but all this was told to him in snatches, and he could not manage to piece them together. She told him more about herself one day when they were sitting under a plane-tree at the edge of a meadow. Down below, at the roadside, a little girl, barefoot in the dust, was grazing a cow. As soon as she saw them she came up to ask them for a few coppers. She held her tattered petticoat with one hand, while with the other she scratched her black hair, which looked like a Louis XIV wig framing her brown face, lit up by a pair of splendid eyes.

'She'll be extremely pretty one day,' said Frédéric.

'What luck for her if she hasn't got a mother!' said Rosanette.

'Eh? What?'

'Why, yes. If I hadn't had a mother . . .'

She gave a sigh and started talking about her childhood. Her parents had been silk-weavers at La Croix-Rousse. She helped her father as his apprentice. The poor man slaved away, but all in vain; his wife railed at him and sold everything to buy drink. Rosanette could still see their room, with the looms standing alongside the windows, the stock-pot on the stove, the bed painted to look like mahogany, the cupboard opposite, and the dark closet where she slept until she was fifteen. At last a gentleman had come along, a fat man dressed in black, with a face the colour of boxwood and a sanctimonious manner. He and her mother had had a talk together, with the result that three days later . . . Rosanette broke off, and with a brazen, bitter look on her face, said:

'The thing was done!'

Then, in answer to a gesture by Frédéric, she went on:

'As he was a married man, he would have been afraid of compromising himself in his own house. So I was taken to a private room in a restaurant, after being told that I was going to be happy and get a lovely present.

'The first thing I noticed when the door was opened was a silver-gilt candelabrum on a table laid for two. The table was reflected in a mirror on the ceiling, and the blue silk hangings on the walls made the whole room look like an alcove. It took my breath away. You can imagine the effect on a poor little thing who'd never seen anything of the world! But although I was dazzled I was frightened too. I wanted to go away. All the same, I stayed.

'The only seat was a divan next to the table. It gave softly under me; I could feel hot air coming up at me from the heating vent in the carpet; and I sat there without touching a thing. The waiter who was standing there urged me to eat. He poured me out a big glass of wine straight away; my head started swimming, and I tried to open the window, but he said to me: "No, Mademoiselle, that's not allowed." And he went away. The table was covered with lots of things I'd never seen before. I didn't like the look of any of them. In the end I fell back on a pot of jam and went on waiting. Something was keeping him. It was very late, midnight at least, and I was tired out. I pushed one of the pillows away so as to be able to lie down more comfortably, and under my hand I found a sort of album, a portfolio; it was full of obscene pictures . . . I was asleep on top of it when he came in.'

She bowed her head and remained lost in thought.

The leaves around them were rustling; in a tangle of weeds, a tall foxglove swayed to and fro; the sunlight poured like a wave over the grass; and the silence was broken every few moments by the browsing of the cow which had disappeared from sight.

Rosanette was gazing fixedly at a point on the ground a few yards away from her, absorbed in her thoughts, her nostrils quivering.

'How you've suffered, my poor love!'

'Yes,' she said, 'more than you think! . . . So much that I wanted to put an end to it all. They fished me out of the river.'

'What!'

'Oh, let's forget about it! . . . I love you, and I'm happy. Kiss me.'

And she picked off one by one the thistle spikes which had caught on the hem of her dress.

Frédéric was thinking above all of what she had left unsaid. By what steps had she succeeded in emerging from poverty? What lover had given her her education? What sort of life had she led up to the day when he had first been to her house? Her last admission forbade any further questions. He only asked her how she had come to know Arnoux.

'Through the Vatnaz woman.'

'Wasn't it you I saw once at the Palais-Royal with the two of them?'

He cited the exact date. Rosanette made an effort to remember.

'Yes, that's right! . . . I wasn't terribly gay in those days.'

But Arnoux had been very kind to her. Frédéric did not doubt it; all the same, their friend was a queer customer, full of faults; he took pains to remind her of them. She agreed with him.

'Never mind! I'm still fond of the old rascal.'

'Even now?' asked Frédéric.

She started to blush, half amused, half angry.

'Oh, no! That's ancient history. I'm not keeping anything from you. And even if it were true, it's different with him. Anyway, I don't think you're being very kind about your victim.'

'My victim?'

Rosanette took him by the chin.

'Why, yes!'

And talking like a nanny to a baby, she said:

'Haven't always been good boy, have we? Been to bye-byes with his wife.'

'Me? Never!'

Rosanette smiled. He was hurt by this smile, which he took for a sign of indifference. But she went on gently, with one of those looks which beg for a lying answer:

'Quite sure?'

'Positive!'

Frédéric gave his word of honour that he had never so much as thought of Madame Arnoux, as he had been too much in love with somebody else.

'Who?'

'Why, you, my precious!'

'Oh, don't make fun of me like that! I don't like it.'

He thought it prudent to invent a love-story. He made up some circumstantial details. But the woman in question had made him very unhappy.

'You certainly don't have much luck, do you?' said Rosanette.

'Oh, I don't know about that,' he replied, implying that he had had several successful affairs in order to enhance her opinion of him. Similarly Rosanette did not confess to all the lovers she had had, so that he should think more highly of her. For in the midst of the most intimate confidences, false shame, delicacy, or pity always impose a certain reticence. We come across precipices or morasses, in ourselves or in the other person, which bring us to a halt; in any case, we feel that we would not be understood; it is difficult to express anything at all with any degree of exactness, so that complete relationships are few and far between.

The poor Marshal had never known a better one. Often, as she gazed at Frédéric, tears came into her eyes; then she would look up into the air or over at the horizon, as if she had caught sight of some magnificent dawn, vistas of unbounded happiness. Finally, one day, she confessed that she wanted to have a Mass said 'to bring luck to our love.'

How was it then that she had resisted him so long? She herself did not know. He asked her this question several times, and she would answer as she clasped him in her arms:

'It was because I was afraid of loving you too much, darling.'

On the Sunday morning Frédéric read Dussardier's name in a newspaper, in a list of wounded. He gave an exclamation and, show-ing the paper to Rosanette, declared that he was going to leave straight away.

'What for?'

'Why, to see him, to take care of him.'

'I trust you're not going to leave me here alone?'

'Come with me.'

'What, to get mixed up in a shindy like that? No, thank you!'

'All the same, I can't . . .'

'Oh, la, la! As if there weren't enough nurses in the hospitals! Anyway, what business was it of his? Everybody for himself, that's what I say!'

He was shocked by this selfishness, and he reproached himself for not being in Paris with the others. His indifference to the country's misfortunes had something mean and bourgeois about it. His love suddenly weighed upon his conscience like a crime. They sulked at one another for an hour.

Then she begged him to wait and not to expose himself to danger.

'What if you were killed?'

'Why, I should only have done my duty!'

Rosanette leapt to her feet. To begin with, his duty was to love her. The trouble was that he was tired of her, she supposed. But what he suggested was madness. The very idea!

Frédéric rang for the bill. But it was no easy matter getting back to Paris. Leloir's mail-coach had just left; Lecomte's berlins were not running; while the stage-coach from the Bourbonnais would not be passing until late at night and might be full – it was impossible to say. After wasting a lot of time over these inquiries, he hit on the idea of hiring a post-chaise. The postmaster refused to let him have any horses, as Frédéric had no passport. Finally he hired a landau – the same which had taken them on their outings – and about five o'clock they drew up outside the Hôtel du Commerce at Melun.

The market square was covered with piles of arms. The Prefect had forbidden the National Guards to go to Paris. Those who did not belong to his department wanted to press on. There was a great deal of shouting. The inn was in an uproar.

A terrified Rosanette declared that she would not go any farther, and once again begged him to stay. The innkeeper and his wife supported her. A good fellow who was having his dinner joined in the argument, saying that the fighting would soon be over, and that, besides, a man had to do his duty. This made the Marshal sob more than ever. Frédéric was exasperated. He gave her his purse, kissed her quickly, and disappeared.

When he reached Corbeil they told him at the station that the rebels had cut the rails in several places; the coachman refused to drive him any farther, saying that his horses were 'dead-beat'.

However, through his influence Frédéric secured a wretched cabriolet whose driver agreed to take him as far as the Barrière d'Italie for sixty francs, not counting the tip. But a hundred yards from the tollgate the driver set him down and turned round. Frédéric was walking along the road when all of a sudden a sentry charged his bayonet. Four men seized him, shouting:

'Here's one! Mind out! Search him! Swine! Scum!'

He was so taken aback that he allowed himself to be dragged to the toll-gate guard-post, which was established at the crossroads where the Boulevard des Gobelins and the Boulevard de l'Hôpital meet the Rue Godefroy and the Rue Mouffetard.

Four huge ramparts of paving-stones formed barricades blocking the entrances to the four streets; torches sputtered here and there; in spite of the clouds of dust he made out some infantrymen and National Guards, all with black faces, dishevelled, and haggard. They had just taken the square, and had executed several men; their anger was still unappeased. Frédéric said that he had come from Fontainebleau to look after a wounded comrade who lived in the Rue Bellefond; at first nobody would believe him; they inspected his hands, and even sniffed his ears to make sure that he did not smell of powder.

However, by dint of repeating the same thing over and over again, he ended up by convincing a captain, who ordered a couple of fusiliers to take him to the guard-post at the Jardin des Plantes.

They went down the Boulevard de l'Hôpital. A strong wind was blowing. This revived him.

Then they turned down the Rue du Marché-aux-Chevaux. On the right the Jardin des Plantes formed a huge black mass; while on the left the Hôpital de la Pitié, with every window lit up, was blazing as if it were on fire, and shadows kept moving swiftly to and fro behind the panes.

Frédéric's two escorts went off. Another man accompanied him as far as the Polytechnic School.

The Rue Saint-Victor was in total darkness, without a single gas-lamp burning or a single light in any of the houses. Every ten minutes one heard the words:

'Sentries! Attention!'

And this cry, shattering the silence, went echoing on, like the reverberations of a stone falling into an abyss.

From time to time the tramp of heavy footsteps could be heard approaching. This was a patrol of at least a hundred men; whispers and vague metallic sounds came from the shadowy mass; and swaying rhythmically as they marched past, they faded into the darkness.

In the centre of the crossroads there was a mounted dragoon, motionless. Every now and then a dispatch-rider galloped past; then silence fell once more. Guns moving along the road in the distance produced a dull, ominous rumble; and these sounds, so different from the sounds of everyday life, were strangely disturbing. They even seemed to extend the silence, which was profound and absolute, a black silence. Men in white smocks would come up to the soldiers, say a word to them, and vanish like ghosts.

The guard-post at the Polytechnic School was packed with people. The doorway was crowded with women asking to see their sons and husbands; they were directed to the Panthéon, which had been turned into a mortuary. Nobody listened to Frédéric. He persisted, swearing that his friend Dussardier was expecting him, was dying. Finally he was given a corporal to take him to the town hall of the Twelfth Arrondissement at the top of the Rue Saint-Jacques.

The Place du Panthéon was full of soldiers lying on straw. Dawn was breaking. The camp fires were going out.

The insurrection had left impressive traces in this district. The surface of every street had been pitted from one end to the other. Omnibuses, gas-pipes, and cart-wheels were still lying on the ruined barricades; there were little black patches here and there which were obviously blood. The houses were riddled with bullets, and their timber-work showed through the holes in the plaster. Blinds, held by a single nail, hung like rags. Staircases had caved in, and doors opened into space. The inside of rooms could be seen, with the wallpaper in shreds; sometimes fragile objects had remained unscathed. Frédéric noticed a clock, a parrot's perch, and some prints.

When he went into the town hall, the National Guards were gossiping endlessly about the death of Bréa and Négrier, of the deputy Charbonnel, and of the Archbishop of Paris.[68] It was rumoured that the Duc d'Aumale had landed at Boulogne, that Barbès had escaped from Vincennes, that artillery was coming from Bourges, and that help was pouring in from the provinces. About three o'clock somebody brought good news; spokesmen for the rebels were parleying with the President of the Assembly.[69]

Everybody rejoiced; and, as he still had twelve francs left, Frédéric sent out for a dozen bottles of wine, hoping that this would hasten his release. Suddenly they thought they could hear firing. The drinking stopped, and they looked at the stranger with suspicious eyes; he might be Henri V.

To avoid all responsibility, they transferred him to the town hall of the Eleventh Arrondissement, which he was not allowed to leave until nine o'clock in the morning.

He ran all the way to the Quai Voltaire. An old man in his shirt sleeves was weeping at an open window, his eyes raised towards the sky. The Seine was flowing peacefully by. The sky was blue; birds were singing in the trees of the Tuileries.

Frédéric was crossing the Place du Carrousel when a bier was carried past. The guard promptly presented arms, while the officer brought his hand up to his shako and said:

'Honour to our fallen heroes!'

This phrase had become almost compulsory; whoever uttered it always appeared to be deeply moved. The bier was escorted by a group of angry people shouting:

'We'll have our revenge! We'll have our revenge!'

Carriages were driving along the boulevard, and women were sitting in the doorways shredding linen. However, the insurrection had been suppressed, or nearly suppressed; this was announced in a proclamation by Cavaignac which had just been posted up. A squad of Mobile Guards appeared at the top of the Rue Vivienne. The prosperous citizens shouted with enthusiasm at the sight; they raised their hats, clapped their hands, danced up and down, tried to kiss the soldiers, and offered them drinks, while ladies threw flowers down from the balconies.

Finally, at ten o'clock, just as the guns started roaring for the attack on the Faubourg Saint-Antoine, Frédéric arrived at Dussardier's lodgings. He found him in his attic, stretched out on his back, fast asleep. A woman tiptoed out of the next room. It was Mademoiselle Vatnaz.

She took Frédéric aside and told him how Dussardier had received his wound.

The previous Saturday a boy wrapped in a tricolour flag had shouted to the National Guards from the top of a barricade: 'Are you going to fire on your brothers?' As they moved forward, Dussardier had dropped his musket, pushed the others away, leapt up on to the barricade, felled the young rebel with a well-directed kick, and snatched the flag from him. He had been found under the debris, his thigh pierced by a copper slug. They had had to cut away the flesh round the wound and remove the bullet. Mademoiselle Vatnaz had arrived the same evening and had stayed with him ever since.

She skilfully prepared his dressings, helped him to drink, anticipated his slightest wishes, came and went as quietly as a nurse, and gazed at him with loving eyes.

Frédéric did not fail to call every morning for a fortnight. One day when he was talking about Mademoiselle Vatnaz's devotion Dussardier shrugged his shoulders.

'Oh, no! It's out of self-interest!'

'You think so?'

'I'm positive,' he replied, without offering any further explanation.

She plied him with attentions, even bringing him the newspapers in which his brave exploit was extolled. These praises seemed to embarrass him. He even confessed to Frédéric the scruples which were preying on his conscience.

Perhaps he ought to have gone over to the other side and joined the smocks; for after all, they had been promised a great many things which had not been given to them. Their conquerors hated the Republic; and then, they had been savagely treated! No doubt they were in the wrong, but not entirely; and the good fellow was tormented by the idea that he might have been fighting against a just cause.

Sénécal, imprisoned in the Tuileries under the waterside terrace, did not share these scruples.

There were nine hundred men there, packed together pell-mell in the filth, black with powder and coagulated blood, shaking with fever and shouting with rage; and those among them who died were left with the living. Occasionally, at the sound of a sudden explosion, they imagined that they were all going to be shot; and they threw themselves against the walls, before sinking back on the floor, so numbed by suffering that they felt as if they were living in a nightmare, a ghastly hallucination. The lamp hanging from the ceiling looked like a bloodstain; and little green and yellow flames produced by the vapours of the cellar flickered here and there. Fear of an epidemic led to the appointment of a commission of inquiry. At the top of the flight of steps the chairman drew back, horrified by the stench of excrement and corpses. When the prisoners came near the gratings, the National Guards who had been posted there to prevent them from loosening the bars thrust their bayonets at random into the crowd.

By and large the National Guards were merciless. Those who had not taken part in the fighting wanted to distinguish themselves; and in an explosion of panic they took their revenge at one and the same time for the newspapers, the clubs, the demonstrations, the doctrines, for everything which had been infuriating them for the past six months. Despite their victory, equality—as if to punish its defenders and ridicule its enemies – asserted itself triumphantly: an equality of brute beasts, a common level of bloody atrocities; for the fanaticism of the rich counterbalanced the frenzy of the poor, the aristocracy shared the fury of the rabble, and the cotton nightcap was just as savage as the red bonnet. The public's reason was deranged as if by some great natural upheaval. Intelligent men lost their sanity for the rest of their lives.

Old Roque had grown extremely brave, almost reckless. He had arrived in Paris on the 26th with the contingent from Nogent; but instead of going back with them, he had joined the National Guards encamped at the Tuileries; and to his delight he was put on sentry duty on the waterside terrace. There at least he had the ruffians under his thumb! He rejoiced in their defeat, in their abjection, and could not refrain from railing at them.

One of them, a youth with long fair hair, pressed his face to the bars and asked for bread. Monsieur Roque ordered him

334

to be silent. But the young man went on repeating in a pitiful voice:

'Bread!'

'Do you think I've got any?'

Other prisoners appeared at the grating, with bristling beards and blazing eyes, jostling each other and howling:

'Bread!'

Old Roque was furious at seeing his authority flouted. To frighten them he aimed his musket at them; and the young man, carried up to the ceiling by the crowd pushing behind him, threw his head back and cried once again:

'Bread!'

'Right! Here you are!' said old Roque, firing his musket.

There was a tremendous howl, then nothing. Something white remained on the edge of the grating.[70]

After this Monsieur Roque went home; for he owned a house in the Rue Saint-Martin in which he had set aside a little flat for himself; and the damage caused to the front of the building by the insurrection had contributed not a little to his anger. Looking at it again on his return, he felt that he had made too much of it. His recent exploit had soothed him, as if he had been paid compensation.

It was his daughter who opened the door to him. She told him straight away that his prolonged absence had made her anxious; she had been afraid that he had had an accident or been wounded.

This proof of filial affection touched old Roque's heart. He expressed his surprise that she should have left Nogent without Catherine.

'I've just sent her out on an errand,' replied Louise.

She inquired after his health, and about this and that; then, with assumed indifference, she asked whether by any chance he had met Frédéric.

'No. I haven't seen a sign of him.'

It was purely on his account that she had made the journey.

Somebody came along the corridor.

'Oh! Excuse me . . .'

And she disappeared.

Catherine had not found Frédéric. He had been away for several days, and his friend Monsieur Deslauriers lived in the country now.

Louise reappeared trembling all over, incapable of uttering a word. She leant against the furniture for support.

'What is it? What's the matter?' exclaimed her father.

She motioned to him that it was nothing, and by a great effort of will pulled herself together.

The caterer across the street brought over the soup. But old Roque had had too violent an emotional disturbance. 'It wouldn't go down,' and at dessert he had a sort of fainting fit. A doctor was hurriedly sent for, and he prescribed a potion. Then, once he was in bed, Monsieur Roque insisted on having as many blankets as possible, to make him sweat. He lay there sighing and groaning.

'Thank you, my dear Catherine! Kiss your poor father, my pet! Oh, these revolutions!'

And when his daughter scolded him for making himself ill worrying about her, he answered:

'Yes, you're right. But I just can't help it. I'm too sensitive!'

II

MADAME DAMBREUSE was sitting in her boudoir, between her niece and Miss John, listening to Monsieur Roque, who was describing the hardships of his military life.

She kept biting her lips and seemed to be in pain.

'Oh, it's nothing! It'll pass off.'

And she added in a gracious voice:

'We have an acquaintance of yours, Monsieur Moreau, coming to dinner.'

Louise gave a start.

'Apart from him, just a few friends of the family – Alfred de Cisy among others.'

And she praised his manners, his looks, and, above all else, his morals.

On this last point Madame Dambreuse was not as far from the truth as she thought, for the viscount was contemplating marriage. He had said as much to Martinon, adding that he was sure that Mademoiselle Cécile would take to him and that his family would accept her.

In Martinon's opinion, for Cisy to risk a confidence of this sort, he must have favourable information about the dowry. Now Martinon suspected Cécile of being Monsieur Dambreuse's natural daughter; and it would probably have been a clever move to take a chance and ask for her hand himself. But this bold step had its dangers; so up to now Martinon had taken care to avoid compromising himself; besides, he did not know how to rid himself of Cécile's aunt. Cisy's remark had decided him; and he had made his proposal to the banker, who, seeing no objection, had just informed Madame Dambreuse of it.

Cisy appeared. She rose and said:

'You're becoming quite a stranger.' She added in English: 'Cécile, shake hands!'

Just then Frédéric came in.

'Ah! There you are at last!' exclaimed old Roque. 'I've been to your house three times this week with Louise.'

Frédéric had carefully avoided them. He explained that he spent every day with a wounded friend. Apart from that, he had been taken up with various matters for a long time; and he racked his brain for some plausible stories. Luckily the guests started arriving: first Monsieur Paul de Grémonville, the diplomat of whom he had caught a glimpse at the ball; then Fumichon, the industrialist whose reactionary zeal had shocked him one evening; and after them the aged Duchesse de Montreuil-Nantua.

Then two voices were heard in the hall.

'I'm positive,' said one.

'Dear lady! Dear lady!' the other replied. 'Please calm yourself!'

It was Monsieur de Nonancourt, an old buck who looked as if he had been mummified in cold cream, and Madame de Larsillois, the wife of one of Louis-Philippe's prefects. She was trembling violently, for she had just heard a barrel-organ playing a polka which was used as a signal by the rebels. Many well-to-do people had similar fancies, imagining that there were men in the catacombs who were going to blow up the Faubourg Saint-Germain, hearing strange noises coming from cellars, and seeing suspicious things happening behind windows.

Everybody did his best, however, to calm down Madame de Larsillois. Order had been restored. There was no longer anything to fear. 'Cavaignac has saved us!' As if there had not been sufficient atrocities during the insurrection, they exaggerated their number. There had been no fewer than twenty-three thousand convicts fighting for the Socialists!

They had implicit faith in the stories of poisoned food, of Mobile

Guards sawn in half between a couple of planks, and of flags bearing inscriptions calling for pillage and arson.

'And something else too!' added the ex-prefect's wife.

'Oh, my dear!' said Madame Dambreuse out of propriety, with a meaningful glance at the three girls.

Monsieur Dambreuse came out of his study with Martinon. She turned her head away and acknowledged Pellerin's greeting as he came towards her. The artist looked uneasily round the walls. The banker took him aside and explained to him that he had had to conceal his revolutionary painting for the time being.

'Naturally!' said Pellerin, whose opinions had been modified by his reverse at the Club de l'Intelligence.

Monsieur Dambreuse added politely that he would commission other works from him.

'But excuse me! . . . Ah, my dear fellow! What a pleasure it is to see you!'

Arnoux and Madame Arnoux stood before Frédéric.

He felt slightly giddy. Rosanette had annoyed him the whole afternoon with her admiration for the soldiers; and his old love awoke again.

The butler came in to announce that dinner was served. Madame Dambreuse ordered the viscount, with a glance, to take Cécile's arm, hissed: 'Villain!' at Martinon, and the company moved into the dining-room.

Under the green leaves of a pineapple, in the middle of the tablecloth, a dolphin lay with its head pointing to a haunch of venison and its tail touching a mound of crayfish. Figs, huge cherries, pears, and grapes, all grown in Parisian hothouses, were piled in pyramids in baskets of old Dresden china; here and there bunches of flowers were interspersed with the gleaming silver; the white silk blinds, lowered over the windows, filled the room with a soft light; the air was cooled by two fountains containing pieces of ice; and tall servants in knee-breeches waited on the guests. All this was the more refreshing for the excitement of the past few days. The guests were enjoying once more the things which they had been afraid of losing, and Nonancourt expressed the general sentiment when he said:

'Ah! Let us hope our good friends the Republicans will allow us to have our dinner!'

'Despite their fraternity!' Monsieur Roque added wittily.

These two worthies were sitting on the right and the left of Madame Dambreuse. Facing her was her husband, between Madame de Larsillois, who had the diplomat beside her, and the old duchess, who was elbow to elbow with Fumichon. Then came the painter, the china manufacturer, and Mademoiselle Louise; and thanks to Martinon, who had taken his place so as to sit by Cécile, Frédéric found himself next to Madame Arnoux.

She was wearing a dress of black barège, with a gold bracelet at her wrist; and, as on the first evening he had dined at her house, she had a red ornament in her hair – a spray of fuchsia twined in her chignon. He could not refrain from saying to her:

'It's a long time since we last met.'

'Ah,' she replied coldly.

He went on, with a gentleness in his voice which attenuated the impertinence of his question:

'Did you think of me sometimes?'

'Why should I think of you?'

Frédéric was hurt by this answer.

'Perhaps you're right, after all.'

But, repenting quickly, he swore that he had not passed a single day without being ravaged by her memory.

'I don't believe a word of it, Monsieur.'

'All the same, you know I love you.'

Madame Arnoux made no reply.

'You know I love you.'

She still said nothing.

'All right, go to blazes!' Frédéric said to himself.

And, looking up, he caught sight of Mademoiselle Roque at the other end of the table.

She had thought it smart to dress all in green, a colour which clashed crudely with her red hair. The buckle of her belt was too high; her collar was a poor fit; and this lack of elegance had probably contributed to the coolness of Frédéric's greeting. She watched him inquisitively from a distance; and although Arnoux, who was sitting beside her, lavished compliments on her, it was all in vain: he could not get a word out of her. Finally he gave up trying to please, and listened to the conversation, which was now on the subject of the pineapple puddings at the Luxembourg.

According to Fumichon, Louis Blanc owned a mansion in the Rue Saint-Dominique and refused to let it to the workmen.

'What I find funniest,' said Nonancourt, 'is the idea of Ledru-Rollin hunting on the royal estates!'

'He owes a jeweller twenty thousand francs,' added Cisy; 'and they even say ...'

Madame Dambreuse interrupted him.

'I think it's dreadful to get excited over politics. And a young man, too – you ought to be ashamed of yourself! You should be talking to your neighbour!'

Next the more serious-minded guests started attacking the newspapers.

Arnoux took up their defence; Frédéric joined in the conversation, describing them as commercial enterprises like all the rest. The people who wrote for them were generally either fools or humbugs; he claimed to know all about them, and countered his friend's generous sentiments with sarcastic remarks. Madame Arnoux failed to see that this was a revenge upon her.

In the meantime the viscount was racking his brains to find a way of conquering Mademoiselle Cécile. To begin with he displayed his artistic tastes, criticizing the shape of the carafes and the chasing on the knives. Then he talked about his stable, his tailor, and his shirtmaker. Finally he broached the subject of religion and found a means of giving his neighbour to understand that he fulfilled all his religious duties.

Martinon showed greater finesse. Talking at a monotonous pace and looking at Cécile all the time, he extolled her bird-like profile, her insipid fair hair, and her stumpy hands. The ugly girl revelled in this shower of compliments.

Everybody was talking so loud that nothing could be heard. Monsieur Roque wanted 'an iron hand' to rule France. Nonancourt even expressed regret that the death penalty for political crimes had been abolished. All those ruffians ought to have been exterminated in a body!

'They're cowards too,' said Fumichon. 'I can't see anything brave about sheltering behind a barricade!'

'Talking of barricades, tell us about Dussardier,' said Monsieur Dambreuse, turning towards Frédéric.

The worthy shop-assistant was now a hero, like Sallesse, the Jeanson brothers, the Péquillet woman, and the rest.

Without waiting to be pressed, Frédéric recounted the story of his friend, which shed a sort of reflected glory over him.

The guests were led very naturally to describe various feats of courage. According to the diplomat, it was not at all difficult to face death, as was shown by all the people who fought duels.

'We can take the viscount's word on that point,' said Martinon.

The viscount went red in the face.

The other guests looked at him; and Louise, more surprised than the rest, murmured:

'What is it?'

'He funked it in a duel with Frédéric,' whispered Arnoux.

'Do you know something about it, Mademoiselle?' Nonancourt asked straight away.

And he passed her reply on to Madame Dambreuse, who, bending forward a little, started looking at Frédéric.

Martinon did not wait for Cécile to question him. He told her that the duel had been over a person of unspeakable morals. The girl drew back slightly on her chair, as if to avoid contact with this libertine.

The conversation had started up again. Fine clarets were served and the talk became livelier. Pellerin could not forgive the revolution for the total destruction of the Spanish museum. That was what upset him most, as a painter. Catching this last word, Monsieur Roque asked him:

'Aren't you the painter who produced a really remarkable picture?'

'Possibly. Which one?'

'It shows a lady in a . . . well . . . rather scanty costume, holding a purse, with a peacock behind her.'

It was Frédéric's turn to blush scarlet. Pellerin pretended not to hear.

'But I'm positive it's by you. For there's your name written at the bottom, and a line on the frame saying it belongs to Monsieur Moreau.'

Monsieur Roque and his daughter had seen the Marshal's portrait one day when they were waiting for Frédéric at his house. The old fellow had even taken it for 'a Gothic picture'.

'No!' snapped Pellerin. 'It's the portrait of a woman.'

Martinon added:

'And a woman who's very much alive! Isn't she, Cisy?'

341

'Eh? I don't know anything about it.'

'I thought you knew her. But if you'd rather not talk about it, forgive me for mentioning it.'

Cisy lowered his eyes, proving by his embarrassment that he had played a sorry role in connexion with the portrait. As for Frédéric, the model could only be his mistress. This was one of those convictions which strike one straight away, and the faces of the company revealed it clearly.

'How he lied to me!' Madame Arnoux said to herself.

'So that was why he left me!' thought Louise.

Frédéric imagined that these two stories might harm his reputation, and he reproached Martinon with his indiscretion as soon as they were out in the garden.

Mademoiselle Cécile's suitor laughed in his face.

'What! Not in the least! It'll help you! Go ahead!'

What did he mean? And why this benevolence which was so unusual in him? Without offering any explanation, Martinon went off towards the far end of the garden, where the ladies were sitting. The men were standing up, and Pellerin, in the midst of them, was expounding his opinions. A well-conducted monarchy was the best form of government from the point of view of the arts. The present day disgusted him, 'if only because of the National Guard', and he looked back regretfully to the Middle Ages and to the reign of Louis XIV. Monsieur Roque congratulated him on his views, even confessing that they had dispelled all his prejudices against artists. But he moved away almost immediately, attracted by Fumichon's voice. Arnoux was trying to prove that there were two sorts of Socialism, a good and a bad. The industrialist could not see any difference between them, for the word 'property' sent him into a fury of indignation.

'It's a right consecrated by Nature. Children cling to their toys; every people, every animal on earth shares my opinion; the lion itself, if it had the power of speech, would call itself a landowner! Take my case, gentlemen: I started with a capital of fifteen thousand francs. Well, you know, I got up regularly at four o'clock in the morning every day for thirty years! I had the very devil of a job to make my fortune. And now they come and tell me that I can't do what I like with it, that my money isn't my money, that property is theft!'[71]

'But Proudhon . . .'

'Oh, don't talk to me about Proudhon! If he was here I do believe I'd strangle him!'

He would indeed have strangled him. After the liqueurs especially, there was no holding Fumichon; and his apoplectic face looked as if it were on the point of exploding like a shell.

'Good day, Arnoux,' said Hussonnet, walking briskly across the lawn.

He had brought Monsieur Dambreuse the first sheet of a pamphlet entitled *L'Hydre*, for the Bohemian had become the spokesman for a reactionary club, and it was in this capacity that the banker introduced him to his guests.

Hussonnet amused them, first by asserting that the candlemakers hired three hundred and ninety-two street-urchins to shout 'Light up!' every evening, and then by poking fun at the principles of '89, the emancipation of the Negroes, and the orators of the Left.[72] He even went so far as to do a skit on 'Everyman on a Barricade', possibly out of a simple-minded jealousy of these well-to-do people who had just dined so well. The joke fell flat. The company's faces grew longer.

Besides, this was no time for joking, as Nonancourt pointed out, recalling the death of Monsignor Affre and that of General de Bréa. These deaths were always being brought up; they were used as arguments. Monsieur Roque declared that the Archbishop's demise was 'absolutely sublime'; Fumichon gave the palm to the soldier; and instead of merely deploring these two murders, they started arguing as to which ought to provoke the stronger indignation. A second parallel followed: that of Lamoricière and Cavaignac.[73] Monsieur Dambreuse extolled Cavaignac and Nonancourt Lamoricière. Except for Arnoux nobody present could have seen the two men at work. Everybody none the less passed an irrevocable judgement on their activities. Frédéric refrained from doing so, confessing that he had not taken part in the fighting. The diplomat and Monsieur Dambreuse gave him an approving nod. After all, those who had combated the insurrection had in fact been defending the Republic; and although the result had been favourable, the Republic was the stronger for it. Now that they were rid of the conquered, they wanted to rid themselves of the conquerors.

They had scarcely come out into the garden before Madame Dambreuse had taken Cisy aside and scolded him for his clumsiness.

Catching sight of Martinon, she dismissed him and asked her future nephew what had led him to make fun of the viscount.

'But nothing.'

'And all for Monsieur Moreau's glory! With what object in view?'

'None. Frédéric is a charming fellow. I'm very fond of him.'

'So am I. I'd like to have a word with him. Bring him over here.'

After a few commonplace remarks, she started by gently criticizing her guests, which was tantamount to saying that he was a cut above them. He did not fail to disparage the other women a little, a skilful method of paying her compliments. But every now and then she left him; she was 'at home' that evening, and ladies kept arriving. Then she came back to her place, and the chance arrangement of the seats prevented them from being overheard.

She was at once gay, serious, sad, and thoughtful. The problems of the day were of little interest to her; there was a whole category of emotions of a more lasting nature. She accused the poets of distorting the truth, then looked up at the sky and asked him the name of a star.

Two or three Chinese lanterns had been hung in the trees; they swayed in the wind, and rays of colour flickered across her white dress. As usual, she was leaning back a little in her armchair, with a stool in front of her; the tip of a black satin shoe was visible and now and then she said something in a louder voice, or even gave a laugh.

These coquettish tricks made no impression on Martinon, who was busy with Cécile; but they caught the eye of Louise Roque, who was talking to Madame Arnoux. The latter was the only woman there whose manner did not strike her as supercilious. Louise had sat down beside her; then, feeling an urge to open her heart, she said:

'Don't you think he talks well? Frédéric Moreau, I mean.'

'Do you know him?'

'Oh, very well! We're neighbours. He used to play with me when I was a little girl.'

Madame Arnoux gave her a lingering look signifying: 'You aren't in love with him, are you?'

The girl's eyes replied without any embarrassment: 'Yes, I am.'

'Then you must see quite a lot of him?'

'Oh, no! Only when he comes to stay with his mother. And he

hasn't been to Nogent for ten months now – even though he promised to come more often.'

'You mustn't put too much faith in men's promises, my child.'

'But he hasn't deceived me!'

'He's deceived others!'

Louise shivered. 'Could he, by any chance, have promised something to her too?' she wondered, and her face puckered up with hatred and suspicion.

Madame Arnoux was almost frightened at the sight; she wished she could take back what she had said. Then the two of them fell silent.

As Frédéric was sitting on a folding chair opposite them, they looked at him – the one discreetly, out of the corner of her eye, the other undisguisedly, with her mouth open; so that Madame Dambreuse said to him:

'Do turn round and let her see you!'

'Who?'

'Why, Monsieur Roque's daughter!'

And she teased him about the young country girl's love for him. He denied it and tried to laugh.

'You're joking! I ask you! An ugly little thing like that!'

All the same his vanity was hugely flattered. He recalled that other party, which he had left with his heart full of humiliation, and he heaved a sigh of relief.

He felt that he was in his natural environment, almost on his own estate, as if everything there, including the Dambreuse mansion, belonged to him. The ladies formed a half-circle to listen to him; and in order to shine he declared himself in favour of the re-establishment of divorce, which ought to be made so easy that people could part and come together again indefinitely, as often as they liked. His audience gave cries of horror. Some of the women whispered among themselves; and snatches of conversation, like the clucking of excited hens, came from the shadows at the foot of the creeper-covered wall. Frédéric went on developing his theory, with the self-assurance that springs from the awareness of success. A footman brought a tray full of ices into the arbour. The gentlemen came up. They were talking about the latest arrests.

Frédéric promptly took his revenge on the viscount by persuading him that he risked being arrested as a Legitimist. The other protested that he had not stirred from his room; his adversary listed all the chances against him; even Monsieur Dambreuse and Monsieur de Grémonville were amused. Then they complimented Frédéric, while expressing their regret that he did not use his talents to uphold law and order; and their handshake was cordial; he could count on them in the future. Finally, as everybody was leaving, the viscount bowed low before Cécile.

'Mademoiselle,' he said, 'I have the honour to bid you good night.'

She answered curtly:

'Good night.'

But she gave Martinon a smile.

Old Roque, in order to continue his discussion with Arnoux, suggested seeing him home, 'and Madame too', since they were going the same way. Louise and Frédéric walked in front. She had seized hold of his arm; and when they were out of earshot of the others she said:

'At last! Oh, what I've been through all evening! How spiteful those women are! What airs they give themselves!'

He tried to defend them.

'To begin with, you might have spoken to me when you came in, seeing that you haven't been home for a year.'

'It isn't a year,' said Frédéric, who was glad to be able to take her up on this point so as to avoid the rest.

'All right! It seemed a long time to me, that's all. But during that horrible dinner anybody would have thought you were ashamed of me! Oh, I can see why. I haven't got what they've got to attract a man.'

'You're wrong,' said Frédéric.

'Really? Swear you're not in love with any of them.'

He swore.

'And I'm the only one you love?'

'Of course!'

This assurance cheered her up. She would have liked to lose her way so that they could roam the streets together all night.

'I was so worried at home! People talked about nothing but barricades! I saw you falling to the ground, covered with blood! Your mother was in bed with her rheumatism. She didn't know what was happening. I had to keep quiet. I couldn't stand it any more. So I took Catherine and we set off.'

And she told him about her departure, her journey, and the lie she had told her father.

'He's taking me home two days from now. Come along tomorrow evening, as if by chance, and take the opportunity to ask for me in marriage.'

Frédéric's thoughts had never been further removed from marriage. Besides, Mademoiselle Roque struck him as a somewhat ridiculous little thing. What a difference there was between her and a woman like Madame Dambreuse! A very different future awaited him! He was certain of that now; so this was not the moment to involve himself, on a sentimental impulse, in a decision of this importance. It was a time for realism; and moreover he had seen Madame Arnoux again. However, Louise's frankness embarrassed him. He replied:

'Have you thought it all over carefully?'

'What!' she exclaimed, petrified with surprise and indignation.

He said that it would be madness to marry at present.

'So you don't want me?'

'But you don't understand!'

And he launched out into an extremely complicated speech, designed to explain that he was restrained by important considerations, that he had endless business affairs to deal with, that even his fortune was in danger – here Louise cut him short with a blunt comment – and finally that the political situation was unfavourable. So the wisest course was to be patient for a while. Everything would doubtless work out all right in the end; at least he hoped so; and, since he could not think of any more excuses, he pretended that he had suddenly remembered that he ought to have been at Dussardier's two hours ago.

Then, after saying good-bye to the others, he plunged into the Rue Hauteville, went round the Gymnase, came back on to the boulevard, and climbed Rosanette's four flights of stairs at a run.

Monsieur and Madame Arnoux took leave of old Roque and his daughter at the end of the Rue Saint-Denis. They walked home without speaking; he was worn out with chattering, while she felt terribly tired; she even leant her head on his shoulder. He was the only man who had shown any decent feelings during the whole evening. She felt full of indulgence towards him. He, on the other hand, still felt a little resentment against Frédéric.

'Did you see his face when they were talking about the portrait?

And you wouldn't believe me when I told you he was her lover!'

'Oh, yes, I was wrong!'

Arnoux, pleased with his victory, pressed home his advantage.

'I'd even wager that he left us just now to go and join her! He's with her now! He's spending the night there.'

Madame Arnoux had pulled her hood down low.

'But you're trembling!'

'It's because I'm cold,' she answered.

As soon as her father was asleep, Louise went into Catherine's bedroom and shook her by the shoulder.

'Get up!' she said. 'Quick! Hurry! Go and get me a cab.'

Catherine replied that there were none to be had at that hour.

'Then you'll take me there yourself, won't you?'

'Where?'

'To Frédéric's house!'

'The idea! What for?'

She had to talk to him. She could not wait. She wanted to see him straight away.

'But you can't do that! Going to a house, just like that, in the middle of the night! Besides, he'll be asleep now.'

'I'll wake him up!'

'But it isn't proper for a young lady.'

'I'm not a young lady! I'm his wife! I love him! Come on, put on your shawl.'

Catherine stood beside her bed, thinking. Finally she said:

'No, I won't!'

'All right, then, stay here! I'm going anyway!'

Louise stole down the staircase like a snake. Catherine rushed after her and joined her on the pavement. Her expostulations were all in vain; so, still fastening her dressing-jacket, she followed Louise. The journey struck her as extremely long. She complained of her old legs.

'After all, I've got nothing to drive me on like you!'

Then she became tearful.

'Poor darling! You've got nobody but your old Cathy, as usual!'

Every now and then scruples affected her.

'Oh, this is a nice thing you're making me do! What if your father wakes up? Lawks above! I only hope nothing awful happens!'

In front of the Théâtre des Variétés a patrol of National Guards stopped them. Louise promptly said that she and her maid were going to the Rue Rumfort to fetch a doctor. They were allowed to go on.

At the corner of the Madeleine they met a second patrol, and when Louise gave the same explanation, one of the citizens asked:

'Is it for a nine-months' illness, ducky?'

'Gougibaud!' cried the captain. 'No smutty talk in the ranks! Ladies, on your way!'

In spite of this order, the witticisms continued.

'Have a good time!'

'My compliments to the doctor!'

'They like a good laugh,' said Catherine loudly. 'They're just boys.'

At last they arrived at Frédéric's house. Louise pulled the bell vigorously several times. The door opened a little way, and in response to her inquiry the concierge answered:

'No!'

'But he must be in bed?'

'I tell you, no! He hasn't slept at home for nearly three months now!'

And the little window of the lodge dropped into place like a guillotine. They stood there in the darkness, under the archway. A furious voice shouted at them:

'Get out!'

The door opened again; they went out.

Louise was obliged to sit down on a gate-stone; and with her head in her hands, she wept copiously, from the bottom of her heart. Day was breaking; some carts went by.

Catherine took her home, holding her up, kissing her, and telling her all sorts of comforting things drawn from her own experience. She mustn't take on like that over a sweetheart. If this one failed her, she would find plenty of others.

III

When Rosanette's enthusiasm for the Mobile Guards had abated, she became more charming then ever, and Frédéric gradually fell into the habit of living at her apartment.

The best part of the day was the morning on their terrace. In a loose batiste, with slippers on her bare feet, she pottered about around him, cleaning her canaries' cage, changing her goldfishes' water, and gardening with a coal-shovel in the window-box from which nasturtiums climbed a trellis on the wall. Then, leaning on their balcony, side by side, they would watch the carriages and the passers-by, sunning themselves and making plans for the evening. He was never away for more than a couple of hours during the day; afterwards they would go to some theatre or other, taking a stage-box; and Rosanette, holding a bouquet of flowers, would listen to the orchestra, while Frédéric whispered jokes or compliments into her ear. On other evenings they would hire a barouche to take them to the Bois de Boulogne, and drive until late at night. At last they would come back by the Arc de Triomphe and the great avenue, drinking in the air, with the stars above them, and all the gas-lamps down to the end of the vista lined up like a double string of luminous pearls.

Frédéric always had to wait for her when they were going out; she spent ages arranging the two ribbons on her bonnet round her chin; and she would smile at herself in her wardrobe mirror. Then she would tuck her arm in his and make him stand beside her in front of the glass.

'We look nice like that, the two of us side by side! Poor darling, I could eat you!'

He was now her property, her chattel. This lent a continuous radiance to her face, while at the same time her movements seemed more languid, her contours more rounded; and he found her changed in some other way, though he could not say what.

One day she told him, as if it were an important piece of news, that Arnoux had just opened a drapery shop for a woman who used to work in his factory; he went there every evening and spent a great deal on her.

'Why, only last week, he actually bought her a suite of rosewood furniture.'

'How do you know?' asked Frédéric.

'Oh, I'm positive.'

On her instructions Delphine had made inquiries. She must be very fond of Arnoux, to take such an interest in him! He contented himself with replying:

'What business is it of yours?'

Rosanette looked surprised at this question.

'But the swine owes me money! It makes me livid to see him spending it on a lot of trollops.'

Then, with an expression of triumphant hatred, she added:

'Anyway, she's making a proper fool of him. She's got three other lovers. Serve him right! And I hope she bleeds him white!'

Arnoux was in fact letting the Bordeaux woman exploit him, with all the indulgence of an infatuated old man.

His factory had closed down, and his business affairs were generally in a pitiful state. To pick them up again he had first of all thought of setting up a music-hall where nothing but patriotic songs would have been sung; the Government would have granted him a subsidy and his establishment would have become both a centre of propaganda and a source of profit. Authority having changed hands, this plan had had to be abandoned. Now he was thinking of setting up a huge military hat-shop. But he lacked the necessary capital.

He was no more fortunate in his domestic affairs. Madame Arnoux was not as gentle with him as she used to be, and was sometimes even a little abrupt. Marthe invariably took her father's side. This increased the discord, and the house became uninhabitable. Often he went out first thing in the morning, spent the day bustling about, to tire himself out, then dined in a country tavern, abandoning himself to his thoughts.

Frédéric's continued absence irritated him. Accordingly he turned up one afternoon at Frédéric's house, begged him to come round as he used to in the old days, and extracted a promise from him.

Frédéric was afraid of seeing Madame Arnoux again. He felt that he had betrayed her. But this was sheer cowardice on his part. He had no excuse for staying away. One evening, determined to have done with it, he set off.

It was raining, and he had just taken shelter in the Passage Jouffroy when, in the light of the shop-windows, a fat little man in a cap came up to him. Frédéric had no difficulty in recognizing Compain, the orator whose motion had aroused so much laughter at the club. He was leaning on the arm of an individual in a red zouave cap, who had an unusually long upper lip, a complexion as yellow as an orange, and a short beard, and who was gazing at Compain with eyes glistening with admiration.

Compain was presumably proud of this admiration, for he said:

'Allow me to introduce this good fellow. He's a friend of mine who's a bootmaker and a patriot. Shall we have a drink together?'

Frédéric having declined, he promptly started railing against Rateau's proposal, which was a manoeuvre on the part of the aristocrats.[74] They needed another '93 to stop their little game. Then he asked after Regimbart and a few other people, equally famous, such as Masselin, Sanson, Lecornu, Maréchal, and a certain Deslauriers, who was involved in the case of the carbines which had recently been intercepted at Troyes.

This was all news to Frédéric. Compain did not know any more about the affair. He left Frédéric, saying:

'See you again soon, because you're a member, aren't you?'

'Of what?'

'Of the calf's head!'

'What calf's head?'

'Ah, you will have your little joke!' answered Compain, giving him a dig in the ribs.

And the two terrorists dived into a café.

Ten minutes later Frédéric had forgotten all about Deslauriers. He was standing on the pavement outside a house in the Rue Paradis; and he was gazing at the light of a lamp behind the curtains of a second-floor window.

At last he went up the stairs.

'Is Arnoux in?'

The maid answered:

'No, but come in all the same.'

And throwing open the door, she said:

'Madame, it's Monsieur Moreau!'

She stood up, as pale as her collar. She was trembling.

'To what do I owe the honour ... of such an ... unexpected visit?'

'Nothing! Just the pleasure of seeing old friends again.'

And, sitting down, he asked:

'How is Arnoux keeping?'

'Very well. He's out.'

'Oh, I see! His old nocturnal habits – a little relaxation.'

'Why not? After working at figures all day, a man's brain needs a rest.'

She even praised her husband's industry. This eulogy irritated Frédéric; and pointing to a piece of black cloth with blue braid which she had on her lap, he asked:

'What's that you're working on?'

'A jacket I'm altering for my daughter.'

'That reminds me, I haven't seen her. Where is she?'

'At boarding-school,' replied Madame Arnoux.

Tears came into her eyes; she held them back, plying her needle vigorously. To keep himself in countenance he picked up a copy of *L'Illustration* from the table beside her.

'These caricatures by Cham are funny, aren't they?'

'Yes.'

Then they fell silent again.

All of a sudden a gust of wind rattled the windows.

'What weather!' said Frédéric.

'Yes, it was really very good of you to come here in this awful rain.'

'Oh, it doesn't worry me! I'm not like those people who let it keep them from their rendezvous.'

'What rendezvous?' she asked innocently.

'Don't you remember?'

She shivered and bowed her head.

He put his hand gently on her arm.

'You made me terribly unhappy, you know.'

She answered with a plaintive note in her voice:

'But I was afraid for my child!'

And she told him about little Eugène's illness and the terrors of that day.

'Thank you! Thank you! All my doubts have gone. I love you as much as ever.'

'Oh, no! That isn't true!'

'Why not?'

She looked at him coldly.

'You are forgetting the other woman! The one you take to the races! The one whose portrait you possess – your mistress!'

'Yes, you're right!' exclaimed Frédéric. 'I don't deny it! I'm a brute! Listen to me!'

If he had made her his mistress, it had been out of despair, like somebody committing suicide. What is more, he had made her very unhappy, to avenge his own shame on her.

'What torments I have suffered! Don't you understand?'

Madame Arnoux turned her lovely face towards him, holding out her hand; and they closed their eyes, absorbed in a sweet, boundless intoxication. Then they sat there, very close, face to face, gazing at each other.

'Could you imagine that I no longer loved you?'

She replied in a low voice, full of tenderness:

'No. In spite of everything, I felt in my heart of hearts that that was impossible and that one day the barrier between us would disappear.'

'So did I! And I nearly died of longing for you!'

'Once,' she said, 'in the Palais-Royal, I passed very near to you.'

'Really?'

And he told her how happy he had been to see her again at the Dambreuses' house.

'But how I hated you, that evening, when I left.'

'Poor boy!'

'My life is so sad.'

'Mine too. If it were just my sorrows and anxieties and humiliations, everything I endure as a wife and mother, I wouldn't complain, since everybody has to die one day. But what is so dreadful is my loneliness, without a soul to . . .'

'But I am here!'

'Oh, yes!'

A passionate sob shook her body. Her arms opened; and, standing up, they clasped each other in a long kiss.

The floor creaked. A woman was beside them, Rosanette. Madame Arnoux had recognized her, and gazed at her with staring eyes, full of surprise and indignation. At last Rosanette said:

'I've come to see Monsieur Arnoux on business.'

'He's not here, as you can see.'

'That's true,' said the Marshal. 'Your maid was right. I beg your pardon.'

And turning to Frédéric, she said:

'So you're here, are you, darling?'

This familiarity, in her presence, made Madame Arnoux blush, like a slap in the face.

'I tell you, he's not here.'

Then the Marshal, who was looking idly round the room, said calmly:

'Shall we go home? I've a cab outside.'

He pretended not to hear.

'Come along, let's go!'

'Why, yes!' said Madame Arnoux. 'Now's your chance! Go! Go!'

They went out. She leant over the banisters to have a last look at them; and a shrill, piercing laugh came down to them from the top of the staircase. Frédéric pushed Rosanette into the cab, sat down opposite her, and did not utter a single word all the way home.

He himself was the cause of this disgraceful incident, with its appalling consequences for him. He felt both the shame of a crushing humiliation and regret for a happiness he would never know; just when at last he had been on the point of winning it, it had escaped him for ever. And all because of this woman, this trollop, this whore! He would gladly have strangled her; he was choking with rage. As soon as they got home he flung his hat on a table and tore off his tie.

'That was a nice thing you did just now, and no mistake!'

She planted herself proudly in front of him.

'Well, and what of it? Where's the harm in it?'

'What! You were spying on me, weren't you?'

'Is that my fault? Why should you go and amuse yourself with respectable women?'

'That's beside the point. I won't have you insulting them.'

'How did I insult her?'

He could not think of a reply; and with a spiteful edge to his voice he said:

'But that other time, at the Champ de Mars . . .'

'Oh, I'm sick and tired of your old flames!'

'You bitch!'

He raised his fist.

'Don't kill me! I'm pregnant!'

Frédéric drew back.

'You're lying!'

'Look at me if you don't believe me!'

She picked up a candlestick, and, pointing to her face, said:

'You know the signs?'

Her skin was unusually puffy, and flecked with little yellow spots. Frédéric did not deny the evidence. He went and opened the window, took a few steps up and down the room, then sank into an armchair.

This event was a catastrophe; first it postponed their separation and then it upset all his plans. Besides, the idea of being a father struck him as grotesque, unthinkable. But why should it? If, instead of the Marshal . . .? And he became so absorbed in his reverie that he had a sort of hallucination. There on the carpet, in front of the fireplace, he saw a little girl. She took after Madame Arnoux and a little after him: dark-haired and pale-skinned, with black eyes, thick eyebrows, and a pink ribbon in her curly hair. Oh, how he would have loved her! And he seemed to hear her voice calling: 'Papa! Papa!'

Rosanette, who had just undressed, came up to him, saw a tear in his eye, and kissed him gravely on the forehead. He stood up, saying:

'Dammit, we'll let the kid live!'

She started chattering away. It was going to be a boy, that was certain! They would call him Frédéric. She must start getting his baby-clothes together. And seeing her so happy, he was moved to pity for her. Since his anger had disappeared, he asked why she had acted as she had.

The reason was that Mademoiselle Vatnaz had sent her, that very day, a bill which had fallen due long ago; and she had rushed to Arnoux's house to get some money.

'I would have given it to you,' said Frédéric.

'It was simpler to collect my money from Arnoux and pay back her thousand francs to the Vatnaz woman.'

'Is that really all you owe her?'

She answered:

'Of course!'

The next day, at nine o'clock in the evening – the hour recommended by the concierge – Frédéric called at Mademoiselle Vatnaz's house.

He bumped into a pile of furniture in the hall. The sound of voices and music guided him. He opened a door and found himself in the middle of a party. In front of the piano, which was being played by a bespectacled young lady, stood Delmar, as solemn as a high-priest, reciting a humanitarian poem about prostitution; and his sepulchral voice rolled round the room, supported by sustained chords. Lining the wall was a row of women, dressed for the most part in dark colours, without either collars or cuffs. Five or six men, all intellectuals, were sitting on chairs here and there. In an armchair there was a former fabulist, a wreck of a man; and the acrid smell of a couple of lamps mingled with the aroma of the chocolate which filled some bowls on the card-table.

Mademoiselle Vatnaz, wearing an Oriental sash round her waist, was standing at one corner of the fireplace. Dussardier was facing her at the other corner; he looked somewhat embarrassed by his position. Besides, he was overawed by this artistic milieu.

Had Mademoiselle Vatnaz finished with Delmar? Perhaps not. All the same, she seemed to be keeping a jealous watch on the shop-assistant; and when Frédéric asked if he might have a word with her, she motioned to Dussardier to join them in her room. When the thousand francs had been counted out before her, she asked for the interest as well.

'It isn't worth bothering about!' said Dussardier.

'Shut up!'

This cowardice on the part of so brave a man pleased Frédéric in that it seemed to justify his own. He brought back the receipted bill, and never mentioned the scene at Madame Arnoux's again. But from then on all the Marshal's failings became apparent to him.

Her taste was incorrigibly bad; she was incredibly lazy; and she had the ignorance of a savage. She even regarded Doctor Desrogis as a great celebrity; and she was proud to entertain him and his wife because they were 'a married couple'. She exerted a tyrannical control over the life of Mademoiselle Irma, an insignificant little thing with a tiny voice, who was kept by 'a real gent', a sometime customs official who was good at card tricks; Rosanette called him 'ducky'. Frédéric could not stand the way she had of repeating stupid phrases such as: 'Nothing doing!' 'Go to Jericho!' and 'You never can tell!'; or her habit of dusting her knick-knacks every morning with a pair of old gloves. He was particularly revolted by her behaviour towards her maid, whose wages were always in arrears and who even lent her money. The days they settled their accounts they squabbled like a couple of fishwives, and then kissed and made up. Being alone with Rosanette was no longer any pleasure. It was a relief to him when Madame Dambreuse's parties began again.

Madame Dambreuse at least was an amusing companion. She knew all about society intrigues, the transfers of ambassadors, and the personnel of the fashion-houses; and, if she made a commonplace remark, she put it in such a banal form that it was impossible to tell whether she had her tongue in her cheek or not. She was at her best in the midst of a score of people talking together – forgetting no-body, provoking the replies she wanted, forestalling dangerous remarks. The simplest stories, told by her, seemed like confidences; her least smile was an enchantment; and her charm, like the exquisite perfume she usually wore, was complex and indefinable. In her company, Frédéric always felt the pleasure of the unexpected; yet every time he saw her she showed the same serenity, like the shimmer of clear waters. But why did she behave so coldly towards her niece? At times she even darted strange glances in her direction.

As soon as the question of marriage was raised, she had told Monsieur Dambreuse that the 'dear child's' health was not good enough, and she had promptly taken her off to the baths at Balaruc. On her return, new difficulties had arisen: the young man had no social standing; this grand passion did not seem serious; there was no harm in waiting. Martinon had replied that he would wait. He behaved superbly. He sang Frédéric's praises. He did more: he told him how best to win Madame Dambreuse's favour, even insinuating that he knew the aunt's feelings thanks to the niece.

As for Monsieur Dambreuse, far from showing jealousy, he lavished attentions on his young friend, consulting him on various matters, and even taking an interest in his future. Thus one day, when old Roque's name was mentioned, he whispered meaningly in his ear:

'You did well there.'

Cécile, Miss John, the servants, the porter – everybody in the house was charming to him. He went there every evening, leaving Rosanette alone. Her approaching confinement had made her more serious, even a little melancholy, as if she were tortured by anxiety. To all his questions she replied:

'You're wrong. I'm perfectly all right.'

It was five bills, not one, that she had signed long before: and, not daring to tell Frédéric after he had paid the first, she had gone back to Arnoux, who had promised her, in writing, a third of his profits from a company providing gaslight in the towns of Languedoc – a wonderful enterprise! – at the same time advising her not to use his letter until the shareholders' meeting; this meeting was postponed from one week to the next.

In the meantime the Marshal needed money. She would have died rather than ask Frédéric. She did not want money from him. It would have spoilt their love. True, he contributed towards the household expenses; but a little carriage, hired by the month, and other sacrifices which had become indispensable since he had started frequenting the Dambreuses, prevented him from doing any more for his mistress. Two or three times, coming home at unexpected hours, he thought he saw masculine backs disappearing through doorways;

and she often went out, refusing to say where she was going. Frédéric did not try to go any deeper into the question. One of these days he would make a definite decision. He dreamt of a different life, nobler and more amusing. This ideal made him indulgent towards the Dambreuse mansion.

It was a sort of annexe to the Rue de Poitiers.[75] There he met the great Monsieur A, the famous B, the intelligent C, the eloquent Z, the wonderful Y, the old stagers of the Left Centre, the paladins of the Right, the veterans of the Middle Way, all the stock characters of the political comedy. He was astounded by their abysmal conversation, their pettiness, their spite, their bad faith; for all these people who had voted for the Constitution were now doing their best to destroy it. They exerted themselves enormously, publishing manifestoes, pamphlets and biographies; the *Life of Fumichon* by Hussonnet was a masterpiece. Nonancourt busied himself with the propaganda in the country districts, Monsieur de Grémonville worked on the clergy, and Martinon rallied the youth of the middle classes. Everybody helped to the best of his ability, even Cisy. Giving his mind to serious matters now, he drove about all day long in a cabriolet, on party business.

Monsieur Dambreuse, like a barometer, always registered the party's latest variation. Lamartine's name could never be mentioned without his quoting the remark made by a man of the people. 'We've had enough poetry!' In his eyes, Cavaignac was nothing but a traitor. The President, whom he had admired for three months, was beginning to go down in his estimation, since he did not think he had 'the necessary energy'. And as he always had to have a saviour, his gratitude, ever since the Conservatoire incident, now went to Changarnier.[76] 'Thank God, Changarnier ... Oh, there's nothing to be afraid of as long as Changarnier ...'

The company were loud in their praises of Monsieur Thiers for his volume against Socialism, in which he showed himself to be a thinker no less than a writer. They laughed uproariously at Pierre Leroux, who quoted passages from the Encyclopaedists in the Chamber. They made jokes about Fourier's disciples. They went to applaud *La Foire aux idées*, and compared its authors to Aristophanes.[77] Frédéric went to see it like the others.

The political verbiage and good food began to dull his sense of morality. However mediocre these people might seem to him, he felt proud to know them and inwardly longed to enjoy their esteem. A mistress like Madame Dambreuse would establish his position in society.

He set to work to do what was necessary.

He stationed himself in her path when she went for a walk; he never failed to go and pay his respects in her box at the theatre; and, finding out the times when she usually went to church, he planted himself behind a pillar in a melancholy attitude. There was a continuous exchange of little notes giving details about curios or concerts, or asking for the loan of a book or a magazine. Apart from his evening visits, he sometimes paid her another in the late afternoon; and he experienced a graduated series of pleasures as he passed in succession through the main gate, the courtyard, the hall, and the two drawing-rooms. Finally he reached her boudoir, which was as quiet as a tomb and as warm as an alcove. One bumped into the padded sides of pieces of furniture, among a medley of assorted objects: chests of drawers, screens, bowls and trays in lacquer, tortoiseshell, ivory, and malachite – costly trifles which were frequently replaced. There were simple objects too – three pebbles from the beach at Étretat which were used as paper-weights, a Frisian cap hanging on a Chinese screen – and somehow all these things toned in with one another. There was even a certain grandeur about the overall effect, which may have been due to the height of the ceiling, the richness of the door-curtains, and the long silk fringes hanging over the gilded legs of the stools.

She was nearly always installed on a little sofa close to the flower-stand in the window-recess. Sitting on the edge of a big tuffet on castors, he paid her exquisitely calculated compliments; and she looked at him with her head a little to one side, and a smile on her lips.

He read her pages of poetry, putting his whole soul into it, in order to move her heart and win her admiration. She would interrupt him with a disparaging remark or a practical comment; and their conversation would constantly revert to the eternal question of love. They asked each other what caused it, whether women felt it more than men, in what way their own ideas about it differed. Frédéric tried to express his point of view without being either coarse or insipid. It became a kind of battle, which was sometimes enjoyable, sometimes tedious.

When he was with her he did not feel that overwhelming ecstasy which impelled him towards Madame Arnoux, nor the happy excitement which Rosanette had caused him at first. But he desired her as an exotic, refractory object, because she was noble, because she was rich, and because she was devout, imagining that she had delicate feelings as exquisite as her lace, with holy medals next to her skin and modest blushes in the midst of debauchery.

He made use of his old love. He told her about all the emotions which Madame Arnoux had once aroused in him – his yearnings, his fears, his dreams – as if she had inspired them. She listened to all this like a woman accustomed to such things; she did not expressly rebuff him, but nor did she yield an inch; and he was no more successful in seducing her than Martinon was in getting married. In order to get rid of her niece's suitor, she went so far as to accuse him of wanting to marry for money, and asked her husband to test him on this point. Monsieur Dambreuse accordingly informed the young man that Cécile, being the orphan daughter of poor relations, had neither a dowry nor any 'expectations'.

Either because he did not believe this was true, or because he had gone too far to draw back, or on one of those stubborn impulses which often prove to be strokes of genius, Martinon replied that his own income of fifteen thousand francs a year would be enough for the two of them. This disinterested attitude touched the banker's heart, it was so unexpected. He undertook to find a post for him as a tax-inspector, promising to put up the necessary caution-money; and in May 1850 Martinon married Mademoiselle Cécile. There was no ball. The young couple left for Italy the same evening. The next day Frédéric called to see Madame Dambreuse. She looked paler than usual. She contradicted him sharply on two or three trivial points. In any case, men were all egoists.

He protested that there were a few – if only himself – who were unselfish.

'Nonsense! You're no different from the rest.'

Her eyelids were red; she was crying. Then, summoning up a smile, she said:

'I beg your pardon. I'm wrong. That was just a gloomy thought that occurred to me.'

He did not understand.

'Never mind,' he said to himself. 'She's weaker than I thought.'

She rang for a glass of water, drank a mouthful, and sent it back. Then she complained that the staff were disgracefully inefficient. To amuse her he offered his services as a menial, claiming that he was capable of waiting at table, dusting furniture and announcing guests

– in short, that he could be a valet, or rather a footman, even though footmen were out of fashion. He would have liked to stand at the back of her carriage, wearing a hat trimmed with cock's feathers.

'And how proudly I should walk behind you, carrying a little dog in my arms!'

'You're very cheerful,' said Madame Dambreuse.

But wasn't it ridiculous, he answered, to take everything seriously? There were enough troubles in the world without creating one's own. Nothing was so precious that it was worth breaking one's heart over it. Madame Dambreuse raised her eyebrows, in a manner which suggested approval.

This harmony of views spurred Frédéric to greater boldness. His earlier disappointments had taught him a lesson. He went on:

'Our grandfathers knew how to live better than we do. Why shouldn't we yield to the impulse of the moment?'

After all, love in itself was not so very important.

'But what you're saying is positively immoral!'

She had installed herself again on the sofa. He sat down on the edge against her feet.

'Can't you see that I'm lying? Because to please a woman one has to display a carefree levity or a tragic frenzy. They laugh at us when we tell them we love them, and nothing more. To my mind the highflown humbug they enjoy is a profanation of true love; so that one doesn't know how to declare that love, especially to a woman who is ... very intelligent.'

She gazed at him with half-closed eyes. He lowered his voice and bent over her face.

'Yes! You frighten me! But perhaps I've offended you? ... Forgive me ... I didn't mean to say all that. It isn't my fault. You're so beautiful!'

Madame Dambreuse closed her eyes and he was astonished at the ease of his victory. The tall trees in the garden, which had been rustling gently, stood still. Motionless clouds streaked the sky with long red ribbons, and the whole universe seemed to have come to a standstill. Then a vague memory occurred to him of other evenings like this, with similar silences. Where could it have been? ...

He went down on his knees, took her hand, and swore eternal love to her. Then, as he was leaving her, she beckoned him back and whispered to him:

'Come back to dinner! We shall be alone!'

Going down the staircase, Frédéric felt that he had become a different man, that he was surrounded by the scented air of hot-houses, that he had finally made his way into the exalted world of patrician liaisons and aristocratic intrigues. To reach the top, all that he needed was a woman like Madame Dambreuse. Greedy, in all probability, for power and action, and married to a mediocrity whom she had served devotedly, she wanted a man of strong personality to guide her. Nothing was impossible now! He felt capable of travelling five hundred miles on horseback, or working for several nights on end, without the slightest fatigue; his heart was brimming over with pride.

A man in an old overcoat was walking along the pavement in front of him. His head was bowed and he looked so miserable that Frédéric turned round to look at him. The man raised his eyes. It was Deslauriers. He hesitated. Frédéric threw his arms round his neck.

'My dear fellow! What! Is it really you?'

And he carried him off to his house, asking him countless questions at the same time.

Ledru-Rollin's former commissioner began by telling him about all his trials and tribulations. Since he had preached fraternity to the Conservatives and respect for the law to the Socialists, the former had fired their muskets at him, while the latter had brought along a rope to hang him. After the events of June, he had been brutally dismissed. He had thrown himself into a plot, the one connected with the arms seized at Troyes. He had been released for lack of evidence. Then the committee of action had sent him to London, where he had come to blows with his colleagues in the middle of a banquet. On his return to Paris ...

'Why didn't you come to see me?'

'You were always away. Your concierge put on mysterious airs, so that I didn't know what to think. And then I didn't want to come back as a failure.'

He had knocked at the gates of Democracy, offering to serve her with his pen, his voice, his energy; everywhere he had been turned away; nobody trusted him; and he had had to sell his watch, his library, his linen.

'I'd be better off dying with Sénécal in the prison-ships at Belle-Isle!'

Frédéric, who was arranging his cravat at that moment, did not seem unduly upset by this news.

'Ah, so our friend Sénécal has been transported, has he?'

Deslauriers, looking enviously round the walls, retorted:

'Everybody isn't as lucky as you.'

'You must excuse me,' said Frédéric, not noticing the allusion, 'but I'm dining out. They'll get you something to eat; order anything you want. And take my bed if you like!'

In the face of such openhanded hospitality, Deslauriers' bitterness vanished.

'Your bed? But . . . that would inconvenience you.'

'Not in the slightest! I've got others!'

'Ah, I see!' said the lawyer, laughing. 'Where are you dining, then?'

'At Madame Dambreuse's.'

'Is it . . . by any chance . . . could it be . . .?'

'You're too inquisitive,' said Frédéric, with a smile which confirmed this supposition.

Then, glancing at the clock, he sat down again.

'That's life! You must never give up hope, my old champion of the people!'

'To hell with the people! Somebody else can look after them for a change!'

The lawyer detested the workers, having suffered from them in his province, a coal-mining area. Every pit had appointed a provisional government of its own to give him orders.

'Come to that, they behaved delightfully everywhere – at Lyons, Lille, Le Havre, Paris. Because, just like the manufacturers who want to exclude foreign goods, these gentlemen demand the expulsion of all workers from England, Germany, Belgium, and Savoy. As for their intelligence, what good did their famous guilds do them under the Restoration? In 1830 they joined the National Guard, without even having the sense to get control of it! And, as soon as '48 was over, didn't the trade unions appear again with their own special banners? They even wanted their own representatives in the Chamber, who would have spoken just for them! Just like the beetroot deputies who never worry about anything but beetroot! Oh, I've had enough of those fellows! First they grovelled in front of Robespierre's scaffold, then it was the Emperor's boots, and after that Louis-Philippe's umbrella. Scum, that's what they are, always ready to serve anybody who'll stuff their mouths with bread! People are always condemning the venality of Talleyrand and Mirabeau; but the messenger downstairs would sell his country for fifty centimes if you promised him a tariff of three francs for every errand he ran! Oh, what a mess we're in! We ought to have set fire to every corner of Europe!'

Frédéric replied:

'The spark was missing. You were just a lot of little shopkeepers at heart, and the best of you were doctrinaires. As for the workers, they've got every reason to complain; for apart from a million taken from the Civil List, which you granted them with the vilest flattery, you've given them nothing but fine phrases. The wages book remains in the employer's hands, and the employee, even before the law, is still inferior to his master, because nobody takes his word. Altogether, the Republic strikes me as out of date. Who knows? Perhaps progress can only be achieved through an aristocracy or a single man. The initiative always comes from above. The people are still immature, whatever you may say.'

'You may be right,' said Deslauriers.

According to Frédéric, the great mass of the people simply wanted to be left in peace – he had kept his ears open at the Dambreuses' house – and all the odds were in favour of the Conservatives. But that party needed new men.

'If you put yourself forward, I'm certain . . .'

He broke off. Deslauriers understood, and passed his hands over his forehead. Then, all of a sudden, he asked:

'But what about you? There's nothing to prevent you. Why shouldn't you be a deputy?'

As the result of a double election, there was a vacancy for a candidate in the Aube. Monsieur Dambreuse, who had been re-elected to the Legislative Assembly, belonged to another district.

'Would you like me to see what I can do?'

He knew a lot of innkeepers, schoolmasters, doctors, lawyers' clerks, and their employers.

'Besides, one can make the peasants believe absolutely anything!'

Frédéric felt his ambition kindling anew.

Deslauriers added:

'You ought to find me a job in Paris, you know.'

'Oh, that won't be difficult, through Monsieur Dambreuse.'

'Since we were talking about coal just now,' said the lawyer, 'what's become of his great company? That's the sort of work I need. And I could be useful to them, while keeping my independence.'

Frédéric promised to introduce him to the banker within three days' time.

His meal alone with Madame Dambreuse was an exquisite experience. She sat smiling at him from the other side of the table, across a basket of flowers, in the light of a hanging lamp; and stars could be seen through the open window. They talked very little, probably because they did not trust themselves; but as soon as the servants turned their backs, they blew each other a kiss. He told her of his idea of standing for election. She approved, and even promised to get Monsieur Dambreuse to help.

Later in the evening a few friends appeared to congratulate and sympathize with her; she must miss her niece dreadfully. It was a good idea, though, for the young people to go abroad; later on there would be children and other difficulties. But Italy did not come up to one's expectations. However, they were at the age of illusions! And then, everything seemed more beautiful on a honeymoon. The last to go were Monsieur de Grémonville and Frédéric. The diplomat showed no inclination to leave. Finally, at midnight, he got to his feet. Madame Dambreuse motioned to Frédéric to leave with him, and thanked him for his obedience with a gentle squeeze of the hand which was more delightful than all that had gone before.

The Marshal gave a cry of joy at seeing him again. She had been waiting for him since five o'clock. He explained his absence by saying that he had had to see to some urgent business for Deslauriers. His face wore a triumphant expression, a positive halo, which dazzled Rosanette.

'It may be because your tail-coat suits you so well, but I've never seen you look so handsome before! How handsome you are!'

In a transport of affection, she swore inwardly that she would never give herself to another man again, whatever happened, even if she had to die of hunger!

Her pretty, glistening eyes sparkled with such a powerful passion that Frédéric drew her on to his knees. 'What a swine I am!' he said to himself, glorying in his wickedness.

IV

WHEN Deslauriers called to see Monsieur Dambreuse the latter was thinking of reviving his big coal business. But the merging of several companies into one was viewed with suspicion; people talked of monopolies, as if they did not know that enormous capital was essential for enterprises of this sort.

Deslauriers, who had just read on purpose Gobet's work and Monsieur Chappe's article in the *Journal des Mines*, knew the subject thoroughly. He explained that by the law of 1810 the holder of a licence had an inalienable right to the profits from it. What is more, they could give a democratic colour to the enterprise by maintaining that any restriction on coal mergers was an attack on the very principle of association.

Monsieur Dambreuse gave him some notes from which to draw up a memorandum. As for the payment for his work, he made him promises which were all the more alluring for being vague.

Deslauriers came back to Frédéric's house to report on his interview. Apart from that, he had seen Madame Dambreuse at the foot of the stairs as he was coming out.

'I congratulate you there, I must say!'

Then they talked about the election. Some plan would have to be devised.

Three days later Deslauriers reappeared with a manuscript intended for publication in the press. It was a friendly letter in which Monsieur Dambreuse gave his approval to their friend's candidature. Supported by a Conservative and extolled by a Radical, he was bound to succeed. But how had the capitalist been persuaded to sign such a document? Without the slightest embarrassment, the lawyer had, on his own initiative, gone and shown it to Madame Dambreuse, who had thought it excellent and done the rest.

This action on his friend's part surprised Frédéric. However, he gave it his approval; and then, seeing that Deslauriers was in touch with Monsieur Roque, he explained how he was placed with regard to Louise.

'Tell them anything you like – that I'm in financial difficulties, that I'll sort things out in time. She's young enough to wait.'

Deslauriers set off; and Frédéric considered himself a man of decision. He also had a feeling of contentment, of profound satisfaction. His delight in the possession of a rich woman was not spoilt by any contrast; his emotions were in entire harmony with his environment. His life, nowadays, was a succession of pleasures.

The most exquisite, perhaps, was watching Madame Dambreuse surrounded by a group of people in her drawing-room. The propriety of her manners made him think of other postures; listening to her talk in a chilly voice, he remembered her stammered words of love; all the respect shown for her virtue delighted him as a sort of indirect homage to him; and he sometimes longed to cry out: 'But I know her better than you! She's mine!'

Their liaison soon became a thing accepted and acknowledged. Throughout the winter Madame Dambreuse took Frédéric into society.

He nearly always arrived before her; and he used to watch her come in, her arms bare, her fan in her hand, and pearls in her hair. She stopped on the threshold, with the doorway surrounding her like a frame, and she made a slight movement of indecision, half-closing her eyes to see if he was there. She brought him back in her carriage; the rain lashed the windows; the passers-by flitted through the mud like shadows; and, pressed close together, they observed all this dimly, with a calm disdain. On various pretexts he would stay at least another hour in her room.

It was out of boredom that Madame Dambreuse had yielded. But this last experience was not going to be wasted. She wanted a grand passion, and she began to load him with flattering attentions.

She sent him flowers; she made him a tapestry chair; she gave him a cigar-case, an inkstand, countless little objects of everyday utility, so that he could not perform a single action without evoking her memory. These little gifts charmed him at first, but soon he took them for granted.

She took a cab, dismissed it at the entrance to an alley-way, and came out at the other end; then, with a double veil over her face, she stole along close to the walls until she reached the street where Frédéric was waiting for her. He quickly took her arm and led her into his house. His two servants were off duty and the concierge was out on an errand; she looked around her; there was nothing to be afraid of; and she heaved a sigh like an exile returning home. Their luck made them bolder. They met more often. One evening she went so far as to appear unexpectedly in full evening dress. He reproached her for her rashness; this sort of surprise might be dangerous. Besides, he thought she looked singularly unattractive. Her low-cut dress showed too much of her scrawny bosom.

He admitted at that moment what he had refused to acknowledge until then – the disillusionment of his senses. This did not prevent him from simulating ardent passion; but in order to feel it, he had to summon up the image of Rosanette or Madame Arnoux.

This atrophy of the heart left his head entirely clear, and he longed more than ever for a high position in society. Seeing that he had this stepping-stone at his disposal, the least he could do was to use it.

One morning towards the middle of January, Sénécal came into his study, and, on his exclamation of surprise, explained that he was Deslauriers' secretary. He had brought Frédéric a letter. It contained good news, but at the same time reproached Frédéric for his negligence; he must come to see his constituency.

The future deputy said that he would set off in a couple of days.

Sénécal expressed no opinion about his candidature. He spoke about himself and the state of the country.

Pitiful though it was, he rejoiced over it; for things were moving towards Communism. To begin with, the administration was going that way willy-nilly, since every day that passed saw more things brought under Government control. As for Property, the Constitution of '48, for all its weaknesses, had been anything but indulgent to it; in the name of the common weal, the State could henceforth appropriate anything it thought fit. Sénécal declared himself in favour of Authority; and Frédéric noticed in what he said an exaggerated version of his own remarks to Deslauriers. The Republican even thundered against the inadequacy of the masses.

'By defending the rights of the minority, Robespierre brought Louis XVI before the National Convention, and saved the people. The end justifies the means. A dictatorship is sometimes indispensable. Long live tyranny, provided the tyrant does good!'

Their discussion lasted a long time, and, as he was leaving, Sénécal remarked – this may have been the object of his visit – that Monsieur Dambreuse's silence was making Deslauriers impatient.

But Monsieur Dambreuse was ill. As a friend of the family, Frédéric was allowed to see him every day.

The dismissal of General Changarnier had upset the capitalist badly.[78] The same evening he had been afflicted with a burning sensation in the chest, together with a breathlessness which prevented him from lying down. The application of leeches brought him immediate relief. His dry cough disappeared, his breathing became more regular; and a week later, drinking some broth, he said:

'Ah, I feel better now! But I nearly went off on my last journey!'

'Not without me!' exclaimed Madame Dambreuse, implying that she would have been unable to survive him.

Instead of answering, he looked at her and her lover with a peculiar smile, which combined resignation, indulgence, irony and even a hint of amusement.

Frédéric wanted to leave for Nogent. Madame Dambreuse urged him to postpone his departure; and he kept packing and unpacking his bags according to the fluctuations of the banker's illness.

All of a sudden Monsieur Dambreuse started spitting blood copiously. The 'princes of science' were consulted, but had nothing new to recommend in the way of treatment. His legs swelled up and he grew steadily weaker. He had several times expressed a desire to see Cécile, who was at the other end of France with her husband, for Martinon had been appointed to a post as tax-inspector a month before. Monsieur Dambreuse explicitly ordered her to be sent for. His wife wrote three letters to this effect, which she showed him.

Refusing to trust even the nun who was nursing him, she did not leave him for a moment, and no longer went to bed. Callers leaving their names at the porter's lodge asked after her admiringly, and passers-by were impressed by the amount of straw that was spread in the roadway, under the window.

On 12 February, at five o'clock, an alarming haemoptysis occurred. The doctor on duty explained the danger. A priest was hurriedly sent for.

During Monsieur Dambreuse's confession, his wife watched him inquisitively from a distance. Afterwards the young doctor applied a blister and waited.

The lamps, hidden by pieces of furniture, shed an uneven light over the room.

Frédéric and Madame Dambreuse, at the foot of the bed, watched the dying man. In one of the window recesses the priest and the doctor were talking in low voices; the nun, on her knees, was mumbling prayers.

At last the death-rattle sounded. The hands grew cold, the face began to turn pale. Every now and then he suddenly drew a deep breath, but this happened more and more rarely. He blurted out two or three incoherent words; exhaling gently, he turned up his eyes, and his head fell to one side on the pillow.

For a moment everybody remained motionless.

Madame Dambreuse went up to the bed; and quite naturally, with the simplicity of a duty to be done, she closed his eyes.

Then she stretched out her arms, twisting her body as if in a paroxysm of controlled despair, and left the room, supported by the doctor and the nun. A quarter of an hour later Frédéric went up to her room.

An indefinable scent hung in the air, an emanation of the exquisite things which filled the place. In the middle of the bed a black dress was spread out, contrasting sharply with the pink coverlet.

Madame Dambreuse was standing at the corner of the fireplace. Without imagining that she was plunged in grief, he supposed that she would be a little sad; and in a sympathetic voice he asked:

'Are you unhappy?'

'I? Not in the least!'

Turning round, she caught sight of the dress and examined it; then she told him to make himself at home.

'Smoke if you like. You're in my house now.'

Then, heaving a sigh, she added:

'Heavens above! What a relief to be rid of him!'

Frédéric was astonished at this exclamation. Kissing her hand, he remarked:

'All the same, we were free enough!'

This allusion to the facility of their liaison seemed to offend Madame Dambreuse.

'Oh, you don't know all I did for him, or what agonies I went through.'

'Agonies?'

'Why, yes! How do you think I could feel safe with that bastard of his always around? She was brought into the house when we'd been married five years, and if it hadn't been for me she'd undoubtedly have made him do something foolish.'

Then she explained her financial situation. They had married under the system of separate means. Her own fortune amounted to three hundred thousand francs. By their marriage contract, Monsieur Dambreuse had guaranteed her, if she outlived him, an income of fifteen thousand francs a year, together with ownership of the mansion. But a little later he had made a will leaving her his entire fortune, which as far as she could tell at the moment, she put at over three million.

Frédéric opened his eyes wide.

'It was worth waiting for, wasn't it? Anyway, I helped to make it. It was my property I was defending; Cécile would have robbed me of it, unjustly.'

'Why didn't she come to see her father?' asked Frédéric.

At this question, Madame Dambreuse looked hard at him; then she said dryly:

'I haven't the faintest idea. Heartlessness, I imagine. Oh, I know what she's like! So she won't get a penny from me!'

But she had caused hardly any trouble, at least since her marriage.

'Oh! Her marriage!' said Madame Dambreuse with a sneer.

And she blamed herself for having been too kind to that jealous, scheming, hypocritical little minx. 'All her father's faults!' She criticized him more and more. He had been as deceitful as could be, ruthless, hard as nails, 'a bad man, a bad man!'

Even the cleverest people sometimes make mistakes. Madame Dambreuse had just made one in giving vent to her hatred. Frédéric, sitting opposite her in an easy-chair, was shocked and thoughtful.

She rose and sat gently on his knee.

'You're the only person I know who's good at heart! I love you, and only you!'

Looking at him, her heart melted, a nervous reaction brought tears to her eyes, and she murmured:

'Will you marry me?'

At first he thought he had misheard. The thought of all that wealth made him dizzy. She repeated in a louder voice:

'Will you marry me?'

At last he said with a smile:

'Can you doubt it?'

Then he felt a sudden compunction, and as a sort of reparation to the dead man, he offered to watch over him himself. But as he was ashamed to admit this pious impulse, he added casually:

'It might look better if I did.'

'Yes, perhaps you're right,' she said, 'on account of the servants.'

The bed had been pulled right out of the alcove. The nun was at the foot, and at the head there was a priest, this time a tall, thin fanatical-looking man with something Spanish about him. On the bedside table, which had been covered with a white napkin, three candles were burning.

Frédéric took a chair and looked at the dead man.

His face was as yellow as straw; there was a little blood-flecked froth at the corners of his mouth. A silk scarf had been tied round his head; he was wearing a knitted waistcoat; and he had a silver crucifix on his chest, between his folded arms.

So that turbulent life of his was over! How many times had he visited ministries, juggled with figures, fixed deals, and listened to reports! How many people had he flattered with smiles and bows! For he had acclaimed Napoleon, the Cossacks, Louis XVIII, 1830, the workers, truckling to every government, worshipping Authority so fervently that he would have paid for the privilege of selling himself.

But he left behind the estate of La Fortelle, three factories in Picardy, the Forest of Crancé in the Yonne, a farm near Orleans, and a fortune in stocks and shares.

Frédéric totted up his fortune again: all this was going to belong to him! First of all he thought of 'what people would say', then of a present for his mother, of the houses he would have, of an old family coachman he would take on as porter. The livery would have to be changed, of course. He would turn the big drawing-room into his study. By knocking down three walls he could easily install a picture gallery on the second floor. It might be possible to fix up some Turkish baths downstairs. But what could be done with that unattractive room Monsieur Dambreuse had used as his study?

These dreams were rudely interrupted by the priest blowing his nose or the nun poking the fire. But reality confirmed them; the body was still there. The eyes had opened again; and the pupils, though sunk in the murky shadows, had an inscrutable expression which Frédéric found unbearable. He thought he could recognize in it a judgement on himself; and he felt something akin to remorse, for this man had never done him any harm; on the contrary, he . . . 'Oh, come now! He was an old rascal!' And he took a closer look at him, to steady his nerves, silently shouting at him:

'Well, what is it? I didn't kill you, did I?'

Meanwhile the priest read his breviary; the nun dozed without moving; the wicks of the three candles lengthened.

For two hours the dull rumbling could be heard of the carts on their way to the Central Market. The windows grew whiter, and a cab went past, followed by a troop of she-asses trotting along the road. Then came the noise of hammering, the cries of street-hawkers, blasts on a trumpet, all these sounds merging already into the great voice of Paris awakening.

Frédéric set to work. First he went to the town hall to register the death; then, when the medical officer had given him a certificate, he returned to the town hall to state which cemetery the family had chosen, and to make arrangements with the undertakers.

The clerk showed him a drawing and a prospectus, the one listing the different classes of funeral, the other showing all the paraphernalia in detail. Did he prefer a hearse with a cornice round the roof or a hearse with plumes? Were the horses to wear bows and the footmen aigrettes? Did he want funeral lamps, and a man to carry the decorations of the deceased? And how many carriages were there to be? Frédéric erred on the generous side; Madame Dambreuse was determined to spare no expense.

Then he went to the church.

The curate who arranged funerals began by criticizing the undertakers' capacity. For example, the man to carry the decorations was utterly superfluous; it would be far better to spend the money on hundreds of tapers. They agreed on a low Mass with music. Frédéric signed the contract, which included a binding obligation to pay all the expenses.

Next he went to the town hall to buy a burial plot. A plot six foot by three cost five hundred francs. Was the grant to be for fifty years or in perpetuity?

'Oh, in perpetuity!' said Frédéric.

He took the matter seriously and went to enormous trouble over it. A monumental mason was waiting for him in the courtyard of the mansion, to show him estimates and plans for Greek, Egyptian, and Moorish tombs; but the architect of the house had already discussed the subject with Madame; while on the hall table there were all sorts of prospectuses concerning the cleaning of mattresses, the disinfection of rooms, and various methods of embalmment.

After dinner he went back to the tailor's to see about the servants' mourning; and then he had to go out one last time, for he had ordered beaver gloves, whereas etiquette demanded floss-silk.

When he arrived the next day at ten o'clock, the big drawing-room was filling with people. Most of them greeted each other with a melancholy air, remarking:

'Why it's only a month since I saw him! Ah, well, it's the fate of us all!'

'Yes, but let's try to put it off as long as we can!'

Then they would give a satisfied chuckle, and even start conversations which had nothing whatever to do with the circumstances. At last the master of ceremonies, dressed in a black coat, knee-breeches, cloak, and weepers, with his sword at his side and his three-cornered hat under his arm, bowed, and uttered the traditional words:

'Gentlemen, at your convenience.'

They set out.

It was the day of the flower market on the Place de la Madeleine. The weather was fine and mild; and the breeze which was gently shaking the canvas stalls puffed out the edges of the huge black cloth hanging over the portal. Monsieur Dambreuse's arms, in a velvet square, were repeated on it three times. They were 'sable, with sinister arm or, and clenched fist gauntleted argent', with a count's coronet and the motto: 'By every path'.

The bearers carried the heavy coffin up the steps, and the mourners went in.

The six chapels, the apse, and the chairs were hung with black. The catafalque at the bottom of the choir, with its tall tapers, formed a single blaze of yellow light. At the two corners, flames of spirits of wine were rising from candelabra.

The most important mourners took their seats in the sanctuary, the others in the nave; and the Mass began.

With a few exceptions, those present were so profoundly ignorant of things religious that the master of ceremonies motioned to them from time to time to stand up, kneel down, or sit. Voices alternated with the organ and the two double basses; in the intervals of silence the priest could be heard mumbling at the altar; then the music and the singing started again.

A dull light fell from the three cupolas; but the open door let in a horizontal stream of white radiance which struck all the bare heads; and in the air, half-way up to the roof, there floated a shadow, pierced by the glitter of the gold paint decorating the ribs of the pendentives and the foliage of the capitals.

To while away the time, Frédéric listened to the *Dies irae*, looked at the people around him, and tried to see the paintings of the life of Mary Magdalen, which were too high up for him to make them out. Luckily Pellerin came and sat beside him, and promptly launched out into a long dissertation on the frescoes. The bell tolled. They left the church.

The hearse, decorated with hanging draperies and tall plumes, moved off in the direction of Père-Lachaise. It was drawn by four black horses with bows in their manes and plumes on their heads, enveloped in great caparisons embroidered with silver which reached down to their hooves. The coachman wore riding-boots and a three-cornered hat with a long crape ribbon. The ropes were held by four people: a treasurer of the Chamber of Deputies, a member of the General Council of the Aube, a representative of the coal-mining companies, and Fumichon, as a friend. The dead man's barouche and a dozen mourning carriages followed. Behind came the guests, filling the middle of the boulevard.

The passers-by stopped to watch; women holding their babies in their arms climbed on to chairs; and men drinking beer in cafés appeared at windows with billiard cues in their hands.

It was a long way; and just as at official dinners where the guests are first reserved, then expansive, the general atmosphere soon relaxed. The talk was all of the Chamber's refusal of an additional grant to the President.[78] Monsieur Piscatory had been too severe, Montalembert 'magnificent as usual', while Monsieur Chambolle, Monsieur Pidoux, and Monsieur Creton – the whole commission, in fact – ought perhaps to have followed the advice of Monsieur Quentin-Bauchard and Monsieur Dufour.

This conversation continued along the Rue de la Roquette, with its double line of shops displaying nothing but coloured glass chains and black disks covered with patterns and gold lettering, which made them look like caves full of stalactites, or china stores. But when they reached the gate of the cemetery, everybody immediately fell silent.

The tombs rose up among the trees: broken pillars, pyramids, temples, dolmens, obelisks, and Etruscan vaults with bronze doors. Some contained a sort of funereal boudoir, with rustic armchairs and folding stools. Cobwebs hung like rags from the chains of the urns; and dust covered the crucifixes and the bunches of satin ribbons. Everywhere, on the tombs and between the pillars of the balustrades, there were wreaths of immortelles, candlesticks, vases, flowers, black disks engraved with gold lettering, and plaster statuettes. These were of little boys and girls, or little angels suspended in the air by brass wires; several of them even had zinc roofs over their heads. Huge ropes of spun glass, in black, white, and blue, hung in long snake-like coils from the tops of steles to the tombstones beneath. The sun caught them and made them glitter among the black wooden crosses; and the hearse made its way along the wide paths, which were paved like the streets of a town. Now and then the axles creaked. Kneeling women, their dresses trailing in the grass, spoke softly to the dead. Puffs of whitish smoke rose from the green yew-trees. They were burning rubbish and abandoned wreaths.

Monsieur Dambreuse's grave was not far from those of Manuel and Benjamin Constant. The ground fell away here in a steep slope. There were green tree-tops immediately below, the funnels of fire-engines further off, and in the distance the whole of Paris.

Frédéric was able to admire the view while the speeches were being made.

The first was made on behalf of the Chamber of Deputies, the second on behalf of the General Council of the Aube, the third on behalf of the Saône-et-Loire Coal Company, the fourth on behalf of the Agricultural Society of the Yonne; and there was another on behalf of a philanthropic association. Finally, just as everybody was moving away, a stranger started reading a sixth speech, on behalf of the Amiens Society of Antiquaries.

All the speakers took the opportunity to thunder against Socialism, of which Monsieur Dambreuse had died a victim. It was the spectacle of anarchy together with his devotion to law and order which had cut short his days. They extolled his intelligence, his probity, his generosity, and even his silence as a deputy, for, if he was no orator, he was endowed with those compensatory virtues which were infinitely preferable, and so on and so forth . . . None of the traditional phrases was omitted: 'Premature end . . . everlasting regret . . . that other homeland . . . farewell, or rather, till we meet again!'

The pebbly earth fell into place; and the world had done with Monsieur Dambreuse.

The mourners did talk about him a little more on their way back through the cemetery; and they did not scruple to say what they really thought of him. Hussonnet, who had to write a report of the funeral for the newspapers, even parodied all the graveside speeches; for, when all was said and done, old Dambreuse had been one of the most accomplished 'palm-greasers' of the previous reign. Then the funeral carriages took the business-men back to their affairs; the ceremony had not taken up too much time, and they congratulated themselves on the fact.

Frédéric went home, utterly exhausted.

The next day, when he arrived at the Dambreuse mansion, he was told that Madame was working in the study downstairs. Files and drawers were gaping open all over the place; account books had been thrown to right and left; a roll of papers labelled: 'Bad debts' was lying on the floor; he nearly tripped over it, and picked it up. Madame Dambreuse was almost invisible, buried in the big arm-chair.

'Hullo! Where are you? What's the matter?'

She sprang to her feet.

'What's the matter? I'm ruined! Ruined, do you understand?'

Monsieur Adolphe Langlois, the lawyer, had summoned her to his office, and had read her a will drawn up by her husband before they were married. He left everything to Cécile; and the other will had disappeared. Frédéric turned very pale. Perhaps she had not searched everywhere?

'Look for yourself!' said Madame Dambreuse, pointing round the room.

The two strong-boxes were yawning open; they had been broken into with an axe. She had turned the desk upside down, ransacked the cupboards, and shaken the door-mats. Suddenly she gave a shrill cry and rushed into a corner of the room where she had just caught sight of a little box with a brass lock. She opened it. There was nothing there!

'Oh, the swine! And I looked after him so devotedly!'

Then she burst out sobbing.

'Perhaps it's somewhere else?' said Frédéric.

'Oh, no! It was there, in that strong-box. I saw it not so long ago. It's been burnt! I'm sure it has!'

One day, at the beginning of his illness, Monsieur Dambreuse had gone downstairs to sign some papers.

'It must have been then that he did it!'

And she collapsed on to a chair, utterly prostrate. A bereaved mother beside an empty cradle could not have been more pitiable than Madame Dambreuse before the gaping strong-boxes. Indeed, her grief, however base its cause, seemed so profound that he tried to console her by pointing out that, after all, she was not reduced to destitution.

'But it is destitution, seeing that I can't offer you a large fortune!'

All that she had left was thirty thousand francs a year, not counting the mansion, which might be worth another eighteen to twenty.

Although this represented affluence for Frédéric, he none the less felt a sense of disappointment. It was good-bye to his dreams and the splendid life he would have had! Honour demanded that he should marry Madame Dambreuse. He thought for a moment, and then said tenderly:

'I shall still have you!'

She threw herself into his arms; and he pressed her to his breast, with a feeling of emotion not unmixed with admiration for himself. Madame Dambreuse, who had stopped crying, lifted her face, which was radiant with happiness, and took his hand.

'Oh, I never doubted in you!' she said. 'I was certain you wouldn't fail me.'

This premature confidence in something which he regarded as a magnanimous action on his part annoyed the young man.

Then she took him to her room and they made plans. Frédéric must concentrate now on making his way in the world. She even gave him some excellent advice on his candidature.

The first thing was to learn off two or three phrases of political economy. Then he should specialize in some subject such as horse-breeding, for instance, write a few articles on a topic of local interest, always have some post office appointments and tobacco licences at his disposal, and perform a host of small services. Monsieur Dambreuse had been exemplary in this respect. Thus, one day in the country, he had stopped his brake, which was full of friends, outside a cobbler's workshop, and bought a dozen pairs of shoes for his guests, together with an appalling pair of boots for himself, which he had actually had the heroism to wear for a fortnight. This anecdote amused them. She told him others, with a resurgence of grace, youth, and wit.

She gave her approval to his idea of an immediate journey to Nogent. Their farewells were tender; then, on the threshold, she murmured once again:

'You do love me, don't you?'

'For ever!' he replied.

A messenger was waiting for him at home with a pencilled note informing him that Rosanette's confinement was imminent. He had been so busy during the last few days that he had forgotten all about her. She had gone to a private nursing-home at Chaillot. Frédéric took a cab and set off.

At the corner of the Rue de Marbeuf he saw a notice-board announcing in big letters: 'Nursing and Maternity Home, under the direction of Madame Alessandri, first-class midwife, former student at the Maternity Hospital, author of various works, etc.' The same sign reappeared half-way down the street on a little ordinary door. It said: 'Madame Alessandri's Nursing Home', giving all her qualifications but omitting the word 'maternity'.

Frédéric banged the knocker.

A maid looking like a soubrette showed him into the drawing-room, which was furnished with a mahogany table, some red velvet armchairs, and a clock in a glass case.

Madame appeared almost immediately. She was a tall, dark woman of forty with a slim figure, fine eyes, and good manners. She informed Frédéric that the mother had been safely delivered and took him up to her room.

Rosanette gave a smile of ineffable joy, and, as if submerged under the waves of a suffocating passion, she whispered:

'A boy. There! There!' pointing to a bassinette by her bed.

He drew aside the curtains, and saw, in the midst of the bed-clothes, a yellowish-red object, hideously wrinkled, which smelt unpleasant and was wailing.

'Kiss him!'

To hide his repugnance, he replied:

'But I might hurt him.'

'No, no!'

He gave his child a grudging kiss.

'How like you he is!'

And with her frail arms she hugged him in a frenzy of emotion such as he had never seen in her before.

The memory of Madame Dambreuse came back to him. He reproached himself for his monstrous behaviour in deceiving this poor creature, who loved and suffered with all the frankness of her nature. For several days he kept her company until the evening.

She was happy in this quiet house; the shutters of the front windows were always closed; her room, which was hung with bright-coloured chintz, overlooked a large garden; and Madame Alessandri, whose only fault was a habit of referring to famous doctors as close friends, lavished attentions on her. Her fellow patients, who were nearly all young ladies from the country, were extremely bored as they had no visitors; Rosanette noticed that she was regarded with envy, and told Frédéric so with some pride. All the same, they had to talk in whispers, for the partitions were thin, and everybody tried hard to eavesdrop in spite of the continuous noise of piano-playing.

He was at last about to set off for Nogent when he received a letter from Deslauriers.

Two new candidates had appeared, one a Conservative, the other a Radical; a third would have no chance, whatever his politics. It was Frédéric's fault; he had let his opportunity slip; he ought to have come earlier and bestirred himself. 'Why, you didn't even put in an appearance at the agricultural show!' The lawyer criticized him for having no connexions with the newspapers. 'Oh, if only you'd taken my advice a few years ago! If only we had a paper of our own!' He laboured the point. Besides, a lot of people who would have voted for him out of consideration for Monsieur Dambreuse would drop him now. Deslauriers was one of these. With nothing more to hope for from the capitalist, he was abandoning his protégé.

Frédéric took his letter to show to Madame Dambreuse.

'So you haven't been to Nogent?' she said.

'Why do you say that?'

'Because I saw Deslauriers three days ago.'

Hearing of her husband's death, the lawyer had come to see her, to return the notes on the coal industry and to offer his services as legal adviser. This struck Frédéric as peculiar; and what was his friend up to at Nogent?

Madame Dambreuse wanted to know how he had spent his time since she had last seen him.

'I've been ill,' he replied.

'You might at least have told me.'

'Oh, it wasn't worth it.'

Besides, he had had a host of things to do, appointments to keep, calls to pay.

Henceforth he led a double life, scrupulously spending every night with the Marshal and every afternoon with Madame Dambreuse, so that he was left with barely an hour to himself in the middle of the day.

The child was in the country, at Andilly. They went to see it every week.

The nurse's house was in the upper part of the village, at the back of a little yard as dark as night, with straw on the ground, hens scratching about here and there, and a vegetable cart in the shed. Rosanette began by kissing her baby frantically, and afterwards bustled about in a sort of frenzy, trying to milk the goat, eating some farmhouse bread, sniffing the dung-heap, and suggesting putting a little of it in her handkerchief.

Then they went for long walks; she ventured into nursery gardens, broke off branches of lilac hanging over walls, shouted: 'Gee up, Neddy!' whenever she saw a donkey pulling a cart, and stopped to admire beautiful gardens through the railings. On other occasions the nurse took the child and put it in the shade under a walnut-tree; and the two women talked the most boring nonsense to each other for hours on end.

Sitting beside them, Frédéric gazed at the square vineyards on the sloping ground, with a bushy tree-top here and there, the dusty paths looking like greyish ribbons, and the houses dotting the green landscape with red and white. Now and then, at the foot of the wooded hills, the smoke of a railway engine stretched out in a horizontal line, like a gigantic ostrich feather whose tip kept blowing away.

Then his eyes fell once more on his son. He imagined him as a young man; he would make him his companion; but he might turn out to be a fool, and he was certain to be a failure. His illegitimate birth would always be a burden to him; it would have been better for him not to be born, and Frédéric murmured: 'Poor child!' his heart swelling with an inexplicable melancholy.

Often they missed the last train home. Then Madame Dambreuse would scold him for his unpunctuality, and he would make up a story for her.

He had to invent some for Rosanette too. She could not understand how he spent all his evenings, and why he was never there when she sent a message to his house. One day when he was at home, the two women appeared almost at the same moment. He got the Marshal out of the house and concealed Madame Dambreuse, telling her that he was expecting his mother.

Soon his lies began to amuse him; he repeated to one the vow he had just made to the other; he sent them two similar bouquets, wrote to both of them at the same time, then made comparisons between them; but there was a third woman who was always in his thoughts. The impossibility of possessing her served as a justification for his deceitful behaviour, which sharpened his pleasure by providing constant variety; and the more he deceived one of his mistresses, the more she loved him, as if the two women's passions stimulated one another and each woman, out of a sort of rivalry, were trying to make him forget the other.

'See how I trust you!' Madame Dambreuse said to him one day, unfolding a note which informed her that Monsieur Moreau was living with a certain Rose Bron.

'Is that by any chance the young lady of the racecourse?'

'What nonsense!' he said. 'Let me see it.'

The letter, which was written in capitals, was unsigned. To begin with, Madame Dambreuse had tolerated this mistress, who served as a cover for their adultery. But when her passion grew stronger she had insisted on his breaking with Rosanette, something which, according to Frédéric, he had done long before. When he had finished his protestations, she narrowed her eyes, which glittered like the points of two daggers seen through muslin, and said:

'All right. But what about the other one?'

'Which other one?'

'The china-dealer's wife.'

He shrugged his shoulders disdainfully. She did not press the point.

But a month later, when they were talking about honour and loyalty, and he was praising his own – in a casual way, for safety's sake – she said:

'Yes, it's true you're a man of your word. You don't go there any more.'

Frédéric, who was thinking of the Marshal, stammered:

'Where?'

'To Madame Arnoux's.'

He begged her to tell him how she had obtained this information. It was through her second seamstress, Madame Regimbart.

So she was familiar with his life, while he knew nothing of hers! True, he had found in her dressing-room a miniature of a gentleman with a long moustache. Was this the man about whom he had once been told a vague story ending in a suicide? But there was no way of learning any more on the subject. Anyway, what was the use?

Women's hearts were like those desks full of secret drawers fitting one inside another; you struggled with them, you broke your fingernails, and at the bottom you found a withered flower, a little dust, or nothing at all! Perhaps he was afraid too of finding out too much.

She made him refuse invitations to places where she could not accompany him, and kept him at her side out of fear of losing him; yet in spite of this relationship which grew closer every day, chasms would suddenly open up between them on account of trivial matters, such as the appreciation of a person's character or a work of art.

She had a hard, correct way of playing the piano. Her spiritualism – for Madame Dambreuse believed in the transmigration of souls to the stars – did not prevent her from managing her financial affairs with admirable skill. She was haughty with her servants; the rags and tatters of the poor left her dry-eyed. An innate selfishness revealed itself in her habitual expressions – 'What do I care? I'd be a fool if I did! Why should I?' – and in countless contemptible little actions which defied analysis. She would have been perfectly capable of listening at keyholes, and there could be no doubt that she lied to her confessor. Out of a spirit of domination she insisted that Frédéric should go to church with her on Sunday. He obeyed, and carried her missal.

The loss of her inheritance had changed her considerably. These marks of a grief which was attributed to Monsieur Dambreuse's death made her more interesting; and, as before, she entertained a great deal. Since Frédéric's electoral discomfiture, she had been scheming to obtain a legation in Germany for the two of them; and the first essential was to accept the prevailing ideas.

Some people wanted the Empire, some the Orléans family, some the Comte de Chambord; but all were agreed on the pressing need for decentralization. Several methods were suggested – dividing Paris into countless high streets with villages round them, transferring the seat of government to Versailles, moving the University to Bourges, suppressing the libraries, or putting everything in the hands of the General Staff – and country life was praised to the skies, since illiterates were naturally more sensible than the rest of men. Hatred abounded: hatred of primary school teachers and wine-merchants, of philosophy classes and history lectures, of novels, red waistcoats, and long beards, of any kind of independence, any display of individuality; for it was necessary to 'restore the principle of authority'. It did not matter in whose name it was wielded, or where it came from, provided it was strong and powerful. The Conservatives now talked like Sénécal. Frédéric was nonplussed; and at Rosanette's he heard the same ideas expressed by the same men.

The courtesans' drawing-rooms – their importance dates from this period – served as neutral territory on which reactionaries of different parties could meet. Hussonnet, who spent his time disparaging the great men of the day – thus helping to speed the restoration of order – inspired Rosanette with a longing to have evening parties of her own, like anybody else. He promised to publish reports of them; and he began by bringing along Fumichon, a serious-minded man; after him came Nonancourt, Monsieur de Grémonville, Monsieur de Larsillois, the former prefect, and Cisy, who was now an agricultural expert in Brittany and more devout than ever.

Some of the Marshal's former lovers came too, including the Baron de Comaing, the Comte de Jumillac, and a few others; their free-and-easy manners offended Frédéric.

To show that he was the master, he put the establishment on a more lavish footing. They engaged a groom, moved house, changed all the furniture. This expenditure had the advantage of making his forthcoming marriage appear less out of proportion to his fortune. But his fortune diminished alarmingly as a result; while Rosanette could make neither head nor tail of his behaviour.

By nature a woman of the middle class, she adored domesticity, a quiet home life. All the same, she enjoyed having an 'at home' day, referred to her fellow courtesans as 'those women', wanted to be 'a society lady', and came to believe that she was. She asked Frédéric not to smoke any more in the drawing-room, and tried to make him observe fast days because it was good form.

However, she failed to play her part properly, for she began to turn serious. She even displayed a certain melancholy every night before going to bed. It was like finding cypress-trees outside the door of a tavern.

He discovered the reason for this: she too was dreaming of marriage! Frédéric was furious. Besides, he remembered her sudden appearance at Madame Arnoux's, and he still bore her a grudge for resisting him so long.

He none the less went on trying to find out the names of her old lovers. She denied them all. A sort of jealousy took hold of him. He took exception to the presents she had been given in the past and was still receiving; and while her personality irritated him more and more, a sensual urge, bestial and violent, would still impel him towards her, producing a momentary illusion which always turned to hatred.

Her smile, her voice, the words she used, everything about her came to irritate him, and particularly the look in her eyes, that limpid, vacant, feminine gaze. Sometimes he was so exasperated by her that he could have watched her die without feeling the slightest emotion. But how could he be angry with her? Her sweet, even temper was utterly disarming.

Deslauriers reappeared and explained his stay at Nogent on the grounds that he had been trying to buy a lawyer's practice. Frédéric was glad to see him again; he was somebody to talk to. He made him the third party in their company.

The lawyer dined with them from time to time; and whenever a slight disagreement arose, he took Rosanette's side, so that Frédéric said to him once:

'Oh, go to bed with her if you like!' – he was so anxious for some opportunity to get rid of her.

Towards the middle of June she received a writ in which Maître Athanase Gautherot, a process-server, called upon her to pay four thousand francs owing to Mademoiselle Clémence Vatnaz, failing which payment he would come the next day to seize her belongings.

The fact of the matter was that only one of the four bills she had once signed had been paid, and such money as she had received since then had been spent on other things.

She hurried round to Arnoux's house. He was now living in the Faubourg Saint-Germain, and the concierge did not know the address. She went to see several friends, found nobody at home, and came back in despair. She did not want to say anything to Frédéric, for fear that this fresh incident might imperil her marriage.

The next morning Maître Athanase Gautherot appeared, escorted by two acolytes. One was a pale, weasel-faced individual, who looked as if he were eaten up with envy; the other wore a detachable collar, tight trouser-straps, and a black taffeta stall on his forefinger. Both of them were revoltingly dirty; their collars were greasy and their coat-sleeves too short.

Their master, on the other hand, was a handsome fellow, and he began by apologizing for his painful mission, at the same time look-

ing round the room, which was 'full of pretty things, upon my word!'
He added: '... apart from those which can't be seized.' At a sign
from him his two assistants disappeared.

He now became even more complimentary. Was it possible that
such a ... charming person should not have a friend to protect her?
A sale by order of the court was an absolute disaster. One never
recovered from it. He tried to frighten her; then, seeing that she was
upset, suddenly adopted a fatherly tone. He was a man of the world;
he had had dealings with countless ladies; and as he gave their names
he examined the pictures on the walls. They had belonged to Arnoux,
and included sketches by Sombaz, watercolours by Burieu, and
three landscapes by Dittmer. Rosanette obviously did not know
their value. Maître Gautherot turned to her and said:

'Look here! To show you I'm a good sort, let's come to an
arrangement. Give me these Dittmers, and I'll settle your debt. Is it
agreed?'

At that moment Frédéric, who had been told what was happening
by Delphine in the hall, and had just seen the two assistants, stormed
into the room, still wearing his hat. Maître Gautherot resumed his
dignified air; and, as the door had been left open, he called out:

'Right, gentlemen, take this down. In the second room, we'll say:
one oak table, with two leaves; two sideboards ...'

Frédéric interrupted him to ask if there was any way of preventing
the seizure.

'Why, of course. Who paid for the furniture?'

'I did.'

'Well, then, put in a claim; it will be so much time gained.'

Maître Gautherot hurriedly finished his inventory, citing Mademoiselle Bron in his report to the court, and left.

Frédéric did not utter a word of reproach. He gazed at the muddy
footprints the bailiff's men had left on the carpet; and, talking to
himself, said:

'I must go and find some money.'

'Lord, what a fool I am!' said the Marshal.

She rummaged in a drawer, took out a letter, and hurried over to
the offices of the Languedoc Lighting Company, to sell out her
shares.

She came back an hour later. The shares had been sold to somebody else! The clerk had examined the paper she had shown him,
Arnoux's written promise, and had told her:

'This document doesn't make you a shareholder. The Company doesn't recognize it.'

In short, he had sent her packing; she was furious; and Frédéric must go to see Arnoux straight away, to clear the matter up.

But Arnoux might imagine that the indirect purpose of his visit was to recover the fifteen thousand francs of his lost mortgage; besides, he thought there was something ignoble about claiming money from a man who had been his mistress's lover. Taking a middle course, he went to the Dambreuse mansion to obtain Madame Regimbart's address, sent a messenger to her, and in that way found out which was the café the Citizen now favoured with his custom.

It was a little café on the Place de la Bastille, where he sat all day at the back of the room, in the right-hand corner, as motionless as if he had been part of the building.

After trying, one after the other, coffee, grog, punch, mulled wine, and even wine and water, he had fallen back on beer; and every half-hour he muttered the word 'Bock!' – having reduced his conversation to the absolute minimum. Frédéric asked him if he ever saw Arnoux.

'No.'

'Oh! Why not?'

'A fool!'

Perhaps it was politics which had come between them; and Frédéric thought it advisable to ask after Compain.

'What an idiot!' said Regimbart.

'What do you mean?'

'His calf's head!'

'Ah! Now do tell me what the calf's head is.'

Regimbart gave a pitying smile.

'A lot of nonsense!'

After a long silence Frédéric went on:

'So he's moved house?'

'Who?'

'Arnoux.'

'Yes. Rue de Fleurus.'

'What number?'

'Do you think I mix with Jesuits?'

'What do you mean, Jesuits?'

The Citizen answered angrily:

'The swine has taken the money of a patriot I introduced him to, and set up as a dealer in rosaries!'

'I don't believe it!'

'Go and see for yourself!'

It was absolutely true. Weakened by an illness, Arnoux had turned to religion – besides, 'he had always been pious at heart' – and, with his innate combination of sincerity and commercial guile, he had become a dealer in ecclesiastical objects, hoping in this way to secure both his salvation and a fortune.

Frédéric had no difficulty in finding his establishment, which displayed a sign reading: 'The Gothic Art Shop. Church Restoration – Ecclesiastical Ornaments – Polychrome Sculpture – Incense of the Magi' and so on, and so forth.

In the two corners of the shop window there stood two wooden statues, painted in gold, vermilion, and blue: a Saint John the Baptist with his sheepskin, and a Saint Geneviève with roses in her apron and a distaff under her arm. Then there were some groups in plaster: a nun teaching a little girl, a mother kneeling beside a cot, and three schoolboys at the communion table. The prettiest was a sort of chalet representing the stable at Bethlehem, with the donkey, the ox, and the Infant Jesus lying on real straw. All the shelves were lined with dozens of medals, rosaries of every kind, holy-water stoups in the shape of shells, and portraits of notabilities of the Church, among which shone the smiling faces of Archbishop Affre and the Holy Father.

Arnoux was dozing behind his counter, with his head bowed. He had aged enormously, and even had a ring of pink pimples round his temples, on which the gold crosses glittering in the sunlight cast a glow.

At the sight of this decline, Frédéric was filled with sadness. However, out of loyalty to the Marshal, he steeled himself and stepped forward; Madame Arnoux appeared at the back of the shop; he turned on his heel.

'I couldn't find him,' he said when he got home.

And although he went on to say that he was going to write straight away for money to his lawyer at Le Havre, Rosanette lost her temper. Nobody had ever seen such a weak, spineless man; while she suffered all sorts of privation, other people lived a life of luxury.

Frédéric thought of poor Madame Arnoux, and imagined the heartbreaking dreariness of her home. He sat down at the writing table; and as Rosanette's voice went on complaining shrilly, he said:

'Oh, for heaven's sake, shut up!'

'You aren't going to defend them, are you?'

'Yes, I am!' he exclaimed. 'After all, why are you so down on them?'

'But why don't you want them to pay? You're afraid of upsetting your old flame; go on – admit it!'

He felt like hitting her with the clock; words failed him. He said nothing. Striding up and down the room, Rosanette added:

'I'm going to have the law on your precious Arnoux. Oh, I don't need your help to do that!'

And pursing her lips, she went on:

'I'll take legal advice.'

Three days later, Delphine came rushing in.

'Madame! Madame! There's a man here with a pot of paste. I'm scared of him!'

Rosanette went into the kitchen, where she found a mumbling, pock-marked ruffian, who was paralysed in one arm and three-quarters drunk.

This was Maître Gautherot's bill-sticker. The objection to the seizure having been overruled, the sale was automatically going to be held.

First of all he asked for a drink, for the trouble he had taken to come upstairs; then he begged another favour – namely some theatre tickets, for he imagined that Madame was an actress. After that he spent several minutes winking unintelligibly; and finally he declared that for the sum of four francs he would tear off the corners of the bill he had already posted on the door downstairs. Rosanette was mentioned there by name – a measure of exceptional severity which revealed the virulence of Mademoiselle Vatnaz's hatred.

The latter had been soft-hearted as a girl; and once, when she had suffered a disappointment in love, she had actually written to Béranger for advice. But the storms of life had embittered her; she had, in succession, given piano lessons, run a boarding-house, written for fashion papers, let rooms, and trafficked in lace among the courtesans of Paris – a milieu in which her connexions enabled her to be of service to a great many people, including Arnoux. Before that, she had worked in a business house.

There one of her duties had been to pay out the wages of the working-girls. There were two account-books for each girl, one of which remained constantly in the care of Mademoiselle Vatnaz. Dussardier, who as a kindness to her kept the account of a girl called Hortense Baslin, happened to come up to the cash-desk just as Mademoiselle Vatnaz was presenting this girl's account. It was for 1,682 francs, which the cashier handed over to her. Now, only the previous evening, Dussardier had brought Hortense Baslin's book up to date; and the sum he had entered in it had been 1,082 francs. He asked for the book back on some pretext; then, wanting to cover up this theft, he told the girl he had lost it. She innocently repeated his lie to Mademoiselle Vatnaz, who, to get to the bottom of the matter, casually asked Dussardier about it. He merely replied: 'I've burnt it'; and that was all. She left the firm shortly afterwards, without believing that the book had been destroyed and imagining that Dussardier still had it.

When she had heard that he had been wounded, she had hurried round to his house to get it back. Finding nothing, in spite of an intensive search, she had been filled with respect, and soon with love, for this young man who was so loyal, so gentle, so brave, and so strong. Such good fortune at her age was utterly unexpected. She threw herself on him with the appetite of an ogress; for his sake she abandoned literature, Socialism, 'the comforting doctrines and the bountiful Utopias', the lectures she was giving on 'The De-subordination of Women' – everything, even Delmar; and she ended up by making him a proposal of marriage.

Although she was his mistress, Dussardier was not in the least in love with her. Besides, he had not forgotten her theft. And then she was too rich. He turned her down. Then she cried and told him of the dream she had cherished, of running a dress shop between them. She had the necessary capital, which would be increased the following week by four thousand francs; and she told him about the action she had taken against the Marshal.

Dussardier was upset on account of his friend. He remembered the cigar-case given to him at the guard-post, the evenings at the Quai Napoléon, the enjoyable conversations they had had, the books he had been lent, Frédéric's countless kindnesses. He begged Mademoiselle Vatnaz to drop her lawsuit.

She laughed at his good nature, revealing an inexplicable loathing for Rosanette; indeed, she longed for riches simply in order to be able to crush her one day under her carriage wheels.

These depths of malevolence alarmed Dussardier; and as soon as he was certain of the date of the sale he went out. The next morning he called on Frédéric, looking extremely embarrassed.

'I owe you an apology.'

'Whatever for?'

'You must think me terribly ungrateful, seeing that . . .'

He stammered:

'Oh, I'll never speak to her again! I won't be her accomplice!'

And as Frédéric looked at him in bewilderment, he went on:

'Aren't they going to sell up your mistress's furniture in three days' time?'

'Who told you that?'

'Vatnaz herself! But I'm afraid of offending you . . .'

'You couldn't, my dear chap!'

'Yes, that's true. You're so good-natured!'

And he shyly held out to him a little leather wallet.

It contained four thousand francs, his entire savings.

'What! Oh, no! No, really . . .'

'I knew very well I should hurt your feelings,' said Dussardier, with tears in his eyes.

Frédéric clasped his hand; and the good fellow went on in a plaintive voice:

'Take them! Just to please me! I'm so miserable! And anyway, isn't everything over now? When the revolution came, I thought we'd all be happy. You remember how wonderful it was – how freely we breathed! But now we're worse off than ever.'

And, fixing his eyes on the floor, he continued:

'Now they're killing our Republic, just as they killed the Roman Republic . . . and poor Venice, Poland, and Hungary![80] What villainy! First they cut down the trees of liberty, and now they've limited the suffrage, closed the clubs, restored the censorship, and put education in the hands of the priests until the Inquisition's ready.[81] Why not? There are some Conservatives who'd like to see the Cossacks back in Paris. The newspapers are punished for arguing against the death penalty; Paris is bristling with bayonets; sixteen departments are in a state of siege; and they've refused an amnesty yet again!'

He put both hands to his forehead; then, stretching out his arms as if he were in terrible pain, he said:

'Yet if only people tried! With a little good faith, they could reach an understanding. But it's no use. You see, the workers are no better than the middle classes. At Elbeuf, only the other day, they refused to help to put out a fire. There are some scoundrels who call Barbès an aristocrat. And to make the people look ridiculous, they're trying to put up Nadaud as a candidate for the Presidency. A stonemason – I ask you! And there's no solution to the problem, no remedy! Everybody's against us. Personally, I've never done anybody any harm; and yet it's like a weight on my stomach. I shall go mad if it goes on! I feel like committing suicide. I tell you I don't need my money! Treat it as a loan; you'll pay me back, I know.'

Frédéric, who was in financial difficulties, ended up by taking his four thousand francs. So, as far as Mademoiselle Vatnaz was concerned, they no longer had anything to worry about.

But shortly afterwards Rosanette lost her case against Arnoux. Out of stubbornness, she wanted to appeal.

Deslauriers wore himself out trying to make her understand that Arnoux's promise represented neither a gift nor a proper transfer; she would not listen, complaining that the law was unfair; it was because she was a woman; men always stood up for one another. In the end, however, she followed his advice.

He had made himself so much at home in the house that he brought Sénécal in to dinner several times. This lack of ceremony annoyed Frédéric, who had been lending him money and even having him fitted out by his own tailor, only to see the lawyer giving his old frock-coats to the Socialist, whose means of subsistence were unknown.

However, Deslauriers would have liked to be of service to Rosanette. One day she showed him a dozen shares in the china-clay company – the one which had resulted in a fine of thirty thousand francs for Arnoux.

'But there's something fishy here,' he said. 'This is splendid!'

She was entitled to sue him for the repayment of her shares. She could prove, first of all, that he was under an obligation to pay all the company's liabilities, since he had passed off personal debts as collective debts, and also that he had misappropriated several of the company's assets.

'All this makes him guilty of fraudulent bankruptcy, under Articles 586 and 587 of the Commercial Code. We'll have his skin, my pet, you can be sure of that!'

Rosanette threw her arms round his neck. The next day he gave her a letter of recommendation to his former employer; he could not take the case himself, as he had to go to Nogent; Sénécal would write to him if necessary.

His negotiations for the purchase of a practice were just a blind. He spent his time at Monsieur Roque's house, where he had begun not only by singing Frédéric's praises, but also by imitating his manner and delivery as far as he could. By this means he had won the confidence of Louise, and was trying to obtain her father's by railing against Ledru-Rollin.

If Frédéric did not come back to Nogent, that was because he was moving in high society; and little by little Deslauriers informed them that he was in love with somebody, that he had a child, and that he kept a mistress.

Louise's despair was immense, Madame Moreau's indignation just as violent. She saw her son spinning towards the depths of a mysterious abyss; her sense of propriety, which was almost a religion with her, was affronted; it was like a personal disgrace. But one day her expression changed. When she was asked about Frédéric, she would reply with a knowing smile:

'He's keeping well, very well.'

She had learnt of his approaching marriage to Madame Dambreuse.

The date had been fixed; and he was already wondering how to reconcile Rosanette to the idea.

Towards the middle of the autumn, she won her case over the china-clay shares. Frédéric learnt this by meeting Sénécal, who had come straight from the courtroom, on his doorstep.

It had been proved that Arnoux was an accessory to all the fraudulent transactions; and Sénécal looked so pleased about this that Frédéric prevented him from going any further, by assuring him that he would deliver his message to Rosanette himself. He went into her room with a scowl on his face.

'Well, I've got good news for you!'

She did not hear.

'Look!' she said.

And she showed him the child, who was lying in a cradle by the fire. She had found him looking so ill that morning at the nurse's house that she had brought him back to Paris.

His limbs had all grown extraordinarily thin, and his lips were covered with white spots; the inside of his mouth looked as if it were full of clots of milk.

'What did the doctor say?'

'Oh, the doctor! He thinks the journey has aggravated his ... I don't know what, some word ending in *itis* ... that he's got thrush, in fact. Do you know anything about that?'

Frédéric promptly replied: 'Of course,' adding that it was nothing. But that evening he was alarmed by the sickly appearance of the child and by the spread of the whitish spots; they looked like patches of mildew, as if life had already abandoned the poor little body, leaving nothing but dead matter on which vegetation had started to grow. His hands were cold; he could no longer drink anything; and the nurse, a new one whom the concierge had hired at random from an agency, kept repeating:

'He looks very low, very low!'

Rosanette was up all night.

In the morning she called Frédéric.

'Come and see. He doesn't move any more.'

He was dead. She picked him up, shook him, hugged him, called him all the pet names she could think of, and covered him with kisses and tears; then she turned on herself in a frenzy, screaming and tearing her hair. She sank on to the edge of the divan, where she sat with her mouth open and tears pouring from her staring eyes. Then a torpor came over her and silence fell on the room. The furniture had been overturned. Two or three napkins were lying on the floor. Six o'clock struck. The night-light went out.

Looking around him, Frédéric almost imagined that he was dreaming. Fear gripped his heart. He felt that this death was only a beginning, that some worse misfortune was going to follow close behind it.

Suddenly Rosanette said in a voice full of tenderness:

'We'll keep him, won't we?'

She wanted to have him embalmed. There were a good many objections to the idea. The most cogent, in Frédéric's opinion, was that embalmment was impracticable in the case of a child as young as this. A portrait would be better. She adopted this suggestion. He wrote a note to Pellerin, and Delphine hurried off with it.

Pellerin arrived promptly, hoping that his zeal would efface any recollection of his previous conduct. At first he said:

'Poor little thing! Heavens, what a tragedy!'

But gradually the artist in him prevailed, and he declared that he could not do anything with those dark eyes, that livid face; that it was a real still-life, calling for enormous talent; and he kept murmuring:

'Oh, it's quite a problem, quite a problem!'

'So long as it's a good likeness . . .' said Rosanette.

'Oh, I don't care whether it's a likeness or not. Down with realism! It's the spirit I'm out to paint! Now leave me alone! I'm going to try to work out what it should be like.'

He pondered the problem, with his forehead in his left hand and his elbow in his right. Then, all of a sudden, he said:

'Ah! An idea! A pastel! With strong half-tints, laid on almost flat, you can bring up the outlines in relief.'

He sent the maid to fetch his colour-box; then, with his feet on one chair and another beside him, he started sketching the main outlines, as calmly as if he were drawing from the round. He praised Correggio's little Saint Johns, Velasquez's pink Infanta, Reynolds's milky flesh-tints, and the distinction of Lawrence, especially as revealed in the long-haired child on Lady Gower's knee.

'Besides, what could be more charming than those little brats? The summit of the sublime – as Raphael showed with his Madonnas – is probably a mother with her child.'

Rosanette, who was choking with sobs, went out; and straight away Pellerin said:

'Well, Arnoux . . . You know what's going on?'

'No. What?'

'Anyway, it was bound to finish like that.'

'What was?'

'Perhaps at this very moment he's . . . Excuse me.'

The artist got up to raise the little corpse's head.

'You were saying . . .' prompted Frédéric.

And Pellerin, half-closing his eyes to take the necessary measurements, went on:

'I was saying that at this very moment our good friend Arnoux may be in jug!'

Then, in a satisfied tone of voice, he said:

'Have a look at that! Have I got it?'

'Yes, beautifully. But what about Arnoux?'

Pellerin put down his crayon.

'From what I could gather he's being sued by a fellow called Mignot, a pal of Regimbart's. Now there's a brain for you! What an idiot! Just imagine, one day . . .'

'But we're not talking about Regimbart!'

'That's true. Well, last night Arnoux had to find twelve thousand francs, or else he was done for.'

'Oh, it's probably not as bad as all that.'

'On the contrary. It looked serious to me, very serious.'

Just then Rosanette returned, with red marks under her eyes, as bright as patches of rouge. She sat down beside the picture and looked at it. Pellerin made a gesture to indicate that he would say no more, on her account. But Frédéric took no notice.

'All the same, I can't believe . . .'

'I tell you,' said the artist, 'I met him yesterday, at seven in the evening, in the Rue Jacob. He even had his passport with him, just in case; and he was talking of taking ship at Le Havre with the whole of his circus.'

'What! With his wife?'

'Presumably. He's too much a family man to live by himself.'

'And you're quite sure?'

'Of course. Where do you think he could lay his hands on twelve thousand francs?'

Frédéric walked up and down the room two or three times. He was breathing hard and biting his lips. Then he grabbed his hat.

'Where are you going?' said Rosanette.

He made no reply, and disappeared.

V

HE had to find twelve thousand francs, or else he would never see Madame Arnoux again; and up to now he had kept an unconquerable hope alive in his heart. Was she not the substance of his feelings, the very essence of his life? For a few minutes he stumbled along the pavement, tortured by anxiety, yet glad to have got away from Rosanette.

Where was he to find the money? Frédéric knew from his own experience how difficult it was to obtain at short notice, whatever the price one offered. There was only one person who could help him – Madame Dambreuse. She always kept several banknotes in her writing-table. He went to see her and asked her straight out:

'Have you got twelve thousand francs you could lend me?'

'What for?'

It was another person's secret. She wanted to know what it was. He would not give way. Both of them stood firm. Finally she declared that she would give him nothing until she knew what it was for. Frédéric went very red. One of his friends had committed a theft. The money had to be given back that very day.

'What is he called? His name? Come now, his name?'

'Dussardier!'

And he threw himself at her feet, begging her not to tell anybody.

'What do you take me for?' retorted Madame Dambreuse. 'Anybody would think you'd done it yourself! Stop being so tragic about it, for heaven's sake! Look, here's the money! And much good may it do him!'

He hurried round to Arnoux's shop. The dealer was not there. But he was still living in the Rue Paradis, for he had two addresses.

The concierge in the Rue Paradis swore that Monsieur Arnoux had been away since the day before; and as for Madame, he could not say. Frédéric bounded up the stairs and pressed his ear to the keyhole. At last the door opened. Madame had left with Monsieur. The maid did not know when they would be back; her wages had been paid; she was leaving too.

Suddenly he heard a door slam to.

'But there's somebody there!'

'Oh, no, Monsieur! It's the wind.'

He withdrew. There was no blinking the fact that there was something peculiar about so swift a disappearance.

Perhaps Regimbart, who was a close friend of Mignot's, could shed some light on the matter? Frédéric took a cab to his home in the Rue de l'Empereur, in Montmartre.

His house had a tiny garden beside it, enclosed by railings which were backed by sheets of iron. A flight of three steps added distinction to the white façade; and passing along the pavement, one could see into the two ground-floor rooms, one of which was a drawing-room, with dresses draped all over the furniture, and the other a workshop for Madame Regimbart's seamstresses.

The latter were all convinced that Monsieur had an important position and grand connexions – in short, that he was a truly remarkable man. When he went along the passage, with his long, solemn face, his hat with the turned-up brim, and his green frock-coat, they all interrupted their work to look. Besides, he never failed to greet them with a word of encouragement, a sententious compliment; and later, in their own homes, they felt discontented because they had adopted him as their ideal.

Yet none of them loved him as much as Madame Regimbart, an intelligent little creature who kept him on the proceeds of her business.

As soon as Frédéric gave his name, she hurried out to greet him, for the servants had told her about his liaison with Madame Dambreuse. Her husband 'would be back in a minute'; and Frédéric, as he followed her, admired the way the house was kept and the lavish use of oilcloth all over the place. Then he waited for a few minutes in a sort of study to which the Citizen used to retire in order to think.

The reception he gave Frédéric was less surly than usual.

He told him all about the Arnoux affair. The sometime chinamanufacturer had convinced Mignot, a patriot who held a hundred shares in the *Siècle*, that the management and editorship of the paper ought to be changed in the interests of democracy; and, under the pretext of imposing this point of view at the next shareholder's meeting, he had asked him for fifty shares, saying that he would pass them on to reliable friends, who would support his motion; Mignot would have no responsibility, and would make no enemies; then, once they had succeeded, Arnoux would get him a good post on the staff, worth at least five or six thousand francs a year. The shares had been handed over. But Arnoux had promptly sold them, and used the money to go into partnership with a dealer in ecclesiastical objects. After that, there had been complaints from Mignot and evasive answers from Arnoux; finally the patriot had threatened to have him prosecuted for fraud if he did not return his shares or pay him what they were worth, fifty thousand francs.

Frédéric's face fell.

'But that's not all,' said the Citizen. 'Mignot, who's a good sort, reduced his demands to a quarter of the sum. More promises from Arnoux – more bunkum of course. In short, the day before yesterday, in the morning, Mignot called on him to pay back twelve thousand francs within twenty-four hours, without prejudice to the rest of the debt.'

'But I've got the money!' said Frédéric.

The Citizen turned slowly to face him.

'You're joking.'

'No, I'm not. It's in my pocket. I was bringing it to Arnoux.'

'You don't waste time, do you? Well, I'm damned! But it's too late; the action has been brought, and Arnoux has gone.'

'By himself?'

'No. With his wife. Somebody saw them at the station at Le Havre.'

Frédéric turned deathly pale. Madame Regimbart thought he was going to faint. He took hold of himself, and even summoned up the courage to ask two or three questions about the affair. Regimbart was upset about it, because when all was said and done this sort of thing harmed the cause of Democracy. Arnoux had always been an unprincipled, irresponsible fellow.

'A feather-brained rascal! He burnt the candle at both ends. It was women that did for him. I'm not sorry for him so much as for his poor wife.'

For the Citizen admired virtuous women, and had a high opinion of Madame Arnoux.

'She must have gone through hell.'

Frédéric was grateful to him for this sympathy; and he shook hands with him warmly, as if Regimbart had done him a good turn.

'Did you see to everything?' Rosanette asked him when he came back. He had not felt up to it, he replied. He had roamed the streets at random to deaden his grief.

At eight o'clock they went into the dining-room; but they sat opposite each other in silence, heaving a sigh from time to time and pushing away their plates. Frédéric drank some brandy. He felt worn out, crushed, prostrate, conscious of nothing but extreme exhaustion.

She went to fetch the portrait. Patches of red, yellow, green, and indigo clashed in violent contrast; the thing was hideous, almost laughable.

For that matter, the dead baby was now unrecognizable. The purple tint of his lips heightened the pallor of his skin; his nostrils were thinner than ever, his eyes more hollow; and his head rested on a blue taffeta pillow, among petals of camellias, autumn roses, and violets. This was the maid's idea; and the two women had devoutly arranged him in this fashion. On the mantelpiece, which had been draped with a lace cloth, there stood some silver-gilt candlesticks, interspersed with bunches of holy box; aromatic pellets were burning in the vases at each end; all this, together with the cradle, formed a sort of altar of repose; and Frédéric remembered his vigil beside Monsieur Dambreuse.

Every quarter of an hour or so, Rosanette drew aside the curtains to look at her child. She imagined him a few months later, learning to walk, then in the yard at school, playing prisoners' base, then as a young man of twenty; and all these pictures which she summoned up made her feel that she had lost so many sons, the excess of her grief making her a mother several times over.

Frédéric, motionless in the other armchair, thought about Madame Arnoux.

She was probably in the train, with her face at the carriage window, watching the countryside gliding past behind her, in the direction of Paris; or else she was on the deck of a steamer, as she had been the first time he met her; but this boat was sailing inexorably towards lands from which she would never return. Then he saw her in a room at an inn, with her luggage on the floor, the wallpaper hanging in tatters, and the door rattling in the wind. And afterwards, what would become of her? Perhaps she would be a schoolmistress, or a companion, or a chambermaid. She was at the mercy of all the hazards of poverty. His ignorance of her fate tormented him. He ought to have prevented her flight, or else followed her. Was he not her real husband? And as it was borne in on him that he would never see her again, that it was all over, that she was irrevocably lost, he felt his whole being torn apart; his tears, which had been gathering all day, overflowed.

Rosanette noticed.

'Ah! So you're crying like me? You're unhappy?'

'Yes! Yes! Terribly unhappy!'

He clasped her to him, and the two of them sobbed in each other's arms.

Madame Dambreuse was crying too, lying face down on her bed, with her head in her hands.

Olympe Regimbart, who had come that evening to try on her first coloured dress, had told her about Frédéric's visit, and how he had brought twelve thousand francs in cash for Monsieur Arnoux. So that money – her money – had been intended to prevent the other woman's departure, to keep his mistress in Paris!

Her first reaction was to fly into a towering rage; and she had made up her mind to dismiss him like a lackey. After weeping copiously, she calmed down. It would be better to conceal her feelings and say nothing.

The next day, Frédéric brought back the twelve thousand francs.

She begged him to keep them for his friend, just in case, and she plied him with questions about this gentleman. What could have induced him to commit a breach of trust like that? A woman, no doubt. Women drove men to commit all sorts of crimes.

Her mocking tone disconcerted Frédéric. He felt extremely remorseful about his slander. But he was reassured by the thought that Madame Dambreuse could not know the truth.

She did her best to ferret it out, however, for two days later she asked again after his young comrade, then after another friend, Deslauriers.

'Is he a reliable, intelligent man?'

Frédéric praised him highly.

'Ask him to come and see me one morning; I'd like to consult him about a legal problem.'

She had come across a roll of papers containing some bills of Arnoux's, correctly protested and signed by Madame Arnoux. These were the bills about which Frédéric had called to see Monsieur Dambreuse one lunch-time, and although the financier had decided not to sue for the money, he had obtained a judgement of the Commercial Court, not only against Arnoux but against his wife as well. Madame Arnoux knew nothing of this, as her husband had not thought fit to tell her.

This was a magnificent weapon: Madame Dambreuse had no doubts about that. But her lawyer might advise her to refrain from using it; she would prefer somebody more obscure; and she had remembered the tall fellow with the impudent face who had once offered her his services.

Frédéric innocently passed on the message.

The lawyer was delighted to be put in touch with such a great lady.

He hurried to see her.

She told him that the estate had been left to her niece, and this was a further reason for getting these old debts settled. She would hand the money over to the Martinons, for she wanted to heap coals of fire on their heads.

Deslauriers realized that there was some mystery behind all this; and he examined the bills thoughtfully. The sight of Madame

Arnoux's signature brought back vividly the memory of her person, and of the affront he had suffered at her hands. Why should he not seize this opportunity for revenge?

He accordingly advised Madame Dambreuse to have the bad debts belonging to the estate sold by auction. An agent would secretly buy them back and carry out the prosecution. He undertook to provide the agent.

Towards the end of November, Frédéric was walking along Madame Arnoux's street when he looked up at her windows and noticed a poster on the door, announcing in large letters:

'Sale of valuable furniture and household effects, consisting of kitchen utensils, personal and table linen, chemises, laces, petticoats, drawers, French and Indian cashmere shawls, an Erard piano, a pair of Renaissance oak chests, Venetian mirrors, Chinese and Japanese porcelain.'

'It's their furniture!' Frédéric said to himself; and the concierge confirmed his suspicions.

He did not know who was having the goods sold. But perhaps the auctioneer, Maître Berthelmot, would be able to give him some information.

At first the official refused to say which creditor had ordered the sale. Frédéric insisted on knowing. It was a certain Sénécal, a general agent; and Maître Berthelmot was kind enough to lend his caller his own copy of the *Petites-Affiches*.

When Frédéric arrived at Rosanette's apartment, he tossed the open paper on the table.

'Read that!'

'Well, what is it?' she asked, with such a calm expression on her face that he was revolted.

'That's right! Pretend you don't know!'

'I don't understand.'

'It's you who are selling up Madame Arnoux!'

She read the advertisement again.

'Where's her name?'

'Oh, it's her furniture all right. You know that better than I do.'

'What's it got to do with me?' said Rosanette, shrugging her shoulders.

'What's it got to do with you? Why, you're taking your revenge, that's all. You're going on with your persecution. Didn't you once carry your insolence to the extent of going to her house? A common

403

whore like you, and the saintliest, sweetest, kindest women in the world! Why are you so set on ruining her?'

'I tell you, you're wrong!'

'Come now! Admit that you put Sénécal up to it!'

'What nonsense!'

Then he flew into a passion.

'You're lying! You're lying, you bitch! You're jealous of her! You've got a judgement of the court against her husband! Sénécal's already had a hand in your affairs! He loathes Arnoux, and your hatred matches his! I saw how pleased he was when you won your case over the china clay. Do you still deny you're hand in glove with him?'

'I give you my word . . .'

'Oh, I know what to think of your word!'

And Frédéric reeled off a list of her lovers, with their names and circumstantial details. Rosanette turned pale and drew back.

'That surprises you, doesn't it? You thought I was blind because I shut my eyes. Now I've had enough. A man doesn't break his heart when he's deceived by a woman like you. If she goes too far, he drops her; it would be degrading to punish her.'

She wrung her hands.

'God Almighty, what has changed you?'

'You, and nothing else.'

'And all this for Madame Arnoux!' cried Rosanette through her tears.

He answered coldly:

'I have never loved any one but her.'

This insult stopped her tears.

'That shows what good taste you've got! A dumpy, middle-aged creature with a complexion like liquorice and eyes as big as manholes – and as empty! If that's what you like, go and join her!'

'That's what I was waiting for! Thank you!'

Rosanette stood motionless, astounded by this extraordinary behaviour. She even let him shut the door behind him; then, with a single leap, she caught up with him in the hall, and put her arms round him.

'But you're mad, you're mad! This is ridiculous! I love you!' She implored him:

'For heaven's sake – in the name of our baby!'

'Confess that you were behind this affair!' said Frédéric.

She protested her innocence once more.

'You won't confess?'

'No!'

'All right! Good-bye – for ever!'

'Listen to me!'

Frédéric turned round.

'If you knew me better, you'd realize that my decision is final.'

'Oh, you'll come back to me!'

'Never!'

And he slammed the door hard.

Rosanette wrote to Deslauriers that she needed to see him straight away.

He arrived five days later, in the evening; and she told him about the quarrel.

'Is that all?' he said. 'That's nothing to complain about!'

At first she had thought that he might be able to bring Frédéric back to her, but now all was lost. The porter at his house had told her of his coming marriage to Madame Dambreuse.

Deslauriers lectured her, and was curiously gay and high-spirited; finally, as it was very late, he asked permission to spend the night in an armchair. Then, the next morning, he set out for Nogent once more, telling her that he did not know when they would meet again; there might be a great change in his life before long.

Two hours after his return, Nogent was in a ferment. It was said that Monsieur Frédéric was going to marry Madame Dambreuse. Eventually the three Auger girls, unable to stand it any longer, went to see Madame Moreau, who proudly confirmed the news. Old Roque was thoroughly upset. Louise shut herself in her room. It was even rumoured that she had gone mad.

In the meantime, Frédéric could not conceal his melancholy. Madame Dambreuse was more considerate than ever, presumably in order to divert his mind. Every afternoon she took him out in her carriage; and one day, when they were crossing the Place de la Bourse, it occurred to her that it might be amusing to visit the sale-rooms.

It was 1 December, the very day Madame Arnoux's sale was due to be held. He remembered the date, and showed his reluctance, declaring that the place was unbearable on account of the crowds and the noise. She just wanted to have a look. The brougham stopped. He had no option but to follow her.

In the yard could be seen washstands without basins, pieces of wood from armchairs, old baskets, fragments of china, empty bottles, and mattresses. There were villainous-looking men in smocks or dirty frock-coats, some of whom carried sacks on their shoulders; they were either chatting in separate groups or shouting noisily to one another.

Frédéric pointed out the drawbacks to going any further.

'Nonsense!'

And they went up the stairs.

In the first room, on the right, some gentlemen were examining pictures, catalogue in hand; in another, a collection of Chinese weapons was being sold; Madame Dambreuse decided to go downstairs again. Looking at the numbers over the doors, she led him right to the end of the corridor, towards a room packed with people.

He recognized straight away the two sets of shelves which had been in the office of *L'Art Industriel*, her work-table, and all her other pieces of furniture. Piled up at the far end, in order of height, they formed a slope stretching from the floor to the windows, while on the other three sides of the room, her carpets and curtains hung on the walls. Underneath, there were rows of seats on which old men were dozing. On the left, behind a sort of counter, the auctioneer, wearing a white cravat, was casually brandishing a little hammer. A young man was writing beside him; and lower down stood a sturdy fellow, looking like a cross between a commercial traveller and a tout, who shouted out a description of each lot. Three men placed the lots on a table, in front of which sat a row of second-hand dealers. The crowd moved around behind them.

When Frédéric came in, petticoats, scarves, handkerchiefs, and even chemises were being passed from hand to hand and turned inside out; sometimes they were thrown across the room and a gleam of white flashed through the air. After that they sold her dresses, then one of her hats with a limp, broken feather, then her furs, then three pairs of shoes; and the distribution of these relics, which vaguely recalled the shape of her limbs, struck him as an atrocity, as if he were watching crows tearing her corpse to pieces. The atmosphere of the room, which was heavy with human breath, made him feel sick. Madame Dambreuse offered him her smelling-salts; she was enjoying herself immensely, she said.

The bedroom furniture was displayed.

Maître Berthelmot would announce the price. The crier would

promptly repeat it, in a louder voice; and the three stewards would calmly wait for the hammer to fall, before carrying the lot into an adjoining room. In this way there vanished, one after another, the big blue carpet with its pattern of camellias which her dainty feet used to touch lightly as they came towards him; the little tapestry easy-chair in which he always used to sit facing her when they were alone; the two fire-screens, whose ivory had been made smoother by the touch of her hands; and a velvet pincushion, still bristling with pins. He felt as if a part of his heart were disappearing with each article; and the monotonous effect of the same voices accompanied by the same gestures numbed him with fatigue, afflicting him with a deathly torpor, a sense of disintegration.

Suddenly he heard a rustling of silk; Rosanette was beside him.

She had heard about the sale from Frédéric himself. Once she had got over her grief, if had occurred to her that she might pick up a bargain. She had come to watch, wearing a white satin jacket with pearl buttons, a flounced dress, tight gloves, and a triumphant expression.

He went pale with anger. She glanced at the woman who was with him.

Madame Dambreuse had recognized her; and for a full minute they looked each other up and down, with scrupulous attention, in search of some flaw or blemish – the one perhaps envying the other's youth, while the latter was annoyed at her rival's good taste and aristocratic simplicity.

Finally Madame Dambreuse turned her head away, with a smile of unspeakable insolence.

The crier had opened a piano – her piano! Without sitting down, he played a scale with his right hand and offered the instrument for twelve hundred francs; then he came down to a thousand, eight hundred, seven hundred.

Madame Dambreuse playfully described it as an old tin can.

The stewards placed before the dealers a little casket with silver medallions, corners, and clasps. It was the casket he had seen at the first dinner-party in the Rue de Choiseul; afterwards it had passed to Rosanette before coming back to Madame Arnoux; his gaze had often fallen on it during their conversations; it was linked with his dearest memories, and his heart was melting with emotion when all of a sudden Madame Dambreuse said:

'You know, I think I'll buy that.'

'But there's nothing remarkable about it.'

On the contrary, she thought it very pretty; and the crier was praising its delicate workmanship:

'A jewel of the Renaissance! Eight hundred francs, gentlemen! It's practically solid silver! With a little whiting you'll get a lovely shine on it!'

She started pushing her way through the crowd.

'What an odd idea!' said Frédéric.

'Does it annoy you?'

'No. But what can you use a thing like that for?'

'Who knows? Perhaps for keeping love letters.'

She darted a glance at him which made the allusion perfectly clear.

'That's another reason for not robbing the dead of their secrets.'

'I didn't think she was as dead as all that.'

She added in a penetrating voice:

'Eight hundred and eighty francs'!

'You're behaving very badly,' murmured Frédéric.

She laughed.

'But my dear,' he said, 'this is the first favour I've ever asked you.'

'You're not going to be a very nice husband, you know.'

Somebody had just made a higher bid; she raised her hand.

'Nine hundred francs!'

'Nine hundred francs!' repeated Maître Berthelmot.

'Nine hundred and ten ... fifteen ... twenty ... thirty!' yelped the crier, looking round the crowd and giving little jerks of the head.

'Show me that I'm marrying a considerate woman,' said Frédéric.

He drew her gently towards the door.

The auctioneer continued:

'Come along, gentlemen, nine hundred and thirty! Any advance on nine hundred and thirty?'

Madame Dambreuse, who had reached the doorway, stopped and said in a loud voice:

'A thousand francs!'

A shiver went through the crowd, and then there was silence.

'A thousand francs, gentlemen, a thousand francs! Any advance? No? Going at a thousand francs! Going, going, gone!'

The ivory hammer fell.

She passed her card over, and the casket was brought across to her. She thrust it into her muff.

Frédéric felt his heart turn cold.

Madame Dambreuse had not let go his arm; and she did not dare to look him in the face until they were out in the street, where her carriage was waiting for her.

She flung herself into it like a thief on the run, and when she had sat down she turned towards Frédéric. He had his hat in his hand.

'Aren't you coming?'

'No, Madame.'

And, bowing to her coldly, he shut the door and motioned to the coachman to drive away.

His first reaction was one of joy at having regained his independence. He was proud of having avenged Madame Arnoux, by sacrificing a fortune to her; then he was astonished at what he had done, and a feeling of infinite weariness overwhelmed him.

The next morning his servant had news for him. A state of siege had been declared, the Assembly had been dissolved, and some of the deputies were in Mazas Prison.[82] Politics left him indifferent, he was so preoccupied with his own affairs.

He wrote to various tradesmen, cancelling several purchases connected with his marriage, which now struck him as a somewhat ignoble speculation; and he was filled with loathing for Madame Dambreuse because he had nearly dishonoured himself on her account. He forgot about the Marshal, and did not even worry about Madame Arnoux, thinking only of himself and nobody else, lost among the ruins of his hopes, sick with grief and discouragement; and, in his hatred of the artificial world in which he had suffered so much, he longed for the freshness of the grass, the peace of the country, a sleepy life among simple-hearted folk, in the shadow of the house where he was born. Finally, on the Wednesday evening, he went out.

Large groups of people were standing about on the boulevard. Now and then a patrol would disperse them, but they would form up again behind it. They talked freely, shouting jokes and insults at the soldiers, but going no further.

'What! Isn't there going to be any fighting?' Frédéric asked a workman.

The man in the smock answered:

'We're not such fools as to get ourselves killed for the rich! They can settle their own affairs!'

And a gentleman, darting a sidelong glance at the workman, muttered:

'Filthy Socialists! If only they could be wiped out this time!'

Frédéric was nonplussed by so much hatred and stupidity. His disgust with Paris increased as a result; and two days later he took the first train for Nogent.

Soon the houses disappeared and the countryside opened up. Alone in his carriage with his feet on the seat, he pondered the events of the last few days, and the whole of his past. The memory of Louise came back to him.

'She at least loved me! I made a mistake in not taking that chance of happiness . . . Ah, well, let's forget it!'

Then, five minutes later, he said to himself:

'Still, who knows? . . . Later on, why not?'

His thoughts, like his eyes, reached out into the distance.

'She was a simple little thing, a peasant, almost a savage, but so good-hearted!'

The nearer he got to Nogent, the closer to him she seemed. When they crossed the meadows of Sourdun, he imagined he could see her under the poplars as in the old days, cutting rushes beside the pools. The train arrived. He got out.

Then he leant on the parapet of the bridge to look once more at the island and the garden where they had strolled one sunny day. Numbed by the journey and the open air, and still weak from the emotional upheavals of the last few days, he was filled with a sort of intoxication and said to himself:

'Perhaps she's gone out. Supposing I were to meet her!'

The bell of Saint-Laurent was tolling; and on the square in front of the church there was a throng of poor people, and a barouche, the only one in the district, which was used for weddings. All of a sudden, under the porch, in a crowd of well-to-do citizens in white cravats, a newly married couple appeared.

He thought at first that he was dreaming. But no! It was she all right – Louise – draped in a white veil which fell from her red hair to her heels; and it was he all right – Deslauriers – wearing a blue coat trimmed with silver, the uniform of a prefect. What was the meaning of all this?

Frédéric hid behind the corner of a house, to let the procession pass.

Shamefaced, beaten, crushed, he went back to the station and returned to Paris.

The driver of his cab told him that there were barricades up from the Château-d'Eau to the Gymnase, and he drove along the Faubourg Saint-Martin. At the corner of the Rue de Provence Frédéric got out in order to make his way to the boulevards on foot.

It was five o'clock, and a thin drizzle was falling. The pavement alongside the Opéra was filled with prosperous-looking people. The houses opposite were closed. There was nobody at the windows. Taking up the whole width of the boulevard, some dragoons rode by at full tilt, bent over their horses, with their swords drawn, and the plumes of their helmets, and their great white capes spread out behind them, were silhouetted against the light of the gas-lamps, which swung to and fro in the wind and mist. The crowd watched them in terrified silence.

Between the cavalry charges squads of policemen came up to drive the crowds back into the side streets.

But on the steps of Tortoni's a man stood firm, as motionless as a caryatid, and conspicuous from afar on account of his tall stature. It was Dussardier.

One of the policemen, who was marching in front of his squad, with his three-cornered hat pulled down over his eyes, threatened him with his sword.

Then Dussardier took a step forward and started shouting:
'Long live the Republic!'
He fell on his back, with his arms spread out.

A cry of horror rose from the crowd. The policeman looked all around him, and Frédéric, open-mouthed, recognized Sénécal.

VI

HE travelled.

He came to know the melancholy of the steamboat, the cold awakening in the tent, the tedium of landscapes and ruins, the bitterness of interrupted friendships.

He returned.

He went into society, and he had other loves. But the ever-present memory of the first made them insipid; and besides, the violence of desire, the very flower of feeling, had gone. His intellectual ambitions had also dwindled. Years went by; and he endured the idleness of his mind and the inertia of his heart.

Towards the end of March 1867, at nightfall, he was alone in his study when a woman came in.

'Madame Arnoux!'

'Frédéric!'

She seized him by the hands, drew him gently to the window, and gazed at him, saying:

'It's he! Yes, it's he!'

In the twilight he could see nothing but her eyes under the black lace veil which masked her face.

After placing a little red velvet wallet on the edge of the mantelpiece, she sat down. The two of them sat there, unable to speak, smiling at each other.

Finally he started asking all about herself and her husband.

They had settled in the depths of Brittany, so that they could live cheaply and pay off their debts. Arnoux was ill nearly all the time and looked like an old man now. His daughter was married and lived at Bordeaux, and her son was garrisoned at Mostaganem. Then she rasied her head.

'But I've seen you again! I'm so happy!'

He did not fail to tell her that as soon as he had heard of the disaster which had overtaken them he had hurried round to their house.

'I know.'

'How?'

She had seen him in the courtyard, and had hidden.

'Why?'

Then, in a trembling voice, and with pauses between her words, she said:

'I was afraid. Yes . . . afraid of you . . . of myself!'

This revelation caused him a sort of paroxysm of delight. His heart beat wildly. She went on:

'Forgive me for not coming sooner.'

And pointing to the little red wallet, which was covered with golden palms, she said:

'I embroidered that specially for you. It contains the money for which the land at Belleville was supposed to be the security.'

Frédéric thanked her for the present, but reproached her for going to the trouble of bringing it personally.

'No. I didn't come for that. I looked forward so much to this visit, and now I shall go home . . . back there.'

And she told him about the place where she lived.

It was a low-built, single-storied house, with a garden full of huge box-trees and a double avenue of chestnuts stretching up to the top of the hill, from which there was a view of the sea.

'I go and sit there on a bench I call "Frédéric's bench".'

Then she started looking with greedy eyes at the furniture, the ornaments, and the pictures, in order to fix them in her memory. The portrait of the Marshal was half hidden by a curtain. But the golds and whites, standing out in the midst of the shadows, attracted her attention.

'I know that woman, don't I?'

'No, you can't!' said Frédéric. 'It's an old Italian painting.'

She confessed that she would like to go for a stroll through the streets on his arm.

They went out.

The lights of the shops illuminated intermittently her pale profile; then the darkness closed in on it again; and they moved among the carriages, the crowds, and the noise, oblivious of everything but themselves, hearing nothing, as if they had been walking together in the country, on a bed of dead leaves.

They talked about old times together, about the dinners in the days of *L'Art Industriel*, about Arnoux and his habit of tugging at the points of his collar and smearing pomade on his moustache, and about other things of a more profound and personal nature. What rapture he had felt the first time he had heard her sing! How beautiful she had been at Saint-Cloud on her name-day! He reminded her of the little garden at Auteuil, evenings at the theatre, an encounter on the boulevard, old servants, her negress.

She marvelled at his memory. But then she said:

'Sometimes your words come back to me like a distant echo, like the sound of a bell carried by the wind; and when I read about love in a book, I feel that you are there beside me.'

'You have made me feel all the things in books which people criticize as exaggerated,' said Frédéric. 'I can understand Werther not being put off by Charlotte's bread and butter.'

'My poor friend!'

She sighed, and after a long silence added:

'Never mind, we have loved each other well.'

'But without belonging to one another.'

'Perhaps it is better so,' she answered.

'No, no! How happy we should have been!'

'Yes, I can believe that, with a love like yours!'

It must have been very strong to survive so long a separation! Frédéric asked her how she had discovered that he loved her.

'It was one evening when you kissed my wrist between my glove and my sleeve. I said to myself: "Why, he loves me ... he loves me." But I was afraid of making sure. Your discretion was so charming that I took pleasure in it as in an unconscious, never-failing homage.'

He regretted nothing. His former sufferings were redeemed.

When they returned, Madame Arnoux took off her hat. The lamp, standing on a console table, lit up her white hair. It was like a blow full in the chest.

To conceal his disappointment, he went down on his knees, took her hands, and started murmuring endearments to her.

'Your person, your slightest movements seemed to me to possess a superhuman importance in the world. My heart used to rise like the dust in your footsteps. The effect you had on me was that of a moonlit night in summer, when all is perfume, soft shadows, pale light, and infinite horizons. For me your name contained all the delights of flesh and spirit, and I repeated it again and again, trying to kiss it with my lips. I imagined nothing beyond your name. It conjured up Madame Arnoux, just as you were, with her two children, tender, serious, dazzlingly beautiful, and so kind-hearted! That picture blotted out all the others. Why, I didn't so much as give them a thought, since in the depths of myself I always had the music of your voice and the splendour of your eyes.'

She rapturously accepted this adoration of the woman she had ceased to be. Frédéric, drunk with his own eloquence, began to believe what he was saying. Madame Arnoux, with her back to the light, bent over him. He could feel the caress of her breath on his forehead, and the vague touch of her whole body through her clothes. They clasped hands; the toe of her shoe protruded a little from under her dress, and almost fainting with emotion, he said to her:

'The sight of your foot disturbs me.'

An impulse of modesty made her get up. Then, motionless, and talking with the strange intonation of a sleepwalker, she said:

'At my age! Him! Frédéric! ... No woman has ever been loved as I have been loved. No, no! What's the use of being young? I don't care about youth. I despise all the women who come here!'

'Oh, hardly any do,' he said, to please her.

Her face lit up, and she asked if he intended to marry.

He swore he never would.

'Really and truly? Why not?'

'Because of you,' said Frédéric, clasping her in his arms.

She stood there, leaning backwards, her lips parted, her eyes raised. Suddenly she pushed him away with a look of despair; and when he begged her to speak, she bowed her head and said:

'I should have liked to make you happy.'

Frédéric suspected that Madame Arnoux had come to offer herself to him; and once again he was filled with desire, a frenzied, rabid lust such as he had never known before. Yet he also had another, indefinable feeling, a repugnance akin to a dread of committing incest. Another fear restrained him – the fear of being disgusted later. Besides, what a nuisance it would be! And partly out of prudence and partly to avoid degrading his ideal, he turned on his heel and started rolling a cigarette.

She gazed at him admiringly.

'How considerate you are! There's nobody like you! There's nobody like you!'

Eleven o'clock struck.

'Already!' she said. 'At a quarter past, I shall go.'

She sat down again; but she watched the clock, while he went on walking up and down and smoking. Neither of them could think of anything more to say. In every parting there comes a moment when the beloved is already no longer with us.

At last, when the minute-hand pointed to a little after twenty-five past, she slowly picked up her hat by the ribbons.

'Good-bye, my friend, my dear friend! I shall never see you again. This was my last act as a woman. My soul will never leave you. May all the blessings of heaven be upon you!'

And she kissed him on the forehead like a mother.

But she seemed to be looking for something, and finally she asked him for some scissors.

She took out her comb, and all her white hair fell over her shoulders.

With an abrupt gesture she cut off a long lock close to her head.

'Keep it. Good-bye!'

When she had gone out, Frédéric opened his window. On the pavement Madame Arnoux beckoned to a passing cab. She got in. The carriage disappeared.

And that was all.

VII

TOWARDS the beginning of that winter, Frédéric and Deslauriers were chatting together by the fire, reconciled once again by that irresistible element in their nature which always reunited them in friendship.

Frédéric briefly explained his quarrel with Madame Dambreuse, who had subsequently married an Englishman.

Deslauriers, without saying how he had come to marry Mademoiselle Roque, told how, one fine day, his wife had run off with a singer. In his attempts to remove some of the ridicule this had brought upon him, he had shown excessive zeal for the Government and thus compromised his position as prefect. He had been dismissed. After that he had been director of colonization in Algeria, secretary to a pasha, manager of a newspaper, and an advertising agent; and at present he was employed as solicitor to an industrial company.

As for Frédéric, he had run through two thirds of his fortune and was now living on a very modest scale.

Then they asked each other about their friends.

Martinon was now a senator.

Hussonnet had an important post which gave him control of all the theatres and the whole of the press.

Cisy, who had become deeply devout and the father of eight children, lived in his ancestral mansion.

Pellerin, after dabbling in Fourierism, homoeopathy, table-turning, Gothic art, and humanitarian painting, had become a photographer; and on all the walls of Paris there were pictures of him in a black coat, with a tiny body and a huge head.

'And your friend Sénécal?' asked Frédéric.

'Disappeared! Heaven knows where. And your great love, Madame Arnoux?'

'She must be in Rome now with her son, a cavalry lieutenant.'

'And her husband?'

'Died last year.'

'Really?' said the lawyer.

Then, slapping his forehead, he went on:

'Incidentally, I met the dear old Marshal in a shop the other day, holding the hand of a little boy she's adopted. She's the widow of a certain Monsieur Oudry, and she's become terribly fat, not to say huge. What a decline! When you remember what a slim waist she had in the old days.'

Deslauriers did not conceal the fact that he had taken advantage of her despair to find this out for himself.

'After all, you did give me permission.'

This confession made up for his silence concerning the attempt he had made to seduce Madame Arnoux. Frédéric would have forgiven him for this, since it had not succeeded.

Although slightly annoyed by his friend's revelation, he pretended to laugh at it; and the thought of the Marshal reminded him of Mademoiselle Vatnaz.

Deslauriers had never seen her, any more than many other members of Arnoux's circle; but he remembered Regimbart perfectly.

'Is he still alive?'

'Only just. Every evening, without fail, he drags himself from café to café, from the Rue de Grammont to the Rue Montmartre, worn out, bent double, finished, a ghost of a man!'

'And what about Compain?'

Frédéric gave a cry of joy, and begged the sometime commissioner of the Provisional Government to explain to him the mystery of the calf's head.

'It's an idea imported from England. To parody the ceremony which the royalists over there used to hold on the 30th of January, a few independent spirits founded an annual banquet at which they ate calves' heads, drank red wine out of calves' skulls, and toasted the extermination of the Stuarts. After Thermidor, some Terrorists started a similar society over here, which shows that stupidity is catching.'

'You seem to have lost a lot of your old political fervour.'

'The effect of age,' said the lawyer.

And they looked back over their lives.

They had both failed, one to realize his dreams of love, the other to fulfil his dreams of power. What was the reason?

'Perhaps it's because we didn't steer a straight course,' said Frédéric.

'That may be true in your case. But I, on the contrary, was far too rigid in my line of conduct, and I failed to take into account a thousand-and-one minor factors which were really all-important. I was too logical, while you were too sentimental.'

Then they blamed chance, circumstances, the times into which they were born.

Frédéric went on:

'This wasn't how we expected to end up in the old days at Sens, when you wanted to write a critical history of philosophy, and I a great medieval novel about Nogent. I'd found the subject in Froissart: How Messire Brokars de Fénestranges and the Bishop of Troyes attacked Messire Eustache d'Ambrecicourt. Do you remember?'

And as they exhumed their youth, they asked each other after every sentence:

'Do you remember?'

They saw once more the school yard, the chapel, the parlour, the gymnasium at the bottom of the stairs, the faces of masters and boys. There was one called Angelmarre, from Versailles, who used to cut himself trouser-straps out of old boots; Monsieur Mirbal with his red sidewhiskers; Varaud and Suriret, the geometrical and artistic drawing-masters, who were always quarrelling; and the Pole, the compatriot of Copernicus, with his planetary system in cardboard, an itinerant astronomer who was paid for his lesson with a free meal in the refectory. Then they recalled a tremendous binge they had had once during an outing, their first pipes, the prize-giving days, the joy of the holidays.

It was during the holidays of 1837 that they had been to the Turkish woman's house.

This was the name usually given to a woman who was really called Zoraïde Turc; and many people actually believed that she was a Mohammedan from Turkey. This added to the romantic appeal of her establishment, which was situated on the river bank, behind the ramparts. Even at the height of summer there was shade around her house, which was recognizable by a bowl of goldfish next to a pot of mignonette on a windowsill. Girls in white dressing-gowns, with rouge on their cheeks and long ear-rings, used to tap on the window-panes as one passed, and in the evening they would stand on the doorstep singing softly in husky voices.

This haunt of perdition enjoyed a remarkable reputation in the whole district. People referred to it by euphemisms: 'You know where I mean . . . a certain street . . . below the Bridges.' It made the farmers' wives of the neighbourhood tremble for their husbands; well-to-do women feared its influence on their maids, because the sub-prefect's cook had been caught there; and it was of course, the secret obsession of every adolescent.

One Sunday, when everybody was at Vespers, Frédéric and Deslauriers, having previously had their hair curled, picked some flowers in Madame Moreau's garden, and then went out by the gate leading to the fields. After a long detour through the vineyards, they came back by the Pêcherie and slipped into the Turkish woman's house, still holding their big nosegays.

Frédéric presented his, like a lover to his betrothed. But the heat of the day, fear of the unknown, a sort of remorse, and also the very pleasure of seeing at a single glance so many women at his disposal affected him so powerfully that he turned deathly pale, and stood still, without saying a word. The girls all burst out laughing, amused by his embarrassment; thinking they were making fun of him, he fled, and as Frédéric had the money, Deslauriers had no choice but to follow him.

They were seen coming out. This caused a local scandal which was still remembered three years later.

They told one another the story at great length, each supplementing the other's recollections; and when they had finished:

'That was the happiest time we ever had,' said Frédéric.

'Yes, perhaps you're right. That was the happiest time we ever had,' said Deslauriers.

NOTES

1

After one of the most famous and controversial murder trials of modern times, Madame Lafarge had just been found guilty of poisoning her husband, and sentenced to life imprisonment on 2 September 1840.

2

These are the creations of Goethe (Werther), Chateaubriand (René), Musset (Franck), Byron (Lara), and George Sand (Lélia).

3

The petitions for electoral reform called for the reduction or suppression of the property qualification for the franchise. The census organized by Humann, the Minister of Finance, in 1841, was designed to increase the number of taxpayers and aroused fierce opposition.

4

The Protectionist party in France argued that Free Trade would help England to the detriment of France.

5

Pritchard was a missionary who acted as British consul in Tahiti. When Admiral Dupetit-Thouars annexed the island to France, he arrested and later expelled Pritchard. Under the threat of war with England, Guizot abandoned the protectorate and paid Pritchard an indemnity, a concession which angered the French public. Flaubert has inadvertently placed the Pritchard Affair, which took place in 1844, in December 1841.

6

Béranger was a Republican, Laffitte was one of the leaders of the Opposition, and Chateaubriand was known to be hostile to Louis-Philippe's régime.

7

Presumably a reference to the riots in the provinces provoked by the Humann census.

8

Two talking-points among French artists of the day: the portrait of Cherubini by Ingres, and Delaroche's decoration of the hemicycle in the Palais des Beaux-Arts.

9

The *National* was an Opposition newspaper under both the Restoration and Louis-Philippe.

10

The National Guard was regarded as the epitome of the middle class, from which it drew nearly all its recruits.

11

Fortifications had recently been built around Paris, ostensibly as a defence against a foreign invasion, but according to the Opposition as a means of cowing the population of the capital. The September Laws, passed in 1835 after Fieschi's attempt to assassinate Louis-Philippe, had imposed crippling restrictions on the Press. Guizot's concessions to England in the Pritchard Affair won him the nickname of 'Lord' Guizot.

12

The recovery of France's natural frontiers, especially the left bank of the Rhine, was one of the Opposition's most frequently stated aims.

13

Armand Marrast was a leading Republican journalist.

14

Odry was a comic actor who specialized in playing simpletons.

15

The Garde-Meuble was the building on the corner of the Rue Royale and the Rue de Rivoli which was later occupied by the French Admiralty.

16

A reference to Augustin Thierry's thesis that the aristocracy was descended from the Franks, and that the French Revolution represented a racial revolt by the oppressed Gauls.

17

The property qualification for a parliamentary candidate was 500 francs.

18

A guest dressed like the hero of Adam's opera *Le Postillon de Longjumeau*.

19

The famine which occurred in France in the winter of 1846–7 resulted in a peasant rising at Buzançais (Indre) and the murder of the leading landowner of the district.

20

In 1846 Louis-Philippe brought about the marriage of the Queen of Spain and her sister to an Italian prince and one of his own sons, thus causing alarm and anger in England. The Rochefort scandal was a case of fraud in which the Government played an equivocal role. The Chapter of Saint-Denis consisted of a number of bishops entrusted with the care of the royal tombs at Saint-Denis; in 1847 the Chamber of Peers voted an increase in the subsidy paid to the Chapter.

21
Barbès was imprisoned several times for Republican agitation during Louis-Philippe's reign. Finally, in the summer of 1839, he was condemned to death; the sentence was reduced to life imprisonment as the result of public indignation, and Barbès remained in prison until the 1848 Revolution.

22
Poniatowski was drowned in the Elster while covering the retreat of Napoleon's Grand Army. In 1831 the Republicans in France called on the French Government to support the Polish insurrection; Louis-Philippe knew that France was no match for Russia, and he therefore abandoned the Poles to their fate, at the same time pretending that he was in favour of intervention.

23
Monsieur de Genoude, the Legitimist director of the *Gazette de France*, had begun demanding the same electoral reforms as the Liberal organ, the *Siècle*.

24
This was the insurrection of 12 May 1839, organized by the secret society known as the Société des Saisons, in which Barbès was wounded and arrested.

25
Lesurques was wrongly found guilty of complicity in the famous Lyons Mail case, under the Directory, condemned to death, and executed.

26
Antony was the pale, melancholy, star-crossed hero of Dumas *père*'s play of the same name, whom a whole generation of young Frenchmen – including Flaubert – took as their model.

27
Bou-Maza was an Algerian chieftain who was captured by the French in 1847 and sent to Paris, where he spent the rest of his life living on a French Government pension.

28
Mickiewicz, who occupied the Chair of Slavonic Languages at the Collège de France, and Quinet, who occupied that of Southern European Languages, aroused the enthusiasm of their students and the hostility of the authorities by their liberal, anti-clerical ideas; finally both chairs were suppressed.

29

The banker Drouillard was found guilty in 1847 of bribing electors. Bénier was a Government official who, on his death in 1845, was found to have abstracted 300,000 francs from public funds.

30

Godefroy Cavaignac, the brother of the General Cavaignac who was to become head of the Executive under the 1848 Republic, was an ardent Republican who campaigned fiercely against the July Monarchy until his death in 1845.

31

Chalier was a revolutionary of Lyons who was guillotined in July 1793. The Société des Familles was a secret Republican society which changed its name in 1837 to the Société des Saisons. Alibaud tried to assassinate Louis-Philippe in 1836, was condemned to death by the Peers, and executed.

32

On 13 April 1834 a Republican insurrection broke out in the Marais district of Paris. It was quickly and savagely suppressed; one incident, in which all the occupants of a house in the Rue Transnonain were butchered by General Bugeaud's troops, was immortalized by Daumier in his lithograph, *The Massacre of the Rue Transnonain.*

33

The leaders of the Société des Saisons were imprisoned in the fortress at Mont-Saint-Michel for their part in the insurrection of 12 May 1839. They were all brutally ill-treated during their captivity; it was in 1841 that the cruelties described here were inflicted on Barbès.

34

Political offences were judged by the Chamber of Peers in the Luxembourg.

35

The year 1834 was marked not only by insurrections in Paris and Lyons but also by serious Government crises.

36

The Carbonari was a revolutionary society originating in Italy and active in France during the Restoration. After 1830 many of its members became supporters of Louis-Philippe's régime.

37

Lachambeaudie was a Republican whose *Fables* enjoyed a considerable vogue. Eugène Sue's sensational novel *Les Mystères de Paris* was the most popular work of fiction of the 1840s. *L'Histoire de Napoléon* by Norvins was widely read at the time, when the Napoleonic Legend was gaining strength. The poet Béranger, who contributed to this Legend, was also idolized by the Republicans.

38
During the last few months of Louis-Philippe's reign the Opposition organized a series of so-called Reform banquets, at which the speakers called for electoral reforms. The year 1847 was marked by intense political agitation in Italy as well as France.

39
At the beginning of his reign, Louis-Philippe had been obliged by pressure from England to deny support to the Belgian provinces which were rebelling against Dutch rule. In Switzerland Guizot backed the conservative Sonderbund, which was destined to be defeated by the Radicals in 1848. In Germany the gradual extension of the Zollverein, a customs union dominated by Prussia, was causing growing alarm to the French.

40
A disillusioned supporter of Guizot's Government declared in 1847: 'What has been done in the past seven years? Nothing, nothing, nothing.'

41
The Jesuits had been expelled from France in 1845, but despite this ban continued their teaching work in many parts of the country.

42
In May 1847 Teste, the President of the Court of Appeal and a former Minister of Public Works, was put on trial for taking a bribe from General Cubières in return for a salt-mine concession. Teste was sentenced to civic degradation and three years' imprisonment, Cubières to degradation and a fine.

43
The Duchesse de Choiseul-Praslin was murdered in August 1847 by her husband, who was arrested but poisoned himself before he could be brought to trial. The Government was widely suspected of having facilitated his suicide in order to avoid the scandal of a peer's being tried for murder.

44
Pope Pius IX, who had succeeded Gregory XVI in June 1846, had instituted a number of reforms in the Papal States which had won him the admiration of the French Republicans.

45

Louis-Philippe had been proclaimed King of the French from the balcony of the Hotel de Ville in July 1830. His 'betrayal' of the Revolution since then was symbolized in a famous cartoon which showed him doing a vanishing trick with two balls labelled 'Liberty' and 'Revolution'. In 1793 he had served under Dumouriez and had gone over to the enemy at the same time.

46

A reference to Buridan's ironic monologue: 'These are great ladies', in Dumas *père*'s play *La Tour de Nesle*.

47

Les Bœufs, one of the most popular songs of the day, was composed by Pierre Dupont, a famous Lyons singer whose political opinions endeared him to the Republicans.

48

The Comte d'Alton-Shée was one of several Conservatives who in 1847 went over to the Opposition.

49

Léotade was a Friar of the Christian Schools at Toulouse who was sentenced to life imprisonment in April 1848 for indecent assault. Palermo had risen in revolt on 12 January 1848, and in February the King of Naples granted the Sicilians a constitution. The Twelfth Arrondissement banquet in favour of electoral reform had been banned by the police.

50

The Pear was the name given to Louis-Philippe by opponents of his régime, on account of his pear-shaped head.

51

The illness in question was croup. Flaubert watched a tracheotomy at the Sainte-Eugénie Hospital, but left before the end of the operation. For his novel he therefore chose the rare but not impossible cure by the spontaneous discharge of the croupous membrane.

52

Speaking at the Hôtel de Ville on 25 February 1848 to the workers who wanted the Republic to adopt the Red Flag, Lamartine declared that the Red Flag had only gone round the Champ de Mars (in 1791) 'whereas the tricolour has gone round the world.'

53

As soon as the revolutionary Caussidière was appointed Prefect of Police by the Provisional Government, he organized a new police force colourfully dressed in blue shirts, red cravats, and red belts.

54

Lamartine was Foreign Minister in the Provisional Government, Ledru-Rollin Minister of the Interior, and the octogenarian Dupont of the Eure Prime Minister. The workers were represented on the Government by Albert, the engineer leader of the Société des Saisons; Louis Blanc was appointed President of the Labour Commission, a body without any power or responsibility; Blanqui was an extreme left-wing Socialist, and the founder of the Société Républicaine Centrale.

55

The royal Château de Neuilly and the Château de Suresnes, which belonged to the Baron de Rothschild, were both sacked in February 1848. In March Ledru-Rollin sent a circular letter to his provincial commissioners, who were encountering considerable opposition, telling them that they had unlimited powers. In the same month the Government took two unpopular financial measures, issuing banknotes at a forced rate and raising taxation by 45 centimes to every franc.

56

Flocon, the editor of the *Réforme* and a member of the Provisional Government, enjoyed widespread popularity on account of his eccentric dress, his distinctive pipe, and his wife, a forthright woman of the people reputed to be a sometime mistress of Lamartine.

57

In March 1848 Proudhon had published two pamphlets on the social problems of the time in which, although a Socialist, he criticized the organization of labour by the State.

58

L'Assemblée Nationale was an Orleanist newspaper founded in February 1848.

59

The name of a revolutionary society which, on 21 January every year, celebrated the anniversary of the execution of Louis XVI.

60

The notorious Public Prosecutor during the Terror of 1793.

61

'Citizens! I greatly appreciate the honour you are paying me, and, great as your kindness is, your attention is even greater. ... From the proclamation of the Constitution of Cadiz, that fundamental contract of Spanish liberty, down to the last revolution, our country has had many heroic martyrs ... Next Tuesday a Requiem Mass will be celebrated in the Church of the Madeleine. And all Spaniards would like to see gathered there the deputations from the clubs and the national militia. A funeral oration, in honour of the freedom of Spain and of the whole world, will be delivered by a member of the clergy of Paris in the Salle Bonne-Nouvelle. Honour to the French people, whom I would call the greatest people in the world if I were not a citizen of another nation.'

62

The offices of Émile de Girardin's newspaper the *Presse* were attacked by a crowd of Republican demonstrators on 29 March 1848. On 15 May there was a demonstration in favour of Poland, and the mob invaded the National Assembly. In both cases order was restored by the National Guard.

63

The Luxembourg conferences were those held by Louis Blanc's Labour Commission. The Club de la Légion des Vésuviennes, in the Rue Sainte-Apolline, was one of many feminist clubs, such as the Club de L'Émancipation des Femmes and the Club des Femmes, founded in 1848.

64

The Napoleon in question here is Louis-Napoléon Bonaparte, who had declared his support for the Second Republic immediately after the February Revolution, and was now preparing to exploit the popularity created for him by the Napoleonic Legend and his supporters in France. Marie was the highly unpopular Minister of Public Works in the Provisional Government.

65

The national bank to which Monsieur Dambreuse refers here was the Comptoir National d'Escompte, instituted in March 1848. The five million francs were intended for the National Workshops, but the Comte de Falloux, whom the Government had appointed to investigate the question, recommended the immediate suppression of the Workshops. Although Falloux's report was not submitted until 23 June, its conclusions were known beforehand. The decree ordering all workmen between eighteen and twenty-five employed in the National Workshops to choose between military service and drainage work in the provinces was signed on 21 June and published in the *Moniteur* on the 22nd; it resulted in the bitter street-fighting and savage repression of 23, 24, and 25 June.

66

The 'lovely ladies who wept in the stage-boxes' were the ladies of the court who, according to Rousseau's *Confessions*, were moved to tears by the production at Fontainebleau in 1752 of his comic opera *Le Devin du Village*.

67

In the evening of 23 June, at General Cavaignac's request, Ledru-Rollin ordered the prefects of the surrounding departments to send all the troops and National Guards at their disposal to Paris.

68

On Sunday, 25 June, the last day of the insurrection, General Bréa, General Négrier, and the deputy Charbonnel were killed by the rebels in different parts of Paris; and Monsignor Affre, the Archbishop of Paris, was killed by a stray bullet in the Faubourg Saint-Antoine, while trying to negotiate a cease-fire.

69

The negotiations took place in the early morning of 26 June. General Cavaignac rejected the rebels' proposals, and at 10 a.m. the Government troops launched an attack on the last rebel stronghold, in the Faubourg Saint-Antoine.

70

A National Guard from the provinces did in fact fire at a prisoner in the Tuileries, and some two hundred lives were lost in the firing which followed.

71

A reference to Proudhon's famous dictum, 'Property is theft', stated in his *Qu'est-ce que la propriété?* (1840).

72

Slavery had been abolished in the French colonies in April 1848.

73

Lamoricière was Cavaignac's second-in-command during the fighting in June 1848.

74

Rateau's proposal, which was adopted by a narrow majority in January 1849, was for the dissolution of the Constituent Assembly and the election of a Legislative Assembly.

75

The so-called Réunion de la Rue de Poitiers was an organization of leading Legitimists and Orleanists which, by means of energetic and heavily financed propaganda, obtained the election in May 1849 of a Legislative Assembly in which the Republicans were in a minority. The members of the Rue de Poitiers committee believed that they were preparing the way for a restoration of the monarchy; they did not suspect that they were in fact helping Louis-Napoleon to lay the foundations of the Second Empire.

76

The retort: 'We have had enough poetry!' had been made on 15 May 1848, when Lamartine had harangued the mob invading the Assembly. General Cavaignac, who after the June insurrection had been hailed as the saviour of France and appointed Head of the Executive, was in fact a Republican; he was replaced in December 1848 by Louis-Napoleon Bonaparte, when the latter was elected President of the Republic. General Changarnier, Commander-in-Chief of the Army in Paris and of the National Guard, had suppressed a left-wing insurrection on 13 June 1849, in which Ledru-Rollin and a small band of supporters had chosen the Conservatoire des Arts et Métiers as their last stronghold.

77
A revue at the Vaudeville which satirized the Republicans.

78
On 4 January 1851 the *Moniteur* announced that General Changarnier, who since October 1850 had joined with the Assembly in opposing the Prince-President's imperial pretensions, had been relieved of his dual command.

79
In February 1851 an extra-parliamentary cabinet appointed by Louis-Napoleon after Changarnier's dismissal recommended increasing the Prince-President's annual allowance by 1,800,000 francs. The Assembly rejected this recommendation by a large majority, and the Prince-President retaliated by making ostentatious economies at the Élysée.

80
A French army under General Oudinot took Rome on 3 July 1849 and restored the Pope's authority. The Venetian Republic, proclaimed in March 1848, came to an end on 27 August 1849, when Venice was recaptured by the Austrians. In Poland insurrections which broke out at the news of Metternich's fall were rapidly crushed. Similarly the Hungarians, who had thrown off the Austrian yoke, were defeated in August 1849 by a Russian army sent to help the Austrian Emperor.

81
Carlier, appointed Prefect of Police in December 1849, had ordered all the trees of liberty in Paris to be cut down early in 1850. In May 1850, alarmed by a series of by-elections which had returned left-wing deputies with large majorities, the Government introduced a law reducing the number of electors by over three million; after a dozen stormy sessions this law was passed on 31 May 1851. The political clubs had been closed after the insurrection of 13 June 1849. On 16 June 1850 the Assembly passed a law imposing new restrictions on the Press. On 15 March 1850

the Falloux law, named after the then Minister of Education, was passed by the Assembly, placing the lay schoolmasters of every commune under the supervision of the local clergy.

82
The time is the morning of 2 December 1851. Louis-Napoleon has just carried out his *coup d'état*, dissolving the Assembly and ordering the incarceration of his leading political opponents in Mazas Prison.